IT CALLS FROM THE SEA

AN EERIE RIVER PUBLISHING ANTHOLOGY

IT CALLS FROM THE SEA

Paperback ISBN: 978-1-990245-19-0
Hardcover ISBN: 978-1-990245-20-6
Digital ISBN: 978-1-990245-13-8

Edited by Alanna Robertson-Webb
Cover design Francois Vaillancourt
Book Formatting by Michelle River

Special thanks to our Jr. Editors Tim Mendees, David Green, Callum Pearce, Chris Hewitt, Shawna Rowan, Kim Rei and S.O. Green.

Foreword

Across the 300,000 years in which human beings have existed on this planet, only five per cent of the ocean has been explored and discovered.

Consider that for a moment.

Out of the five per cent of explored sea water, we know of approximately 220,000 different types of marine animals. Scientists predict there may be as many as 2 million species of underwater creatures living in the ocean. That leaves a great deal to the imagination of what awaits discovery down below.

Personally, I've always had a great respect for the sea. If you've ever trodden the gentle foams of the shore—shells, rocks, and pincered-creatures biting into the hardened soles of your feet—you know what I'm talking about. Even a gentle lick of the ocean is enough to leave an impact on you. If you've ever strayed farther from the safety of the golden sands and experienced the strength of the waves and the undertow, then you'll know the heart-racing surge of adrenaline that comes from being nothing more than a piece of flotsam in the sea's vast clutches. A ragdoll caught in the midst of a whirlpool. You have no say. The ocean has you.

I've nearly drowned twice in the sea. I've cut my shins on jagged rock. I've been flicked off the back of a banana boat in the Mediterranean Ocean and felt the brush of something unknown speed past my thigh as I bob on the tides and await rescue. I've been caught as the tide rushes in, feet squelching in muddy sand, the ground trying to stick me so the salty waters can swallow me whole.

Suffice to say, this anthology speaks to me.

There's a lot to love about the ocean, and there's a whole lot more to fear. Whether it's the monolithic toss of the tides, waves cresting as tall as cathedrals, or the pounds of ambient pressure which has the ability to turn the human brain to soup, or the myriad of predatory creatures with teeth, claws, tentacles, skills, and gifts honed from aeons of evolving in some of the most hostile reaches of the planet, there's something to make everyone's skin prickle and turn their throat dry.

Ironic, really.

In the pages ahead of you, you will embark on a journey of oceanic discovery. The stories which have been collected by the Eerie River team will take you across the Seven Seas, have you exploring forgotten civilizations, swimming with unimaginable, forgotten creatures, and tackling some of the harshest disasters in the most remote regions of the world. They will strip away all that you thought you knew of the great big blue and leave you with a trembling hesitation every time you return to the shores and stare out across the waters at the setting sun.

There is beauty in the deep, my friend.

But there is much horror, too.

Can you hear it? The sirens calling? The whale song reverberating through the currents?

Listen closely, dear reader.

For, It Calls From the Sea...

Daniel Willcocks
14 May, 2021
www.danielwillcocks.com

Stories & Authors

Abyssal Horror

Trey Dowell

The great whale took one final breath and slipped beneath the azure surface of the Atlantic. His tissues and organs now pulsed with enough oxygen to stay submerged for an hour, more than enough time for the hunt. The sperm whale's massive, squarish head tipped forward, and for a moment his body held perfectly still, vertical in the silent, blue expanse. Then one giant sweep of his twelve-foot-wide tail propelled the whale in the only direction that mattered.

Down.

The large male descended slowly at first, letting 70 tons of body mass do most of the work. At 250 meters the undulating tail helped accelerate the dive, pushing deeper and deeper into the darkening void. By 1000 meters even the sun's strongest rays could penetrate no farther. The whale continued the dive in complete darkness, every square centimeter of his thick skin under constant assault by water pressure that would jellify a human being instantly.

Even in the endless black the whale wasn't blind. Soft clicks—generated in the front tip of the elongated head—projected a sonic wave through thick spermaceti toward the rear of the great whale's skull. The bony rear plate, shaped like a satellite dish, focused the wave and reflected the energy forward, into the deep. The clicks fired ahead of the whale at over 230 decibels, more powerful than a jet engine's roar, in a tight beam less than a foot wide. This built-in sonar allowed him to 'see' everything that waited in the dark.

At 2000 meters the great whale sensed the first returning clicks—sound bouncing off something far below. Something almost as long as the whale itself, but thinner, with long appendages trailing behind: a giant squid, the length of a city bus, meandered through frigid water almost a kilometer below.

Food.

The tail flicked harder now, pushing the excited predator faster. At the same time his eco-location clicks increased in frequency, giving the sperm whale a clearer picture of his next meal. As the whale closed to within 500 meters of his prey the clicking was a constant stream of energy. A human being placed in the path of this sonic assault would have been vibrated into pieces. The squid, though, lacked the ability to detect ultrasonic waves—it had no idea it was even being tracked from above. Nearly a half-ton of fat and muscle, the squid swam in a lazy circle squarely in Death's crosshairs.

Two hundred meters from the prey and closing fast, the great whale rolled to position his jaw for the kill. The mouth cracked open and 48 teeth, each the size of a man's forearm, felt the rush of icy water.

150 meters...

100 meters...

Without warning the sonar image of the squid changed. It wriggled violently from side to side, thrashing in the water. The long, thin body was being torn apart at the midsection, and the two pieces simply...disappeared.

The whale slowed, shifting its head to reacquire the prey, but its sonar sensed nothing. Well, not quite *nothing*. The clicks bounced hard off the only remaining obstacle: the bottom. Confused at his prey's disappearance, the sperm whale swept its sonar all along the ocean floor, searching.

Then the bottom moved.

The whale stopped. More clicks confirmed the impossible: sonic echoes returning faster and faster, as though the ocean floor itself was rising up through the deep.

Slowly.

Steadily.

The great whale wasn't afraid, only confused. As the largest apex predator in the history of the planet it had never known fear, which is why the sperm whale barely moved when it sensed a flash of movement on the rising seafloor.

Something sharp punched through the thick blubber

of the whale's belly, something large enough to shove the animal upward. The whale shuddered, feeling more shock than pain at first.

Then warmth enveloped him in a cloud. Some part of the animal's brain knew what that meant—hundreds of liters of its own blood were gushing out into the cold, remorseless black water—but the great whale no longer cared. It died sending a weakening series of clicks in all directions as it spasmed, trying to understand what had attacked him in his own hunting ground.

The truth was far beyond the great whale's ability to reason, or even detect: an enemy large enough to mimic the ocean's limitless bottom.

Something powerful.

Something hungry.

Something that now continued in the only direction that mattered.

Up.

Alex Matteson was used to jolting awake. Used to the drenched sheets, the rapid breathing and the beeping heart-rate alert from his Apple Watch. A buzzing iPhone at 4:30AM, however, rarely became part of Alex's routine. He stared at the screen for the first four vibrations, assuming *a patient.* By the fifth, curiosity got the better of him.

"Hello?"

"Alex? This is Bob Rouse. Did I wake you?" The voice

sounded tinny and slightly muffled.

Alex ran his free hand through sweaty hair, felt the long seam of a scar running underneath. "Sheriff? I'm... no...not asleep. Bad dreams."

Rouse issued a tired sigh. "After tonight, I might have a few of those myself."

The man's tone burned off the last of Alex's sleep fog. "What can I do for you, Sheriff?"

"I know it's late, or, well, early, I suppose, but I sure could use you down at Judson Pier."

Alex swung his long legs out from under the sheet, thumping bare feet down on the cold wood floor. "What's happened?"

After a pause, Rouse asked "You know *The Crystal Marie?*"

Alex's brow furrowed as he tried to place the name. "Is that Munson's boat?"

"Yep. Teddy Munson. Got a crew of seven, plus him. There's been, well uh...an accident."

Alex started searching the floor for a semi-clean pair of pants. "Is this a grief-counseling kind of accident?"

"More like a what-the-fuck kind of accident," Sheriff Rouse said. "I need you to help me interview Teddy. He's a goddamn mess, totally out of it. Paramedic says he's okay physically, but..."

"If he's okay, who got hurt?" Alex grabbed some jeans from the floor, tried to stab a leg through, almost tripped. "One of the crew?"

"That's the thing, Doc. There is no crew. They're all

gone."

The disheveled psychiatrist stopped trying to force the jeans onto his legs and stood straight. "Whaddayou mean 'gone?'"

Rouse waited a full three-count before answering. "Come ask him yourself, because what he's telling me doesn't make any sense."

"Be there in fifteen minutes," Alex said, ending the call.

It took less than five for him to make it out the front door, cursing the chill of April mornings in Maine the whole time. He twisted the cap off of a Mountain Dew and backed the Jeep out of the driveway. By the time he made it to the harbor the sugar and caffeine had worked enough of their magic to clear his head. In the predawn darkness it was easy to spot the flashing lights of Rouse's cruiser and the ambulance down at the far end of Judson Pier. The sheriff stood at the ambulance's open back door, and as Alex approached the lawman adjusted his cap and gave an apologetic shrug.

"Sorry, Doc. Wouldn't have called if I didn't need you. He's all clammed up now."

Alex peered around the heavyset sheriff and saw Teddy Munson huddled within the ambulance, swaddled in a mylar blanket. Behind the emergency vehicles the dark hull of his boat *The Crystal Marie*—now secured safely to the pier—flickered in the red-and-blue lights.

The paramedic saw Alex and hopped down off the rig. "Hey, Dr. Matteson," she said, voice low to avoid Munson's earshot. "Mild shock, exposure, fatigue—nothing too bad, but he's pretty shaken up."

"You taking him in?"

The medic nodded, then blew warm air into her cupped fists. "Yep. Gotta get him signed off at Mercy."

Alex took a look at Munson's glassy eyes and unfocused stare. "Alright, but lemme talk to him first."

"Have fun," Rouse whispered. "At least he's not ranting like a psycho anymore."

Alex winced. "In my profession that's a bad word."

"Psycho?"

"Fun," the psychiatrist deadpanned. He grabbed the door handle and hefted himself into the rig. Munson barely registered the arrival.

"Teddy? It's Dr. Matteson, from North Point Mercy. Can you hear me?" Alex drew an index finger back and forth between Munson's eyes, looking for pupil tracking. None. The whites of the boat captain's eyes were clouded by broken capillaries and tears. He'd either been crying too much or staring too much, probably both. Alex gently removed Munson's hands from the folds of mylar. He grasped both of the captain's wrists, applying warm pressure to the undersides with his fingers. "Teddy," Alex said, the single word more command than question. The pupils moved, registering Alex's presence for the first time.

"What?" Munson finally croaked. His hands pulled back beneath the blanket. "What did you say?"

"What happened out there?" Alex felt Sheriff Rouse behind him, moving closer to hear.

"It's like I told him already. The crew. My boys...

they're just...they just..."

Alex knew plenty of boat captains. In Portland, Maine they weren't hard to find, which meant he also knew how they thought. Every last one was a navigator at heart. "Start with the basics, Captain. Where were you?"

Munson's gaze flicked left and right like a biological hard drive searching for data. When the movement stopped, he said "The Abyssal Shelf, 50 miles east of Luckes Sound."

"Good. And then what?"

"We'd finished taking in the last line of nets," he said, sucking in a deep breath. "Just after midnight. Secured the catch. I was on the bridge checking for the nav buoy when I heard all the deck chatter just stop cold. Everybody shut up, like someone turned off a switch."

Behind him Alex heard Rouse scribbling in his notepad from outside the rig; apparently Captain Munson's story had more detail now that he was warm and calm.

"So I look out the bridge windows and there's all seven of 'em," the captain continued. "The whole crew leaning against the port rail, looking down into the water."

"Looking at what?"

Munson's eyes flashed angrily. "I have no fucking clue what they saw, but...they were standing, all of 'em the exact same with arms hanging at their sides and heads down. No sound, like seven identical statues. Made no sense. Looked..." The captain ran both hands over his facial scruff, pulling the skin taut until his expression mimicked an anguished scream.

"Looked rehearsed? Like they were screwing with the boss at the end of the shift?" Alex offered.

"Yeah, exactly like that. I killed the engine and ran out on deck to give them an earful, but..."

Rouse climbed up into the rig, no longer satisfied to eavesdrop.

"...but it wasn't a joke. The closest man on the rail was Joey Riggins. Hell, he didn't even flinch when I screamed at him. Just kept staring at the water."

"What did Joey see, Captain? What was in the water?"

Munson's volume increased. "Not a goddamn thing! Middle of the night in open ocean, and not one man had so much as a lit flashlight. I stared over Joey's shoulder, figuring it had to be something incredible, something unbelievable, and...nothing. Black nothing. So I'm getting ready to yank that silly fucker away from the rail when the kid says two words, 'Warm. Safe.' Just like that. He smiles like they're the two best words he's ever heard, then the rest of the crew says it too."

"Warm and safe?"

"No. Not like that. No 'and.' Just the two words, without any feeling. My entire crew." Munson choked up, swiped a hand across his quivering lips. "So I'm screaming at Joey, telling him the North Atlantic might be a lot of things, but none of 'em are 'warm' or 'safe,' and it's like he doesn't even hear me. Without a sound that boy goes headfirst right over the port rail."

Alex took a look back at Rouse. The lawman's only response was a slow, sad nod.

"I just about shit myself," Munson continued. "Started to yell 'Man overboard,' but more splashes stopped me. Six more. Each one was another man going into the water."

"I don't understand. Did they fall overboard? Maybe a swell hit—"

Munson's glare cut him off. "There wasn't any Goddamn *swell.* They didn't fall, they *dove.* Then kept right on going, straight down. None of 'em even came up for air."

Alex's attention shifted from Munson to the sheriff, then back. "So they all drowned? On purpose?" he stammered.

"I threw everything that could float overboard," Munson said, almost pleading. "Life preservers, coolers, barrels, even seat cushions—then stayed on the rail praying for anybody to surface. Shot off every rescue flare on my boat. Waited for two hours straight. They never came back up, not a one."

"Jesus." Alex leaned back, mouth agape.

"Canadian trawler out of Nova Scotia spotted the flares," Rouse said. "Radioed for help. Coast Guard brought *The Crystal Marie* in an hour ago, left Teddy in my custody."

Munson's head dropped into his hands. He muttered "Dove right over," in disbelief. "Like they were hypnotized or something."

Alex squeezed the grieving man's shoulder. "Rest now, Captain. We'll talk again tomorrow." He jumped down and gave a quick nod to the EMT, who climbed back in to secure Munson for the trip to North Point Mercy.

Rouse flipped his notepad closed. "Well, what do you think?"

"Makes no damn sense."

A mirthless chuckle rumbled out of the sheriff's throat. "I don't need a medical expert to tell me that."

"If you're asking me if he's telling the truth, I'm pretty sure he is. As much as he remembers it, anyway."

Rouse pulled a flash drive out of his coat pocket, rubbing it between his fingers like a lucky rabbit's foot. "He's got a security cam that covers most of the foredeck on an eight-hour loop. I'll have our tech guy scan through the footage this morning—hopefully it caught enough of what happened to clear Munson. I'd hate to find out he got careless, hit a swell, and sent those boys into the sea. Seven counts of manslaughter hung around Munson's neck would make him sink faster than his crew."

"Ouch."

"Just sayin'."

The two men watched the ambulance pull away. Alex fought back a yawn. Sheriff Rouse noticed and slapped him on the back. "Go get some sleep. We'll talk later today, okay?"

Alex hopped back in the still-warm Jeep and waited for Rouse to pass him before making a U-turn to head back home. As he did the psychiatrist caught a glimpse of a solitary figure at the far end of Judson Pier. Whoever they were they stood motionless right at the edge, against the railing, facing out over the harbor. A jogger? Harbor security? Could have been either one, but all Alex could picture was Joey Riggins on the deck of *The Crystal Marie*—waiting to jump. *Wanting* it. He shuddered before turning the wheel and heading home.

To the east the harbor opened into the vast Atlantic. The first glimmer of dawn made a thin band of sea water at the horizon glow light blue, but everything below that was unrelenting blackness.

Six hours of sleep put him in a better mood, but Alex still dreaded his Tuesday meeting. An hour of weekly group therapy for anxiety disorders—an unpaid hour—which satisfied his annual licensing requirements but little else. Listening to ten people moan about their fears and dreams was no more interesting for him than anyone else who valued their time and their patience. Plus, from his experience, group therapy often blossomed into group dysfunction; each person tried to one-up the other with their own embellished tale of woe.

Still, bills needed to be paid. A valid medical license made that a Helluva lot easier.

When the last attendee entered the St. Sebastian's meeting room Alex took a seat in the pre-arranged circle of chairs, motioning for everyone to join him.

"Well, who would like to start this week?" he said, pen tip hovering above his open notebook. For the first time in several weeks no one volunteered. "Really? C'mon folks. We're here to *share*," he admonished. Finally a nervous, red-headed woman in a gray suit raised her hand.

"Joyce, thank you. How have things been this week?"

Joyce Russo cleared her throat, sitting straighter against the vinyl back of her chair. "I've gotten out of the house three times. Well, four, if you count today." She blushed as the clapping started, the wave of applause simultaneously seeming to invigorate and embarrass.

"That is *excellent,*" Alex said, truly enthusiastic. "Each time brings you a little closer to the independence you want. Agoraphobia is a bitch, I know. And the nightmares?"

Joyce's smile faded. When she spoke, her voice wavered. "Still there. Twice this week."

"And the lucid dreaming strategies we talked about last time?"

Her lips pressed together in a hard line, Joyce shook her head. "Nothing. I still can't control the nightmares. I'm always trapped in an endless open plain, alone. No ability to move, or even call for help. It's like I'm...like I'm—"

"It's okay, Joyce. Control your breathing, focus on my voice." An anxiety attack during group never helped anyone, so Alex tried to relieve some of the stress before it snowballed. Joyce's car accident five years ago might not have caused her agoraphobia, but the brain surgery and three-week hospital stay had definitely kicked it into a higher gear.

After a few minutes of deep breathing she'd recovered enough to say thanks and receive supportive comments from the group.

Alex made his notes and asked "Who's next?" Not one hand went up. Even after the requisite polite delay, no one said a peep. "Seriously?" He pointed to a stout man in coveralls and work boots. "Charlie? We talked a long time about your issues with confined places last week. Any progress there?"

Charlie Beckham looked embarrassed for a second. His shoulders sagged like he was ready to unload serious emotional baggage, but instead he laughed. A rare happy laugh for him.

"I gotta be honest, Doc. This has been a pretty great week."

"How so?"

The dockworker leaned forward, almost excited to share now. "I've slept better these last few nights than I have in years. Maybe ever—"

The woman next to him, Renata blurted "Oh my god, yes! So have I! It's been wonderful."

Around the circle others nodded and murmured their agreement. Jennifer, the tight-laced receptionist at Mercy's outpatient clinic looked visibly relieved. "Thank God. I was afraid to say anything. I didn't want to piss anybody off."

Every person in the meeting was suddenly rainbows and unicorns—all except Joyce, who looked like she'd been the only person left out of a lottery win.

"Guys, please," Alex said, reeling everyone back in. "Charlie, why do you think you've slept so well?"

"To be honest, I think it's my dreams. And I'm saying

'dreams' for once, not nightmares. Last night was amazing. I was a kid again, riding with my grandpa in his Bonneville, going for ice cream at City Square."

Alex kept up with Charlie's imagery, scribbling notes as the big man spoke.

"Being in that huge car, his arm around me the whole time? Man, I felt incredible," Charlie said. "I can't even describe it. So… So…"

"Warm. Safe." Renata said the words with a beatific smile.

Alex's pen froze on the pad. "What did you say?" he whispered.

Jennifer repeated Renata's words.

As did the next person in the circle. And the next.

"That's exactly how it felt," Charlie said.

Holy shit.

Alex let everyone go a half-hour early.

Alex called the sheriff's department from the Jeep on his way home. Bob Rouse sounded happy enough when he picked up.

"Munson's in the clear," the sheriff said. "Video backed up his story. The crew dove in, pretty as you please."

When Alex told him what had happened at group, and the exact words used, Rouse was distinctly less pleased. "That can't be a coincidence, can it?"

Alex turned down Stanton Road, shaking his head. "I

don't know, but I almost fell out of my chair. Has anything else strange happened today?"

"Strange how?"

"I don't know, unusual? Rare?"

"Lemme check the log." After a delay, Rouse came back on. "A couple of missing persons, that's it."

Alex guided the Jeep onto McPherson, then started climbing the bluffs above the harbor. "And that's normal?"

"We get a few every season. Usually turn up drunk and contrite the next day."

The psychiatrist pinched the bridge of his nose, refocused on the road. "Do me a favor and let me know if you hear of anything else, will ya?"

As the Jeep came around the last curve before Alex's street he saw two women standing on the bluff, on the opposite side of the safety rail. Inches apart. Motionless. "What the Hell?" He stopped, lowering the passenger window, and honked. Five full seconds of blasting the Jeep's horn broke their trance. The women looked at Alex, confused. "You two okay?" he shouted through the window. Both pedestrians eyed him suspiciously, then each other. They walked off in opposite directions.

Rouse's voice came through the car's speakers. "Everything alright?"

"Yeah, it's just..." Alex put the Jeep back in gear, rolled up the window. "I'm starting to get a bad feeling about this."

The sheriff grunted in agreement. "I got a bad feeling the second Teddy Munson opened his mouth. Welcome to the club. You sound tired Doc. Go home, try to get some sleep."

"'Try' is the operative word," Alex said, then ended the call.

The nightmare started as it always did—a bright, sunny morning full of promise and joy.

Alex sat on the wooden bench across from the beach, checking his wetsuit one last time. Ocean mist tickled his face as he looked at the slate-blue horizon. Paradise all around. On any other of the thousand nights this nightmare had invaded his sleep Alex would have been unable to resist the water's pull—lucid dreaming strategies be damned. He'd have grabbed his surfboard and trudged across the sand, dread increasing with every unsteady step. The sky would darken right before he entered the surf, and he'd realize too late that beneath the shimmering surface of paradise terrors waited.

But not tonight.

Instead Alex felt rooted to the bench, unable to rise or leave, as though his only purpose was to bask in the sun and the sound of rolling waves breaking against the shore. He wanted to lean back, actually enjoy the warm glow for once, but as a veteran of disturbing nightmares he knew better; if he waited long enough all pleasant dreams eventually turned south, often with surprising speed.

"Hello, Alex."

He turned. Behind him a young woman perched atop the split-rail fence which rode the border between sand dunes and coastal scrub. In her twenties, wearing gingham shorts and a green bikini top, the girl lazily kicked her legs to a rhythm only she could hear. A golden necklace with red jewels hung around her tan neck, causing a twinkle of reflected sunshine strong enough to make Alex squint.

"Do I know you?" he asked.

Her laugh tickled the hairs along his spine. "Not yet." She pushed off the fence and bopped through the sand to join him on the bench. As she sat down the smell of coconut and brine bloomed around them both. Up close he could see she was pretty: the sun-kissed complexion, green eyes to match the jade-tone bikini top and her golden-brown hair, lighter at the tips, was dancing in the sea breeze.

"A name would be nice," he teased, feeling younger every second he sat next to her. She smiled and gazed at the ocean. Balanced on the front edge of the bench, hands curled over the lip, the woman looked ready for a starter's pistol. Rather than bolt for the beckoning surf, though, she eyed Alex with a side glance.

"Why can't you hear my song?"

He cocked his head to one side. "I don't understand. What song?"

She shrugged. "All eventually will. You just need to come closer."

He looked at the five inches of bench separating them. "Um, this is about as close as we can get."

"Silly man. We can get so much..." She let the words drift, then edged nearer, cupping his chin with her hand. Her voice dropped three octaves. "...*closer.*" As she spoke Alex saw the green eyes shimmer into deep black, then roll over milky-white. Her smile grew large—too large—until both jaws distended past her lips, each now sporting a row of triangular, serrated teeth. Alex pinwheeled off the bench, skittering backward across the sand like a crab. Before he could regain his feet the woman pushed violently off the bench. For a panicked second Alex expected her to attack, teeth gnashing, but she didn't.

Instead she strode toward the water, back arched. Confident. When she turned once more to Alex her face had resumed its former appearance.

"I know what scares you, love," she said. Before sprinting to the surf, the woman winked. "See you soon."

The instant she slipped below the waves, Alex woke up.

Screaming.

Warm. Safe.

The whole damn group in Heavenly Dreamland, Alex thought while driving to the hospital the next morning. Well, not exactly the whole group. Not Joyce, and after last night's horror show certainly not him.

What did the two of them have in common? Fear? Clinical anxiety? Clearly, but so did the rest of the group.

Joyce had been in a car accident, but he'd never so much as had a speeding ticket. She'd sustained heavy injuries to her—

Alex's hand darted to his scalp, fingers searching for the uneven scar beneath his dark hair.

The brain.

Joyce's accident had caused a subdural hematoma—a brain bleed—which pushed against several sections of her cerebral cortex. Alex's own...accident...had forced the neurosurgeons to use 127 stitches and three steel plates to reform his skull. Massive swelling in both brain hemispheres meant it took Alex two full weeks to relearn how to use a spoon.

Maybe traumatic brain injuries protected people from whatever affected Joey Riggins?

Alex needed to check Munson's chart first thing—if the fishing captain had head trauma in his past it'd be more proof that he was on to something. The psychiatrist pressed the Jeep's engine a little harder. The whole drive into work his questions kept piling up, turn after turn.

If not for laying on the horn the day before, would those two women have wound up at the bottom of the harbor? Was the horn a temporary solution? Permanent?

And the worst, most important question of all:

What-in-the-actual-fuck is out there, calling people down?

After the Jeep squealed into the hospital's parking lot Alex went straight to Medical Records and asked the clerk for Munson's file.

Three pages in, the trauma practically jumped off the page: a seizure, ten years prior. Serious enough to hospitalize Munson for a week. Alex slapped the file back down on the counter and reached for his pocket. The phone vibrated before he could even grab it—an incoming call from the sheriff's department.

"Doc, you're not gonna believe this," Rouse started, practically out of breath from the first word. "I just got off the phone with the Coast Guard, who just got off the phone with the goddamn U.S. Navy. Apparently they've got sensors buried in the sea bed all along the coast, constantly searching for large underwater objects—enemy warships, submarines."

Alex nodded, waiting for an opportunity to share his own news, but Rouse barely paused.

"So the Navy says the detectors in the Gulf of Maine just went batshit crazy. Something huge is coming straight in."

"Straight in where?"

"HERE. Portland Bay. Coast Guard says it's already past the Diamond Islands, it should be practically in the harbor within twenty minutes. Coast Guard is sending a cutter and a helicopter to intercept whatever the Hell it is. My guess is the Navy won't be far behind."

Alex turned toward the window, looking out to the east. He couldn't see the ocean from the ground floor of the hospital, but what he saw disturbed him more. Dozens—no, more than that—*hundreds* of people walking along the bluffs and over the road, headed east toward the water. All walking in a trance, not even swinging their arms. Like dead fish being pulled in on a line.

All those people. How much power does this thing have, how large would...

"Sheriff, how big?' Alex asked.

Rouse yelled at someone in his office, then got back on the line. "Christ, it's crazy in here. Say again?"

"How big is it?" Alex said, voice shaky and louder than he wanted.

"So big that the Navy's software won't tag it as a single object," Rouse said, almost gleeful. "At least a half-mile across."

"Oh, my God."

"I know, right? I'm going down there now. Gotta assess the situation, keep everybody safe."

Alex shouted "No!" into the phone, but Rouse had already hung up.

Alex drove as fast as he could, blasting the Jeep's horn the whole time at the lines of people streaming toward the harbor. No one responded like the day before. Everyone on the bluff, Hell, maybe the entire city, couldn't hear anything anymore except whatever pulled them toward the water.

As the Jeep came up over the rise Alex had to use both hands to swerve away from a group of human lemmings walking right over the bluff's edge. In the two-second break from continuous horn blasts Alex gathered himself and managed his first look down at Portland Bay. His breath caught in his throat.

A giant, circular shadow, almost as big as a stadium, churned the sea just outside the harbor mouth. The thing was far too wide to enter the harbor, but Alex saw quite clearly that it didn't matter. Boats from every marina pulled into the channel and headed for the shadow. Pleasure craft, commercial, even rowboats. Still docked, the huge Portland Ferry was a hub of activity—hundreds of people walking along the wharf in that direction. And at the entrance sat one sheriff's car, Rouse's number "01" on the roof.

"Goddamit."

Alex slammed the Jeep into gear and raced down the hill.

By the time he reached the wharf the crowd was almost on top of Rouse's car. Alex parked next to it and jumped out, frantic to find the sheriff—provided he was still the sheriff and not a suicidal swimmer on autopilot. A shout from the top deck of the ferry provided an answer.

"Doc, you still got your marbles?"

Alex breathed a sigh of relief and yelled back "So far!"

"Then get up here and help me shut off these goddamn engines. I'm not letting 500 people turn into lunch for whatever that thing is."

Alex took a final look at the approaching crowd and ran without thinking, jumping from the dock to the ferry's transom. The deck was already partially filled with passengers, all huddled against the rail staring longingly into the bay. Alex ran up to the top deck, searching for the bridge. When he found it Alex took a look over the side before walking through the hatch, and saw the bow and stern lines were untied, leaving the ferry free to navigate. He ducked onto the bridge to find Rouse alone.

"Hey, why are the lines untied? We don't need to sabotage the engines, let's just tie up instea—"

Rouse punched him square in the mouth, dropping Alex to the deck.

Sprawled on the cold, metal, Alex saw the sheriff's face go slack. Rouse knelt beside him and fastened his handcuffs—one side on Alex's left wrist, the other on a bulkhead's metal handrail. "She wants you," the sheriff muttered before pushing the throttle forward.

Alex groaned as the ferry accelerated away from the dock, headed into the channel.

"Bob, please." The psychiatrist stumbled to his feet, pulling at the cuffs and begging. "You don't have to do this—think of all the people. You're killing all of us," he whined, blood seeping from his nose. His pleas fell on deaf ears; Rouse was no more communicative than Joey Riggins had been.

Alex peered through the bridge windows at the frightening scene ahead. Dozens of boats headed toward the shadow, now hovering in the shallows just outside the harbor, each filled with people ready to die. Rouse threw the throttle wide open and the ferry moved that much faster toward the end.

On the far side of the shadow a Coast Guard cutter approached at flank speed, steel-gray deck gun gleaming in the sun. The cutter and the ferry reached the shadow at almost the same time. Hope flared in Alex's chest—but died just as quickly. The cutter's entire crew spilled out over the port and starboard railings without hesitation, leaving the ship to continue unmanned into the harbor. The armored bow sliced through two yachts before it even entered the channel.

"No...no...no," Alex wailed, tears forming. As if in response Rouse cut the throttle, and, much to Alex's surprise, unlocked the cuffs. The surprise wasn't pleasant though. Rouse threw the psychiatrist against the bulkhead, then manhandled him through the bridge hatch onto the deck—ready to pitch Alex into the ocean, right on top of whatever wanted him. Before the sheriff could, a Coast Guard helicopter came in high over Diamond Island, heading their way. Rouse didn't look up, but he did pause, almost as though waiting for orders.

Alex elected not to wait. He threw his body backward, thunking the sheriff against the bridge hatch and stunning the bigger man. The psychiatrist turned, grabbing Rouse's head with both hands and ramming it into the metal two times, then a third for good measure. The sheriff slumped to the deck.

It's not too late. Start the engines. Get the Hell out of here, Alex thought.

Above him the Coast Guard helicopter pitched forward, then dove straight for the middle of the shadow. It hit the surface and exploded in a white-orange fireball. The shockwave hit the ferry amidships and blew Alex off the top deck into the water.

The cold hit him first. An intense burst of pain, followed by every nerve ending screaming in protest. Then Alex's own thrashing flipped him over in the water, and in an instant he no longer cared about the cold at all.

It stretched out beneath him, 20 feet below the surface, farther than Alex's vision could carry in the murky coastal water. A titanic mass, shifting and roiling like an amoeba under a microscope, except it was a half-mile wide. An oily film clung to the surface that clouded any details of the thing's actual skin. As Alex drifted lower the section nearest to him shimmered. The oil dissipated enough for him to finally see.

To see that it didn't have skin.

It had mouths.

Everywhere.

Dozens in just the small section he could see. Gaping mouths two feet wide, each with vicious, needle-like teeth over six inches long. Jaws snapping open and shut, over and over. Even worse, Alex recognized the jaws.

Angler fish.

Denizens of the deepest ocean trenches, where no light penetrated. The ocean's oldest predator, hunting by drawing prey to those jaws with a bioluminescent lure. Except in real life they were barely two feet long; these were ten-foot long monsters, layered over one another, but not as individuals. They were *fused*, with no beginning or end. Thousands of them.

Millions, a voice echoed in his head. *Gathered in the deep for eons, Alex. Evolving. Telepathy works so much better than bright light, don't you think?*

Alex wanted to claw at the water, scramble to the surface, but the voice paralyzed him—gave him only enough strength to hold his breath. A strength that was fading.

Now we're ready to ascend. To taste all the delicious fear humans have to offer. And you, Alex, have so much, don't you? The oldest fear.

An inky plume of oil erupted from the surface of the creature, stretching through the water to envelope him completely. There, in the monstrosity's grip, Alex breathed in the oil, surrendering to it. To his surprise he didn't choke or convulse; instead his lungs expanded and relaxed.

I can breathe, he thought. Then wished he couldn't.

The darkness around him coalesced into pure blackness, like a night dive. Like the last dive he'd ever made.

He searched the blackness like he had ten years ago, feeling a presence but unable to see. A dead flashlight on his hip. Only the sound of the scuba tanks and his own breath bubbling into the limitless ocean. Alone.

But not quite.

A gentle brush of water pressure against his face. Something swimming nearby.

His hand dropped to the flashlight, desperate for one

more glimpse.

Alex clapped the light against his hand, hoping for one more flicker. The light beamed for one second. Long enough to see it come for him.

Now, in the creature's grip, the light shines once more.

The great white's jaws distend, coming for his face. Alex managed to duck his head, the way he'd saved himself last time. The teeth had clamped down, some on skull and some on his regulator valve. Now though, the shark tastes nothing but flesh.

Alex feels his own head separate, tastes his own blood in his mouth just before the shark swallows. Then, somehow, he doesn't die. The scene repeats, and it happens again.

And again.

And again.

Each time the voice in his head groans in pleasure.

The inky sphere pulls Alex down gradually, keeping him alive, sinking slowly toward hungry, gnashing jaws where real death awaits.

Trey Dowell

About the Author

Trey Dowell is an award-winning author of both short and novel-length fiction. His short stories have been published in Ellery Queen Mystery Magazine, as well as several anthologies, and his debut sci-fi novel The Protectors was published by Simon & Schuster in 2014. You can learn more at www.treydowell.com.

Hostile Territory

Steve Neal

Kat nestled into the side of her new fiancé, Anders, her head on his shoulder and their fingers interlaced. They sat on a wooden bench with no back, shaded from the mid-day Louisiana sun by a cloth canopy held up by thin, metal rods. To their right a small dock, made up of bobbled and uneven planks, led out over an opaque strip of water to a sparkling airboat, seemingly brand new. Nailed to one of the dock's posts was a picture of four men surrounding a massive alligator: a beast too huge to be real, its head alone was larger than a five year old child, and a tail long enough that anyone would mistake it for a fell trunk floating in a swamp. A creature more befitting a prehistoric world, far too monstrous to still exist around people.

"There's no way it's actually that big, right?" Anders asked. "I mean that thing could swallow me whole."

"I don't think they're using a lot of photoshop out here, dearest. We're going to find out, anyhow. Excited?

You're excited," she wiggled further into him.

"Terrified. Excited. Same thing, right?"

"Aw, but I need my big, strong husband to protect me against the scary dinosaur. Gotta be brave to impress me, you gotta win me over," she said, failing to suppress the smirk on her lips, her cheeks pushed upward with each word that came out her mouth.

"Think I've impressed you plenty," he brought up her left hand and let her engagement ring glimmer in the light. "Plus, we're not going anywhere unless fella shows back up," he used their intertwined hands to point over at the dilapidated shack that'd served as both ticket office and gift shop.

On arrival Marlon had greeted them - a lanky, leathery man who might have been twenty or forty. He'd told them that the tour would start up soon, and to wait by the dock while he prepared. Instead of returning within ten minutes he'd been inside the crooked shack for nearly half an hour, with no sign that he'd re-emerge any time soon. Still, the couple were more than happy to lounge around with one another and test the resilience of the mosquito spray they'd coated on themselves before leaving the house.

Looking around at the world was enough to keep Kat engaged. Everything from the thickness of the blades of grass to the size of the bark on the surrounding trees was different from home; a place where the sun came out for two months a year, and tropical things only existed on screens or billboards. This was as close to an alien planet as she'd experience. She lost three whole minutes watching a yellow-and-black striped spider the size of her hand dangling from one of the crooked tree limbs across from them, examining it, watching as it made jerked movements as it spun its web. She smacked her hand into Anders' thigh, pointing over to it. His whole body tensed, and tongue shot from his mouth.

"Oh Christ, why on Earth would you show me that?" He shivered and got up, taking a step to his left and sitting back down on the bench. "You're my first line of defense against that."

"Alright, folk," Marlon burst through the back door of the shack, a portly man rushed after him, gripping a styrofoam cooler in both hands. "Looks like ain't nobody else showin' up, so why don't we get this boat on the road," he said with a wide, blisteringly-white smile. "Under the back bench," he told the man following him. "Now, couple rules. Nothing fancy. One, don't get in the water or leave the boat for any reason. Two, don't touch the gators, they familiar with me, but y'all smell funny to them, smell a little funny to me too," he said with a nod and a grin. "Third, ear protection on at all times unless I'm standin' in front of ya chattin' 'way like I do to ya now. Questions?"

He spoke fast, giving little time for the out-of-towners to decipher his accent. Both nodded regardless of how many words they'd missed from his rundown.

"Let's board this beauty then," Marlon hopped onto the boat with a small leap that made the vessel rock with the impact.

At the back of the boat, near the driver's podium

adorned with a myriad of switches and dials, the shorter man cursed as he snatched for the back row of benches to steady himself. A string of nonsensical utterances followed as he scowled at Marlon, shaking his head before walking off the boat and past the couple, up the dock.

"Just stay away from Willy's zone. Don't go searchin'," he yelled over his shoulder before continuing his march.

Marlon didn't react. His smile remained, hand extended to help the couple onto the craft.

"Is Willy the huge one?" Kat asked as she took a seat in the front row and looked down the tight corridor of water in front of her.

"No, ma'am," Marlon said as he walked to the back of the boat, grabbing an oar and pushing them off from the dock. "Mongo's our big man, makes Willy look like the runt. Willy rambunctious as all Hell, but he taken himself off somewhere, maybe grumpy with me, maybe sick of these waters. We feed into the gulf so most other gators steer clear. Mongo don't care. Ain't a bit o' salt in the waters gon' bother a big man like him."

Marlon plunged the oar into the water as he spoke, digging into the sediment below the surface to push the boat forward into the natural tunnel that had formed around the stream; a canopy of wizened branches were twisted and entangled with other limbs. All trees were decorated by thick clumps of dangling, Spanish Moss that hung like natural draperies, obscuring what came next. With a deft touch he navigated the various roots that rose out from the water and dipped back under like elusive serpents, each threatening to lodge the boat between their curves. Little light made it through the foliage above, though God-rays burst through in sparse locations, making the dingy water sparkle in certain places.

"Now, we can go see big man first, or I can show y'all some of the other critters-"

"I want to see Mongo," Kat interjected, turning around on the bench with a child-like glee to her voice. "Please."

Marlon laughed. "Alright. If ya want, I'll let ya feed big man. Toss him some chicken if ya got an arm on ya. Big man might even do a trick for us. He basically a big ol' puppy. Used to feed him marshmallows when I was a kid."

"I didn't know alligators could be so cute," Anders said.

"Hell, brother, he the size of truck, yet I seen his leg twitch when I rub his belly more times than I can count. He's the family pet 'round here."

"You're already having fun," Kat nudged her elbow into Anders' side to accentuate each word.

He smiled and the pair went back to scanning the water, their heads snapping to each tiny ripple, expecting a gaping maw to emerge from the deep. All they saw were dozens of bugs skirting along the surface, a constant motion to the water, a whole ecosystem interacting and thriving. Clumps of gnats buzzed in the air, shifting in communal swings and dodging through the air as if they called out motions before performing them. Marlon pushed the oar into various trees and clumps of mud, letting the boat glide down the serene river while the couple sat with their heads bouncing from side to side until unabated sunlight appeared in the distance.

"Gonna need y'all to put on the muffs now. Hold on tight, backs flat against the seat."

Both gave a thumbs up once the padded headphones were on, and the world's humming and buzzing became a murmur. The peace only lasted for a few seconds as a soft whine coincided with the boat lurching forward. The sound came in waves, the throttle feathered as they made their way toward the light. They accelerated comfortably as ripples moved out from the sides of the boat, and a soft foam formed around the point of the ship.

Sunlight kept the world ahead of them a mystery, bleached into a textureless whiteness. Kat squinted and leaned forward to see what lay ahead, the fan's whining turning into a roar, the sudden force of acceleration shoving her back into the seat as they rocketed into the light. She grabbed ahold of the seat's lip, white knuckling as wind whipped at her face, stinging her eyes so she had to look through her eyelashes. Underneath her she could feel the boat shifting back and forth, cool sprays of water dousing her exposed shins to accentuate the turns.

When her eyes adjusted to the light she saw a gorgeous world blurred in front of her. Long grass formed a wall around the waterway, carved through frequent use, the boat battering the vegetation aside. The water sparkled under a cloudless, pale sky. Sparse trees dotted the skyline, gnarled and leafless things that housed curious birds with twisted necks who watched the boat speed through their world.

Kat leaned into the turns, bobbing up and down like she was controlling the boat's actions with the twists and turns of her body. For a brief second she looked over at Anders and saw the giddy smile on his face that wobbled with air and inflated his cheeks. Various splits in the waterway promised other views and tours around the expanse, which turned Kat's head and made her try to catch a glimpse of where the paths led. There seemed to be no end to the swamp, the world's horizon hidden behind the grass' tips, the natural maze cut into the water and reeds making it seem all encompassing. Miles grew between them and the dock, twenty minutes of high-speed turns and blurred landscapes; an extended thrill ride that seemed to have no end.

The fan shut off, the whirring calming to a stop as the boat approached an open expanse of water; a wide lake with a few patches of earth erupting through the surface. It was decorated with stubby blades of grass and mud to form little islands while towering swamp grass stared inward from the edges like a curious but tepid crowd. Unlike the stream, the water sat still here. Nothing tested the surface, nothing moved around or skidded atop it. A lake of dark glass, shining under the sun, its contents obscured.

"Sorry, folk," Marlon said once he walked back up to the front, "that's a long go without a break. Usually we see Willy first. Break up the drive. Y'all good?"

The pair nodded, eyes wide and hair swept in all manner of directions.

"That was fucking awesome," Anders leaned in toward her, whispering.

She grabbed his knee and shook it back and forth as a sign of solidarity.

"Alright, well, time to meet the star of the show. You can see him already, over there," Marlon pointed to the edge of the lake, a part in the tall grass where the blades sat bent.

Kat stood and squinted out to the distance while Anders hung onto her belt loop. Only the gator's head was visible from where they sat, and even that was enough to show its gargantuan size. From snout to neck the reptile's head would've been as long as a basketball player's torso, and as wide as a bodybuilder's. Beady eyes stared back, making direct contact with her. She slapped at Anders.

"Do you see this thing? Holy crap," she pointed and flailed before grabbing his head and directing it toward Mongo.

"That's real?" Anders stood, and turned to Marlon with his mouth agape.

"Very real, older than all us combined they reckon. Y'all wanna meet 'im?"

"Please," Kat burst out in excitement.

Marlon walked to the back and returned with the cooler in his arms. He placed it between the feet of the couple. Inside, packed between pounds of ice, were a few bottles of water, a few beers and chunks of uncovered chicken breast.

"Drinks?"

"No, thank you," Anders held up his hand.

Kat shook her head, unenthused by the idea of sipping on a beer can coated in the slime from raw chicken. Marlon shrugged and dove his hand into the cooler, removing three chunks of chicken in one swoop. He knelt and dipped one of them into the water, swirling it around.

The grass in the distance rustled as Mongo lurched forward. Ridges rose above the surface of the water as he emerged from the grass. In, what seemed like a cruel joke, an endless procession of protrusions kept coming no matter how many seconds passed. Even as the ridges tapered inward, and the wake from Mongo's swishing tail became visible, his size still seemed like an impossibility to Kat.

"How freaking big did you say he was?" Anders asked, shuffling around the bench into the back row.

"About nineteen feet or so, we don't measure him very often," Marlon said, standing up.

"Can I stay up here?" Kat asked.

"'Course, ain't nothin' to be 'fraid of. He just want his chicken. Eatin' us too much a hassle to the lazy thing."

The alligator stopped a few dozen feet away from the boat. Its eyes and nostrils were among the few things visible above the water. Marlon bent back down again, splashing the chicken around in the water.

"Dinner time, my friend," he called out, extending his arm forward over the edge of the boat.

Mongo burst forward again, serpentining in the water, fluid motions that closed the distance. Kat watched in amazement, marveled by the grace of a creature larger than the boat she stood upon. Everything worked in tandem to bring him closer to them. Kat's mouth hung open, passing trembling exhales over her lips as beads of sweat formed on her palms. Little details became visible as the weathered and scarred leviathan neared, every crack and dimple on a hide that had greyed from decades of living.

In one fluid movement Mongo rose his head out of the water, jaws wide open as he bent back on himself and snapped down at the water near his midsection. A great splash mixed with Kat's yelps and Anders' string of curses, creating an appropriate din to the sudden flash of violence. Mongo started to roll, spinning in place and sending out miniature waves that bobbled the air boat.

"Take ya seats," Marlon shouted out, as he grabbed the oar and tried to move the boat away from the mayhem. "He got sumtin."

Kat had already flung herself onto the bench to avoid the turmoil. No fear bubbled inside of her. A curiosity rose instead; the wonderment of seeing an apex predator kill in person. She tried to look at his mouth, to see what he'd caught between his jaws, but couldn't see many details through the plumes of water and foam. All she could make out was chunks of grey and occasional bits of white as the alligator's underbelly became visible as it spun. Streaks of red appeared, and the foam around Mongo gained a pink hue as blood mixed with the swamp.

"Marlon," she cried out, grabbing at the man's arm once she noticed the lines across Mongo's stomach.

The spins of the gator came slower, its motion restricted.

"What the Hell," he stopped pushing the boat backward, digging the oar into the sediment to stop them.

"What're you doing, wrong way," Anders said from the back seat. "Get us away from it."

"Quiet ya ass down. Sumtin's wrong with the big man."

Mongo's spin stopped entirely, the gator floating belly up in the water. Once the water settled, Kat could see the ropes or weeds wrapped around its stomach and legs that held him in place.

"He's caught on something," she called out.

"We'd like to leave now," Anders said from the back.

"Nah, man," Marlon put the oar down, and reached down to his ankle, unsheathing a blade nearly as long as his shin. "That's my friend. Not gonna let him drown for y'all."

Kat swiped at him, trying to latch on to part of his shirt or a flailing limb before Marlon jumped into the waist-high water, but he began to wade toward the trapped alligator with his arms outstretched in front of him.

"Get back here," Anders slapped against the benches in protest, but Marlon ignored the demand.

Traversing through the water seemed an arduous affair as Marlon struggled to step more than once every second or two. Mongo's stomach began to bulge, the grip of whatever he'd caught himself on tightening with each passing second. More of the giant's legs and tail disappeared, covered by an increasing number of the fibers until almost none of his limbs were visible.

"Please come back aboard, I don't think-" Kat's plea

didn't make it all out of her mouth before Marlon shouted back at her.

"I ain't leavin' without freein' him, lady. Now row the boat over."

Anders shook his head viciously from side to side. "Don't you dare."

Mongo's body began to move. Not thrashing like it had before, but subtle bumps and twitches before the center of his stomach started to rise above the rest of it like something bent it in half. It reached a sharp peak before the reptile's skin split, something bursting up and out of the reptile's stomach. Through the spray of blood and innards Kat saw what had punctured the hide: a worm-like creature, grey and segmented, yet as thick as a grass snake. It was tipped with a beak that opened, blossoming after it'd pierced through the flesh and anchoring itself around the exit wound.

"Mongo," Marlon screamed.

"Get back," Kat pleaded.

Anders started fiddling around with the controls on the driver's podium.

More peaks and protrusions warped Mongo's skin, pushing more of his massive body out of the water. The beaked tentacles continued to wrap themselves around the alligator, pushing their tips through its body until dozens of them had pierced Mongo, holding him a few inches above the water as if they were displaying their kill like a fisherman holding his catch above his head. Marlon continued to stride toward them, either familiar with the creatures or unperturbed by them. He cursed every step, promising Hell and vengeance once he arrived.

Kat started making her way over to the side. "Please, just come back now. It's dead, Marlon. The gator's dead, come on," she cried as the tearing began.

Like a hundred zips being undone in unison a cacophonous few seconds followed as the worms pulled Mongo apart, rendering the massive beast into hunks of meat of all sizes and flinging them in opposing directions. A soft pattering filled the air as droplets of blood rained from the sky, accentuated by louder splashes as chunks of Mongo landed in the water. A feeding frenzy commenced as the tendrils darted beneath the surface, attacking the remains from below and breaching through the flesh with their beaks before flattening to fasten themselves against the lumps of meat to drag them below.

Kat grabbed the oar on the deck. "Get the fuck back here," she called out to Marlon, extending the oar out to him. "Grab on. Grab on now."

Marlon stood frozen in the center of the swamp, covered in the remains of his friend, staring wide-eyed at the spot where the colossal beast had lay only seconds earlier.

"Move, you dumb hick," Anders screamed. "I can't figure this out," he'd started smacking every button and nozzle on the podium, hoping something would cause the fan to roar to life and jettison them far from whatever killed such a beast.

"Marlon, follow my voice," Kat tried to keep her words calm, hoping that serenity would cut through the chaos and bring him back into the waking world.

Marlon trembled as he looked at a piece of Mongo bobbing on the surface. Small waves emanated from around his hips as he shivered. Kat saw the movement in the water, a slight bulge in the surface heading toward him. She gave a final cry, a last-ditch effort to snap him out of it. Only the contact of the tentacle fought off the freezing grip of shock and made him slice at the water blindly with his knife, but the first tendril already wrapped itself around his waist. He cursed and stabbed down into water, plunging his arm down to the elbow.

He cried out again and ripped his arm back up, now with one of the beaks having impaled the inside of his forearm. It blossomed, flattened and began to pull him downward as if an angler reeled him in. The force bent Marlon down, unable to yank his arm upward without the anchored beak tearing an even greater hole in him. More tentacles reached up from the water, wrapping around his neck and bursting through his chest to anchor into his back.

Kat turned away, not wanting to watch Marlon get pulled under, or apart. Instead, she carefully stepped over to Anders and hugged him, burying her face in his clavicle.

"Don't move an inch," she said.

"Let go," he tried to pull his arms free, but she'd wrapped him up in hers.

"It's the movement. They attack movement."

A piece of Marlon flew out of the water, an unidentifiable chunk of meat that arced through the air before splashing down. Immediately a beak pierced it, dragging it down.

"Let's just get outta here," Anders' growled, shaking free of her grasp and stamping toward the back of the boat.

"You don't know how to start it, let alone drive it," she matched the venom in his voice.

"Better than just waiting around to die," he said as he looked over the panel.

His movement only bobbed the boat slightly, but it garnered an immediate response from the horde. A series harsh impacts shifted the entire vessel to its right with enough force that Anders lost his footing, the boat's slick deck offering no friction, no way for him to stop his feet flying out from under him. A slip bounced his backside off the lip of the boat and dumped him into the water.

Kat rushed straight for the oar and slapped it against the water several feet away from him. "Anders, move, move now."

She continued to smack the water in quick succession, moving the oar away from him with each hit, trying to cause as many different ripples and points of interest in the water as possible. Within a matter of seconds two of the creatures had pierced through the oar's plastic, spreading their beaks and yanking the oar from her hands with a vigor that nearly dragged her with it.

Anders got his upper body onto the deck with the time she'd bought him, kicking his feet as he struggled to pull the rest of himself on board. Kat latched onto his arms and started to pull. Six more cracks rang out around the swamp, the boat's hull pierced by the things. She ignored them; only getting Anders out of the water mattered. Adrenaline allowed her to drag his body on top of hers as she fell back onto the deck, only the toes of his boots touching the water. He continued to crawl over her, eventually flopping to her side and curling up next to the driver's podium. He began to laugh, a heaving belly laugh that made his shoulders bounce. She slapped her hand into his chest, a flat palm into his sternum.

"This is so fucked," he said through the laughs.

"Stop laughing. Stop it," she said rolling onto her side.

The front of the boat looked like the beach at low tide as copper-tinged water lapped at the deck, rolling over the lip as an early warning sign of the inevitable.

"If you'd just," she slapped him again, "have," again, "listened," her final smack boomed before she pulled herself up to a stand and looked out at the swamp around them. "You never just listen to me."

It didn't stop him from laughing. It'd only grown more raucous, the man rocking in a fetal position.

All around them the water moved, kicked up into a foam as a frenzy commenced under the surface, most volatile in the spot that Anders had fallen into a few seconds prior. She could see the tendrils snapping at nothing, some launching vertically out of the water like fountain jets. Everything else around rushed in that direction, waves forming on the surface as countless predators rushed to a prey's last known position.

"What is so damn funny?" She snapped again.

"He took the keys."

"What?" She turned her head to look at him on the floor, an arm extended upward, his finger pointed at an ignition half-way down the podium.

"Nearly died for nothing," the phrase finally stopped his amusement, two more monosyllabic laughs came out to signal the end.

Kat extended her hand down toward him and helped him to his feet. The pair stood side-by-side and watched the swamp's movements as the tide licked an inch higher up the deck. Every few minutes another crack rang out, a testing probe. They let minutes dribble by without so much as a word or prolonged sigh, their fingers intertwined.

As a unit they took careful steps, sitting down on the back bench with their feet up on the front one, a comfortable seat for oblivion. Both seemed content to exist in the silence, unmoving, unthinking, as if becoming voids would grant them freedom.

"You think they're connected to something?" She asked.

"I..." Anders shivered and didn't respond further.

"Sorry," she said under her breath, regretting putting the mental images in her own mind, let alone his.

"No. Fuck this. Don't be sorry," his head darted from side to side, searching for something. Instead, he reached down and began to undo his shoelaces.

"Are you okay?"

"Water's still, right? Has been?" With his shoe off he cocked back his arm and launched it as far off the east side of the boat as possible.

He held out a finger, the international sign for 'wait'.

"Yeah, they'll attack it. They attacked the oar."

As predicted a few tentacles darted through the water, impaling and constricting the shoe. Anders swung his finger around to the other side of the boat and pointed at the swamp on the opposing side of the shoe.

"See?" He said, smug.

Shimmers moved through the water. Visible surges on the surface as the speed of their attack warped the surface. They moved in a direct line, passing under the boat as if it hadn't been a target for them earlier. Every tentacle in the vicinity descended upon the shoe with a passionate desperation that only the starving could understand.

"So, they all go after it? Like a hive mind?" Kat scowled, unsure that he was making a point worth making.

"If the splash is big enough, I think they all try and get a piece, yeah. We can use that."

Kat laughed. A single, dismissive 'ha' that threw her head back as it came out.

"It's not far," he only moved his outstretched arm a few degrees, and pointed at one of the small humps of land that protruded from the swamp; a mix of grass and mud that promised salvation. "Forty, fifty feet?"

"And the second we move we're dragged under water, no way," she shook her head.

"We've got a couple of hours max before this thing sinks, right? Then we'll be in the water anyway."

"There was the other guy at the shack. He'll come looking for us when we don't return, and we can get the fuck out of here. Maybe there's a radio or-" Kat readied herself for a stand.

"Already looked, there's not," Anders put a hand on her shoulder, keeping her in place.

"Well, I'm still waiting. That's suicide."

Kat expected him to reply, to forge a rebuttal, but instead he nodded and stared out at the floating remains of his shoe. Together they studied the swamp's glass-like flatness, as not even bugs dared to land and disturb the water. The deception of a dangerous world, one that began to change as shadows grew long and laid out across the swamp. A landscape that, at a glance, had nothing wrong with it, deceptive enough that some might've considered it picturesque; home to nothing more than man-eating alligators, flesh-rotting bacteria and venomous snakes. Things that, in hindsight, didn't seem so scary.

"Pass me a drink, yeah?" Kat said after over an hour of reticence.

The water lapped further up the boat; a portion of the front permanently submerged. On certain rolls of the tide the water made its way up to the cooler. To avoid a stray wave slapping against his soles Anders clambered over the benches to get to the front seats.

"What do you fancy, beer or-" he held the lid to the cooler in his hands but stopped looking down at the contents halfway through his sentence. "Catch," he said, and waited a solid second before tossing one of the water bottles through the air at her.

Kat's eyes burst open, and her hands flailed outward,

snatching the plastic bottle in a firm, two-handed grip as she stared daggers at him. Her lips peeled back; all teeth bared before a guttural tirade started. "Do you even think? If that had hit the floor-"

"Every one of those things within a mile would've bore down on us. Exactly my point," he said as he climbed back to his original position.

"Nope."

The pair passed the bottle back and forth, taking little sips every few minutes, welcoming the respite from the oppressive swamp air. Both shirts had darkened around their armpits and lower back, all hairlines damp and pasted to their foreheads. Long exhales became the most common sound.

Kat grew restless once the sun started to caress the top of the long grass, the inevitability of darkness posed an additional threat that made it impossible to sit still. Unlike Anders, she was unable to look at one spot and zone out. Her head always bobbed around, looking for some kind of movement. Part of her wanted the mayhem to return, or a bird to land on the water and remain untouched, but nothing happened. Nothing in the world spoke. Nothing moved. Time just ticked by.

"He's not coming, is he?" Kat said once the bottom edge of the sun became blocked out behind the long grass.

"We have to try. We'll be underwater in the dark," the glee in his voice had gone, the excitement over a devised plan eroded into a despondency.

"Sell me on it."

"Alright," Anders took a long step from the back bench onto the one in front. "It all depends on this," he held up a single ice cube before whipping his arm and sending the chunk into the water with a thick 'plonk'.

As expected, the tentacles investigated the splash, rushing to it, some crashing into the side of the boat in feverish excitement.

"We can do this," he turned and smiled. "There's at least," he paused, bobbed his head from side to side. "Forty ice cubes in here. Plus the drinks, plus the chicken. All we do," he rested his arms across the back of the bench as he spoke, "is throw a few big things far. Get in the water, stay still. Throw another thing, move. Repeat."

"And if they notice us?"

"We hope they don't."

"Maybe it's possible the boat hits the bottom and we're not fully submerged. Or, or-"

"Stop," he cut her off. "This is our only option. Just have to stay still. Are you ready?"

"Now?" Her head cocked forward, eyelids peeling back as far as they could go.

Anders shrugged. "It's either that, or we wait to go down with the ship."

"Alright," her voice trembled out the words.

With shuffled, tandem steps, they moved the cooler to the western side of the boat, placing it down on the edge. Both lowered themselves into a sit either side of it. Kat closed her eyes. Breathed. A steady inhale. Hold. A steady exhale. A way to make the automatic process labored and thoughtful, to steal her mind away from worry, to slow her heart rate down from the blasting in her chest; a thumping so vigorous she worried the creatures would sense it in the water.

"I'm going to throw one as far as I can, then lower yourself in. Be careful, okay? If I see them coming I'm pulling you out."

"Sure," she kept her eyes closed.

A splash came a couple of seconds after. A deep sloshing in the distance.

"Now. Go now," Anders said along with the impact.

Kat pointed her toes and placed her palms flat on the deck as she began her slide into the water. When her toes dipped into her water she bit down, ground her teeth into their counterparts, not wanting to scream or curse, trying to stay as focused on her movements as possible. Warm water enveloped her feet, then her ankles, then calves, as she lowered herself in a controlled descent from the deck.

"You're fine. You're doing fine. Nothing's coming," Anders told her as her hips disappeared below the surface.

She kept her eyes closed tight, hard enough that creases spread out to her temples. Vision would only betray her. Without it she could pretend to be doing anything else at all: wading through the ocean, or dipping herself into a hot tub with a cold beer sat on the tile next to her. She kept herself in the fantasy until her toes hit the mud at the bottom. When her feet flattened the water lapped against her sternum; a soft current that caused a constant sensation of motion against her chest and back. She kept her arms raised above her head, taking that group of muscles out of the potential traitors due to an unwarranted spasm.

"I'm in," she whispered, afraid of speaking with too much conviction or bass.

"Throwing another."

Kat watched as the chicken breast sailed through the air, beyond the sloshing as the tentacles battled over the original piece of meat. When it landed near a hump of land by the grass, a gush of movement followed it. Anders didn't wait for them to reach it before sliding himself into the swamp, doing so in half the time it'd taken her. She didn't focus on him. Instead she watched the feeding, mentally timing it to see how long a small hunk of meat would keep them distracted.

Anders made it in just before the splashing ceased. Without saying a word, he grabbed the cooler from the deck and thrust it in her direction.

"Why me?" She asked.

"I need to throw. Now's not the time for a debate."

Kat held her arms out flat, ready to bear the weight, her muscles tensed so that its addition didn't change her posture. A slight tremble started in her arms as Anders lowered the cooler onto her, the box heavier than she'd expected, sending a surge of panic through her; a paranoia over whether it'd moved her or wobbled the swamp enough to send a curious tentacle through the water to prod at her. All she could do was stay still, keep her arms strong and the cooler directly in front of her face. It blinded her, kept her unaware of her surroundings except her periphery, leaving her clueless to how close their island salvation sat.

"Tell me before you reach in, okay? Don't scare me. Don't make me jump. Please? Okay?" She spoke through a clenched jaw, worried that even the muscles in her neck may reverberate through the water.

"You're okay. I'm going to take a few drinks and throw them in time with our steps. I'll call it all out to you, you're safe," his voice had a measure of certainty about it. An unearned calm about a dire situation.

Part of Kat wanted to lambaste him, demand he panic and show the same amount of anxiety that swept through her, but she kept her mouth shut, remaining focused on her breathing and giving him an affirmative 'mhm'.

"Grabbing now," he said.

Kat flexed her forearms and biceps, expecting a downward force as Anders' hands ruffled through the cooler. Only the sound of ice brushing against ice followed as he used a gentle touch to grab the cans.

"Step when you hear the splash. Throwing," he said.

The wait for impact seemed to last forever, to the point where she started to believe she'd missed the window and expected admonishment from Anders to follow. When the splash came her right leg glided forward without any consideration, an automatic movement executed without pause. Her left leg followed suit. When she stood still in the new spot she felt a twinge of relief. No pain or tightness came. The only sensation was that of the water brushing past her shins when she moved.

"Do you see any?" She asked, partially thankful that

she couldn't see the state of the water. A gloomy surface that promised secrets below, a sight that would've only increased her paranoia and heart rate.

"Nothing's coming," a hint of smug celebration existed in his voice. A gloating tone Kat never thought she'd be thankful to hear. "Ready? Throwing now."

Another step came and went without any hassle. Anders warned Kat and grabbed another two cans. He threw both, and they completed two more steps without any complications or indication anything lived in the water. A dangerous thing started to swell: belief. Kat stopped fearing every step, believing that they'd make it to the mound of earth without any interference from the ravenous tentacles. She'd stopped thinking about them entirely by the eighth step, finding herself in a rhythm that followed Anders' directions reflexively. They operated in tandem, a well-oiled machine, human intelligence overcoming the creatures' innate barbarism.

But then she felt it against her exposed skin. A feathered touch that wrapped around her, a solid loop tickling her ankle. She yelped and twitched at the contact.

"Fuck," she squeaked. "Throw. Throw now. Help. Throw," she said through grit teeth, expecting a searing pain to run up her leg in response to her movement.

Anders moved quicker this time, his hand pushing down into the cooler to grab as much as possible. Multiple splashes followed, one after another.

"It's got me, keep throwing," she said, prompting Anders to dive his hand back in.

Even more pressure pushed down on her from his digging this time, more of his body weight pressing into the cooler as he searched deeper inside. Two more large splashes followed, then a dozen smaller ones.

It writhed up and down her ankle, stroking it with a delicate touch. Gentle movements that she'd not expected of the creatures, perhaps a stray or a runt, curious and unsure how to proceed. "It's still there, Anders, please."

"We, uh, we need to step, okay? On the next throw, you have to step forward for me, alright?"

"It'll kill me, it'll kill me if I move, please, just get it off me."

"Hold still. Just..." he trailed off, sighing before digging his hand back into the cooler. "Shit. Alright. You're going to feel me grab your leg, don't freak out."

A few splashes followed. Small ones, like pebbles dropping into a bucket. Kat groaned as she felt the movement around her leg, a muffled scream that lasted until she no longer felt tension around her ankle, and heard Anders pop out of the water. Before he said anything he threw another ice cube.

"Step," he called out.

"Did you get it?" She said, following his order. "Is it dead?"

"Yep. Dead. Got it. Focus on moving, okay?" A terseness arrived in his voice, hidden beneath a purposeful softness, one that she would've felt the need to address had the situation been different.

The splashes continued to come, minute sounds that

barely registered in Kat's ears, making her doubt whether she should step or not.

"Just walk," he told her. "Don't stop."

Instead of the well-timed impacts of the water they came in a constant barrage. One after another. She felt him digging around in the cooler multiple times, tipping it on its side to reach further inside. The rapid splashes only lasted so long, about ten steps, before gaps started to form between the noises.

"Keep going. Don't stop," Anders said as he ripped the cooler from her hands.

For the first time since entering the water she was able to see. They'd only made it halfway to their island savior, a pastoral patch of green set ablaze by the sinking sun. Anders stood directly to her left, a piece of frayed rope dangling from his right hand. He dug around in the cooler for half a second before he began to smash it into the water, wading back toward the boat as he smacked it against the surface.

"Swim. Go. Go now!" Anders screamed between hits.

"What're you-" she began to ask.

"Fucking swim!" he yelled.

There wasn't time to argue. A couple of dozen feet in front of Anders a wave surged toward him. Both of her feet kicked as hard as possible, her body twisting with every stroke as knife-edged hands propelled her toward the shore. She didn't hear him splashing any more, her own noise and motions drowning him out. Between strokes she gained glimpses of a nearing mound of dark earth. A tangible goal. Something to strive toward and ignore her brain's insistence that they'd pull her back at any moment.

A cold, hard surface struck her fingertips mid-stroke, causing her to lift her head to see the mound inches in front of her face. She clawed at it, struggling to find grip, not able to bury her nails in the dirt the way she imagined. She flailed, slapping her limbs against the surface and scrambling to get all of her body out of the water. No grass grew on this mound, the smallest of the ones around them, just a brownish-grey patch of earth, perhaps a rock, poking up from the water. A few feet to her right was the land they'd aimed for.

Kat looked across the swamp expecting to see Anders still slapping the cooler into the ground, or standing atop the deck, having escaped the wrath of the creatures. Instead she saw the cooler, bobbing up and down in the water a few feet away from the boat. She called out for him, screaming twice at the top of her lungs, hearing her own voice echo back to her. A third attempt to call out passed between her lips as a shaking whimper, then she collapsed down to her knees. She continued to scream and smack her hands into the surface until what little energy she had ran out, leaving her to watch as a few tentacles punctured the cooler and tried to drag it under the water. Its buoyancy kept it afloat as the tentacles dragged it toward her.

"I'm sorry," she stammered out. "I should-"

A sudden shift from below stopped her words, her island moving beneath her, grazing against her knees. She stood and looked down, expecting to see the rocks and dirt parting, drifting away from one another under the duress of her weight. Instead, she saw vague movements that required a squint to examine. The brown and grey appeared to unravel, like intertwined pieces of yarn freeing themselves from one another, then she saw two beaks passing by her feet. Kat shifted her movement, ready to sprint, to dive into the water and make a final break for the island, but her body didn't move. Her feet sealed to the surface, enveloped by the grey strands that spiraled up her leg.

A moment of pandemonium followed. Flailing limbs slapped against the water, waves and splashes surrounding her body as the tentacles dragged her directly down into the water, and under the surface. Localized, stabbing pains began. Plumes of red rose around her, wafting in the murky depths of the swamp. She fought and struggled to the best of her ability, but lacked the necessary strength to free herself. A haze of colors appeared through the cloud of disturbed dirt in the water. Just out of reach, gold and silver swirled in front of her. All of her floundering stopped as she stared into the colors revolving around a black slit in the center. The tentacles pulled her closer, and proximity provided clarity and form to the colors. An eye as large as her head stared at her.

The being that Kat had dragged herself onto slunk beneath the surface, sending a few final ripples across the water. Within a matter of seconds the undulations dissipated, and the swamp regained its motionless calm with only the sinking airboat as evidence of what had occurred.

Steve Neal

About the Author

Steve Neal is an English-born writer living in America. A lifelong horror fanatic who enjoys poking at the unknown and seeing what he uncovers. With a passion for the bizarre, horrifying, and bewildering, he aims to make readers reconsider what they think about the natural world. Follow him over at twitter @SteveNealWrites.

Xook

Dan Le Fever

Rebecca looked up at the glittering light that reflected down at her from around the underside of their boat. She felt sorry for Scott; he was going to have to spend the afternoon fishing while the dive team got to explore the cave system off the coast of Quintana Roo. The sense of joy she had as she felt the ocean pressure pushing down on her was indescribable, almost akin to an embrace. She savored it for a moment before she swam to catch up to the dive lights slowly fading inside the large cave entrance.

Using the radio inside her mask, she said, "Don't get too far ahead. Over."

"Roger," came back two high-pitched voices that made her laugh. The two men, Dennis and Eduardo, typically had deep voices, but the gas in their tanks made everyone sound like they'd been sucking on helium-filled balloons.

Unclipping her light, Rebecca swept it along the cavern wall as she glided along, now leisurely kicking her legs. Algae and ocean grasses had grown thick near the entrance, making it hard to see at first, but beyond the opening it cleared out. She was able to see the sandy, almost rust colored stone all around her, and she followed the glowsticks Eduardo was placing for the other divers who were waiting just where the tunnel took an almost ninety degree turn to the south.

Eduardo stretched an arm out and pointed at her, then with the other he pointed at Dennis, indicating that she would lead while Dennis would follow behind her and he'd bring up the rear. Rebecca made the 'okay' sign, grasping at the cave wall to help guide her around the corner. Stalagmites and stalactites greeted her in the ten-foot-wide tunnel, and she felt the swelling of excitement in her stomach. Rock formations like this could only mean these caves had once been above the surface.

"The scientist was right. Over," she radioed.

"He's going to be jealous. Over," Dennis responded.

"I'd rather be fishing with him," Eduardo said.

"Over. Over," Rebecca chided.

"*Dios mio!* Over," Eduardo mumbled over the radio. When Eduardo's light came around the corner and bounced off the jagged rocks, he added, "Looks like a shark's mouth. Over."

"Let's get swallowed then. Over," she said.

"Roger," they said in unison.

The three divers carefully worked their way through the low-hanging stalactites one at a time, while the others watched in case their tanks or regulators got snagged.

Even though the cave was wide it was only about five feet from floor to ceiling. Once Eduardo was through Rebecca swung around, leading the team for almost a quarter of a mile. Pale fish darted in and out of their pools of light as they swam deeper, and for a while her breathing and the swishing of water lulled her into the sense of perfect calm she often achieved while diving. It wasn't the most exciting cave she'd ever explored, she had to admit, and really hoped they weren't swimming into a dud. Then the tunnel took another ninety degree turn to the west. She paused, using the rough cavern wall to slow her momentum. "This is strange. Over."

"What is? Over," Dennis asked.

"Never seen a cave like this. Over." She pointed at the new direction the tunnel was taking with her dive light.

Eduardo swam up on the other side of the tunnel. He pulled a trowel from his tool belt and started to gently scrape at the wall, removing sediment that had built up in the cracks over time. Cloudy puffs filled the water around him before the sand resettled to the cave floor. Rubbing his hand over the surface he'd just cleared, Eduardo radioed, "Seems like a normal cave. Over."

"Should keep going. Over," Dennis urged.

"Stand by," she said and pushed off the wall towards the next turn in the cave. She stuck her head and light around the corner, the illumination disappearing down an unusually square-shaped corridor. *Ninety degree turns and ninety-degree angles?* "I think this could have been another one of those mines. Over," she said. It was the only thing that made sense.

"An ochre mine?" Dennis' voice somehow became even more high-pitched. He'd been jealous of the team that had found the eleven-thousand-year-old mine last year; he was supposed to be with them, but had gotten a stomach flu the week before they were to set sail.

"Over. Over," Rebecca turned around, looking at him.

"Sorry. Over," he responded a bit glumly.

"Air check. Over," Rebecca said.

"Thirty in tank one. Forty-five in tank two. Over," Dennis said, checking the small readout on his wrist.

"Same. Over," said Eduardo.

"Affirmative. Over," she said. "Let's go for another twenty, and then go for the backups. Over." They had tethered additional tanks to their drop line just outside the cave entrance so they could explore without having to return to the surface.

"Roger," they said.

Using the wall to crawl forward, Rebecca continued around the corner. It was a little disorienting at first. Entering the oddly-shaped tunnel she looked back at the natural cavern behind them, but as it faded into the darkness the feeling disappeared too. Besides its shape the rock of the tunnel was a lighter color than the cavern, almost tan compared to the rust outside. Also, no fish were swimming around their dive lights. Several minutes passed, and while the tunnel never deviated it did slope gradually down. Sometimes Dennis would come up next to her, and she could tell by his body language how excited he was. He really wanted to come up with an important finding, a finding he could put his name on.

Eduardo was commenting about some striations he found, thinking they might be tool markings, when her hand bumped into something. She turned to see what it was, and she screamed in her mask. A face in the carved rock wall leered back at her. It was almost human in appearance. Small, green flat stones were fitted together in a way that appeared scale-like. Strange, bright orange rocks made up the irises of otherwise black sockets, and shark teeth jutted from its gaping mouth. She reeled back from the visage, her heart thumping. Usually she was not so easily startled, but this was the last thing she'd expected to find in an undersea cave.

"*Dios mio,*" Eduardo said after he hurried to her side and spotted the stone face.

"I think it's safe to assume that isn't a natural formation," Dennis stated.

Staring at the grotesque image, Rebecca felt goosebumps forming under her wetsuit. "Affirmative," she breathed out in response.

Eduardo had his mask close to the face, studying it in detail. He was mumbling something that she couldn't make out over the radio. "Say again," she asked.

Pointing at it, Eduardo said, "This looks like *Xook*, but there's too many teeth."

"Shock?" Dennis asked.

"*Xook.* A Mayan deity," Eduardo said, kicking his legs to turn himself around to face them.

"Oh, shit. Oh, shit," Dennis said quickly over the radio.

"Calm down before you use up all your air. Over," Rebecca said putting her hand on Dennis' arm.

"Do you have any idea what this means?" Dennis' eyes were practically bugging out of their sockets behind the clear glass of his mask.

"It's not possible," Eduardo piped in. "This whole area went under the waves over eight thousand years ago, before the Mayans even existed."

Pointing at the inhuman image, Dennis said, "Maybe this is where the idea of this deity came from. We could be in a pre-Olmec temple."

"*Tal vez*," said Eduardo and looked back at the mosaic depiction.

"If we're going to stay down here any longer, we'll need more air. *Over*," Rebecca stressed the last word, annoyed at the two for abandoning protocol.

"Sure, sure," Dennis said staring now at the tunnel ahead.

"Let's go, *idiota*," Eduardo tapped him on the shoulder.

Reluctantly Dennis followed them out of the cave. Rebecca took the time to remind them about proper procedure with these dives. "That includes radio communication. Over."

"Roger," the men said.

Outside the cavern they quickly helped each other swap out their tanks. There was always that moment of panic for Rebecca when she knew she couldn't take a breath. For a scuba diver it wasn't a good phobia to have, but she'd worked on it over the years so now it was just a dull pressure in her chest, rather than the body-shaking tremor it used to be.

"How's it looking down there?" Scott's voice crackled in from up above.

"Fine. Just fine. Over," Rebecca sighed.

"Find anything?" Scott asked. "Oh, Over."

"Uncertain, but could be something of historic significance, investigating further. Over," she answered.

"Alrighty, well, keep me posted. Over," he radioed back down.

"*Que imbécil*," Eduardo muttered.

"*Hablo español*, Eduardo. Over," Scott reminded him. It was hard to make out over the radio, but Rebecca thought it sounded as if Scott was laughing.

"Noted. Over," Eduardo said sheepishly.

Dennis was already waiting for them impatiently at the mouth of the cave, and they returned to the last glowstick that Eduardo dropped by their discovery. Calmer than before, Rebecca examined the mask-like face closer and realized whoever made it had used real shark teeth. They looked fresh, as if placed there in the last few years.

"It's amazing how well-preserved this is," she said. "The teeth haven't even discolored yet. Over."

"They aren't buried in sediment, that could be why. Over," Dennis said.

Rebecca stared into the orange irises and suddenly

felt a chill. It was always cold in the ocean, but this went to her very core. It felt that this Xook, or whatever, was staring right back at her. She breathed before turning away and leading them deeper into the tunnel. She hoped for the return of her perfect calm, but she was too on edge. Somewhere ahead of them she thought she heard the occasional sound of rocks clicking against each other through the water. "You hearing that? Over," she asked.

"Stop and stand by," Dennis requested.

They were another quarter mile from where they had found the primitive sculpture. Rebecca slowly spun around and looked back. The trail of glow sticks Eduardo had dropped behind them sloped upwards in a relatively straight line until they drifted from view.

"I don't hear anything. Over," Dennis said.

"Same. Over," Eduardo said.

"Okay. Maybe it was my nerves. Over," she sighed.

"The Steel Lady gets nervous?" Eduardo joked.

"I *am* human, Eduardo. Over," she chuckled and twisted back around to continue.

She quickly forgot about the clicking sound when an opening appeared to their right in the tunnel. Another perfect square carved into the rock. She came to a stop by grabbing the edge of the doorway, Dennis bumping into her as he excitedly swam to see what she'd found. He mumbled an apology over the radio and began to shine his light quickly in all directions. Rebecca had a hard time making out anything with his dancing orb, so she relied on her own, sliding her dive light slowly around the small room. It was a ten-by-ten-foot room built into the rock. Shelves had been carved along the walls in even rows. Earthenware pots lined the shelves, each one about the size of a large vase, and adorning them were human skulls, much like a cork in a wine bottle.

"It's a burial chamber!" Dennis said. "This is amazing."

Eduardo swam into the room and moved closer to one of the pots. "I can't believe none of these are broken. I've seen photos from other finds, but it's usually fragments and bone chips."

"Yes. That is odd," Rebecca said more to herself than to the two men. She peered down the tunnel and thought she saw another opening just past the edge of her dive light. When she turned to say something Dennis was lifting a skull from one of the ancient receptacles and shining his light into the hole. "What are you doing?!" She shouted.

Dennis said, "Seeing what's inside."

Astonished by his abruptness, she said, "You shouldn't touch anything until we catalogue our findings. We're going to need more divers, a scientific vessel, a research team—"

"Or we can just look inside for a second and see there's some beads and stone tools. And now we know," Dennis said, interrupting her.

"Same here," Eduardo said, looking in another one on the other side of the room.

She stared dumbfounded at the two. She'd never seen them act this way before. Granted they'd never made a huge discovery before, but she always thought they would have acted more professionally than this. Feeling betrayed, she left them and made her way down the tunnel to the other opening. More shelves with pots and skulls. She saw another entryway again at the edge of her light.

"If you two are done grave robbing there are more rooms ahead. Over," she said.

"Rebecca, come on. Don't be like that," Dennis said over the radio.

"She's right. We've got to respect these people's resting places. Let's go, *puta*," Eduardo said.

"Hey! I know that one," Dennis grumbled.

"*Dios mio*. You come to Mexico and you only learned the Spanish swear words?"

"Didn't think I was going to need it underwater."

She waited for them to catch up with her before continuing. Rooms appeared at regular intervals on either side of the tunnel. Shining their lights inside they found more of the same. That is, until they came across a room where one of the skulls still had wisps of hair floating around it. The three just stared at the thin hair for several seconds before Eduardo said, "I don't understand. That shouldn't be here, *especially* here."

"Maybe the further back we go the newer the graves are? This could have been placed hundreds of years after the first one." Dennis said.

"No, that's not what I mean. Look at the hair. You ever seen any light-haired, indigenous Mexicans?" Eduardo reached out and pulled some of the hair closer to his light, showing them the blonde strands.

"I'm confused. What are you saying?" Rebecca asked, the cold feeling returning.

Eduardo gently lifted the skull and peered inside. He quickly let it go, and the pot fell to the cave floor. The sound of it cracking filled the water around them.

Stunned, Rebecca looked at the shattered pot where something black and reflective was sticking out from between some of the shards. She carefully removed the pieces, and then understood why Eduardo dropped the pot. The black thing was a rectangular shape, with four buttons at the top. The reflective part was silvery letters that spelled *Sony*. It was a Walkman.

"What the fuck?" she said as she stared at it.

"This doesn't make any sense," Dennis said. He swam over to another pot and looked inside. He let it fall just as Eduardo did, and another crack boomed around them. A small, rubbery horse figure slid out from between the broken pot towards Rebecca. It floated towards the ceiling and in the light, she could see the pinkish skin and rainbow-like hair of a *My Little Pony*, just like one she had when she was a little girl.

"We have to get out of here," Eduardo said, panic in his voice. He was swimming backwards towards the door as a loud rumble emanated from further down the tunnel. The three remained still until it grew quiet again. Then the clicking noise Rebecca had heard before returned, and it didn't sound like just one rock striking against another. This time it sounded like a landslide.

"Go!" she shouted.

The three swam into the tunnel as the sounds grew louder. Rebecca pointed her light in both directions, nearly letting go when multiple pinpoints of orange reflected back at her in the murky depths. A strong hand pulled at her shoulder. Eduardo beckoned her to follow, and they kicked with all their strength. Dennis was ahead of her and Eduardo; she could see his yellow flippers frantically moving through the water, spurred on by the growing clicks behind them.

Eduardo cried out and disappeared next to her. Something had dragged him backwards. His radio, still sending, let them hear his horrible screaming. She chanced a glance back and regretted it instantly. Flashes of greenish scales darted through and around a swirling mass of dark red. She'd seen something like that before, when she'd dove near some sharks and witnessed a feeding frenzy. "Oh, God. Eduardo!" she called out, but his radio had gone silent.

A form shot out of the spreading cloud of blood towards her, and she pumped her legs as hard as she could. She had to get out of there. *Focus on the glowsticks*, she demanded of herself. She needed to follow the path to safety. Dennis had already disappeared somewhere ahead of her, and she hoped it was the turn that led back into the cavern. Something bumped into her leg and she gritted her teeth, adrenaline coursing through her. She had to go faster. Quickly unclipping her tool harness she let her equipment fall to the tunnel floor.

The clicking around her grew in intensity, and for a moment she hoped that whatever was chasing her was distracted by what she'd dropped. But then a scaley shape shot past her and turned around ahead of her, darting back at her headlong. She swam quickly down, her light shining on a yellowish underbelly as she managed to get below it. Whatever it was brushed against her tanks and pushed her further to the tunnel floor. Grasping at the ground she dragged herself forward and found the cave. *Not much farther. Now, swim!*

Ahead of her Dennis' light was dancing frantically along the cave walls through the large clouds of sediment he must have kicked up. Behind her the noises seemed to be receding, but she couldn't let herself relax.

"Fuck! I'm stuck!" Dennis cried over the radio.

She couldn't afford to waste the energy by speaking; she focused on getting to the cave entrance. That focus was what took her so long to become aware of the beeping in her helmet. It was the warning indicator that she was almost out of air. She'd either have to slow down to conserve her air, or go all out and hope she'd have enough to reach the surface. Her decision was made for her when green scales appeared at the edge of her light along the sides of the cave next to her. They hadn't stopped chasing her, they'd only stopped talking to each other.

Fuck. If I can just make it to the tanks we left outside I'll be okay. Her fear of not having any air was quickly trumped by the fear of being torn apart. Things buffeted against her out of the darkness, jostling her in their wake.

Strands of seaweed floated into her mask, obscuring her vision. A tug on her flipper almost ripped it off her foot, but she kept going. The whole time Dennis was groaning over the radio.

She soon found out why. He was trapped between two stalactites. She hurried over to help him just as the clicking began again behind her. "I've got you," she said.

"Hurry," he grunted as he tried to free himself. His arms were pinned at his sides so he couldn't push himself back out. She tried pulling his legs at first, but he was wedged in tight. She swam to the other side and tried pushing, the two divers locking eyes just as she got him free. He had a look of relief just before he disappeared into the watery darkness.

Then came his screams.

There was nothing she could do for him, and with tears burning in her eyes she picked her way through the teeth-like rocks until she came to the other side. The light from outside of the cavern was a welcoming sight. She rushed for the entrance, her lungs pulling at the last bits of air in her tanks. She began unstrapping them before she even got out of the cave, leaving them to the ocean depths. Without their added weight she was able to swim faster, and she reached one of the nearly-empty tanks they'd left earlier. With trembling hands she struggled to get the lead connected to her diving helmet, her eyes bulging as she felt her chest ready to explode.

Finally she was able to take a deep breath. She looked back at the black hole of the cave where green forms were circling around the tanks she'd left behind. She didn't waste their distraction, kicking for the surface as quickly as she could. Her muscles screamed as her head shot out of the water, but she'd rather deal with diver's bends than whatever those things had in store for her.

She pulled off her mask and started gulping in the cool air, fighting to stay conscious. Patches of darkness entered her vision, but she found the boat and dragged herself onto the small, plastic platform on the back of it while she croaked out, "Help..."

She lay there for a minute, breathing and staring at the sky as her vision slowly cleared. Tears mixed with the saltwater on her face as the screams from the others echoed in her head. The sound of something splashing in the water made her reflexively lift her head, and she raised herself up on her elbows. On the deck of the ship she saw Scott standing with his back to her, looking at something out on the water, his hands on his hips. "Scott..." she said, her voice louder this time.

That got his attention and he turned, his balding head beet-red with sunburn, his pink Hawaiian shirt unbuttoned and flapping in the breeze. He looked so normal, and Rebecca couldn't help but to begin laughing while he rushed over and pulled her onto the deck. "What the Hell's the matter with you? You know better than this," he chided her. He helped her to a bench and sat her down. Another splash sounded off the starboard side. "Where's Eduardo? I don't think they understand my accent."

Her head turned slowly to where he was looking and

she saw a smaller boat alongside theirs with two stout, dark-skinned men on it. Their deck was lined with gray earthenware pots that they were tossing over the side. Scott stood again, hands back at his hips before he gestured at the two men. "I keep asking them what they're doing, and they just point at the water and say something that sounds like 'shock.'"

Again, tears fell on her cheeks as she watched the men. One gave her a small wave after he dumped a pot. Something rocked their boat from underneath, some of the pots clinking together, and both men laughed. From the other side of the smaller craft Rebecca heard a lone click, and she screamed.

Dan Le Fever

About the Author

Dan Le Fever is just a guy from Lynn, MA who puts one word after another in the hopes that they make sense in the end. His first story, PANIC, can be found in One Night In Salem by Fundead Publications. His second story, Land of Promise, is included in Exquisite Aberrations, a Gothic anthology, also by Fundead Publications. He is currently in the process of querying his first full length novel, The Ashen War, an alternative history/post-apocalyptic adventure.

https://twitter.com/LefeverDan

The Ocean Sings Softly

Christopher Bond

Hazel Coolidge sat on the front porch of the rented cottage wrapped in a brightly-colored afghan she had crocheted herself, her wrinkled hands holding a cup of steaming coffee, soaking up its warmth. It was a cool morning, much cooler than was typical so late in the summer on the thin splinter of New Hampshire that bordered the Atlantic. A wind was coming off of the water, salty and gentle, and it pushed her silver hair around her head and face, though she hardly noticed. Her phone and a book sat neglected on the small table beside her chair. Her eyes, as always, were on the ocean.

I've been away from it for too long, she thought.

Muffled footsteps approached slowly through the house, and the screen door creaked open. Hazel sat up, her eyes drifting from the shore to the blonde-headed girl who stood beside her chair. The girl's eyes were as gray as the morning sea, the skin around them red and puffy. She had been crying again. Only nine, but already she possessed the grace of an adult, Hazel noticed with a tinge of sadness. Loss has a way of doing that, making you grow up faster than you should. Hazel knew. The girl was the spitting image of her mother, and it tore a little at the hole in Hazel's heart whenever she looked at her.

"Good morning, Katie. How'd you sleep? Better than yesterday?"

"Yes, much better, Grandma. I could hear the ocean all night."

"It's nice, isn't it?"

Katie nodded. "Mmm-hmm. How did *you* sleep, Grandma?"

Hazel chuckled softly. "I slept good, too, little one. Are you hungry?"

"Not really."

"Okay. There's milk and orange juice in the refrigerator, and cereal on the counter. You know where, whenever you feel like it."

"Thanks. What are you doing out here?"

"I like to watch the waves in the morning, listen to the water sing."

"Sing?"

"Sure. All of nature sings, darling, if you take the time to listen. The ocean sings a very beautiful song."

Katie smiled. She knew sometimes grownups said crazy things, and she had learned that, if you smiled afterward, they usually didn't expect anything else. She turned to go back into the house, but paused, her face bunched up in concentration.

"Grandma, what does Persephone mean?"

Hazel's blood turned cold; her heart hiccupped in her chest.

Persephone. The name burst into her mind like a hand thrusting through the packed earth above an old grave, dragging with it the memories of another life she had buried long ago.

Persephone. Echoes of screams and decades dissolved, and she was eleven years old again. Tears blossomed at the edges of her eyes. Her whole body trembled.

"Grandma, what's wrong?" Katie asked, putting her hand on Hazel's arm. Concern filled the young girl's face. "Are you okay?"

Hazel shook her head, staring blankly at her granddaughter. For one scary second Katie thought her grandma didn't recognize her. Then Hazel's eyes softened, the corners of her mouth lifting slightly.

"Sorry, dear, I...my mind must have slipped out of the schoolyard for a second. Where did you hear that name, Persephone?" It felt odd to say it out loud after so many years, the vowels rusty and foreign on her tongue.

"It was on some television show, I think. Or maybe it was something on Youtube." She shrugged her shoulders. "I can't remember. It just sounded like a funny word...I never heard it before."

"Ah, I see." Hazel stammered. "Yes, it *is* a funny word, isn't it? I don't...I...I think she was a queen or a goddess. Something like that, dear."

"Oh." Katie frowned. "You scared me, Grandma. You

looked like you saw a ghost."

Hazel smiled what she hoped was a convincing smile. A reassuring smile. "I'm fine. Really."

Katie went back into the house, and when the door shut, Hazel turned back to the sea, her heart still racing. Her fingers found the familiar bumpy edge of a long scar on her forearm.

Maybe I did see a ghost, she thought. *Maybe I saw a lot of them.*

She knew.

Katie walked through the living room and into the kitchen and she poured herself a glass of orange juice. She sat down on one of the little stools that bordered the countertop. Grandma Hazel's face had told her the truth of it.

She knew, Katie thought, *and then she lied.*

But why would Grandma lie to her? Did she still think of her as a little kid, like the snot-nosed brat she was the last time they saw each other? Because she wasn't seven anymore. She was nine–almost ten–just a stone's throw from being a teenager. Katie's face grew hot, the pressure of forthcoming tears building behind her eyes. She missed her mom, and she missed her friends. She missed her old house and the familiar streets she used to ride her bike on. Heck, she even missed the neighbor kid, Jarvis, even though he was a couple of years younger and a real pain in the butt most days. Katie sighed. It had been a terrible year, the worst year of her short life by leaps and bounds. Her mom was gone, and Grandma Hazel was all she had left.

And now Grandma was lying to her.

She had no right to be upset, she told herself. After all, she had lied too. She hadn't heard the name *Persephone* on television or on YouTube. Katie wanted to tell Grandma Hazel the truth, but she just couldn't; the man had told her not to - the big man with the wiry beard and the eyes as black as panther fur, the man on the rowboat with *Persephone* stenciled on the side who had beckoned her to climb aboard and go on an adventure.

The man from her dreams.

She had *thought* it was a dream, anyway, when she first woke up while the sky was still black. She had thought it was a dream, until she turned on the light and saw the sand on the carpet and on her bedsheets. Her feet were covered in it. She had cleaned up as quietly as she could while Grandma slept, and then she sat on her bed and thought of her mom.

She cried until the sun came up.

Hazel stayed on the porch long after her coffee had gone cold in her mug. Thunderheads were forming at the edge of the horizon, promising one Hell of a storm, and the angry ocean mirrored the dark clouds. The conversation she'd had with Katie had unnerved her more than she cared to admit, and it had unmoored dark thoughts inside of her head she'd kept tied down for so long. "Dammit," she said to the ocean. She shook her head and sighed. "Foolish woman."

It was happening, she felt it in every joint of her old bones. It had been so long though! She had *waited* so long to return to the sea. Over sixty years, decades upon decades of denial and anxiety and worry, countless shrinks and psych meds and always the feeling that she was running away from her problems.

Sixty years of worrying, and now it was happening again.

It was Dr. Hutchinson in Boise who had suggested she take the trip back to New Hampshire. He said it was important that she face her fear, to go back to the source of her trauma. He said it was the only way for her to fully heal, the only way to move on, so she did. Hazel found the cottage on the beach, only two miles from her childhood home, and she booked a four-night stay at the cost of an entire Social Security check.

That was back in January.

In May Laurie had been killed in a hit-and-run accident just a mile from the house she and Katie shared. Laurie's death had been so sudden, so painful; no one expects to die at forty-one.

Hazel had planned to take the New Hampshire trip alone.

Life, as always, had other plans.

⟡

The storm started just after lunch, as the menacing clouds promised it would, and by evening it still showed no sign of letting up. The falling rain beat a frantic cadence against the roof and the siding of the cottage, and Hazel and Katie spent their time together in the living room on the couch, Hazel crocheting and Katie on her phone, the television left on to drown out the wind and the pandemonium outside. Neither had much to say, but it felt good to be together.

Or, more accurately, it felt good not to be alone.

When the wall clock edged over midnight Hazel could hear Katie softly snoring under her blanket. She lifted the girl up and took her into her room, surprised at how heavy she was. Hazel laid her on the bed and kissed her on the forehead, and when a burst of lightning flashed outside the little girl's face changed for a second. It was like Laurie lying there when she was just nine years old, and Hazel's heart broke a little bit. When she closed the bedroom door softly behind her her face was wet with hot tears.

Hazel lay in bed listening to the howl of the wind and the crashing of the rain, like waves against a ship's hull, and she remembered another time when it was dark and the sound of the ocean around her carried doom and destruction on the crest of each whitecap. The wind was wailing outside her window, and just under the shriek she thought could hear the cries of screaming children. Her breathing quickened, and cool sweat beaded along her forehead. She scratched absentmindedly at the scar on her forearm that burned. She didn't think she'd be able to sleep, not on a night like this with her mind so restless, but sleep took her eventually, dragging her unwillingly into memory.

The boat's diesel engine is old, and its worn pistons clang so loudly and so violently in their cylinders that when the power is cut Hazel feels as if she's gone deaf. Then the sounds filter in slowly, the way the music does on an old radio once the tubes start to warm and crackle to life. First small waves broke against the vessel's battered, steel sides, rocking her and the others. The floor and the ceiling pitch to and fro, never steady. Then comes the clinking of rusty lobster traps tucked away in the dark of the ship's hull, out of the reach of the feeble, orange light thrown from the bare bulb hanging from the ceiling.

Then came the voices, and the crying. Her brothers Henry and Tate, plus her sister Louise, all huddled around her, their bodies trembling. Not from the cold, though it is a chilly night and everything is damp, their clothes nearly soaked through. Their little wrists and ankles, like Hazel's, are bound by heavy rope that rubs their skin red. Lastly she hears the heavy, booming steps from above pounding across the creaking deck. The lumbering footfalls of a monster. Each thunderous crash makes her heart spasm like a dying fish about to be gutted.

The scent of diesel fuel and long-dead fish hang heavy in the air, mixing with the stiff, salty brine that coats everything like a polluted snowfall. Beneath it all there's another scent: more subtle, but more primordial. Blood; and with it, Death.

The hatch above the staircase opens, letting in a glimpse of starlight, and Hazel wishes desperately in that brief moment that *she* was a star somewhere out in space; somewhere far away from the sweat, salt and death that surrounds her, somewhere she could be safe from the monster that's descending into the dank, dark hull of the ship.

The monster that killed their mother.

It booms down each metal step, then pauses in the darkness. They can hear it breathing; they can almost hear it thinking. Pondering. It walks into the swaying, orange light, and the children shrink away from it. They press even closer together, though they are already pushing so hard that it hurts them, so hard that if they lived through the night their skin would be covered in dozens of angry bruises. The monster runs his black-hole eyes across them, *into* them, and he smiles beneath the bulk of his coarse, black beard. It's a joyless smile, one Hazel no longer recognizes. A warning. He reaches for them with giant, calloused hands, then he laughs when they shudder, crying out and trying to pull away.

"Dad, stop!" Hazel screams, and the monster hesitates, his brutish hand already gripping the collar of Tate's shirt. She should have yelled louder, been more aggressive, *MADE* him listen, she'll think later. His coal-black eyes are empty and bottomless, and Hazel can see her own face reflected back in those midnight pools. "Please," she says in a much smaller voice. A flash of recognition bursts briefly across the blackness like a signal flare, but then it disappears. The monster drags the young boy away from his siblings and across the dirty floor toward the stairs. Tate's face is red and wet with tears, snot leaking from his nose, and he screams and screams. He calls out for Hazel, their big sister, his protector, to save him, but she can't move as his shoes disappear through the doorway.

Sometimes she tries to remember his face, but it's the shoes she remembers the most.

Screams echo down to the children, tiny screams muffled by the ceiling, the ocean and the night. They don't seem like real screams at all. The boat tumbles back and forth like a pendulum, and then Hazel, Henry and Louise are all screaming, drowning out the cries from above or perhaps joining them. The boat rocks harder and the single orange bulb bounces and flickers and sputters like torchlight, the dried casing of its lone wire cracking along the seam. The children are too afraid to scream now. They are so close together they act as one person, one entity, instead of three individuals. They sit silently, expectantly. A heavy shroud has been pulled around the boat. Nothing moves.

Hazel thinks that maybe something has happened to the monster. Her fingers are crossed, but she doesn't dare to wish aloud; saying your wishes out loud ensures they'll never come true. Images of her mother flash through her mind; of her mother smiling at her, of her mother rocking Tate to sleep, of her mother lying on the bed naked - the sheets are all red, and so is her body. The monster is there too, next to the bed, his hands as red as the sheets.

Hazel tries to block them out, these images, but they're tenacious. She squeezes Henry and Louise and they feel much too small, her arms much too weak to hold them. The heavy footsteps lurch across the deck above, like distant thunder. The hatch opens. When the monster comes down he is alone. The children scream again; it's the only thing they can do.

First Tate, then Henry, then Louise. From youngest to oldest the monster drags his prey out of the bowels of the boat and into the murderous gleam of starlight, the killing twilight. One-by-one the screams of terror are suffocated by the blackness in the sky and in their father's eyes. Hazel is alone and dried out on the inside. A husk, a withered shell, leftover skin from a molting snake. She is somewhere outside of herself. She has cried a lifetime of tears in the thin span of time from when she first found her mother's body until now, more tears than an eleven-year-old should ever have to cry.

The boat heaves under her – not just pitching, but *lifting* this time – and the rusty lobster cages and loosely-stacked crates clatter to the ground. The single bulb sputters and goes out, the worn wire sparking. Hazel rolls into the wall and the frayed rope on her wrists stretches and snaps, and she's struggling in the dark to untie her feet and lift herself up. Her hands search blindly along the ground for something that can help her, for *anything* that can save her, another unspoken wish she keeps safely inside of her.

When her fingers wrap around cold, worn metal a weight lifts from her. The tumult has opened the hatch above the stairs, and she makes for the square of starlight and the cool, ocean air. She is still outside of herself, but she is no longer a husk, no longer the discarded skin of a snake. She is the snake, and the hollow spaces inside of her are filled with a boiling anger.

She is alive.

After the blackness in the belly of the ship the moon and the stars are as bright as stage lights, and the ship's deck and the angry, churning waves that surround it are the stage. The wind wails ferociously. Hazel creeps along, watching for the monster in the shadows. She tiptoes around the cabin toward the bow of the boat with footsteps as fragile as spun glass. When she finally sees her brothers and her sister all feeling goes out from her arms and legs; she collapses onto the deck, all boneless flesh, a deflated balloon.

They're side-by-side, hands touching, leaning over the waist-high metal railing like seasick sailors. Their arms are stretched out along the railing to either side of their bodies, a crucifixion in reverse, their wrists tied tightly to keep them from going over into the water or falling back onto the boat. Tate's legs are too short. He has an extra rope fastened around his waist, and his shoes float a few inches above the deck. Their heads are hanging low, their faces pointed down to the roiling ocean. Blood, like oil, drips into the tainted water. Hazel can tell from the way they swing back and forth at the whim of the waves that her siblings can't see the angry ocean; they can't see anything anymore.

And that's a blessing, Hazel thinks. Because there *are* things there, swimming just below the surface. Big things, slimy and glistening in the pale light, thick cables of dead flesh coiling and twisting together, a thousand tiny beaks like barnacles gasping along each ghoulish tentacle, pulsing grotesquely beneath the waterfalls of blood trickling from the row of small, ruined necks.

With all the activity around the boat Hazel hardly notices the monster standing there. He's facing the water, one car-battery sized hand on the railing, the other holding his serrated fillet knife at his side. He's as tall as a mountain, as the sky, as the whole world. The wind dies for just one fateful second, and the deck creaks under Hazel's soft step. The monster turns his head, one baleful, black eye piercing her, and then he turns to face her. In one movement the hooked point of a harpoon plunges into his chest. He looks down in shock, but he doesn't cry out. Hazel's hands are trembling, the harpoon is twice as heavy as her, but she pushes harder, pushes with the strength of her, her siblings and her mother.

The shaft sinks in, but still the monster doesn't speak, only grunts. The back of the monster's dirty, blue sweater – the same sweater his children bought him two birthdays ago when he was still just *Dad*, before the dark times, before the ocean called to him and changed him and stole him – sprouts an evil-looking barb. The dirty, blue fabric turns black around the spike, and blood seeps out around the monster's waist, over the cuff of his pants and onto the deck. When the stream runs over the edge into the water the tiny beaks on the dead cables scream in a hideous chorus, and the ocean bubbles and explodes around the ship. The air is alive with furious intent and too-many shadows. A graying tentacle, as thick as a telephone pole, reaches up and wraps around the wounded monster's chest, snapping the harpoon.

"Dad! No!" Hazel yells, but the words are stolen by the wind, and she tries again. "Dad, I'm sorry!"

But her dad is gone already; he has been for a long time. The thing in front of her is no longer her father. It is a monster in her father's skin, and it stares at her with hate-filled eyes. The sacrifice is unfinished; the changing incomplete. The ocean is unsatisfied. The monster opens its mouth, black blood pouring over its beard like spoiled molasses.

"You ruined it, Hazel," it spits out between stained teeth. Its breathing is wet and ragged; its chest rattles and knocks like a broken engine. This thing is *not* her father, but it speaks with his voice, and it hurts her to listen. "You ruined...everything...I've worked for. You ungrateful... little bitch..."

Her dad never talked to her that way, had never called her a nasty name or raised his hand to her. But when he says *bitch* it rocks her as hard as if he had slapped her. Hazel tries to step away, but her back is against the wall of the cabin and she can't go any further.

"This isn't over, girl...my work isn't finished. I'll come back for you. I'll come back...and I'll *take you*."

It gasps the last words like a curse, and the tentacle around its chest constricts. A million tiny beaks bite into his flesh, and he's pulled over the railing and into the rioting water. Dozens of glimmering tentacles flash up and over the railing around the boat, grabbing onto the exhaust pipes, antennas and the roof of the cabin, sliding over the gunwale and latching onto whatever the tiny beaks can sink into.

A tentacle hits Hazel's forearm, and the beaks are like daggers when they dig in. She lays her arm against the deck and stomps the slimy cable. The beaks wail, popping like spoiled grapes. The cable retreats to the water and Hazel runs for the shelter of the cabin. All around her the air is alive with the sound of rending metal and splintering wood, the boat tearing and breaking like a child's toy beneath the power of the creature, or creatures, that live beneath the dark waves. She staggers out of the cabin toward the stern of the ship, and climbs up into the rowboat that hangs there from heavy chains. She falls over the edge and onto the floor of the small boat. The *Persephone* shudders, and the rowboat tips precariously to one side.

Hazel grips the higher edge of the boat, and when she does the larger boat shudders again under her and tips even further, its starboard side already taking on water. Her feet dangle five feet above the mass of writhing tentacles. The wood is wet, making her grip weak. The scent of spilled fuel rises from the battered engine compartment, and somewhere below the single wire is still sparking. A crack like a cannon shot splits the night; the boat pitches the other way, slamming Hazel's head against the wood. Flames ignite along the edge of the ruined cabin, setting the night ablaze. Oranges, reds and yellows dance along the water. Dazed, her fingers fumble along the chain until she finds the release cable and she pulls the cord. The rowboat falls, and when it lands Hazel's head hits the floor again - the darkness takes her.

Hazel woke up with a start. The world was black, and for one terrible second she was only eleven, still adrift on the tiny rowboat with *Persephone* stenciled on the side in block letters. The scent of diesel fuel and burning wood lingered in the air like brooding ghosts. The bed sheets were soaked through with sweat, her nightgown clinging uncomfortably to her skin. "Only a dream, Hazel, only a dream," she said to the empty bedroom. Tendrils of the nightmare still stuck into parts of her waking mind, refusing to let go.

She sat up, shaking her head and trying to loosen them. "A bastard of a dream, but only a dream. You survived. He didn't get you." She pulled her legs up and wrapped her arms around her knees. "You survived."

She *had* survived.

The coast guard had found Hazel the day after that terrible night, unconscious and adrift five miles off the coast of New Hampshire. They had followed the smoke, but the *Persephone* was long gone by the time they reached her. Her thin body was covered in bruises, and her nose was broken, but she was alive. A nasty cut on her forearm was red and swollen, already in the middle stages of a terrible infection. Delirious and inconsolable, Hazel screamed at the men who were rescuing her that her skin was burning, that her dad was burning and that the whole world was on fire. She screamed about a monster who ate her brother and sisters.

She had been in the hospital for a month. The police found her mother's body at their house and a few charred pieces of her father's boat floating near her rowboat, but not much else. They filled in the rest with their own deductive reasoning. They got it all wrong, of course, but Hazel didn't correct them. She didn't want to talk about it, didn't want to talk at all. Let them think that her dad and mom were divorcing, that her dad feared a drawn-out custody battle and that he'd been drinking too much and too often. Let them believe that the engine in his fishing boat was old and it had caught fire, that Tate, Louise and Henry died by drowning, burning or were eaten by sharks. Anything was better than the truth.

Not that they would have believed her, anyway.

The rain hammered relentlessly on the other side of her bedroom window, and the cottage shook with the wind and the chaos of the storm. Hazel leaned across to her nightstand and found the switch for her light. She clicked it once, twice, three times. Nothing. The soft breeze of the ceiling fan had stopped, and the green glow of her alarm clock was absent too. She groaned. The power had gone out.

Groping along next to the useless lamp Hazel found the familiar shape of her phone and flicked it on, the light making her wince after the darkness of the room. 2:13 flashed on the screen, juxtaposed above a picture of her and Katie.

KATIE. The thought came with a suddenness, an urgency, and Hazel's mouth went dry. She struggled out of her covers and swung her feet over the side of the bed. When her socks touched the carpet a thunderous knocking boomed from the living room: the front door. Hazel held her breath. Her legs went numb. Her bedroom was the hull of the *Persephone*, and the front door was the hatch above the staircase. "No," she said in a small voice.

KATIE!

Fighting the urge to hide, Hazel stood up; she listened for any foreign sound beyond the reach of the storm, but the knocking had stopped. She forced herself to take a deep breath, trying to still her racing heart. Her steps were silent as she crept toward the bedroom door, and then it came again, three loud crashes. *Only the storm, only the storm.* She swiped her finger, and the phone's flashlight burst into life. She reached for the doorknob with a shaking hand and turned it.

Katie's bedroom door was directly across the hall

from hers. It was open. Hazel ducked inside, where Katie's crumpled pillow lay on the floor like a forgotten doll. The bedsheets were tangled and askew, the bed empty. The booming knock came again from the front of the house.

Hazel ran out of the bedroom on feet still tingling with sleep, her mind racing frantically. "Katie!" she screamed, panic edging into her voice. "Katie, where are you!?"

The wind hit her first, and then a peppering of cold water, like the spray from a ship's wake, stopped her halfway through the living room. The front door was wide open, the floor already drenched. The wind gusted and the open door slammed against the wall of the room, crashing like a pair of giant, wooden cymbals. Beyond the empty door the night awaited, the void beckoning to her like the open maw of some hungry beast. She rushed into it.

Hazel ran toward the ocean, as she knew she must, the light from her phone bouncing along in front of her. The power of the storm was immense, as if the sky were being ripped asunder, every gust and gale threatening to knock her off of her feet and into the swirling sand.

It didn't take long to find her. Katie was standing in the shallow surf near the water's edge, small waves spilling around her ankles. With her back toward Hazel she was just a silhouette of white floating amid a sea of the deepest black. Her blonde hair was drenched, matted to her shoulders, and her arms hung loosely at her side. She didn't turn when the flashlight's beam shone upon her, casting dancing shadows along the shore.

"Katie!" Hazel screamed into the wind. "Katie, thank God!" Freezing-cold water pooled around her bare feet. She reached out for her granddaughter and placed a hand on one thin arm. The girl's skin was cold, prickled with goosebumps. *Slimy.* Katie flinched away from Hazel's touch and turned around. Hazel gasped, crying out in horror.

The girl's eyes were black saucers mirroring the night, her lips a pale blue. Across her throat ragged skin hung loose from where the fillet knife had sawed through the tender flesh. She was still nine, just like the last time Hazel had seen her, just like she always would be in Hazel's memories - and in her nightmares. A white hand gripped Hazel's arm, burning her with its coldness, and Hazel dropped her phone into the water.

It wasn't Katie, it was Louise. Poor, sweet Louise.

"Hello, sister," Louise said. "We hoped you would come back. You've been away for so long."

"No," Hazel said softly, falling to her knees in the water. "No, no, it's not you, Louise...it *can't* be you."

The girl's smile widened, a row of mossy, green teeth like tumbled down tombstones peeking out between her pale lips. Ropes of soggy, brown seaweed were braided through her blonde hair, and bits of sand and broken shells fell from the tangled mass when she spoke.

"But it is, dear sister. Of course it's me. That's why you came back, isn't it? To see us again? To *be* with us? The others will be so excited."

Hazel felt a crippling pain in her chest, and it radiated

outward toward her shoulders and down her arms. Her old heart was galloping erratically inside of her, buckling beneath the strain. It was too much; the pain was too much. She leaned forward, her forehead just above the surging tide.

"Are you ready, Hazel?" the thing that had once been her sister said, "Are you ready to go?"

"No," Hazel whispered to the ocean. She lifted her head, pulling a leg up underneath her until she was in a crouch. She closed her eyes against the pain in her chest, gritting her teeth. She opened her eyes and the rain fell into them, but she didn't falter. "No, Louise, I'm not going anywhere. Not until I know that Katie is safe."

Louise's face darkened, her smile gone. She nodded behind her to a dark shape slumped over in deeper water. It was Katie, her body twisted in a way so that only her face and one hip stayed above the waves. Hazel couldn't tell if the girl was breathing, but her cheeks were flushed, which she took as a good sign.

"She's fine," Louise said, "for now. If you aren't ready to go then she'll have to take your place. Father has been very patient with you, Hazel, but I think he's grown weary of your disobedience."

"No, Louise...not Katie. You can't take her!"

"Oh, Hazel, you still think of yourself as a protector, don't you? The strong big sister? Even after you left us to die out there?"

"It wasn't my fault, Louise! You have to know that... there wasn't anything that I could have done to save you,

I–"

"Yet *you* still live, don't you?" Louise bared her teeth in a snarl. "*You* survived, sister. *You* got away."

Hazel's body quaked. She lowered her head, sobbing, her mind reeling.

"I'm sorry, Louise. I didn't want to survive, Louise. I didn't want to live."

A small hand touched her shoulder, and a new voice said, "But you did, Hazel, and now you can live forever with us. We can be a family again."

Hazel looked up. Her brothers were there, Henry and little Tate on either side of Louise, the four of them together for the first time in sixty years. It was Henry who had spoken. Even with black eyes, and a mangled throat, she still recognized him. The tips of his fingers ended in jagged stumps, the flesh nibbled and gnawed away to reveal knobs of pearly white bone. Hazel tried to shrink away from his touch, but the boy was surprisingly strong. Tate placed a hand on her other shoulder.

Little Tate.

A line of thick barnacles clung to the side of his neck and ran up to his cheek, pulling the skin loose from his skull and making his left eye droop. With Hazel on her knees they were all nearly the same height.

"Come with us, Hazel. Please come with us," Tate said. His eyes were as black as the others, the skin beneath the cluster of barnacles just as white. "It's lonely down there, but we have so much fun. It's so fun to see the world swimming from beneath, to listen to the hungry things chewing and chewing forever, to hear the sacred ones sing as they die. All of nature sings, sister, and every living thing returns to the sea in the end. Father taught us that. It's *your* time to return to the sea now. We've been waiting an awfully long while, and it's so lonely down there."

Hazel shook her head. "I can't, Tate. I can't come with you."

"Why not?"

"Because, I...I'm needed here. I belong here now."

"No!" Tate screamed, his voice like grinding metal. Henry and Louise grabbed Hazel with both of their hands, their cold skin burning her. Tate's small face contorted in anger. The barnacles on his cheeks shook with every word. "You can't leave us again, Hazel! You belong to Father... you belong to the sea!"

Three pairs of hands grasped and pulled, and Hazel fell forward. Pain exploded in her face as she hit the wet sand under the water. Warm blood gushed from her nose. They were dragging her away from the beach, toward the sound of the crashing surf. She struggled against them, but they were too strong and her old muscles too weak. Once she had tried to hold them, to keep them safe, but now they held her and wouldn't let go. Not ever. The saltwater stung wickedly in her broken nose and her eyes. It covered her ears, and all Hazel could hear were the sounds of rushing water. Her lungs struggled to hold on to her last breath as the brine filled her mouth.

All but two of the hands let go, Tate's tiny hands still clinging, and Hazel pushed herself up out of the water, gagging and choking. The night was as liquid-black as the ocean. Hazel had a hard time telling the difference. It was too dark out, the ocean too powerful. *Where were the stars?* She thought. *Where was the moon? Why did she come back here?* The children were looking off into the distance, not paying attention to her. Louise raised one skeletal-thin arm out toward the violent sea, an undead scarecrow.

"He's coming."

And he was.

Lightning flashed, and Hazel saw him. His back was to them as he rowed, but Hazel recognized the bulk of his shape crouched inside the small boat that had once been her salvation. She recognized his blue sweater, even at that distance, a large, familiar stain spreading along the back of it. Her father. The monster. Beyond him in the distance the *Persephone* waited in the dark water, like a crouching sphinx. Hazel wasn't surprised to see that the boat had been made whole. The water churned around it hungrily and her chest constricted, the air all gone in a single breath.

It was time. The sacrifice must be completed; the ritual made whole. The beast returned.

Tate leaned in behind her, rotted wood and decay on his breath.

"It's going to be fun, sister, just like before. We'll have all the time in t – "

His hands jerked away from her suddenly, and the biting cold of his fingers left with them. A primal scream tore through the sound of the rain and the crashing surf. Hazel spun around, and Henry and Louise did the same.

Tate was lying on his back in the sand, just outside of where the waves diminished into nothingness. He was squirming, his face etched in panic and pain. An arm was around his throat, and another around his forehead. Katie was beneath him. Tate's teeth gnashed, biting at the open air, and Katie struggled to keep him still. "Let me go!" the boy screamed, a note of terror in his voice. "Please, let me go! It hurts, it hurts!"

"Katie!" Hazel yelled. Henry and Louise rushed past her toward their fallen brother, but they stopped where the water ended, a couple feet from where their brother struggled. He screamed and screamed, each cry louder and wilder, less human. The girl was bigger, but the boy was a maelstrom of movement. Katie's arm was bleeding, cut by the cluster of barnacles on the boy's cheek. Her grip was slipping in the blood on his wet skin, the pallid flesh splitting like grated cheese under the pressure.

"Let him go!" Henry yelled, tears streaming down his face, his feet planted firmly in the thinnest bit of water. "You let my brother go, or I'll rip out your eyes and pack your stupid skull with sand!" Louise stood beside Henry, unmoving. "Let him go, you bitch!" she screamed.

But Katie held on.

Tate's hands were scrabbling at the girl's fingers, trying to pull them free. Hazel rushed forward, but stopped. Tate's hands were changing. *Melting*. The flesh on the tips running downward like the wax on a burning candle, revealing the bone underneath. The skin melted, and he screamed. When the last of his fleshy palms dissolved his hands were just bones, as if they'd been dipped in acid. When his wrists continued to liquefy the boy's black eyes fixed on Hazel.

"*You! You* did this! You were supposed to save us, Hazel, but you didn't! Save me, Hazel! Drag me back to the water before I'm gone completely."

His eyes nailed her to the shore. She spared a glance over her shoulder. Something monstrous was coming beneath the dark water, pushing the waves up colossal swells that rose and fell like tiny mountains. And, on the crest of one large wave, the rowboat came closer. She looked back to her brother, agony pouring out of him in every pitiful scream. She couldn't take it anymore, couldn't listen to it anymore. She had heard that scream her entire life.

"I'll do it, Tate! I'll save you." Her legs were weak, but her arms felt strong, hopefully stronger than Katie's. "I'm sorry it took so long."

She lunged toward her granddaughter and her brother. As she swept by Henry and Louise she wrapped an arm around each of their waists, pulling them off of their feet and out of the water. They fell in a tangled heap beside Tate and Katie, faces planted in the sand, arms and legs wind-milling. The screams started at once. They were strong, but Hazel was strong too, and she had the advantage of being on top. Their thin bodies writhed beneath her like pinned pythons. They kicked at the sand and clawed at her arms, every scratch a small fire.

Hazel watched as their hands dissolved first, then their feet, and when their arms and legs started to go the struggling died down to a whimper. Beside her Tate was half gone. She grabbed what was left of his deteriorating body and dragged him off of Katie. The girl rolled over, gagging and coughing. Her arms were bleeding in a dozen places. Hazel gathered her siblings in her arms and huddled them together, hugging them to her body. The fight was gone from them. They were almost weightless.

Tate was all but gone, only a few bits of flesh left on his skull, his black eyes withered to small marbles. Henry and Louise were crying. Hazel clutched them tighter, putting her head against theirs. "Shh, shh," she said, "it's almost over, little ones. Your pain is almost through." She held them until their crying stopped, until they stopped moving in her arms. When it was finished she didn't get up. She was freezing cold in her damp nightgown, and her whole body ached, but she didn't get up. The storm had quieted; the stars had returned, along with a thin sliver of moon peeking between the clouds.

"Hazel Marie Coolidge," a hollow voice said from the water. Hazel knew it was the monster, though it spoke in her father's voice. "I told you I would come back," the voice said.

He was as tall a mountain, as tall as the whole world. He stood in the water just past where the waves dissolved into the sand, a great, black shape blotting out the stars. From his chest a rusty barb of a broken harpoon protruded outward. He stared at Hazel, and at the bundle of bones and dirty rags she held in her lap. He held out a hand the size of a grizzly bear paw.

"Give them to me," the monster said. "Give my children to me, let them return to the ocean where they belong. Where *you* belong."

"No," Hazel said, shaking her head. "You can't have them."

"They're not yours. They belong to *me* now, to the ocean and its masters."

"No, that's where you're wrong. They were never yours."

The monster growled, feinting a lunge. Hazel didn't flinch. He screamed at her, ripping the barb from his chest and flinging it into the sand. A swarm of gray tentacles slithered out of the water behind him, climbing up his back and spreading out around his shoulders like the wings of a fallen angel. The beaks opened and closed like the hungry mouths of baby crows.

"Give them to me, or I'll take them from you...it's too late to save them. *You're* too late."

"Why do you want them? You killed them, Dad. You *killed* them. How could you?"

"I gave them *eternal life*!" the monster roared, spittle flying from his mouth. "The same as I offered to you, but you were too frightened to accept it. You ungrateful little wretch." The tentacles pulsed around him with every heave of his chest.

"You killed them, Dad!" Hazel was shouting now, that old anger filling her up inside. "You killed them, and you killed Mom, too! Goddamn your soul for that."

"You're just like your mother, Hazel...too stupid to

see how things really are, too scared to face your destiny. That cunt tried to stop me...stop my transformation into greatness. She wasn't ready. She wasn't...*worthy* of the gift."

"Fuck you," Hazel said. She grabbed Katie and pulled the girl close. "Your power ends at the shore, and so does your legacy." She cradled the skeletons of her siblings to her chest. "As for Henry, Tate and Louise...they'll never touch the ocean again. I'll make sure of it. They'll be buried beside Mom before the sun goes down tomorrow."

The monster glowered, his voice hissing steam. A million beaks screeched around him.

"The sacrifice *must be completed.*"

Hazel shook her head slowly, her eyes pooling with sadness.

"Fuck your sacrifice. My family has given enough!" She turned, and with her back to the monster she walked toward the cottage. Katie stood and walked with her, glancing back at the horror in the surf.

In the distance the *Persephone* burst into flames, a floating inferno. The tentacles coiled and pushed at the beast, launching him out of the water. The monster screamed like a thunderclap before falling onto Hazel and Katie like a tidal wave. His stocky frame barreled into them, slamming them into the sand. A beefy hand closed around each of their throats, his iron grip like the bite of a tiger shark on their windpipes. Hazel's head swam, her vision darkening. She felt her heart seizing. On the shore the tentacles were whipping the water in a frenzy, slapping at the waves. "I love you, Dad," Hazel choked out with the last of her breath.

Just when it felt like the world would end and her chest would collapse, the mighty hands softened under her chin, their grip relaxing. The weight of her dead father's body disintegrated into nothingness. Hazel grabbed her father's bones, and the ratty, blue sweater, then threw them into the sand.

The night was silent again, the sea calm. The water's surface was glassy and unbroken, mirroring the moon and the endless starlight like flakes of crushed opal.

"I'm sorry, Grandma, I'm so sorry," Katie stammered. "I should have told you about him...I wanted to! But he said...he said he could take me to Mom. He said she was waiting for me." The girl shook her head and sobbed. "I'm so sorry."

"Oh Katie, no, it's my fault. I should have never brought you here. I haven't been to the ocean since...since I was nearly your age. I shouldn't have brought you here."

Katie wiped her face. "I'm glad we came, Grandma. I'm glad you could save them."

They trudged up the beach, every step heavier than it should have been. Something glimmered in the sand, and Katie bent and picked it up. It was the rusty shard of the harpoon. She looked back at the pile of bones stuffed inside the moldy sweater.

"What about him, Grandma?"

Hazel sighed. "We'll let him stay there for now, little one. He deserves a rest, and if the ocean wants to take him in the night I won't lose any sleep over it."

Katie started walking, but Grandma Hazel wasn't moving. She was staring back at the water, tears spilling down her cheeks and shining in the light of the moon. She was smiling.

"What is it, Grandma? What's wrong?"

"Nothing, dear. Nothing's wrong. Can you hear it?"

Katie paused, cocking her head. The night was still and calm, aside from the gentle lapping of waves on the shore. "Hear what?"

"The ocean," Hazel said, "it's singing to us."

Christopher Bond
About the Author

Christopher Bond is the author of dozens of stories encompassing the speculative fiction genre, including tales of high fantasy, urban fantasy, horror, and science-fiction. He has spent most of his adult life living between Hawaii and the Midwest. He currently lives in Ohio with his wife, Emily, and their three kids, Kailie, Oliver, and Milo.

You can find him on Twitter @CbondKauai

The Hunter and the Prey

McKenzie Richardson

They found Brody's bike in the pond, though they never did find Brody's body.

"You'd look even prettier if you smiled," the boy said, striding up to me with an air of confidence. He looked about sixteen, the beginnings of coarse hair jutting out from his face in stubbly patches. The rest of his skin was fair and smooth, at odds with his blemish-covered peers. He was clearly the handsomest boy there, a fact punctuated by the swarm of girls always giggling in the periphery of whatever space he inhabited. Even now they were watching through lowered lashes, jealousy and suspicion plainly written upon their round faces, half-masked by layers of runny makeup.

His eyes watched me carefully from beneath dark, fuzzy brows as he tilted his chin to scrutinize me.

When I did not respond, or alter my face to abide by

his words, he introduced himself. "My name is Brody. Is this your first time at camp?"

His blue eyes looked deeply into mine. They were pretty eyes; the kind of blue that reminds you of the sky as you're floating on top of the water, ears just below to drown out all other sound.

I did not answer Brody.

"This is my third summer here," he went on, eyeing me suspiciously. "I know all the good places. Maybe I can show you sometime." He kind of leered at me before wiggling his eyebrows in a way he probably thought looked attractive, but just reminded me of the dark, woolly caterpillars before they turn into giant leopard moths.

He kept talking as though, if he just funneled enough words at me, I would have to react eventually. "It's alright, I suppose. Would be better if we could swim in the pond, but it's a rather nasty thing, don't you think?"

He continued babbling on, examining me through those sky-blue eyes, ever-watchful of some reaction that would let him know what I was thinking. I remained silent, watching as he dug the tip of his shoe into the dirt. Next he kicked at a stone, his confidence dwindling with each unrequited phrase.

"What's your name?" He bit his lip as he waited for my reply.

I looked back into those sky-blue eyes, then I walked away. Brody watched me go.

That was not the last time Brody spoke to me. He made a habit of running into me in the mess hall, near the latrines and at the edge of the pond. On those occasions he always asked me questions.

"What's your name?"

"Where are you from?"

"Why don't you speak?"

"You deaf or something?"

I never answered. After a while Brody stopped asking questions, and just started talking at me. As we sat on top of a picnic table he told me about his family back in New Jersey: a mother, a father, a sister and a dog he didn't much like.

"I prefer big dogs," he explained. "Poodles are yappy little things."

He told me about his hobbies: video games, dirt biking and hunting. I looked up at the last one, the first indication I'd ever given him that I heard what he was saying.

"You like hunting, too?" he asked.

I did not respond, but my involuntary reaction was enough for him. He went on about his collection of guns and knives, his favorite places to hunt and what game he often sought.

"Foxes are the best to kill. The way the blood speckles on their red fur is kind of pretty."

The image of crimson dotting a scarlet coat popped into my mind. It made me kind of sad to think about, poor fox.

For the most part the other campers ignored me. Once a girl with carrot-colored hair mumbled an anxious warning about Brody. She told me he liked the new girls best, until they were no longer new. He lost interest quickly, she said, an assertion I took to come from her own experience. She was pretty in a very natural way, a way that can make one self-conscious at times, a way that can be easily manipulated by boys.

No one else ever looked at me or spoke to me. No one else, except Brody. Even though I did not speak to him he always had something to say to me.

Halfway through the summer I noticed a change in Brody. His sky-blue eyes stopped looking at my face. Instead he openly noted the curves in my body, the way my shirt fit over my breasts, the places where loose clothing clung to me. Brody began to talk to me about other things besides family and hunting.

"You really are very pretty," he said. "It's a shame you can't speak." His tone revealed his opinion that I was defective, a cast off, but I never said I couldn't speak. I just didn't have anything to say to Brody.

As the summer wore on he told me other things. He told me that he wanted to touch me, to taste me and to fuck me. He told me things he wanted to do to me. He said he'd like to peel off my clothing like an orange and suck all the juices from me. I did not comprehend all the things he said, but I understood his intent.

I gazed back into his sky-blue eyes, clouds marring their once-perfect clearness, less pretty in their malicious desire.

"I bet you're delicious," he whispered, licking his lips as he stared down at my lap. His eyes were intense, a fire burning in them that I could not quite explain.

Finally, when the summer was nearly at an end, Brody made his move.

"Come to the pond with me," he demanded, riding along beside me on his bike. It was a shiny blue, deeper in hue than his pale eyes. Similar to the feathers of a blue jay, but more metallic, like some sort of iridescent bug. It reminded me of dragonfly wings skimming the surface of the water before soaring up into the endless sky.

Night was approaching slowly, the sky darkening and stars beginning to open their eyes, watching us as we headed toward the pond.

We walked together, about a foot apart, Brody wheeling his bike between us like a protective barrier. I was not sure who it was protecting.

As we walked I could hear Brody breathing. His heart boomed in his chest, excitement written all over his face at the expectation and anticipation of long-awaited relief. I knew the feeling.

The camp counselors said the pond was too dirty for water activities. It had once been a swimming hole for the camp, for fishing and specimen collecting, but over time nasty things had grown in it. Its surface was green and slimy, the water beneath nearly black. Now it was used more as a landmark, a way to measure distance on group hikes.

When we arrived at the pond we both looked out over its scummy surface. Algae and weeds prevented the water from reflecting the brightening star-faces that dotted the sky above, lending their light to the scene.

We headed to the far end where abandoned beer cans peeked out from snaggles of weeds. In the encroaching darkness I registered movement on the surface of the pond. A little frog's head popped up, the water rippling around it. The creature blinked once, then retreated back into the oily liquid, having better things to do than witness what we were up to.

"They say there's a monster in the pond," Brody said. "All scales and teeth. They say it enjoys the taste of human flesh." His mouth twisted up into a grin as he watched me from the corner of his eye.

From his tone I could tell that Brody was trying to scare me, to frighten me so he could comfort me.

"If I ever saw the thing, I'd kill it. Something so hideous has no right to be alive. The world should only have pretty things."

Silence.

Grasshoppers sang around our feet, and a slight breeze wafted the smell of stagnant water toward us where it danced along our skin.

When I did not take the bait Brody reached out and clasped my hand, spinning me to face him. My hand ached under his tight grip, his too-long fingernails digging into my flesh. His face hovered close to mine, so close I could feel his breath against my cheek. It smelled of bologna sandwiches, and I wrinkled my nose at the odor.

"You really do look yummy." Brody smiled at me. Then, still holding my hand in one of his, the other clasped my breast. His grip was hard against the tender flesh and I winced, his fingers like claws burrowing through my shirt, clumsily trying to find the skin beneath.

I pulled away, but he yanked me toward him so that our lips met.

He tasted like bologna, too.

When he finally separated his face from mine he looked at me with those sky-blue eyes, trying to read my expression.

It was then that, for the first time, I smiled at Brody.

Brody screamed at the sight of my mouthful of pointed teeth, the rows of sharp, jagged prongs that filled my jaw. I licked my lips, reminiscing the taste of his kiss, then lunged toward him.

He continued to scream as I bit a mouthful out of his cheek. A second bite revealed a hole in his face that went all the way through to the cavern of his mouth. Through it I could see his tongue thrashing about. It looked delectable, like a fresh, wiggling grub.

He kicked at me, tried to push me away, but I clamped onto him, holding fast to my prey. With a bite to the throat I severed his vocal cords and he was no longer able to scream.

Still, his mouth opened wide like he was calling for

help, the only sound the wet flop of his tongue. I ate that next, savoring its meatiness, blood gushing from the stub left in his mouth.

My stomach rumbled as I fed it little pieces of Brody bit by bit. It was thrilled to finally have a feast after waiting for so long. The hunt can take time, but the results are nearly always worth the wait.

I peeled off the skin from his jawline, stubbled with the short hair of pubescence. The fine bristles tickled my mouth, and I squirmed at the delightful sensation.

I ate the skin from his face, then those sky-blue eyes which popped in my mouth so delightfully, like the cherry tomatoes in the camp garden. Bite by bite I filled my stomach, which stretched to hold its newest cargo. Bite by bite Brody disappeared.

When all the skin and flesh was gone I cracked the bones and slurped the marrow. It was a delicious feast, a satisfactory meal long awaited. I gnawed on the bone fragments, then used a few shards to pick stray meat from between my teeth, sucking them down to join the rest.

By the time I'd finished eating only a few slivers of bones remained to dot the water's edge, indistinguishable from the scattered rocks and debris that littered the shore. I kicked off my shoes and gathered up the torn remains of Brody's clothes. Balling them up over his sandals I wedged them into the spokes of his bike until they were secure.

Then I threw Brody's bike in the pond where it met the water with a splash. The green algae on the surface opened up like a doorway, welcoming me back home.

Wiggling my bare feet in the dirt I dove through the opening, spun around, and turned my face to the sky. Up above the stars twinkled down like pretty little shells, or like hundreds of eyes watching over me, witnesses to my victory at the end of the hunt. I floated on the surface for a moment, my full belly protruding from the water; big, round and gorged.

Then with a final gasp of air I let my head slip beneath the blackened water. The gills on my neck unsealed and I drank in the liquid. It had been so long since I breathed in the deliciousness of my home.

The webbing grew back between my bare toes and I flexed them, relishing the freedom I experienced now that they were no longer bound in shoes. Each practiced kick of my feet took me further into the muddy waters.

As I swam dark green scales pierced through the vulnerable skin I had worn, rippling over my entire body to form a protective shell, my very own armor. I'd missed the hard casing, abhorring the fleshy covering I'd had to don to fit in with the campers.

Tiny, frightened fish darted away at the sight of me, but I was already sated. I wouldn't need another meal for a few months or so. It was best to fill up during the summer, as you never knew when the next big meal would arrive.

My eyes were already heavy with sleep as I swam to the bottom of the pond. At the opening of the cave I deposited Brody's fancy watch in my pile of trinkets, souvenirs from other satisfying meals. A golden necklace, a fraying friendship bracelet, shoes, teeth and even a yo-yo without a string. Then I settled myself for a good, long nap to digest my latest catch.

Brody and I had had something in common: we both enjoyed the hunt. He'd always been so sure that he would catch his prey. He was used to getting whatever he wanted, one way or another, and something about that confidence had been especially satisfying. It had made his skin more tender, more supple, as though I could taste his fear. Toying with him had made his meat sweeter. It was the best meal I'd had in a while.

Brody had said he thought I would be delicious. He said that I looked yummy, but it was Brody who had been delicious. I had savored every bite.

McKenzie Richardson
About the Author

McKenzie Richardson lives in Milwaukee, WI. A lifelong explorer of imagined worlds on the written page, over the last few years she has been finding homes for her own creations. Most recently, her stories and poetry have been published in anthologies from Eerie River Publishing, Black Hare Press, Iron Faerie Publishing, and Dragon Soul Press. In addition, she has published a poetry collaboration with Casey Renee Kiser, 433 Lighted Way, and her middle-grade fantasy novel, Heartstrings, is available on Amazon. McKenzie loves all things books and is currently working towards a master's degree in Library and Information Sciences. When not writing, she can usually be found in her book hoard, reading or just looking at her shelves longingly. For more on her writing, follow her on: Facebook: facebook.com/mckenzielrichardson/ Instagram: instagram.com/mckenzielrichardson/ Blog: craft-cycle.com

Fronds

Tim Mendees

"Hey, Ruth?" Martin called above the crash of the waves. When he got no reply from the woman further down towards the coastline he tried again, a little louder this time. "Doctor Jenkins?"

Ruth didn't turn from the rock pool that she was currently engrossed in. "Hmm?"

"Just what is it we are looking for?" Being an undergraduate on loan from Aberystwyth University, Martin found a lot of what Doctor Ruth Jenkins did at the marine biology research centre outside of Betyls Cove a complete mystery. She did, after all, deal with the weird and the wonderful. Hers was a program that looked into cases of strange mutations among sea creatures and local flora.

"I mean, 'anything unusual' is pretty vague... all of this stuff is pretty unusual if you ask me... I've never seen crustaceans like this one before." He picked up a small crab by the back end of its shell and peered at it. The crab snapped its pincers indignantly and managed to squirm from his grasp... it landed in the pool with a *plop* and quickly scuttled under a rock.

Ruth didn't reply. This wasn't unusual; she tended towards the silent when something grabbed her attention. She reached over to her satchel, retrieving a pair of tweezers and a sample pot. "What do we have here?" She whispered to herself as she replaced the lid, taking another pot and started rummaging in the rock-pool again.

Martin sighed and returned his attention to the unusual crab. He knew it was futile to try and grab Ruth's attention when she was working; he had tried many times... and failed. This was a problem as, throughout his placement, Martin had cultivated a Great Barrier Reef-sized crush on his mentor. It mattered not that she was in an on-again-off-again relationship with a medical doctor, and it mattered not that she was twice his age. What did matter, however, was the fact that she thought he was a complete turnip!

"... Are you receiving me?" Ruth called in a slightly irritated manner. "Earth to Martin... Come in, you bloody space-cadet."

Evidently, his mind had been wandering again. It was a common problem. As a healthy, young man swirling with barely contained hormones, all he had to do was think about the way her lab coat clung to her curves and he was instantly away with the faeries. "Ugh... Yeah, sorry... Miles away... What's up?"

"Come over here, would you? Bring the camera."

"Found something?" Martin slipped as he got up

from his crouch, submerging one of his boots in freezing seawater. It was his own fault; Ruth had told him to wear his standard-issue Wellington boots, but *no*, he was far too cool and hip for canary-yellow Wellies. He cursed under his breath and chalked it up as a well-earned life-lesson.

"I should say so." Ruth grinned and shook a plastic tube in his direction. He was too far away to see what was inside, but whatever it was it caught the sun in an unusual way, seeming to almost shimmer. "I want you to take a picture of me with the samples in situ. I need to document this properly."

Martin fished the digital camera out of his pocket and started randomly poking it until it made a twittering sound and started working. "What is it?" Excitement had started to build up inside of him. If they had found a new species it could be his meal ticket; he would be the envy of marine biologists all over Britain.

Ruth beamed as he took the first snap. "Seaweed!"

"Seaweed?" His voice must have betrayed a slight, but palpable, disappointment as Ruth's brow creased into a frown.

"It's very exciting seaweed." She stated somewhat petulantly. "It looks to be a completely new species... Here," she passed him the largest sample. "Look."

It was indeed an unusual specimen. It sat somewhere between the tough flatness of bladderwrack and the almost finger-like fronds of thong-weed. Its length was peppered with grotesque, tumour-like bladders to aid its buoyancy. Martin shuddered involuntarily. It seemed to exude sickness, like it was somehow the harbinger of a dreadful plague. He studied it for a second and began to marvel at the weed's unusual colouring. Where most seaweeds are dull browns and muddy greens, this was a shade of pale blue that brought to mind the lips of an asphyxiated cadaver in a TV murder mystery. Veins of deep greens and crimsons ran its length, and it seemed possessed of a pearlescent quality that gave it different hues depending on the position of the sunlight.

"It's bloody weird, I'll give you that," Martin stated flatly after his intense scrutinisation. "I wouldn't like to get that sprinkled over my eggrolls on a Saturday night." Like many students Martin lived on takeaways; he did try cooking once, but it was a complete disaster. He fell at the first hurdle, actually getting the baked beans out of the can. The can opener slipped, and he ended up with beans all over the floor. The ones that he did manage to get into the pan he burnt.

Ruth ignored his flippancy and instead started to gather the specimens into her satchel while Martin took pictures of the rock-pool. It was immediately adjacent to a large outcrop, colloquially known as the Blasted Crag. The crag reached out into the sea and towered above, bathing the beach in shadow. It was from this geological oddity that Betyls Cove not only took its name, but also its distinctly outré ecosystem. At some point in the middle ages the crag was struck by a meteorite, which imbued the cave below with strange mineral deposits. Those, in turn, bred a strange type of fungus known only to grow in that cave.

The Pluto Cap, as it was known, was highly hallucinogenic. It was considered to be dangerous, as it was believed to possess parasitic properties similar to the *cordyceps* fungus. Not that this had stopped a healthy black-market trade on its fleshy, blue caps. Where the *cordyceps* kills its hosts outright the Pluto Cap acted in a symbiotic fashion, mutating the creature into a new species. Ruth postulated that the fungus may be a significant building block in future evolutions, one that needed to be monitored closely.

The rhythmic suck and spit of the waves signalled that the tide was on the turn; in less than an hour this section of the beach would be submerged all the way back to the sea wall. "Come on," Ruth instructed. "Let's get back to the lab so I can get this lot under the microscope..." She paused to glower in Martin's direction; he was drifting again. "Oi, Martin... Let's go."

Martin shook himself out of his reverie and handed the sample back to Ruth. "Sorry...I was just watching the way the colours shifted with the sunlight... It's beautiful, in a creepy sort of way."

Ruth hoisted her satchel over her shoulder and led the way back to the steps. She snorted derisively as she walked past Martin, "What could possibly be creepy about a hunk of seaweed?"

Martin sighed and prodded a frond of the unusual seaweed with a pair of tweezers. No matter how hard he tried he just couldn't summon up even an ounce of enthusiasm for Ruth's discovery. There was just something deeply uninteresting about seaweed, even a specimen as unusual as this. It just sort of floated around, not doing anything. It wasn't even dangerous. In fact, it was considered healthy. This added to Martin's mindset; nothing *healthy* was remotely *cool.*

Ruth, on the other hand, was like a small child in a sweet shop. Her hazel eyes twinkled with excitement as she ran the specimens through a number of elaborate tests. The hours sped on by, until she finally looked over at Martin and grinned. "Definitely a new species!"

Martin rolled his eyes, "Whoopee!"

"Don't be like that..." Ruth frowned. "It's an important discovery." She paused for a second before the gleeful smile spread back across her lips. "Hey! If it is confirmed a new species then we will get to name it!" She adopted a school mistress tone, "If you're a good boy I might name it after you."

"What, Martin?"

Ruth laughed. "Martin Seaweed? No, I don't think so...I was thinking more of *sulkius bollocksus* or *miserablis gittus.*"

Martin's face finally cracked, and he roared with laughter. "Sorry... I guess I am being a bit of a killjoy. I get that it's an important discovery and all that, but it's not something cool like a crab..." He gestured towards a tank at the back of the mobile lab. Ruth's crowning achievement had been the discovery of an unusual sub-species of shore crab that has a symbiotic relationship with the fungus from the cave. She had given it a fancy Latin name, but the one she kept as a pet was called Gerald.

"True, but this weed has some very strange properties. It might have some interesting medical applications... Plus, hang around here for a while longer and you might get your crab, after all."

"Why is that?" Martin's interest suddenly became piqued.

"The mutations seem to be on the rise again. The fungal growth in the Twilight Cave under the crag flares up every now and then; it sometimes gets dangerous and starts infecting the whole coast-line. We have to get the Army in to flame the place from time to time, but it always grows back. When that happens we usually find an unusual specimen or two...hence this weed."

"So you reckon it came from the cave then?" Martin toddled over to Ruth and peered over her shoulder.

"Undoubtedly..." She held up a sample in her tweezers and pointed at the base of the frond. "See here? ... This is where it was attached to a rocky surface, and see those spores? Definitely Pluto Cap spores, I'd recognize them anywhere."

Holding the sample against the bench Ruth reached for a scalpel. She intended to slice the frond along the stem to get a better look at the cell structure, but she was startled when it moved.

"What the Hell?" The seaweed twisted against the prongs in a seemingly desperate attempt to evade the knife. "The damn seaweed is moving!"

Martin stood with his mouth agape as Ruth held the squirming strand of seaweed up in the air. It was flexing and twisting, like some kind of worm. The colours on its surface rippled and pulsed almost hypnotically; Martin had to wrench his eyes away from it.

Ruth had never encountered seaweed that reacted to stimuli like this before, and it seemed possessed of a rudimentary intelligence of sorts. Unsure as to how to continue she instructed Martin to prepare one of the vacant tanks for the samples. "I think we need to monitor what happens when they are left to their own devices." Ruth mused as she plopped sample after sample into the saltwater. The tanks were all kept at conditions as close to those on the coast as possible.

"*They?*" Martin raised an eyebrow. "You sound as though it's alive... I mean, I know it's *alive*. I mean alive in the human sense. Like it has a mind?"

Ruth said nothing. What they had just witnessed shouldn't have happened. Seaweed *shouldn't* behave like that. Once it was back in the water the unusual weed had settled on the bottom of the tank, and its color had returned to darker shades. In the murky water it almost looked *normal*.

"What now?" Martin asked, looking at the clock. It was almost time to finish for the day.

Ruth sighed. "As much as I don't want to, I'm going to have to call the bureaucrats at Truro... I'll have to tell them about Weedy here..." She almost spat the last words like they were poison. This was the last thing she wanted. Truro would, in turn, have to notify the government, and before you could say 'intrusive' the place would be swarming with suits.

Martin was aghast. He knew what that meant. "What? ... Won't they take our discovery away?" The prospect of getting to name the weed had become suddenly attractive, now that it had the possibility of being sentient.

"Probably," Ruth answered grimly. "We need more samples though, and it's the only way to get them."

"We could go down into the cave," Martin said with barely constrained excitement. "I've heard that there are tunnels under the shops, we could get in that way..."

Ruth held up her hand to cut him off mid-flow. "Nope... Don't even think about it. It's ridiculously dangerous down there...Besides, the tunnels have been blocked off. The only way in is from the sea."

Martin opened his mouth to argue, but Ruth stopped him in his tracks. She explained the penalties for going into the cave, and how stupid an idea it was. Martin sulked. After a few moments of silence Ruth announced that they were done for the day. She seemed deflated by the prospect of calling in an outside agency, and decided that a few drinks were in order. Once the lab was locked up she bade Martin a good night after making him promise to forget about the cave. Martin smiled and assured her that he would before heading back to town...though he had no intention of listening to her.

Martin shivered as the cold wind blew off the waves, whipping his face with spray. It was only now, as he guided the small dinghy around the jagged rocks, that it became obvious what a stupid idea this was. He had completely ignored Ruth's warnings, and had hired the vessel with full intentions of getting more seaweed samples. He'd hit on his plan while talking to one of the local fishermen over a drink. Isn't it strange how even the stupidest of ideas seem like strokes of genius after a couple of pints?

"Don't capsize... Don't capsize... Please, God, don't capsize!" He repeated as the swell tipped him sideways. His stomach lurched as the boat dipped suddenly, the sea roaring and roiling around the rocks. Currents swirled, and the surface bubbled with grey foam. The tide was at its height, the waves slamming against the Blasted Crag. His fisherman friend had assured him that it was a good time to try, but Martin had doubts about the man's sincerity.

The small, outboard motor sputtered and chugged against the flow. The man at the rental shed had taken a hefty deposit on the loan of the boat, and Martin had been forced to dip into his student loan yet again.

Still, Martin was now certain that the initial outlay would be worth it. After much thought, and much beer, the prospect of being the co-discoverer of some kind of new life-form seemed like his golden ticket. No university would turn him down after that! He could go where he wanted, work where he wanted. Not only that, but if *he* made it happen by getting the sample then surely Ruth would fall at his feet. She would be so impressed with him that she would fall madly in love with him... wouldn't she?

Finally the rolling waves worked in his favour. As the water crested his boat was sent surging between the rocks and into the mouth of the cave, the boat thudding against the stone as it followed the inlet. Martin turned on his waterproof lamp and gasped. "Bloody Hell!"

Never in his wildest dreams had he expected a sight like this. The cave rose in an almost pyramidal way to a centre point, which was presumably where the meteor had hit. The walls were thick with a disgusting fungal growth glowing with an eerie luminescence, and clumps of sickly mushrooms sprouted from the floor and clustered around cracks and fissures. Towards the far corner, next to where the tunnel had been sealed with a rusted iron gate, grew a huge clump of the mystery weed.

"Jesus..." Martin muttered as he manoeuvred the boat towards a natural ramp. "This place looks like a seventies album cover." Once the boat was secured by tying it to a large rock Martin stepped out onto the slimy rocks. After giving himself a mental pat on the back for remembering his Wellies this time, he picked up his bag containing gardening shears, a trowel and a roll of bin liners.

Picking his way over the uneven surface Martin marvelled at the growth on the walls. It was almost as though he was inside the mouth of a giant creature; no trace of rock was visible under the shimmering blue fungus. It looked to Martin like the cave had been decorated with wallpaper designed by H.R. Giger. Huge, bulbous clumps of it lined the walls like boulders. It was unnerving, like standing in a fever dream.

By far the worst aspect of the cave, however, was the smell. The sickly-sweet scent of decay mingled with an almost meaty sourness that, along with the iodine smell of stagnant seawater and a metallic taint from the rusty gate, created a foulness that could have come straight from the Devil's rectum. It took all of Martin's strength not to throw up.

The weed rippled as he approached, the fronds dancing with unearthly colors. It would have been beautiful, if it didn't look like rotting fingers. Martin tore off a strip of plastic and laid it on the floor before kneeling down. Next he tore off another length and opened it out before taking the shears from his bag.

Leaning forwards Martin grabbed hold of a clump of the weed and prepared to snip it off just above the root. It rustled and shook furiously as it tried to pull itself free from his grip, but Martin was too fast. With a loud *snip*, which echoed off the walls, he cut away clump after clump of the weird vegetation. It could have been his imagination, or a strange effect caused by the whistling wind, but Martin was sure that the weed screamed. It was a high-pitched, barely-audible cry of pain that set his teeth on edge.

Stuffing the cuttings into the bin liner, Martin decided that he had been in there long enough. The atmosphere had grown oppressive, like the growth was closing in around him. He noticed that the walls had joined the weed in swirling and undulating with color. Martin put the shears back in the bag before dumping it, and the bag of weeds, back into the dinghy.

Reaching out to grab the lamp, Martin screamed as a thick frond shot out from the plant and coiled around his wrist. Martin tried to yank his arm away, but the plant was unnaturally strong. It contracted tighter and tighter until it cut into his flesh. Thrashing around in pain, Martin tried to free himself with his free hand. He groped behind himself for the bag, but it was too far out of reach. The momentary lapse of concentration cost him dearly as the weed yanked him forwards, and he fell into it face-first.

The shimmering color of the weed enveloped his vision as he gasped for air and tried to get his balance. The fronds bristled around him and writhed like serpents, coiling around his head. Thick, finger-like strands clamped him firmly as several of the disgusting bladders loomed in front of his eyes. They throbbed and pulsed to a steady rhythm, as though they were in tune with some unholy cosmic melody.

Martin screamed as the bladders opened as one. A dense cloud of sticky spores shot up his nose, into his eyes and into his mouth. He coughed and sputtered as it finally let him go. He twisted his body and landed on his back a couple of feet away from the shrub. Gasping for air he pawed at his face to clear away the ghastly excrescence, blood from his wrist only adding to the mess.

Sitting up, Martin cupped his hands and splashed his face with seawater. The salt stung his wrist and seared his nostrils. It took several more splashes to clear the substance from his skin.

Clack!

Martin yelped as a sharp sound came from the nearby wall.

Clack! ... Clack! ... Clack!

"Holy shit!" Martin sputtered as he saw the source of the rhythmic clacking. It was from the clumps of fungus that lined the walls. Only, they weren't clumps of fungus or boulders... they were oysters. Huge, craggy oysters filled with thrashing, blue tendrils.

Clack! ... Clack! ... Clack!

On every beat the cave flashed with colors that his mind couldn't comprehend. He got to his feet and found that his legs had turned to jelly. The clack of the oysters and the flash of the light quickened with every second, his vision swimming and his guts doing backflips. His head rolled on his shoulders as the sensory assault left him disorientated. Left and right, up and down...all had lost all meaning. He was adrift in a maelstrom of kaleidoscopic visions.

CLACKCLACKCLACK...

The light strobed, and time slowed to a crawl. Martin's knees buckled and his body pitched forwards... He was falling... It seemed like an eternity. As the beat hammered on he hit the freezing water with a deafening *splash!*

Martin plunged headlong into the icy abyss. He felt weightless and content as he passed shimmering columns of blue fungus and flashing weeds. Twisted growths that looked like human faces leered at him on his descent. It was like another world that seemed to go on forever. Strange anemones and ghastly urchins clung to deformed and sickly corals. Huge, alien-looking jellyfish tumbled and danced with the currents, their frond-like tentacles waving below them.

There was a sound down here. It was almost like a voice, but it spoke no words. It seemed to beckon him further down, urging him to greater depths. It was useless to resist. Whatever it was, it was already in his head... planted by the spores.

Everything in this strange, twilight world was lit with the same luminescence as the cave. Everything was covered in the spores; everything carried the taint of the Pluto cap. Martin's chest burst as the pressure overwhelmed his body. His head felt like it was being slowly crushed in a vice. It was useless to struggle against the pull of the sea. All Martin could do was quietly fade into the darkness as oblivion took him...

Bang! ... Bang! ... Bang!

"Martin, for fuck's sake, answer me... I know you're in there, you tosser!"

The angry yelling and the loud banging on the door jolted Martin awake. His room was in darkness and reeked of seawater. He was fully clothed, soaking wet and still wearing his Wellies. His mind raced. He had no recollection of getting home. The last thing he remembered was hitting the water, and that was hazy at best. There was a voice... wasn't there?

"Right, that's it... I'm coming in." The irate voice belonged to Amir, one of his housemates. He was usually such a placid sort of chap, so whatever Martin had done it must have been bad. The door swung open with a glare of yellow light from the bare bulb on the landing. Amir was dressed as though he had just got in, and in his right hand he held a white towel that was dripping with blue slime. "What the Hell are you playing at?" Amir boomed. It was unusual to hear such a big voice come from such a slight figure. "This shit is everywhere!"

"Ugh... Sorry... I don't know..." Martin was startled and vague. His words came out in a jumble of guttural grunts as he tried to stand. His legs were weak, and he had to grab his bedside table for support.

"Jeez," Amir said, his tone softening. "Are you alright? ... What the Hell happened to you?" He clicked on Martin's bedroom light and looked at him. Martin looked like a cadaver that had recently been fished from the river. His hair was clogged with sediment, and his body had taken on a pale blue tinge.

"I... I... Don't ... Seaweed... Where?" Martin's eyes rolled.

Amir, a medical student, moved towards him and looked in his eyes. "Are you on acid again?" He said, judgement dripping off every letter. "You know what happened last time, right?"

"No... No drugs..." Martin said, his mouth gaping like a beached guppy. He shook his head and rubbed his eyes with his thumb and forefinger. "Can't remember... I think I fell in the sea..."

Amir looked at his sodden clothes. "You think?" He asked sarcastically. "What the Hell have you been up to, you idiot?" Concern had subsumed his anger by this point.

Martin rummaged through the wreckage of his memories. "Collecting seaweed... From the cave..."

Before Amir could inquire as to which cave he was talking about, a large *thump* from the bathroom made them both jump. It was followed by a disgusting gurgle. "What the Hell was that?" Amir asked in alarm.

Martin shook his head dumbly.

Amir turned and walked towards the bathroom at the end of the hall. Martin silently followed, noticing the trail of blue goo that led from the stairs to his bedroom. His foot touched one of the puddles, and a flash like a camera bulb went off in his head... it heralded memories...

Martin had somehow washed up on the beach clutching the bag of seaweed. The chill wind cut at his flesh as he traversed the sands and headed to the esplanade. He hadn't a clue what had happened, but he felt strangely elated. He looked down at the plastic bag stuffed with evil fronds and smiled. His ticket to fame, fortune and, most importantly, love, was in his grasp.

After locating his car Martin had driven home to the house he shared with Amir and one other fellow student, Zoe. Nobody had been around as he made his way inside, trailing filth and slime from his saturated clothes and the bag of seaweed. All he had to do now was look after it until morning.

To this end, he wandered into the kitchen and picked up the tub of cooking salt. He couldn't let the weed dry out, and he didn't have an aquarium... the bath would have to do. He dragged the leaking bag up the stairs and went towards the bathroom. Unfortunately, it was occupied. Zoe was evidently having one of her legendarily long baths. He and Amir had often compared her to a prawn as she normally came out pink and wrinkly after a prolonged soak.

Martin's memory became hazy as he recalled picking the bag of weed up in his arms and creeping towards the door...

Now, as Amir neared the closed door, Martin felt a surge of guilt and terror. "Don't go in there!" He screamed as Amir's hand twisted the doorknob.

Amir let out a cry of panic as he gazed through the doorway. Thick fronds of seaweed climbed up and out of the bath. They swayed and writhed as they continued to creep up towards the ceiling. "What the Hell?" Fat, greasy clumps of fungus dripped over the edge of the tub and landed on the tiled floor with a sickening *splat.* Amir took a step towards the bath... and instantly wished that he hadn't.

The mass of growth suddenly sat up!

"Zoe!?" Amir bellowed in disbelief.

The weed that Martin had dumped on top of her had

burrowed into her flesh and taken root. Fronds spilled from her mouth as she wailed at Amir, who babbled as the sight blasted his sanity. Zoe reached out her arms for Amir, thick tendrils tasting the air inches from his body. He tried to back away, but he was suddenly shoved from behind...

"Martin?" Was the last thing Amir said as Zoe dragged him under the water.

Ruth sighed and folded the printed email over before jamming it into the pocket of her lab coat. She had received the message late last evening, and had printed it off to show Martin. It was from the M.O.D: they had told her, in no uncertain terms, that she wasn't to so much as look at the odd weed. They feared another disaster, like the one that occurred when some silly devil decided to sell Pluto cap fungus as compost, and were sending a containment team to flame the cave and destroy the samples.

As much as it took the wind out of her sails, Ruth knew it was for the best. She had been here long enough to know a hazard when she saw it. It was Martin that was going to be the problem; she had seen his eyes twinkle when she said he might get to name it. She chuckled derisively to herself. "Martin the Seaweed... silly sod."

She locked the car and stepped towards the lab. It was a nice day, for a change, and a fresh breeze shook out the cobwebs from last night's gin. Martin's car was parked next to the lab in its usual spot, but he was nowhere to be seen. This was odd, as he didn't have a key; nobody did except Ruth. It was only upon reaching the door that she noticed that the lock had been forced.

"What the living fuck!?" She fumed as she swung it open, ready to give Martin a sound bollocking. Her mounting stream of venom died on her lips as she took in the interior of the lab.

Seaweed sprouted from the floor, hung from the ceiling and draped down the walls. One half of her usually pristine laboratory was now a forest of shimmering fronds. She gasped, then took a step inside. It was everywhere. It grew from between the keys on her computer, and out of the eyepiece of her microscope. Everything was infected.

The letter had told her that it was her duty to contain the infection. Ruth swallowed and thought about all of her lost data before remembering that most of it was backed up to the Cloud. She had no other choice than to set fire to the lab.

One thing that wasn't being toasted, however, was Gerald. Her pet crab's tank was, luckily, on the side of the room away from the growth. She quickly unplugged the filter and lugged the tank outside. Once it was safely in the trunk of her car she went back inside clutching her cigarette lighter.

Ruth started piling all the paper and flammable material she could find by the weeds. It was then that the wall moved...

Two hollow, black orbs opened in the largest clump

of weed. They glared at her as she screamed and went crashing into the desk, sending test tubes and microscopic slides tinkling to the floor in a shower of glass.

The man-size patch of weed detached itself from the rest and shambled towards her unsteadily. Ruth knew that what lumbered towards her, with arms outstretched, was Martin. The silly bugger had defied her and gone to the cave. Martin was infected by the Pluto spores.

Martin was doomed.

"Back!" She demanded, throwing a beaker at the clump that was Martin's head. "Keep back!"

Martin's mouth opened, and a long tentacle of weed that grew out of his tongue thrashed towards her, cracking the air like a bull-whip. Ruth swatted it aside with a metal clipboard and raced towards the back of the room. The Martin-shaped weed monster shuffled towards her, shrieking and howling. The high-notes hurt her ears, and somewhere she could hear a rhythm throbbing that was like the heartbeat of some unspeakable leviathan.

It was almost on her when he spotted the gas tap. With a decisive movement she leapt across the room, simultaneously tearing off the rubber hose to the Bunsen burner and flicking open the valve.

Martin sent out multiple long fronds from his fingers in an attempt to snare her, but Ruth showed her agility by managing to duck and dive out of their path. Once she reached the door she ripped the metal guard off the lighter and jammed the gas open before lighting it, placing it on the floor and slamming the door.

Ruth Jenkins had just got into the safety of her car when the mobile laboratory exploded in a ball of flame and debris. She gunned the engine and sped down the driveway before pulling onto the road. Once she was a safe distance away Ruth took out her phone and called D.S. Finch. Once she had explained the situation she sat, calmly awaiting the fire engines... At least she had saved the Army the job of disposing of the samples...

Tim Mendees
About the Author

Tim Mendees is a horror writer from Macclesfield in the North-West of England that specialises in cosmic horror and weird fiction. He has had over seventy published stories in anthologies and magazines with publishers all over the world. His debut Lovecraftian novella, Burning Reflection is out now from Mannison Press.

When he is not arguing with the spellchecker, Tim is a goth DJ, crustacean and cephalopod enthusiast, and the presenter of a popular web series of live video readings of his material and interviews with fellow authors. He currently lives in Brighton & Hove with his pet crab, Gerald, and an army of stuffed octopods.

https://timmendeeswriter.wordpress.com/
https://tinyurl.com/timmendeesyoutube
https://www.facebook.com/goatinthemachine

Buoy 21415

T. M. Brown

A bitter wind rattled at the tavern's windows, as if searching for a way inside. Ian Rhodes tapped at a half-empty beer bottle as he watched the snow drift across the gravel parking lot. He'd always found the snow mesmerizing. Having grown up in central Georgia it wasn't the kind of thing you saw often. It was the stuff of cheesy Christmas movies, holiday displays at the local mall and dreams. Lately, softly-falling snow had come to feature prominently in the musings of his unconscious mind.

Janet Reynolds was seated directly across from Ian in a shadowy corner booth, but he paid her little more attention than he did his tepid beer. The aging survey technician droned on endlessly about one thing or the other. Janet had clung to him like a drowning cat since the moment he'd introduced himself to the crew of the *McKinley*. The way she prattled on you'd think nobody had listened to a word she'd said in years; perhaps nobody had. The rest of the crew avoided her like the plague.

Every few minutes Ian would respond to her ramblings with a 'yeah' or a 'huh'. He didn't bother to look away from the window, and he certainly didn't listen to whatever it was she was saying, but Ian figured that he owed her at least that much. As the senior Hydrographic Survey Technician aboard the *McKinley*, Janet was technically his boss. She was also one of his only remaining social contacts. Whether Ian liked it or not, he, Janet and the other nerds of the survey team were always looked at as being separate from the rest of the ship's crew.

Ian leaned close enough to the window to feel cold air emanating from behind the glass. He watched as the orange glow of a nearby streetlight struggled against the snow and gloom. Something about the scene was otherworldly. The dying light, the blackness, and the snow... It felt so alien, yet so familiar. A shiver ran the length of his spine.

"You want another?"

Ian's thoughts derailed all at once, piling around his mind in a smoldering heap. He turned from the window to see Janet standing beside the table. She stared back at him expectantly.

"Do you want another?" She repeated.

"I...uh...I'm alright." Ian picked the half-empty beer bottle up off the table and sloshed the contents from side to side. "Still workin' on this one."

Janet's expression harshened. She snatched the bottle away from him and examined it in the tavern's soft light. "Jesus, Bass..." She sighed, pressed the mouth of the bottle to her lips, and tilted it back. Beer dribbled down the contours of her weathered face. She finished and slammed the bottle back to the tabletop. It reverberated with a distinctly hollow sound, suggesting that it had been emptied. "You're gonna need something stronger." Janet turned and walked toward the bar without saying another word.

Ian didn't protest. Perhaps she was right, perhaps he did need something stronger. He hadn't slept well since departing Kodiak, and he had a bad feeling about the voyage from its very outset. It had all the hallmarks of a Hollywood tragedy, and to begin with the weather was shit. The sea was restless and showed no signs of calming in the near future. A sense of foreboding hung in the perpetually overcast skies off the coast of Alaska.

The NOAAS *Fairweather*, on which Ian had been stationed since he'd taken the job several months ago, had been diverted to Anchorage for maintenance. The *Fairweather's* duties were therefore passed off to the NOAAS *McKinley*. The *McKinley* was an old vessel—the oldest in NOAA's chronically underfunded fleet— and singularly ill-suited for the unforgiving waters of the North Pacific. It had been built in the 1940s and had been decommissioned twice before, only to be refurbished when politicians realized the cost of replacing it. The aging vessel's electrical system was temperamental at best, its crew was unwelcoming, and its low hull seemed to invite the ocean onto its exposed decks.

There was also the unusual nature of the mission itself. Two months ago, a buoy equipped with tsunami warning equipment had begun malfunctioning 175 nautical miles off the coast of Attu Island. Remote troubleshooting proved incapable of fixing the problem. The Deep-ocean Assessment and Reporting of Tsunamis program—DART, for short—initially considered the buoy's repair to be a tertiary priority, one which could easily wait until conditions in the North Pacific improved the following season. Fate intervened, however, and after a tsunami destroyed several million dollars' worth of infrastructure in Valdez the functionality of DART buoy 21415 became a top priority for both of Alaska's senators.

The mission to buoy 21415 had been unscheduled, and most members of the *Fairweather's* survey team had been on shore-leave when the *McKinley* put into port. Only Ian and Janet had been pathetic enough to be readily available. Beyond his personal misgivings about traveling to the one of the most remote Aleutian Islands in the dead of winter, Ian had no good excuse as to why he couldn't participate. He climbed aboard, choked down copious amounts of dramamine and melatonin, and tried his best to swallow the growing sense of unease that had taken hold inside him.

Ian and Janet were the only two members of the *Fairweather's* survey team on board. The remainder of the crew was made up of individuals permanently assigned to the *McKinley*. They seemed competent and professional enough, but after several unpleasant days at sea they remained little more than strangers. Ian would have been hard-pressed to identify a single interaction that had been anything more than the terse exchange of necessary information.

The crew certainly looked the part of hardened mariners. They smoked cheap cigarettes, hid weather-worn faces behind greasy facial hair and unabashedly displayed the kind of cheap tattoos a more self-conscious person would almost immediately have come to regret. There was something about these men—and they were *all* men—however, that rubbed Ian the wrong way. They were unusually quiet, joyless individuals. When they spoke at all it was in hushed tones and on matters strictly relating to the performance of their duties. Their stares always seemed to linger just a little too long for comfort.

The *McKinley* was now three days into its voyage. Its stop in Dutch Harbor would only be long enough to refuel and resupply; they'd depart long before the sun could peek above the horizon.

Janet returned from the bar with two glasses in hand. Each was filled to the brim with ice and clear liquid that Ian doubted was water. "Here you go, Bass. Drink up." She sat down and slid one of the two glasses across the table.

"Thanks," Ian replied absently. He didn't like how his boss had taken to referring to him as *Bass*. Supposedly the name derived from the fact that the largemouth bass was the state fish of Georgia. He'd never taken the time to verify the claim, nor was he certain that a 'state fish' was even a thing. It hardly mattered, however. The bass was a freshwater fish, and amidst the ceaselessly roiling waters off the Alaskan coast it seemed distinctly out of place. The nickname was a constant reminder that Ian was out of his depth—a humble pond fish adrift in an infinite, hungry sea.

Ian raised the glass to his lips and inhaled. The aroma of pure rubbing alcohol singed his nostrils. He winced and recoiled. "What's in this? Straight vodka?"

Janet smiled and took a sip from her glass. "And ice..." She added. "My mother's favorite cocktail."

"Well, your mother sounds like quite the lady."

"Indeed she is..." Janet's voice trailed off as she leaned back in her chair.

"She's still alive?" Ian tried his best to mask genuine surprise with a playful tone. "That'd make her what? Like, 200?"

The lines on Janet's face compressed into a scowl. "Not quite... but the Reynolds are quite hardy folk." She took another sip from her glass. "Maybe it's the vodka?"

Ian eyed his own glass. "I guess things do last longer when they're pickled..." He flashed his boss a smile, and for the first time in weeks it wasn't entirely forced.

Janet smiled back. Her teeth glistened in the neon-blue of the promotional beer sign hanging in the window. Ian couldn't help but wonder if they were dentures. "Well then, let's drink to the Reynolds." She raised her glass. "May we stay pickled forever."

Ian joined her in the toast and their two glasses clinked upon impact. Ice-cold vodka sloshed over the rim and ran down his fingers, burning as it slid down his throat. Ian did his best to disguise his desire to spit the vodka back into his glass; letting an old woman outdrink him was simply too emasculating to accept. He placed the glass back on the tabletop and waited for Janet to speak. It rarely took long.

"Best drink up," Janet said before downing what remained of her drink. When she placed the glass back on the table only partially melted ice cubes remained. "It's only going to get worse from here."

Ian knew she was right. All the weather models predicted nothing but rough waters for a week. Still, it didn't make him feel any better to hear it. *Was it that obvious that he was feeling uneasy about the voyage?* He said nothing and took another sip of his drink. It burned less than the first. Ian had never seen his boss as eager to drink as she was this evening. *Was she nervous too?*

"I'm just saying..." Janet's voice was uncharacteristically sympathetic. Her expression was one of concern. "You already look like shit, Bass, and we're not even halfway there. You need to get a good night's sleep, or this trip is going to be *very* unpleasant."

"Yeah... I know," Ian muttered. He desperately wanted to share his misgivings about the voyage with *someone* but couldn't help feeling his boss wasn't the right person. It was pointless to complain about the weather, the remoteness of buoy 21415, or the last-minute change in vessels. Janet already knew all that. He suspected she wasn't happy about it either, but what could she do? What could either of them do? It was simply part of the job.

Telling Janet about his recurring dreams seemed

equally pointless. She wasn't a shrink, nor was she likely to understand. At best she'd listen attentively as Ian described snow drifting amidst a pitch-black sky. She'd nod thoughtfully as he explained that a distant, muted light drew him toward it like a moth to the porchlight of his childhood home. More likely she'd see him as a mere boy unqualified for his job—a little fish hopelessly out of his depth. Either way, no good would come of it.

Better to keep his mouth shut.

"This will be your first time out as far as Attu, won't it?"

"Yeah, I've been as far as Adak before, but-"

Janet didn't let him finish. "Should make for one Hell of a first experience. It's bound to be a bit rough, but you'll come out all the better for it." She paused a moment, as if waiting for Ian to say something. When he remained silent, she continued. "The feed from the buoy is pretty strange, don't you think?"

Ian had expected his boss to ramble on about her good ol' days in the Bering Sea, or offer him long-winded advice from an experienced mariner. He'd already anticipated slipping back into his occasional 'yeah' and 'huh' responses as he gazed out into the drifting snow, so the question threw him off. "No. I hadn't seen it... What's strange about it?"

Ian wasn't exactly sure how the data reported back from a DART buoy could even *be* strange. There were certainly remote stations that reported all kinds of diverse datasets: windspeed, atmospheric pressure, temperature, etc. Buoy 21415, however, didn't have such an advanced payload. It was designed solely to detect tsunamis, and reported back only water depth at fifteen minute intervals. That was it.

Technically the buoy itself was little more than a relay. The actual measurements came from three miles below the water's surface, where an array of instruments transmitted pressure readings from the inky abyss of the Aleutian Trench. The readings fluctuated considerably during a seismic event—otherwise they scarcely varied at all. The buoy either reported a tsunami, or it didn't. *How could that particular line of data even be strange?*

"It's been pushing reports every 15 seconds for months, as if there had been a seismic event." Janet lifted her glass and drained the dregs left by the melting ice.

"And was there an event?" Ian leaned forward across the table. She'd managed to pique his interest.

His boss sighed. "It's been months, Bass. It just keeps transmitting in event mode. Every 15 seconds like clockwork. Mild seismic activity may have triggered it, but none of the other buoys picked anything up." Janet glanced down at her glass. She seemed annoyed that it was empty. "It should have reset on its own, but it never did. The remote overrides failed as well..."

"Huh." Ian leaned back and took another sip of his vodka. "I guess that is kinda strange."

"Right? But that's not even the weird part."

"Yeah?"

"The numbers it's transmitting don't make any sense.

They're not depths, and they're not defaults or factory presets. I don't know. They're just...random." Janet glanced back at the bar longingly. "Well, kind of."

"So... they're random, but not random? Not sure I follow."

Janet stood up from her chair. "Hold on to that thought," she instructed. "I'll be right back." She turned and made her way back toward the bar, leaving Ian alone with his thoughts.

Great. Just another thing to add to his growing list of apprehensions about the voyage. Still, he couldn't deny that he desired to know more. *What, exactly, could be so strange about data transmitted from a buoy at the edge of the world?* Ian's curiosity nagged at him and he glanced about the bar impatiently.

The Bilge Rat was a small tavern, furnished in the ramshackle manner characteristic of far-flung Alaskan settlements. Fishermen, roustabouts, and mariners clustered around a dozen or so tables. The interior was bathed in the unnatural glow of neon signs affixed to the walls and windows, and the corrugated tin roof rattled in the relentless wind.

Several members of the *McKinley's* crew huddled around the pool table. He recognized Captain Ferguson, the portly medic and a handful of others. Each held a bottle of beer in hand, but Ian had yet to see any of them take so much as a sip. They leaned in toward one another, as if they were engaged in conversation, but it didn't appear as if any of them actually spoke. Ian's eyes met the captain's for a brief moment; the man's expression was as cold as the wind outside.

Ian averted his gaze to find that Janet had returned to the table. She carried four glasses on a plastic serving tray and began working on the first no sooner than she took her seat. "It's repeating the same data every transmission. The folks back in Palmer can't make heads or tails of it."

"Wait... what?" Ian struggled to shake the feeling of unease he'd experienced when he'd stared into the captain's eyes. There was something undeniably strange about the *McKinley's* crew.

"Buoy 21415..." Janet's eyes narrowed. "You asked about the transmission right before I got up."

"Oh, right. Probably just a malfunction..."

"Probably," Janet replied before taking another drink of her vodka. Her tone suggested she was not entirely confident in that assessment.

Ian choked down the contents of his glass. The melted ice reduced the burn, but the vodka still tasted like shit. He looked intently at Janet. She'd become uncharacteristically sullen. "Well, what is it then? If it's not a malfunction, what could it be?"

Her expression grew serious. "I never said it wasn't." She slid another glass toward Ian. "There's no other explanation for it."

Ian remained unsatisfied by her response. She was holding something back. "And if you had to? If you *had* to explain it?"

Janet took a gulp of vodka and wiped her mouth with

her shirtsleeve. "I'd say... that if you're so interested, you should check out the feed yourself. It's up in the lab."

"Maybe I will." Ian leaned back in his chair and picked the glass up off the table. There was no ice this time—just straight liquor. He sighed, flashed Janet a forced smile, and drank deeply. He shrugged off the burn and the foul taste. He was going to need it.

That night Ian's dreams returned. He'd hoped the booze would send him into a dreamless, blackout slumber, but instead, it weighed upon him. Where he had once felt a sense of disembodied weightlessness he now felt as if he was being crushed. Immense, phantasmal weight pressed in on him from every direction. He could see more clearly now and further than before, as if the alcohol had sharpened the edges of his subconscious. What had first appeared to be snow was the steady rain of particulate matter drifting toward the seabed. The night sky was the perpetual gloom of the ocean's depths.

A vast, abyssal plain stretched out before him. Pale, otherworldly creatures slithered, swam and crawled their way across a landscape of lifeless grey. Invertebrates illuminated in bioluminescence drifted soundlessly by. Malformed, pelagic monstrosities descended from overhead; rows of uneven, needle-like teeth protruding from gaping maws. Ian recognized some of the creatures from childhood textbooks and visits to the Atlanta Aquarium, while others were entirely alien, their bodies contorted and misshapen in a manner than defied logic.

The only source of visible light, beyond the muted bioluminescence of the surrounding creatures, emanated from a distant point in the abyss. It was faint, but somehow warm. Despite the blackness that enveloped him, Ian could see around him all the same. He could do more than just see: he could *feel.*

Ian could feel denizens of the abyss gathering all around him. He could feel himself being drawn to that distant point of light. They were all being drawn— the wriggling invertebrates, the blind, ghoulish fishes and the pale, drifting behemoths. All of them were being summoned to that distant, haunting beacon.

Ian drifted through the gently-falling marine snow, accompanying the grotesque menagerie on their silent pilgrimage. The light grew larger the nearer Ian drew to it, but never became intense. Eventually the light revealed itself to be the size of a large building. *No, not a building, a ship...* or at least the skeletal remains of one.

The light was not as it first appeared. It didn't emanate from a single point, but rather from the bodies of thousands, perhaps millions, of individual creatures. One-by-one the procession of abyssal monstrosities added themselves to the throbbing, pulsating tangle of life. The ship was all but engulfed by the swarm, distinguishable only by its silhouette against an otherwise featureless landscape.

A glowing pillar extended upward from the wreck

before fanning out into five distinct columns, parallel with the seabed. The symmetry of their orientation struck Ian as unnatural, and it took him a moment to recognize that the five columns aligned exactly with the pressure sensors of a DART array. He didn't have to guess to which buoy the sensors belonged. He knew immediately that he was in the depths of the Aleutian Trench, three miles beneath buoy 21415.

Sun-starved leviathans circled overhead like buzzards. Something deep within the earth trembled, and the assembled mass grew brighter than before. All at once the monsters circling overhead stopped moving. The marine snow ceased its descent and hung suspended in the water around him. For what seemed like an eternity nothing moved. Ian would have known; he would have felt it. It was as if time itself had stopped. Ian was left reminded of the pervasive cold and the crushing weight bearing down upon him.

With time still frozen a great tendril of pure blackness coiled around the shipwreck. It was massive, yet it displaced no water. Ian would have felt it if it did. He could feel everything around him. He could feel the creatures suspended in the water. He could feel the bulk of the shipwreck and the manner in which the sands had shifted around him. *Why couldn't he feel that?*

The tendril was made visible only by the bioluminescence that winked out in its wake. Against the surrounding gloom it was as if the alien appendage was not even there, as if it existed only as the absence of light, of water...

of anything. It was there, and yet it was not there. It was the sort of negative matter that weighed heavily on the cosmos. Whatever it was, or wasn't, it wound its way up the DART pressure array, swallowing the light as it went.

The parts of the array not suffocated by grasping coils pulsed with light, then dimmed. Several seconds later they pulsated yet again. The process continued, repeating in a slow, rhythmic fashion. As Ian looked on, an unsettling realization came to him. The array didn't just glow every several seconds, it glowed every *15* seconds.

"Ian." A deep, resonant voice echoed through his mind. It repeated with each pulse of the array.

"Ian." The voice didn't merely state his name—it called him, beckoned him, *commanded* him.

Ian couldn't say exactly how long he basked in the presence of his summoner. Time twisted, bent and blurred. The next thing he remembered the pressure relented, and he felt momentarily weightless. He was pulled from the abyss—torn from the light, the array and the Summoner. The rapid transition was not a comfortable one. He tasted blood and harsh, intrusive light burned through his tightly-closed eyelids.

"Ian."

The voice was different now. It was softer, weaker and vaguely familiar. It came from outside of him. Ian opened his eyes to reveal a small room awash in light. A figure loomed over him, obscured by the disorienting intensity of the glow.

"Ian, can you hear me?" The voice belonged to a man.

"Yeah... I-I can hear you." Ian reached for his aching head and felt a bandage had been wrapped around it. "Could you turn down the lights a bit? It's too damn bright in here."

"I..." The figure began to protest, but hesitated. "Sure." A moment later the room darkened, and Ian felt comfortable enough to take in his surroundings. He was in the McKinley's infirmary, and the shipboard medic was in attendance. The room shifted under him, indicating the vessel was already in open water. Ian couldn't remember the medic's name; he'd scarcely spoken with the crew.

"Thanks." Ian groaned as he struggled to sit upright. "That's better."

"No problem," the medic responded in a detached tone that suggested he was merely fulfilling the requirements of his job. "You remember what happened?"

"Honestly... no. I don't really remember anything after leaving the bar." Ian's mind felt as if it were in a cloud. Echoes of his nightmare lingered. He struggled to shake the visions of abyssal creatures and the Summoner's grasping tendrils from his mind. His forehead throbbed in pain, and he still felt impossibly light in the absence of the ocean's crushing weight. Nothing that took place since leaving the Bilge Rat made any sense.

"Doesn't surprise me." The medic sighed and began rummaging through a metal cabinet. "You and Miss Reynolds were pretty hammered. You fell outta your bunk and hit your head good. There was quite a bit of blood, and I was afraid you might have a concussion. If you didn't wake up by this evening, we were going to have to divert to Adak." He removed a pill bottle from the drawer and handed it to Ian. "The captain will be glad to hear that won't be necessary."

"Oh..." Ian was slow to respond. He took the bottle offered to him and tried to read the label. The letters were blurry. His head ached when he tried to interpret what he was seeing. "What is this?"

The medic shrugged. "Ibuprofen. Take two in the morning. Take another two before bed."

"That's it? No offense, doc, but do you have anything a bit stronger? I'm feeling pretty rough, and the light feels like it's piercin' my brain."

The medic's beady eyes looked him over skeptically. "Fraid' not. Not for this sort of thing, anyway. NOAA's pretty restrictive about the use of opioids." He scribbled something down on a clipboard before looking back up at Ian. "You might still be feelin' the effects of the hangover as well as the fall. Make sure you hydrate."

"Great." Ian blinked wearily and cradled his forehead. "I'll make sure to do that." Seconds later a wave crashed against the *McKinley's* starboard side. The infirmary tilted, and several loose objects on the nearby desk clattered to the floor. A plastic coffee cup dumped its contents across the room.

"Damnit," the medic muttered to himself. When he

bent over to clean up the mess the overhead lights flickered, then shut off entirely. The room went pitch-black for a brief moment before the emergency lighting kicked on, bathing the infirmary in red. When the medic sat back up in his chair his appearance had changed drastically.

His general form remained consistent, and he wore the same clothes as before, but his skin now appeared waxy and paper-thin. What had previously appeared to be pink, hairy flesh was now little more than a damp, transparent membrane. Beneath the surface squid-like invertebrates were compacted to form a semi-solid human facsimile. Tentacles and strange, tubular masses shifted beneath the medic's supposed skin. His pupils had swallowed his already beady eyes, and they shined with a haunting, bioluminescent glow.

The overhead lights flickered back to life and the second-mate's voice played over the intercom. Ian didn't bother listening to the announcement; he simply stared at the overweight man seated in front of him. The medic's skin was once again pink and sweaty, accented by patches of greying hair. There was no sign of alien invertebrates writhing about beneath his flesh. His expression was one of concern.

"You're not lookin' too good." He wiped spilt coffee from his clipboard and scribbled something else down. "Listen, you can stay here as long as you need. I don't think you're ready for the stairs yet." He stood up from his chair and walked to the door. "I've got to go to the bridge. Just relax, I'll be right back." He exited the room and closed the door behind him.

Another wave struck the *McKinley*. It wasn't as strong as the last, but it was still enough to send several pens and a plastic jar of cotton swabs falling back to the floor. It was also enough to make Ian flash a panicked glance at the overhead lights. They were still obnoxiously bright, but, to his relief, they stayed on.

Ian spent the next several days avoiding the rest of the crew. The task was easy enough. The *McKinley* was designed to be manned by at least fifty personnel, but impulsive decision-making ensured the vessel departed with scarcely half that number. It didn't hurt that there was little work for him to do while the ship was still en route to its destination, and that both Janet and the medic had prescribed him bedrest for the next several days.

During the day Ian would lock himself away in his cabin. The ceaseless thrashing of the waves caused him to throw up what little he managed to eat. Late at night he would venture down to the empty survey lab, scrolling through weeks of buoy 21415's data feeds. He could feel himself growing weaker with each passing day. He became increasingly desperate to get off the *McKinley* and away from its crew; he wanted nothing more than for the journey to come to an end.

Festering anxiety and the constant battering of the waves ensured Ian didn't receive much sleep. *How could he?* Every time he closed his eyes he saw the Summoner coiling itself around the shipwreck, or squid-like creatures moving beneath the medic's paper-thin flesh. If things became too quiet, he could hear whispers echoing in his mind. He had no idea if the crew were, in fact, invertebrate parasites stuffed into human husks, or if he was simply going insane. Either way he had no interest in exploring the subject further. Ian became convinced that whatever was happening to him could be traced back to the DART buoy, and that single line of data it transmitted time and time again.

It was the seventh night of their journey, and the *McKinley* drew near its destination. Ian sat alone in the empty survey lab, watching data come in from buoy 21415. Every 15 seconds it reported the same numbers: 0090.114. Taken literally, it meant the Aleutian Trench was just over 90 meters deep. That, of course, was impossible. Unfortunately, none of Ian's alternate theories seemed to work out either. Coordinates, times, frequencies… none of it made sense. He was mere hours from the buoy, and he'd failed to decipher what it was trying to tell him.

He'd solved *nothing*.

He understood *nothing*.

A door slammed shut behind him and the overhead lights turned on. Ian was instantly blinded. He shielded his eyes and ducked behind an instrumentation rack in an attempt to hide himself from his unwelcome visitor. Nobody entered the survey lab this late at night; most of the crew shouldn't even have had access. He listened for footsteps, but heard nothing beyond the groan of the ship's hull.

"Ian?" A woman's voice called out. "Bass, is that you?"

Ian peeked out from behind the steel rack, trying his best to shield his eyes. "Turn off the lights, Janet."

"Jesus, Bass," Janet gasped. Her voice sounded more than concerned—it sounded frightened. "What happened-"

"Turn off the lights," Ian repeated, his tone growing more demanding.

"Alright..."

A few seconds later only the soft light of the screens and emergency signs remained. Ian emerged from behind the instrumentation rack and scanned the room for any sign that his boss had been accompanied by other members of the crew.

She appeared to be alone.

"You're up late," Ian muttered.

"You weren't answering your door." Janet took a cautious step forward. She balanced herself against a beam as the ship rocked to one side. "We're starting to get a bit worried about you."

"Who's we?"

"Well, me—for one—and Thompson as well."

"And who's Thompson?"

"The medic, Bass... he's been asking about you. I think you should go see him."

"No!" Ian shouted louder than he'd intended. He took a deep breath and repeated himself in a calmer tone,

"No."

"What are you doing here, anyway?" Janet gestured toward the screen displaying buoy 21415's data feed. "Is that what you're down here about?" She sighed. "Listen, I know the message can be interpreted to be a bit... strange, but there's nothing supernatural about it. Seriously, you're letting all this get to your head. You *need* to get some sleep."

Ian paused a moment as he contemplated Janet's words. "What do mean, 'interpreted'?"

A look of regret washed over Janet's tired features. "I just meant..." She shook her head. "Don't worry about it. I shouldn't have said anything."

"What do you mean, interpreted!?"

"Forget it, Bass." She swallowed deeply. "You need to see Thompson."

Ian rushed toward his boss and pressed her back against the beam on which she was leaning. "Tell me!"

Janet's eyes went wide. She offered no resistance. "The data—it *could* be interpreted as a form of alphanumeric code." Janet regained her composure and pushed Ian back away from her. "If you read the numbers as alphabetical placeholders, you get a short, but coherent, message."

Ian backed away slowly. "What's the message?"

Janet exhaled and straightened her posture. "It spells I-A-N, alright? It spells out your name."

Ian's stomach sank. He collapsed back into a chair and stared at the numbers displayed on the screen before him—*09, 01, 14...* His mind was reeling but the interpretation seemed reasonable. Janet's tone suggested she wasn't telling him this because it was what she wanted him to hear. *How had he missed it?* Buoy 21415—no, the Summoner beneath it—was beckoning *him* into the abyss. His hands began to shake.

"I want off..." He whispered to nobody in particular. He looked up at Janet with desperate, pleading eyes. "I want the ship to turn around." To his surprise she nodded in nervous agreement.

"Yeah." Tears formed within her faded eyes. "Yeah, I think you do. Adak's only a couple of days away. Can you make it?" She steadied her breathing. "Can you make it if you know we're on our way back?"

Ian nodded. "I can... I just have to get out of here." Tears welled up in his own eyes and he looked away. Even in his diminished state he couldn't stand to be seen as a failure—as weak and incapable of doing his job. "The crew, the storm and the message... We're close... too close." He wiped away his tears and did his best to compose himself before turning back toward Janet. "We have to turn around *now*. You have to tell the captain to turn around *now*."

"Alright, Bass." Janet undoubtedly intended her tone to be reassuring, but a shakiness in her generally confident voice made it all the more disconcerting. "I'll tell the crew." She shot Ian a final, pity-filled glance and turned back toward the doorway. The door closed behind her, and the room shifted beneath Ian's feet. He was alone with the buoy's data feed once more.

Ian waited anxiously in the survey lab for Janet's return. The waves and buoy transmissions continued to arrive at regular intervals, the ship's aging hull moaning a sorrowful tune. An hour passed with neither sign of his supervisor, nor any indication that the *McKinley* had changed its course. Even as he became increasingly convinced that something horrible had happened to Janet, Ian understood that he didn't have the luxury of time; he couldn't wait any longer. The ship needed to turn around before it reached buoy 21415.

He opened the door to the survey lab and stepped into the blinding light of the corridor. He squinted and felt his way along the cold, steel hull, instantly recognizing the shaft of the emergency axe under his hands. He wrenched the weapon from it's banded, steel frame, making his way toward the stairway that led up several decks to the bridge.

Ian took a deep breath at the base of the stairs. His hands were shaking, and his head throbbed enough to leave him disoriented. He had grown weak over the last several days, and the axe felt far heavier than it should have. The steps groaned and shifted ahead of him. Ian held tight to the handrails and began his ascent.

It was nearly three in the morning, so not a soul interrupted his approach. Ian reached the door to the bridge, turned the lever and pushed it open. The room smelled stale and damp and his eyes struggled to readjust to its dark interior. Instrument panels illuminated the silhouettes of the bridge crew in muted red and green light. Ian took several tenuous steps into the room, tightening his grip of the emergency axe he now wielded with both hands.

"We have to turn around," Ian stated in a far less authoritative tone than he had intended. His voice trembled nearly as much as his hands. "We have to go back, *now*. We're not supposed to be here."

Numerous silhouettes rose from the shadows at the base of the room to join those of the bridge crew. There had to be at least a dozen of them. Ian took a nervous step back, only to be met by the feeling of someone standing behind him. Another wave struck the *McKinley,* and Ian struggled to keep his footing. The silhouettes appeared unphased, a voice speaking from amongst them.

"Quite the opposite, *Bass*." The voice belonged to Captain Ferguson. "We're exactly where we should be." He paused. "Well, almost..."

"Less than two miles out, Sir." A familiar voice spoke from the shadows.

Ian's eyesight began adjusting to the gloom. The shadows melted away and revealed their secrets, just as they had in his recurring nightmare. The floor glistened with moisture. The entirety of the McKinley's skeleton crew stood in front of him. Their skin appeared waxy and damp as their interiors pulsed and throbbed beneath vaguely human forms. Their eyes emitted a faint, sickly glow.

Janet's body lay crumpled on the deck beneath them. Her mouth had been opened impossibly wide. Her eyes were missing—replaced by hollow pits of obsidian blackness. The moisture that glistened in the reds and greens of the instrument panels issued from every available orifice. It flowed easily and plentifully from her ruined face. The vile liquid was impossible to define, but was far too thin to be blood.

The crew of the *McKinley* stared at Ian with hollow, absent eyes. Only one bulging figure was conspicuously absent from the gathering, and Ian knew exactly who stood behind him. He wheeled around and brought his axe down at the medic. He was stopped mid-swing by a hairy, pink hand that held the axe's shaft with an iron grip. The form of the obese medic swallowed the narrow doorway, and in the light of the corridor he still appeared human.

Ian struggled to regain control of the weapon, but the medic pushed him violently backward. He lost his footing on the slippery deck and collapsed to the floor. When he tried to climb back to his feet something pressed him downward. He gasped for air, only to inhale the liquid pouring from Janet's face that was accumulating on the deck. It had the unmistakably brackish taste of saltwater.

Ian could feel the presence of a crew member lingering inches from his face. The abomination neither drew breath nor spoke, but he knew it was there all the same. It reeked of mildew and cheap cigarettes. It held him against the deck and did not relent. Janet's cavities continued to belch seawater, which threatened to drown him. He took gasping breaths when the waves tossed the ship to its side. Finally, the rumbling of the *McKinley's* main engines died away and a hand pulled him from the flooding deck.

"Now," the captain spoke in a guttural, inhuman voice, "you're *exactly* where you need to be."

Ian didn't respond. He no longer struggled against his captors; he had finally reached his destination. The *NOAAS McKinley* had finally arrived at buoy 21415.

Without the main engines to stabilize the ship, the *McKinley* rocked violently in the waves of the North Pacfic. Frigid water left the deck encased in sheets of ice, but the crew made their way across it without difficulty. They gathered on the stern, forming a semi-circle around Ian and Captain Ferguson. Waves crashed over them time and time again. Ian feared he would be swept away, but the captain's grip on him remained unshakable. He was not dressed for the weather, and his clothing was soaked. If the ocean didn't see fit to drown him, he was just as likely to die of hypothermia.

Eventually, buoy 21415 came into view. It was a tiny, pathetic thing—an insignificant piece of orange plastic amidst a ravenous, infinite ocean. Yet there it was, all the same; riding the surface of the black, churning waters. Ian couldn't imagine a more forlorn object. He cried at the loneliness of it, and at the brutal, unfair nature of his own fate. His tears only froze in his eyes. His desperate pleas for mercy were swept away on the relentless, arctic wind.

The buoy drew near, and Captain Ferguson dragged

Ian by the arm to the ship's railing, where the hungry ocean crashed against the *McKinley's* hull below them. The captain leaned in close and whispered in Ian's ear, his word's standing out over the din of restless sea.

"You are truly blessed amongst men, little Bass... the chosen of Vhaaxha the Eternal." The captain's eyes burned with a cold, distant light, and he flashed something akin to a smile. "Now, heed your summons." The captain heaved Ian effortlessly over the railing.

Ian plunged into water, his senses immediately overcome by cold. He struggled back to the surface and gasped for air, swells rising and falling high overhead. He reached for something—anything—of substance. When he finally felt something firm press against him, he grabbed hold of it with the desperation of a dying man.

He spat out seawater and looked around him. The *McKinley's* stern loomed above, the hollow, glowing eyes of its crew glared down at him. He was not clinging to the ship, but rather to the tiny DART buoy which had lured him to his fate. Ian quickly determined that it was far better to drown than to die clinging to the damned thing; he could feel it was what the Summoner wanted.

He could still choose to die on his own terms.

Ian pushed himself off the buoy. He prepared to embrace the icy waters of the Pacific for a final time, but only slammed against the buoy's hard, plastic hull. A shooting pain, intense enough to momentarily drown out the sting of the frigid water, climbed up his leg. His foot had become stuck in the buoy's lift handle, and in his desperate attempt to escape Ian had driven his femur through his flesh. He reached down to free his leg, only to have water rush over him. He waited for the swell to pass, only to discover that the entire buoy was descending deeper beneath the waves.

Ian pulled and twisted at his shattered bone—not so much in an effort to survive, as much as to simply deny the Summoner and its monstrous servants the satisfaction of claiming their prize. Despite his best efforts, however, his leg could not be freed. He could only watch as the bioluminescence of the crew's eyes faded from view. Eventually Ian could hold his breath no longer, and he reluctantly invited the frigid seawater into his lungs.

Ian could not be sure if he died during the descent, or if he was merely transformed. The crashing waves gave way to the silence of the abyss, the blinding light replaced by eternal dark. The fear, the desperation and the loneliness of life gave way to something new and wholly different. When the dark tendrils of Vhaaxha finally coiled around him, Ian welcomed their embrace. One day buoy 21415 would return to the surface with a new message, and a disciple would rise with it.

T.M. Brown

About the Author

Trevor Brown, who writes under the pen name T.M. Brown, serves as an officer in the U.S. Army. He currently lives in Colorado Springs, Colorado with his beautiful wife, Anna, and his two dogs, Fry and Zapp. Although Trevor has long held a passion for speculative fiction, he has only recently taken up writing for publication. His preferred genres include horror, strange fiction, and dark fantasy.

T.M. Brown's debut novella 'The Gloam' is currently available on Amazon in both paperback and Kindle formats. He also has a variety of dark fiction under contract with independent publishers including: Black Hare Press, Burial Day Books, Cosmic Horror Monthly, Eerie River Publishing, Kyanite Publishing, Nothing Ever Happens in Fox Hollow, Sinister Smile Press, and Terror Tract.
https://www.facebook.com/RavenousShadows
https://twitter.com/TMBrown_Author

She Calls From the Sea

Alanna Robertson-Webb

"*Come to me, join me...*"

Captain Mal 'Parlay' Brineheart's head whipped towards the sea, the disembodied voice causing her guts to churn. She had been letting her arms droop across the starboard rail, her positively barbaric posture hidden from the scrutinizing eyes of her crew as they bustled about their day, but now she was on high alert. This was the only railing on the *Barnacled Prow* not overlooking the main deck, so she could allow herself a minute of relaxation whenever she managed to temporarily escape her crew, and for the moment she was glad that they couldn't see the widening of her eyes, or her fretful, darting glances.

She stretched, her line-of-sight flicking to the vast expanse of churning, sapphire water that ebbed and flowed just out of reach. Her gaze was drawn to the frolicking waves, her sense of peace shattering further the longer she stared.

"You know I hunt you. Afraid prey is the sweetest of

meals, and it has been too long since I tasted your terror. You cannot outrun me, no matter how hard you try or how far you sail..."

"Those are just fish in the water, nothing more is out there..."

Her plea-like words did nothing. An occasional glint of sunlight on blackened scales sent a shiver skittering up Mal's spine, her hands scrunching into a white-knuckled grip that threatened to splinter the railing, her inner reassurances failing to quell the surge of panic constricting her chest. The ocean had always held a deep fascination for her, but even as a small child she was raised to fear the teeth and fins lurking below the waves.

The mermaids who stalked her small, coastal village had been her biggest worry until age eight, when her drunk, penniless father sold her to a pirate ship that needed a new cook's assistant. Even then the semi-freedom of the high seas couldn't erase the memory of Mal's mother, nor could it smooth the scars that puckered the flesh of her back.

"I tasted you once, and no quarry escapes me. Your fear is delectable, and I shall have more..."

An involuntary tear slid down Mal's cheek as often-buried memories floated in front of her mind's eye. Beautiful, cinnamon-hued sand stained crimson by flecks of gore, jagged teeth stripping flesh from her mother's exposed bones, wails of anguish as her mother's intestines were sliced from her still-breathing body. Little Mal, hidden behind a sea-hewn boulder, could still vividly picture the jade scales of the monster that feasted on the only kind person in her life.

The crouched child had tried to stifle her own cries, tiny hands clasped desperately over salty lips, but she knew it was too late. When she next dared peek around the boulder the thing was gone, along with her mother's corpse. She turned to flee, to get as far away from the ocean as possible, but fate was not so kind. She slammed right into a second creature, this one covered in black scales, that had crawled up the beach while she was distracted.

Claws.

Pain.

Shrieking.

Fleeing.

Scars.

That had been over a decade ago now, and since the crew had voted her in as the new captain a fortnight back Mal felt that she had true control over her life for the first time. Granted things had not gone as smoothly as planned since taking the mantle of captain, and she had been bombarded with one issue after another, but she would not trade her lifestyle for the world. Scream-inducing nightmares of grasping claws and stiletto fangs still plagued her, but her fear of the flesh-eating fishwomen had faded over time after years at sea without encountering any of the vile creatures.

The end of Captain Two-Fingers horrific dictatorship, a monster among men if Mal had ever seen one, had left the crew in near-ruin. None of the remaining members, those whom he hadn't beaten to death for his sick entertainment, had seen a lick of booty or a smudge of land in weeks. Some of them were falling victim to scurvy, among other injuries and illnesses, and she knew that they needed to find a port soon; that, or things could turn fatal. Rations were running low as much as irritation was running high, but even so the crew was still happier than they had been in several years.

There wasn't time to be worrying about brainless fish.

Mal was the only female pirate the Barnacled Prow crew had even seen, and was initially a common subject for their superstitious scorn, but she had earned their respect countless times since joining them. They placed their unwavering trust in her, and were ready to follow her to the depths of Davy Jones' Locker itself if it meant never having another captain like Two-Fingers. She was determined to do right by them, and that meant focusing on the most important issues.

"Captain Parlay, I 'pologize for intrupptin' yer quiet time, but ye should see this."

Mal instantly straightened, her face beet-red from being caught relaxing. Thankfully it was Cask, her recently-appointed boatswain. Two-Finger's closest men had all been cruel, the kind of sea-scum who delighted in slaughtering innocents, and the moment she was hailed as captain Mal had made chum of them. With a new pirate's Code of Conduct in place her revised crew now consisted of men who, while still regularly indulging in their love of plundering, had been happy to demonstrate restraint when it came to killing and violating civilians.

"Yet you remain a killer, like I am..."

She pointedly ignored the voice, just like she did every time the oozing whispers curled about her ears. Her crew had become the kind of men who could terrorize, without going as far as to leave a trail of bodies behind them, and that was a rare commodity on the high seas. They now showed mercy to all whom they captured, and Mal had even taught them to be quite hospitable to their prisoners. What little bloodlust the crew still had was satiated by fighting the Navy or other pirates, and she was determined to keep them on the, well, relatively straight and narrow.

"Greetings, Cask. How fare you today?"

"I is well, Captain, thank ye."

"Please, call me Mal. Unless we are in a more formalized setting, then you can feel free to go all-out with my title."

"As ye wish, Capta...uh, Mal."

"Now, what business brings you to me?"

"Gulls spotted a strange island, and wants ye ta see ifin we should make sail for it afore nightfall since the fog is rollin' in. There ain't 'upposed to be nothin' here, so says the map, meanin' this be odd. But food is food, eh?"

She nodded, striding behind the short, grizzled man as he led her to the foremast. There, in the crow's nest, was a young lad of about ten years. His anxious, gap-toothed grin flashed down to Mal, and she easily caught the spyglass that he tossed to her.

"Oy, Cap! I know we be needing rations, but this place ain't on me map. Cask was steering us towards it, which is all fine an' dandy since line-o-sight is worsening, but should we make port?"

"Yes, you are so close to me. My voice guides you ever nearer..."

With the cold, salt-crusted metal of the monocular pressed against her cheek Mal surveyed the island. It was a small place, but there was enough lush forest peeking forth for her to suspect that there would be food and fresh water available. She couldn't see the reflection of the sunset off of any window panes, or smoke from a fire, so it wasn't likely to be naval territory, and there weren't any huts or other buildings in sight. She yearned for a brief respite on land, away from the cloying roll of the sea.

"So we know nothing about this island, nothing whatsoever?"

Cask and Gulls shook their heads in unison, their replies overlapping like waves.

"Nothin'."

"Nope!"

"You shall soon..."

She sighed, her petite brow furrowing.

"Very well. We need a fresh stock of water more than we fear danger, so I suppose that we shall drop anchor there. I do not want to linger long, no more than it will take to get the crew rested up."

"Aye aye, Mal."

"Well done. I can almost reach you..."

Cask began barking orders, his old lungs still able to bellow out enough hot air to put the younger pirates to shame. The sailors bustled about, whispers of landfall jumping from ear to ear as they speculated about any potential inhabitants. Within the hour, just after the stars had blanketed the crystalline sky, the rasp of wood on sand resounded around the tiny cove as the Barnacled Prow kissed the beach. The fog was rolling in behind them, obscuring any fins from sight, which merely served to make Mal more uneasy.

With a flurry of unfurling rope ladders the crew disembarked, the men marvelling at the darkening sky bleached the edge of the shore in pale blues, whites, and fading yellows. The rowboats soon reached the sand, and for the first time in weeks Mal could smell something other than fish, salt and body odor. She surveyed the land, her curious eyes drinking in the sight of solid ground. A thick web of mangrove roots had thrust out of the forest soil decades earlier, snaking their way from the edge of the trees into the relentless jungle. The roots clawed and crept their way across the golden sand, almost entirely covering what looked to be an old game trail.

She made her way towards it, halting just shy of the treeline. The surrounding vegetation was in full bloom, shades of vibrant reds and greens juxtaposing the cool blue hues of the ocean. The tops of the trees were swathed in undulating leaves, which grew from the branches like a million tiny masts reaching for the sun. The plants were alive and vivid, except for their fruit. Her hopes drooped at the sight of the dead coconuts, their hairy shells blackened and cracked, and the rotted bananas hadn't fared any better. Hopefully there would be fresher fruit deeper inland.

"Yes, fall into my net my little minnow..."

If the voice in her head wanted her there, then she would meet it head-on; no more running, or pretending that it didn't exist. She sent up a silent prayer to the gods of the sea, hoping that they would help protect her from whatever trial lay before her. Mal's shoulders clenched, the sweat on her brow unrelated to the tropical sun. The island was too quiet, too devoid of birdsong or monkey chatter, and something about it just felt wrong.

"Cap, maybe we should leave, eh? This place gives me the willies."

Mal startled, her senses so focused on the strange island that she hadn't heard her crewman come up behind her. Gulls' voice was tiny, and the boy clenched his small fist around the hem of Mal's shirt. As much as every nerve screamed at her to run, to flee from some unseen danger, she held still, taking deep breaths to calm herself. When she spoke her voice was kind, and she gently ruffled Gulls' hair.

"We are pirates, correct? We are tough, and resourceful! We are feared, and we always win, yes?"

He looked up at her, his emerald eyes clouded by an uncertainty that threatened to spill down his cheeks, but he did offer a weary nod.

"I will make you a deal: I will only lead us five minutes into the treeline. If, by that point, we do not find anything edible then we will only gather enough water for drinking and cooking before we ship out. Do we have an agreement?"

"A-alright. I trust y-ye, Cap, but if we-e sees a ghos-st or somet-thing I'm running-g, and I'll d-drag ye with m-me if I ha-ave ta!"

"Deal! At least ghosts cannot hurt us, though we should make a Pirate's Cross just to be safe."

"That will do nothing. All you do is draw nearer to my home, where my power is strongest..."

The little lookout tried to give her a brave smile, but it was as shaky as his voice. With a nod he made the sign of a skull and crossbones with his fingers: first by drawing a circle in the air around his face, then by drawing an X shape from each shoulder to the opposite side of his rib cage. Mal kept a wary eye on the beach behind them, but with the fog beginning to blanket the waves there wasn't anything odd in sight. She didn't believe that the old superstition actually brought pirates luck, or protected anyone, but she knew that those on the sea placed firm belief in it. She followed his example, her fingers half-heartedly tracing the symbol.

The duo trudged into the treeline, and as soon as they stepped across the forest threshold the temperature dropped drastically. An eerie melody began to echo about them, the very leaves reverberating with each haunting note. Mal glanced down, tossing Gulls a reassuring grin, but as she reached for his hand she saw the young boy's body jerk violently. Fog swirled in a cloak-like fashion about him, streaming into his ears, eyes and mouth. His grip tightened tightened around her fingers, heedless of her attempts to yank herself free of his painful grasp. The boy stared straight ahead, his unfocused gaze a compass as he began dragging her across long-dead logs and under vine archways.

"Gulls? Gulls! Are you alright? If this is a joke then I command you to stop! It is not funny..."

The answering silence was more unnerving than any words that could have been uttered.

The boy, never one to be so unresponsive, dragged Mal through the jungle at a break-neck pace. She tried to break free of his grasp, but all she succeeded in doing was hurting her fingers as they twisted in his grip. His strength was supernatural, his tiny muscles straining as though he were a full-grown man, and when he finally stopped the movement was so sudden that Mal heard a bone in her arm crack.

Her scream pierced the foliage, the leaves trembling in the wake of her wail. Gulls reached up, a small hand clamping firmly across her mouth.

"You will sssssoon sssssee her..."

His sibilant tone, reminiscent of a cobra, caused the hammering of Mal's heartbeat to speed up. The boy pointed ahead, where the last dying slivers of sunlight glinted off of something between a copse of trees. The sound of laughter slithered through the foliage, caressing her sweat-soaked skin and squirming into her ears.

Mal's eyes glazed over as the fog enveloped them. Still resisting Gulls, her fingers already bruising, she was forced through the last of the trees, emerging into a luxurious lagoon. A nude woman was partially-submerged in the cerulean water, her hair glistening in the ruby light. Vibrant shades of black, calling to mind the ground at the base of a volcano, tinted her scaled skin. A pair of doe-like eyes turned upon the pirates, glowing with malice as the final piece of the song slithered from between the thing's fangs.

The fishwoman's excited breathing was coming in fast, shallow bursts from her necklace-draped chest, and with a dainty wrist she waved the pirates into stillness.

"Well done, my tasty morsel! You even brought me an extra supper..."

She began to sing once more, her angelic voice mimicking the ebb of the lagoon as she swam in slow, lazy circles. Mal saw the flash of scales in the water, spiked fins peeking out from the churning ripples, but she was unable to react. Gulls, his salt-crusted boots shuffling through the underlying foliage, marched closer and closer to the pool of death. Some deeply buried part of her wanted to scream at him to stop, to run far from the thing's clutches, but Mal couldn't speak.

She watched in horror, her face remaining stone-still, as Gulls halted at the edge of the lagoon. All it took was a heartbeat. A clawed hand shot from the water, burying itself in his chest. A scarlet blossom spread across his shirt, and Mal's eyes widened inexorably as teeth raked his chest to ribbons. As his flesh was stripped Gulls seemed to come back to his senses, and he began screaming.

"Delicious..."

"Ahhhhhh! Cap, help me! Uggghh..."

His frantic voice sliced through the air, the boy's usually jovial tone drowned in fear. Something snapped inside of Mal, her limbs finally obeying her as she shook the apathetic cobwebs from her mind.

"No!"

Her frantic shriek echoed across the lagoon, her adrenaline-filled limbs giving her the strength to yank Gulls from the mermaid's gaping maws. She dragged him backwards, her pounding steps heedless of the flora as she tried to get him to safety. Her screams never ceased until the shore was in sight. The crew's answering footfalls crashed over the dunes as the distant cackle of the mermaids mocked the *Barnacled Prow's* youngest crew member. The world spun in slow motion as Mal collapsed, her hands trying to stem the flow of blood as his limbs twitched sporadically.

Life-giving lungs failed him.

She clutched his crimson-splattered hand in the only gesture of comfort she knew how to give, her throat scrunching down another wail that threatened to spill from her trembling lips.

"Guess this is my last sunset, ay Cap?"

She couldn't respond, and even if she could she didn't know what to say. A final, wet breath wracked his body, and Gulls was gone. Mal didn't remember the crew dragging him down to the shore, and she didn't notice the men gathering around her. She didn't hear their sniffles as they tried not to cry, nor did night falling fully upon them register. She didn't hear the fear-filled speculation about ocean demons, nor did the sound of her own wails breaking free make sense in her mind. She didn't feel the unnatural chills wracking her body as bulging eyes watched them from the shadows, and she didn't answer the softly-spoken questions that sometimes came her way about what had happened.

"You failed to save him, just like your mother. I will wear you down until you come to me, surrender the only thing on your broken mind..."

All Mal saw was red.

Revenge wasn't in her nature, and it was a fire that she never allowed herself to play with, but in that moment all Mal wanted to do was burn that cursed forest to the ground. She was finally shaken from her stupor by Cask, who was gently prying Gulls' rigid fingers from her hand while the rest of the crew made ready for a sea burial.

"Mal, come. We managed ta gather fresh water, though there ain't no food 'ere, and the crew won't go in deeper. Not after..."

He swept a limp hand towards the stretch of blood-soaked sand that had pooled around the boy.

"What be yer orders, ma'am? The crew no wants ta spend more time here."

"Burn it."

"Eh?"

"Burn it to the gods-forsaken ground!"

Her command was a roar, the words bouncing clearly off of the too-still trees. Her tone brooked no argument, and Cask simply nodded. He was turning away, the briney air tugging his beard towards the safety of the shore, when Mal dug her nails into his wooden leg.

"That sea-wench will pay, Cask. Even if she is something we cannot kill, something not of this world, then I will be damned if we do not at least make this place less tempting for anyone to ever set foot on again."

Her boatswain reached down, giving her fingers an awkward, gentle pat.

"Ay, Mal, we shall burn it all."

"I know. Just please, do not let any of the men set foot into the trees. I cannot lose anyone else..."

Mal wanted to see the bones of the creature dripping flesh as it was cooked alive in the lagoon, and she wanted to hear it scream as it was boiled like a lobster. She imagined eyes popping, hair crackling and fins roasting as her tormentor succumbed to the heat, pain the last thing that the fishwoman would know before death came. Yet, instead of helping the men gather barrels, she scooped Gulls up while shoving down her desire for retribution. She lugged the boy carefully onto the ship, her mind turning to how best to get him ready for a proper sea burial.

As the stars dotted the bruise-hued sky Cask tossed

the last flaming barrel of rum into the treeline. He had expected there to be more dissent from the crew, but Gulls had been cherished by everyone. The men, even as gruff and stone-faced as they could be, tended to hide soft spots for unexpected attachments, such as children and animals. Cask brushed the sand from his palms, taking one long, last look at the fire-brightened silhouettes of the roasting trees.

The mermaid he served would still be there, hiding among the currents of the lagoon, her voices wiggling into his mind any time he ventured near the ocean. The fire wouldn't be enough to kill her, just as he hadn't been convincing enough to lure Captain Two-Fingers to the island as an offering. The mermaid had ensnared him over a hundred years ago, her vile magic commanding him to bring her food whenever possible.

If he did not she would eat his descendants instead.

Cask had been able to scrape by with bringing the disgusting flesh-eater evil men, those who had fled from naval justice after committing atrocious crimes, and never had he imagined that an innocent boy would get caught in the crosshairs. Now it would be another decade or two before Cask would need to set foot on the island again, and he prayed wholeheartedly that it wouldn't be a young child who heard her song next.

Alanna Robertson-Webb
About the Author

Alanna Robertson-Webb is an author and editor who enjoys long weekends of LARPing, is terrified of sharks and finds immense fun in creating new stories for the world to enjoy. She one day aspires to run her own nerd-themed restaurant, as well as her own LARP game.

She has edited over ten books, such as Infected by Blair Daniels, A Cure for Chaos: Horror Stories from Hospitals and Psych Wards by Haunted House Publishing, The Deliverer by Tara Devlin and all of the current Eerie River Publishing anthologies. Alanna's writing has been published in over ninety different collections, and her work can be found at:

https://arwauthor.wixsite.com/arwauthor
https://amazon.com/author/alannarobertsonwebb

Please Leave

Watt Morgan

After he plunged her below the surface with the blade of his oar she climbed back up, standing on the flat-bottom hull of the boat and looking down on him.

She wore the tea-stained, organdy princess dress she'd bought at the thrift store, the layers of which now swirled around her in the saltwater. She spoke in interruptions of bubbling giggles, halting and nervous. She wouldn't stop saying 'sorry'.

"Please leave," he stared through the surface at her. She shook her head, brushing dark hair from her face. She looked like she'd been crying, but now she laughed.

Each morning he would watch the heavy milk bloom in the dark coffee, carrying it in mugs down to her bench on the rocks. She'd be there already, staring out across the choppy whitecaps. His kiss grazed her forehead, her rouged lips keeping a permanent stain on the rim of the ceramic. Every morning went like this, until the last one.

With the mugs emptied she'd put out her right hand, and he'd help her up the rocks for the house. Some steps were getting rotten. "I'll have to replace these boards soon," he'd say. He helped her over them.

He'd tried to till and sow the earth by their home, but nothing would grow. With the exception of some sea grass the ground had become barren where he'd inherited the house. The only good money they made were from the few items he could fix and sell, but it had been enough to afford small charms for them both. She read pulp westerns and dreamed out loud about living in the frontier, having sunshine all year and wearing ghost-white hoop skirts that made her smallest movement seem as though she hovered across the floor.

After breakfast, when the fog had faded, he would disappear into his shop. She never knew what he did in there, but she heard the results echoing and blending with the crashing of the surf. Until lunch all else turned to void.

At lunch he would emerge, and she'd have sandwiches already made. White bread with butter, a bit of meat and whatever else might be left over. They'd lean on the outside deck that overlooked the rocks. Sometimes she would speak, but he rarely did. The lemonade always tasted thin, and every afternoon went like this until the last one.

Afterwards they'd go down to the rocks where the boat floated. He'd untie it from the mooring and guide it to the surf, then help her in. Settling each oar into its lock he'd row them out into the middle of the flat bay where variegated buoys bobbed. Some of the buoys were his, had his colors in stripes across them, and these he'd pull up. Soggy, dripping traps were lifted out, heavy with seaweed and kelp, but sometimes a few were filled with skittering crabs that latched to the inside mesh. She'd hold their bucket out for him, and he'd toss the adult ones in and throw back anything too small.

When the five or so buoys they owned were checked and the bait reset, he'd row the boat back to their place on the surf and help her onto the shore. While she walked to the steps he'd tie the boat onto the mooring and cast it into the bay. If the weather looked to get worse he'd drag the boat up the beach and flip it onto the sea grass, leaving long gouges in the sand that faded with the tide.

He'd haul the bucket of crabs up the steps, then hurry back down to help her up. She always waited, knowing he'd come for her. In the kitchen he'd set the bucket on the floor and go to wash his hands, then the crabs were hers to deal with. She always set a pot to boil.

While the crabs cooked he climbed the stairs to the small room just off their bedroom. He shut the door and latched it from inside. She never said so, but she could hear the dull clapping sounds that he made inside. Like waves collapsing underneath the keel of a boat. He'd come back down with his shirt tucked in tight and buttoned to the neck.

As the day ran off, down the endless curve, she'd read from her books while he stared at the television. Long after his interest died away he'd rise from the creaking seat, then climb the stairs to bed. She'd finish her chapter and follow after him into the darkness of the room. His breathing betrayed the sheets in the moonlight. She'd climb in after him, pretending she couldn't see the dark, blooming bruises that wrapped across his lower back and belly.

Every night went like this until the last one.

⸻

His eyes opened to a hazy light.

She lay there next to him. This hadn't happened in years; she'd always been gone when he awoke. She was always out by the first light of the day, and always down at the bench on the rocks. He always brought her the coffee with the bloom of heavy milk. She always drank it with her rouged lips on the reddened rim of the mug.

Today she stayed there in the room, in the bed.

Reaching over, brushing the sheet down off her nape, he felt her skin. Cold. He touched her neck, her wrist and held a cheek over her open mouth.

Breathless.

He lay there a while, staring up at the rafters and the spider webs.

He climbed out of bed. He touched the sheets, rubbed his hands on them, then bunched them up in his fists. He ripped the sheets from the bed, pulling a wave of air across her body, swirling her hair up in a wind to settle again as a mask over her face.

Throwing the sheets to the floor and stamping on them, he fell to his knees by the side of the bed and wept into his palms. One hand reached out for hers, pinching each finger, searching for reaction. He got to his feet. He slapped her face, but she lay there still.

The stairs moaned underneath his weight. He ran the water in the tub hot and climbed in. When he felt scrubbed clean he emptied the tub, then filled it again. Upstairs, he pulled on clothes, whatever sat at the top of the drawer. His hands slid under her pale legs and back as he carried her downstairs into the tub. Using the natural loofah she had bought and never used—it would have been a shame to waste it, she'd said—he scrubbed her body clean. When he finished he drained the tub again and carried her back upstairs.

In the closet, he found the tea-stained, organdy princess dress she'd bought at the thrift store. It slipped down over her body without work. He leaned back and admired her. She looked delicate, calm. He picked her up again and carried her to the door; pressing her in against him he could just manage to open it. He carried her down the rotten steps and across the rocks, then set her on the bench. She faced out across the choppy whitecaps.

Back in the house he brewed the coffee, watching the heavy milk bloom in the dark. When he returned he set her mug on the rocks before her, turning the mug so that the rouge stain on the rim faced her. He sat back on the bench and let the fog dissipate. When it all had gone he dumped both mugs of coffee into the ocean, then climbed the rotten steps again to return them to the kitchen.

He watched her out the window, staring into the sea, as he washed the mugs and placed them upside-down on the rack to dry. When he had exhausted the list of words he knew he wandered back down to the rocks and picked her up. The boat had run itself up onto the sand, so he set her down in the bottom. He paused, looking up, trying to see the grim sky the way she did. He untied them from the mooring, then used the tip of the oar to push off into the bay.

The water fought him with every row. He passed by the other boats in the harbor. He passed by the buoys, rowing beyond the point any crab pots would go. He rowed out of the bay and into the open ocean.

She watched him row. Before he'd left the shore he had leaned her up against the rear thwart so he could look at her. Sweat and tears rolled down his face. He rowed until his arms ached; it had been years since he'd gone farther out than the crab pots and the buoys. He continued on as he watched her calm face.

She watched him row.

He didn't stop rowing until the land became a dark line on the horizon, then he stopped. He leaned over her and kissed her forehead. Her skin felt cold. Holding her tightly against his body he knelt over the edge, and let her drop in. She sank down into the cold, dark water, arms outstretched toward him, falling away into the void.

He knelt there at the edge of the boat watching where she'd gone. When she didn't appear again he leaned back on his thwart and began the long row back to shore. His shoulders ached, his arms throbbed and his heart thudded. Still he rowed, until the splashes of the saltwater and the interminable beating of the sun became white noise.

Without a break he rowed back into the bay, past the buoys marking sunken locations, toward the shore and the mooring. When he got to the beach, before he climbed from the boat and onto the sand, he looked up toward the rocks and the bench. No sign of her. His gaze followed the rotten steps up to the house and the deck that overlooked the rocks.

No sign of her.

He dragged the boat up the beach and flipped it onto the sea grass. Looking back he'd left long gouges in the sand. They would fade with the tide.

Arms at his side, shoulders sore, he ascended the steps to the deck that overlooked the rocks. He had left the door unlatched. He pushed it open and looked over into the kitchen. The mugs were there on the drying rack where he'd left them. He looked beyond into the den. The television had been turned on, the light murmur of a laugh track going. He went in and leaned over to switch it off. Something moved in her chair.

He turned to look.

She sat there, reading her pulp westerns. She looked up at him and smiled, her gaze returning to the book.

"What," after watching her for a little while, "What are you doing here?"

"Hmm?" she flipped a page, didn't look up.

He took a step back and looked around the room. He felt his skin. Touched his face. "I thought." He stopped. "I thought you..." He went to the entryway and looked out into the kitchen, toward the two mugs in the drying rack. The clock ticked. He went to the front door and looked down the rotten steps toward the rocks, water lapping the rocks where the bench sat. He turned back to the den and went in. Still there. In her chair. Reading her book.

"You thought what?" setting the book aside. "Are you okay?"

"I thought..." He pressed his forehead into his hands. "I don't know." Rubbing his temples. "I don't know what I'm thinking anymore. I'm tired. I'm going to bed."

"Okay," smiling, she picked the book back up, "I'll finish my chapter and be right up."

"No. It's. Well," holding himself up with the wall, "Take your time."

"I'll finish my chapter and be right up." She didn't look up at him.

He crossed to the stairs and went up to the bedroom. The window looked out at the new moon. A dark, clouded sky. He unbuttoned his shirt, slipped off his denims and crawled in under the sheets. He looked up at the rafters.

Some time later she came creaking up the stairs. She had the tea-stained, organdy princess dress already half-way off as she came in the door, and he watched her naked silhouette round the foot of the bed and climb in between the sheets on her side.

He lay there in the dark, listening to the surf, listening to the house creak and listening for breathing. He let his hand fall to his side to touch her skin. She felt cold, very cold. She moaned and rolled over, putting one hand on his chest. A chill poured into him through her hand, cascading down his stomach and sides. He shivered.

He listened for her breath, but none could be heard.

The bed lay bare when he awoke. He got out of bed and pulled his clothes on. Something stopped him when he got to the doorway, and he turned and walked to the window. The bench by the rocks sat bare. No sign of her.

He went downstairs and walked through the rooms of the house. Empty. He took a deep breath and went outside and down the rotten steps. No sign of her anywhere. He lifted the boat on the sea grass and looked inside. Nothing. He rubbed his temples and paced on the beach, the waves erasing the footprints he left in the sand.

"Are you looking for me?" her voice startled him.

"You." She wore the tea-stained, organdy princess dress she'd bought at the thrift store. He put his hands on her shoulders. She felt cold in his grip.

Her eyes were clouding. Where they once appeared dark green, with flecks of gold, they became a pale blue.

"Your eyes," touched her face, "Can you see okay?"

"Sure. Why?"

"They're different now."

"How so?"

"Light blue."

"Oh. Yes. That's a side effect."

"A side effect? Of what?"

She smirked.

"Of what?"

She turned from him and walked down the beach. Her feet were bare. She'd hated the feeling of sand in her toes. She looked back and smiled. "Coming?"

He shook his head. "No. You go on without me."

She frowned. "Okay."

He watched her leave, then he pulled the boat down from the sea grass, flipped it right-side up, and pushed it into the water. Waves clapped the hull as he climbed in and pushed off with the tip of the oar.

As he rowed out into the bay she stepped from the surf onto the rocks, then sat down on the bench. With her hands in her lap, she looked out at him. He watched her as he rowed.

He rowed back out past the harbor and the crab pots and buoys, out of the bay and into the open ocean. When he reached the point where he had watched her sink, he settled the oars into the flat-bottom of the boat and leaned against the gunwale. He dipped his hands into the saltwater. Cold.

The fog dissipated, the sun lifting in the sky.

He sat against the gunwale until the heat from the

sun became more than he could bear, then he pulled the oars up, set them back in their locks, and began the return. His back ached. His arms throbbed.

When he got back to the shore the bench sat empty. He couldn't find her along the surf, or the steps to the house. He climbed from the boat, tied it to the mooring and walked up the rotten steps. She sat at the dining table, and looked over at him when he entered.

"Where did you go?"

He shook his head, "I don't know who you are, but you're not Her."

"Why would you say that?" She got to her feet, her arms outstretched for him.

"You know why. I don't know who you are. You're not Her."

"How could you say that? I'm your wife!" Her lip trembled. "Don't you recognize me? Haven't you seen me every day of the last twenty years?"

"My wife died." He pressed his hands into the corner of the counter top. "She died, and I don't know why you're pretending you're Her. I saw Her go. I saw Her body slip underneath the waves. I watched Her sink. You're not Her."

She went to him, tried to touch his shoulder. He pulled away.

"I'm here." She reached out and turned his face to hers. "See?"

"Your eyes." He looked away. "Your eyes are different. Your hands are cold. Your heart has stopped."

She gripped his wrist and pressed it to her heart. "Has it really?"

He held his hand there. He felt nothing. He shook his head.

"What about here?" She pressed his hand to her neck. "What about here?"

He shook his head.

"Nothing?" Her lip trembled.

His palms bore indents where he'd pressed them into the counter. He rubbed his temples.

With a yell he grabbed the mugs from the drying rack and threw them at the wall. The two mugs smashed and became one pile of shards on the floor.

He turned to her. "Please leave."

The next morning her side of the bed lay empty. He went downstairs and searched for her. No sign of her. He walked out onto the deck that overlooked the rocks. She sat on the rotten steps, holding her leg on her lap.

He stepped down to her. "Are you okay?"

"What do you care?" Her voice stabbed at him.

He took a deep breath and knelt one step below hers. "Let me see."

She looked into his eyes. Hers had grown more pale. Little of the dark green with gold flecks remained. She sighed and let go of her leg. "I don't know what happened. I try to be so careful. That last step, though. It gave way underneath me. I collapsed, and then..."

He took her leg in his hands. Her ankle had snapped. A sharp piece of the bone poked through the skin. No blood had come to the surface, no hint of red. "This is no good, no good at all. You can't walk on this. Here, let me carry you back up."

"No." She shook her head. "No, I want to sit on the bench."

"Here. Your ankle is broken."

"I don't care right now. It'll stay broken. I want to sit on the bench."

He sighed and picked her up. She felt heavy, and the back of her tea-stained, organdy princess dress dripped with saltwater. He carried her down the rest of the way to the rocks and set her on the bench.

When he got up to leave she asked, "Aren't you going to stay?"

"No."

"I want you to stay."

He shook his head, turning to go, but a shriveled, water-logged hand gripped his forearm.

"Stay."

He looked down at her. Her eyes had gone full pale. Her skin sagged and wrinkled. She dripped saltwater. A strand of seaweed clung in her hair. How had he not seen that before?

His jaw hurt. He pressed a hand to it. Throbbing.

"Stay."

"No."

The throbbing persisted. She smiled.

"You'll stay." She let him go and turned to look out across the water.

His mouth ached. He felt along his teeth. Some movement. Reaching into his mouth he pressed on each tooth. One wiggled. He grasped it between his fingers and tugged. He felt the root loosen and give, leaving a dry gap. The tooth sat in his palm, bloodless. When he dropped it it rattled down the rocks to the water.

She closed her eyes. "You'll stay."

He sat on the bench next to her. "Please leave."

He woke to a thudding from the foot of the bed. She had climbed out by herself. He watched her hobble around on the sharpened tibia, loose foot dragging behind her. Little indentations in the wood floor marked her path.

"That doesn't hurt?" his voice startled her.

"No." She leaned over the foot board of the bed. "Should it?"

He closed his eyes. "Please leave."

"Should we check the crab pots?" She sat at the dining table.

"Fine."

He picked her up and carried her down the rotten steps. The boat bobbed on choppy waves. Untying it from the mooring he guided it away from the rocks, then tugged it up onto the beach. She gripped him as he lifted her onto the rear thwart. He pushed off with the tip of one oar, then settled both oars into the locks.

All the crab pots were empty. He reset the bait and dropped them back in.

"Too bad." She looked in at the bottom of the bucket.

He started to row.

"Where are you going?"

He rowed away from the shore. He wouldn't speak.

"This isn't back to the beach. Where are you going?" Her voice grew fizzy with distress.

He rowed out of the bay and into the open ocean.

"No, no, no." Her hands gripped at the gunwale. "No, no, no."

He halted his rowing, letting the waves push the boat back and forth. She wouldn't let him lift her up, her grip too tight on the gunwale.

"Please leave." He rubbed his throbbing jaw.

"No, no, no. Why are you doing this? Why do you do this to me?" Her pale eyes pleaded.

"Please leave." He loosened one of her hands finger-by-finger and tugged. She wouldn't come away. His grip on her slipped. He reached out again. "Please leave." He got hold of her fore and middle fingers. Tugged again. Her forefinger pulled out of its socket at the knuckle. The skin tore apart and maggots spilled out into the bottom of the boat. He dropped the finger and stared at it.

"Please don't." She tried to pick up the finger and put

it back on her hand, but it wouldn't stay attached. "I'm sorry. Please don't."

Her grip had loosened. He picked her up and threw her over the side of the boat.

"Please." Her voice gurgled as she struggled back to the surface. "I'm sorry. Please let me back in the boat."

He pushed her down under the surface with the blade of the oar. Her voice shuddered with saltwater. She watched him push her down. She watched him as she sank back into the dark water. He picked up the finger and dropped it down after her. He sat back down on his thwart, settled the oars back into their locks and rowed for home.

When he got back to the shore he capsized the boat, rinsed the maggots out of it and then dragged it up the beach to the sea grass.

He woke with a start. Something in the bed moved. He lifted the sheets. Maggots. All through the bed were maggots. On top of him, surrounding him, a mess of them squirmed in the shape of Her on her side of the bed.

He leapt out of bed and threw the sheets off. Maggots spilled down, squirming across the floor, sinking into the indentations she had made with her bone and falling between the cracks in the boards. He threw up, getting saltwater all over the floor. The maggots swayed in the tidal pools that formed.

Rubbing his throbbing jaw he rushed to the bathroom and twisted on the hot water. Cold saltwater poured from the spout. He let it run, and let it run. Cold saltwater poured from the spout. He stepped underneath and washed the maggots from his skin, scrubbing his skin red with the natural loofah she had bought and never used. He watched the last of the maggots spiral down into the copper drain.

His throat felt raw from throwing up saltwater. He threw up again into the tub, saltwater and maggots spilling down the drain. He threw up again. More saltwater and more maggots. He threw up again. Nothing this time but yellow bile.

He put on clothes and went downstairs. He could hear the television on in the den. He went in. She sat in her chair, reading her pulp westerns. She looked up at him when he entered.

"Hi, dear." She smiled, maggots spilling from her mouth as she spoke.

"Please leave." He walked out of the room.

He went out and stood on the deck that overlooked the rocks. She hobbled out and stood at the doorway. "I'm sorry. I won't. Will you make me coffee?"

"No. Please leave."

"Please?"

He pressed his head into his palms. He rubbed his throbbing jaw. "Okay."

She smiled and began down the rotten steps.

He made coffee, but there were no mugs to put it in.

He looked at the pile of shards on the floor, still where he had thrown them against the wall. One whole piece had the rouge stain. He picked it up and looked at it. He put it in his pocket. He poured her coffee into a plastic cup he found in the back of the cupboard. He watched the heavy milk bloom in the dark.

When he set the plastic cup beside her on the bench, she pointed at his pocket. "Something to remember me by?"

He fingered the shard.

She lifted the cup to her lips, but her skin had pulled away from itself, and she couldn't get her mouth around the rim. Coffee spilled down her chin as she poured it in. She wiped it away with the hand that lacked a forefinger. She smiled at him. She laughed.

"When did you last eat?" She sat in her chair, reading her pulp westerns. The television had been turned on, though he hadn't been the one to do it.

He shrugged. "Doesn't matter."

"You must be so hungry." She got to her feet. "I'll cook you something."

"No, thank you. I'm not hungry."

"Nonsense. You have to be hungry. You haven't eaten in so long. Here. Let me cook you something."

He watched television.

She came in later. "Okay."

He got up and went into the dining room. She had set a plate on the table. He sat before it. She placed a steaming pot down on the table before him. He sniffed, but could smell nothing.

"What is it?"

"It's okay. It's not very good. I'm sorry."

"What is it?"

"I'm sorry. I'm sorry."

He opened the lid. Maggots in a broth of saltwater. He put the lid back and stood up. He returned to the television.

"I'm sorry."

She came into the bedroom after him. "I'm sorry."

"Please leave. Please."

"I can't. I'm sorry."

"Why can't you? Why can't you leave me? Why can't you let me live with Her memory? Why can't you leave and let me remember Her with love? Why must you torture me with Her?"

"I'm sorry."

"Why won't you stop saying sorry?"

"I can't leave. I can't be Her. I'm sorry."

"Please."

"Please love me."

"Please leave."

"Please love me like you loved Her."

"Please."

"I'm sorry."

She wouldn't stop saying sorry. He'd carry her up the rotten steps. She wouldn't stop saying sorry the whole way up. He'd put her in bed. She wouldn't stop saying sorry as he pulled the sheets up over her nape. He'd draw her a cold, saltwater bath. She wouldn't stop saying sorry.

Twice more he'd taken her out to the open ocean. Twice more he'd ripped her away from the gunwale. Twice more he'd pushed her down into the dark water with the blade of the oar. "Please leave." Twice more he'd dragged the boat up the beach and flipped it onto the sea grass, leaving long gouges in the sand that faded with the tide.

He'd wake up and she'd be there in bed next to him.

He tried tying her down to the bed, but she would be in her chair with the television on when he came in from the deck that overlooked the rocks. He tried locking her in the room, but she would be seated at the bench when he went down the rotten steps. He tried making love to her, tried kissing her retreating lips, tried to penetrate her void. Her cold ran through him so deep that he lost his heat. She grasped for him with her arms, trying to hold him inside, but his strength pulled him away from her.

"I'm sorry."

More of his teeth fell out, replaced by white maggots that wriggled around his gums and lips. He could feel them in there, squirming in the dry sockets. He pinched them and spit them, but there always seemed to be more.

"Why can't you be Her?" He fingered the shard of mug with the rouge stain. "Why can't you be Her?"

She looked at him with those pale eyes. "I can't. I want to. I can't."

He nodded.

His thumb felt cold as he woke. She had it against her tongue. She licked it.

"Hey," in a soft voice, "I figured it out."

"You figured what out?"

"I figured it out. How we can stay together."

"That's not-"

"How we can be okay. Stay together and be okay."

"What?"

"You join me." He thought she'd said it, but he couldn't quite hear through the rising tide.

"What did you say?"

"You can join me."

"What do you mean?"

"The ocean. My body. Become a part of me."

"You mean..."

"It would bring us together. Completely together."

"You mean."

"I would pull you into me. The way the ocean pulled me into it."

"You mean..."

Her tongue ran up one side of his thumb and down the other. She tested her teeth on the flesh between his forefinger and thumb. "You could join me. Then we could be together for all eternity."

"If it's what I think it is then no, thank you." He made a move to climb from bed.

She gripped his wrist. Tighter than he thought she should be capable. Her tongue licked up to the tip of his thumb. "You could join me." Her mouth felt cold.

He tried again to pull away. "I won't." He couldn't.

"You could." Licking.

"Please leave."

"Join me." She drew the thumb into her mouth. Tested her teeth on the flesh underneath the base knuckle. "You can join me."

"I won't. Please leave." His heart thudded in his chest. "Please."

"Join me."

He tried to pull away again. Her grip held. He felt her hand squeezing his wrist. He felt the blood constrict in his fingertips. He tried to pull away.

"Join me."

She slid his thumb into her mouth again.

"No."

"Join me." She pressed her teeth into his flesh just underneath the base knuckle.

"Ow. Please. Ow."

She bit harder. "Join me." Her voice muffled by his skin.

"No. Please. No. Ow. Please."

"Join me." Blood ran out through the cracks between her teeth. "Join me." Dribbled down her lips.

"Please. Please."

She bit harder. "*Join me.*"

"Ow. Please no. Please stop. Please." He clenched his jaw. His eyes teared up. His heart thudded. He stared into her pale blue eyes, no more sign of the dark green with gold flecks. "Please stop."

She pulled the thumb from her mouth. "You'll join me." She put the thumb back in her mouth. She bit down on it.

He felt her teeth sink down into the flesh below the base knuckle. Felt her teeth sink into the muscle underneath that. The ligaments that lined the muscle. She ground her teeth back and forth, sawing through the gristly tissue. Blood and maggots ran down her chin and neck. Ran down her nape. Ran down between her breasts and behind and underneath the tea-stained, organdy princess dress she'd bought at the thrift store.

"Please. Please stop. Please. I'll- I'll-" He tried to pull away.

She stared into his eyes. Shook her head. She bit harder. She ground her teeth back and forth until she found the place between the bones in his hand. She sawed through the ligament with her teeth.

When the thumb came loose in her mouth, her grip released. He fell back off the bed, free hand going to his wrist. He screamed. He looked up at her from the floor, gasping. She sat on her haunches on the bed, a triumphant look on her face. Then she closed her eyes. Neck straining, face pinched, she forced the thumb down her own throat. She smiled.

"Join me."

He shook his head and scrambled for the door.

"Join me." She climbed down off the bed. The tea-stained, organdy princess dress that she'd bought at the thrift store fell down around her knees. She wiped blood from her chin with the hand that lacked a forefinger. "*Join me.*"

He grabbed for the doorknob. Blood covered his palm, and his grip slipped. His face smacked against the floor.

She moved forward. The tip of her tibia dug into the floorboard. "*Join me.*"

He smeared his blood-wet hand on his underwear and reached for the knob again. It twisted.

She moved forward. "*Join me.*"

"Please. Please." He begged. He got the door open a crack. It slammed shut.

She moved forward. Her tibia thudded into the floorboard. "*Join me.*"

"No. No." He gripped the knob again, turned it. This time, he shoved his hand through the crack and leveraged it open.

Her good hand reached out for his ankle. "*Join me.*"

He felt her cold, blood-wet fingers curl around his ankle. He tugged it away. Her grip slipped. He scrambled out the door. He ran for the stairs. Slipped down a step. Stumbled to the bottom. His ankle cracked. A wiry pain threaded up his leg. He tried to stand on it. His ankle wobbled underneath his weight.

She had come out of the room. "*Join me.*" She thudded toward the staircase.

He fell to his knees and crawled for the door. With every thudding step behind him, the stairs creaked out, "*Join me. Join me. Join me.*"

He got to the door at the same time she got to him. Her hand wrapped around his broken ankle and twisted. He screamed and kicked with his free leg. Her pale eyes stared into him. Her lips pulled back in a permanent grin. She yanked him toward her. Her tongue dangled and lapped the air. His back slid across the cracked, drying floorboards. Splinters drove up into his skin, tearing and embedding themselves in him. He kicked at her. His foot hit her shoulder. Hit her face. He kicked. His foot connected with her arm, at the elbow.

She let go and he withdrew his ankle, but she reached out and grabbed him again. Pulled him again. A nail in the floorboards had come loose. She dragged him across it. The head of the nail pulled at the open skin of his back, tearing free a strip of his flesh.

He kicked at the arm that held his ankle.

"*JOIN ME. JOIN ME.*"

He kicked again. The elbow broke. She dropped, smacking her face on the floor. He scrambled to the door and pulled it open. Already, she had gotten to her feet, and thudded toward him on her bloodless tibia.

He crawled along the deck that overlooked the rocks, grasped the edge of the rotten steps. He turned to look at her.

"*JOIN ME.*"

He rolled off, letting his body bump down each step one-by-one, curling up to control his descent. Every step shuddered through his body. Across his ripped and bloodied back. Down his hips and into his legs. Through his ankle which now dangled on the bone. He bumped and thudded down until he reached the base of the steps. He looked up toward her.

She started down. Her arm hanging limp where he had kicked it. Her tibia sank into each rotten board. "*JOIN ME JOIN ME JOIN ME.*"

He crawled across the beach on his hands and knees. His breathing rasped. His heart shuddered. He felt his head weak with bloodletting, his muscles ached and quivered underneath him. His hands pulled him across the sand toward the boat.

He reached the sea grass as she stepped down onto the second to last step. The rotten board broke underneath her, driving her down to the rocks they were built above. Her bone snapped away at the knee.

Gasping for air, he heaved the boat right-side up. He pushed with his good leg, getting the boat a foot down toward the white-capped saltwater. Closer with every push. He turned to look at her.

She'd climbed out between the broken board, dragging herself toward him with her last good arm. "*Joinme-joinmejoinmejoinme.*"

He screamed at her to stop. To go away. He screamed at her to leave him alone. "Please leave."

"*Joinmejoinmejoinmejoinme.*"

Halfway into the water he climbed up over the gunwale and into the flat-bottom. He pulled himself up onto the center thwart. She pulled herself down the beach toward him. Her lips stretched back, teeth clacked and gnashed, blood dried in dark streaks down her chin.

He pushed off using the tip of one oar. Her hand seized the rear transom. He set the oars into the locks and rowed. She dragged herself up the transom, her body swaying in the wake of the boat. When she'd gotten up over the edge, she gripped onto the rear thwart and slid face-first into the flat bottom. He rowed.

"Please." She reached for him with her good hand. He kicked it away and continued to row. "I'm sorry."

She began to cry. Sobs that shook her body. Cold saltwater dripped from her skin, from her hair, down her face, off the tea-stained, organdy princess dress that she'd bought at the thrift store. She wailed. "I'm sorry. I'm sorry. I'm sorry." She wouldn't stop saying sorry.

He rowed. He rowed past the variegated buoys and the crab pots. He rowed past the harbor and the boats. He rowed past the marker buoys.

"I'm sorry. I'm sorry." She wouldn't stop saying sorry.

He rowed out into the open ocean. The fog hadn't lifted today. He rowed into it. He rowed until the dark line of land disappeared.

White caps, clapping waves, fog.

He rowed until the grip of his thumbless hand could no longer hold an oar.

He lifted each oar out of its lock and settled them on the flat-bottom. She lay there in the space between the rear transom and the rear thwart, her head resting against the gunwale. She wouldn't stop saying sorry.

He put his good hand in his pocket and fingered the shard of mug with the rouge stain. He brought it out into his palm. He looked at it for a while, then threw it out beyond the fog. It splashed into the ocean. He slid to a knee between the center and rear thwart. Slid both hands underneath her. Lifted her. His back throbbed. Pain stabbed up through his arms and neck.

He turned to the sea, looked out into the fog and the chopping waves. He heard her soft whimpering apologies. "We could still... We could still be in love."

"Please leave."

He dropped her in. He reached for one oar.

After he plunged her below the surface with the blade of his oar, she climbed up to stand on the flat-bottom hull of the boat and looked down on him.

She wore the tea-stained, organdy princess dress she'd bought at the thrift store, the layers of which now swirled around her in the saltwater. She spoke in interruptions of bubbling giggles, halting and nervous. She wouldn't stop saying sorry.

"Please leave," he stared through the surface at her. She shook her head and brushed dark hair from her face. She looked like maybe she'd been crying, but now she laughed.

Watt Morgan

About the Author

Watt Morgan is a 35 year old writer living as on-the-road as he can with his wife and dog. He loves baseball, hobby game development, and the lull of nature.

Dead Ships

Georgia Cook

It washed up at dawn, drawn in on the morning tide from around the curve of the bay; a fishing boat, small enough for a cabin and a crew of three, but of no make or name we recognized. It curved gently towards the beach, its path haphazard and aimless, engines silent and windows dark. By the time it hit the shingle and plowed to a juddering halt a small crowd of us had gathered on the dockside to watch.

There's something about an empty boat—something dragged in off the tide like that, all slow and sedate—you get to feeling it after a certain time at sea, like a second sense. That's why none of the old fishermen made a move when it finally came to rest; they already knew what we'd find.

Perhaps it started with the snow.

Great, driving fistfuls were what we got that month; merciless, relentless, day after day. A frigid wind howled it down off the clifftops, swamping the roads and transforming the surrounding hills into impenetrable, white monoliths. Nobody arrived in town, nobody left; that's how things go around here come winter.

There's a saying in these parts that it takes a special kind of madness to move here from out of town, and another kind to stay. The seas and the cold breed a particular type of person—it settles in the bones, then squeezes the lungs; sharp and cloying in every breath. This far north the cold is bitter.

Or perhaps it started before that, and none of us noticed.

Some of us tried to sail that week, but only made it as far as the curve of the bay before we were forced to turn back. Battered by the gale and the driving snow, there was no thought of casting our nets. Cutting through the snow was like cutting through ice; nothing in either direction but tumbling flakes and shifting, black sea.

We watched the snow fall, watched it settle on the water and sink, and out of it all we watched the boat arrive.

Philip Abernathy was the first to climb abroad, shimmying up the side like a boy climbing a drainpipe. Twenty-three that May—newly promoted, the youngest Constable in a town of sturdy fishermen and grey-faced old men—possibly he felt it his duty to take charge, or at the very least be the first to check. He was, after all, vastly on his own up here until the snows cleared and the mountain roads became accessible again.

He'd been our Constable for all of two months, and up until then had contended with nothing worse than the odd Drunk and Disorderly on a Saturday night. It was too cold, too dark, to expect any trouble worth hurrying for.

He disappeared inside the captain's cabin, calling nervously, then stumbled out a moment later and was violently sick over the side

The old fishermen knew, and now we knew too: no ship so silent has ever been manned by the living.

Once he'd been helped down, pale and trembling, Abernathy directed a few of us up to find the body. It was slumped across the wheel, he said, tilting back and forth with the rock of the ship, its boots dragging in a slow, steady rut across the floorboards. It might have been a man once, but that was an estimated guess. It no longer had a face, just a slumped, desiccated skeleton.

Its hands, Philip whispered, *its hands were clasped so tightly to the wheel.* So tightly he couldn't pry them open.

We found the rest of the crew below deck.

There's a reason so many fishing communities boast smokeries and salt houses; salted things keep. Salted things keep for a long time, and add to that the conditions of an arctic winter...

There were three of them in total.

Being unprepared means it's all too easy to get lost at sea. Sometimes a storm blows in, sometimes machinery malfunctions. Sometimes human incompetence causes one awful misstep, and suddenly the land vanishes behind you. The ocean stretches out endlessly in all directions, waves slapping the sides of the boat in a long, relentless dirge as the sky sits flat and white.

A man can live like that for a few months, if he's lucky, but once the food runs out, once the water's gone...once there's nothing left but you and your crew and miles of endless black ocean, with nothing but the crackle of dead air over the radio and the cry of the wind...

Ghost ships, they're called. Vessels crewed by the dead; testaments to maritime tragedy and the depths of human error, drifting across the ocean on forgotten tides.

Some boats aren't found for years. Some boats never come back at all.

We dragged the fishing boat up past the waterline and left it there for the authorities from out of town. We took the remains to the mortuary up on the high street, and agreed, collectively, that there was nothing more we could do. The weather was getting worse; time to hunker down, unassisted, from October to March, and pray the snows would clear enough to let us sail again.

It was a horrible thing, someone said, a terrible thing, but sometimes ships wash up. Sometimes it's a small mercy to find a body at all. We all agreed, glad to have the excuse not to think about it, and we went back to our lives, pausing only to glance at the slanting, grey hulk of the fishing vessel up on the waterline, and to think of the skeletal remains in the mortuary freezers.

The next one had a name.

It drifted into the bay with its sail held high a few

days after the first, a smooth, white smear against the grey morning sky. The name 'Mary Teal' was painted in deep-green across its side. It was a good-sized sailing yacht—a passenger boat— and we clustered silently on the jetties to watch. We knew, we already knew: we'd found another one.

How could there be another one?

Constable Abernathy had to be hoisted up on deck by a couple of fishermen, their breaths steaming in the freezing air. The radios had been out all week—Abernathy hadn't heard back from his counterparts down south.

There was nobody coming to relieve us of these rotten ships.

This time he wasn't sick; he simply climbed up from below deck and had to be caught as he hit the railing.

There were passengers down there, he said. More passengers, but he couldn't tell us how many.

"They're just..." he managed this time, his hands twitching incoherently. *"They're just..."*

The two men who steadied him ventured below deck themselves, down into the dark, and came back pale and solemn. Sturdy, solid fishermen, with more than fifty years on the sea between them, were unsettled.

There were, they estimated, six people down there—possibly five adults and a child—but like the others they'd been at sea for too long; the corpses were stuck together, one great, shapeless mass of bones, skin and mummified muscle. Like they'd died clasping one another—clasping for so long they'd fused.

None of us volunteered to look this time. We shored the yacht next to the fishing vessel up on the beach and left it there, making excuses of the cold, the snow and the need to preserve evidence. Really none of us wanted to touch what lay below deck on that horrible, dark boat. None of us wanted to know how two Dead Ships had found their way to us just two days apart.

We left that beach shaken, every man among us, and none more so than poor Constable Abernathy.

The snow came down harder that night. The sky the next morning was pure white from top to horizon, filled with fat, drifting flakes. Some even settled on the beach to be nipped at by the waves and carried away on the surf. It hadn't stopped in almost a week.

No news from the towns, no news from the coast. The weather was once again too terrible to cast out the boats, and so we sat in our homes and in pubs and waited.

It was nearing midnight when Abernathy stumbled into the Whaler's Arms, shivering and pale, his eyes wild. We helped him to the bar and offered him a drink, which he refused, but then gulped down as if his life depended on it.

It took five of us to get the story out of him, but between mad-eyed stares and soft, breathless laughter he told us this:

He'd paid a few local boys to help him dredge through the mess of papers and belongings in the beached ships, hoping to preserve what little they could and to correlate any paperwork or official IDs before the damp got to them; he tried to work out who these people were, and whether they'd been reported missing.

They'd been working at it since first light, picking through the freezing mess in the passenger yacht. They uncovered bags in the cabins packed for only a few days—shorts and hats and swimwear, frozen solid—meagre rations in the galley, no navigational equipment, no working radio. Provisions for a quick trip, or a crew with no experience or business being out on the ocean.

Finally they found the ship's log. The dates were written in fumbling, desperate scrawl: The Mary Teal had left port just two days ago, two days before washing up on our beach.

They weren't old bodies, Abernathy whispered, ashen white in the gloom.

Only a day at sea, only a day to turn the passengers into a fused tangle of bones and flesh.

Only a day.

Nobody had an answer. None of us knew what to say. We sat in silence until William, the bar landlord, cut the lights and told us to go home. We stumbled across town, our eyes downcast, our gazes averted from the deep, black thrashing of the waves in the harbour, from the skeletal silhouettes of the beached ships.

Only a day.

The wind off the sea that night blew bitter cold, and brought with it a sweet, cloying scent.

The next tide brought a new ship.

It was a plastic canoe, still yellow in patches. There

was a tiny skeleton inside, bleached white from the sun, curled up tight at the bottom. We buried that one right there in the sand. Nobody spoke as we did it, nobody said a word.

Folks began to whisper. Hesitant at first, as if saying it might make it real.

Nobody had arrived from out of town in over a week. The roads were still blocked, and every day the snow kept falling. No letters, no news, no shop supplies. Abernathy's radio crackled, but the signal was stuck on dead air. That's not unusual for us, as we can go for weeks up here without a soul.

But...

But...

Then Marie Wilson's boys—all three of them—announced they were taking a truck and driving to the next town five miles over. To find news, or at the very least a phone signal. They headed out at dawn as new snow spiralled down across the roads, and vanished into the white hills above town.

That was a fortnight ago.

During that time more ships have arrived. We stopped pulling them in after the fifth. They crowd the beach like broken toys covered in seagulls, peeling and grey, their sails limp and their windows black and watchful, staring up at us. The Dead Ships, sailing in from whatever awful harbour lies just beyond the curve of the bay.

Poor Constable Abernathy walked out into the sea two days ago. Walked right in until the currents swept him away, and none of us tried to stop him. Instead we sit in our homes and on the dock, watching the line of the sky, waiting for that next ragged silhouette, waiting for the snows to clear.

Dreading the day when they do.

We try the radio, hoping to hear from someone, hoping the static will clear and we'll finally learn what has happened in the world beyond the cove.

We haven't heard back, yet.

Georgia Cook
About the Author

Georgia Cook is an illustrator and writer from London, specialising in folklore and ghost stories. She is the winner of the LISP 2020 Flash Fiction Prize, and has been shortlisted for the Bridport Prize, Staunch Book Prize and Reflex Fiction Award, among others. She can be found on twitter at @georgiacooked and on her website at https://www.georgiacookwriter.com/

Heaven's Lake

Holley Cornetto

The yard was littered with the rusted-out corpses of vehicles — relics, like the house. I parked my rental car behind a Ford F150 that hadn't been on the road in years.

I hadn't been back to Alabama since I was a teenager. My old home was haunted by a past I couldn't face, with memories I didn't dare dredge up from the muck of Heaven's Lake. I'd never even thought about returning, until Earl called to tell me about the cancer. We hadn't done a good job of keeping in touch, but every year, without fail, he'd always sent me a birthday card with a five-dollar bill inside. Those birthday cards were the reason I came. He'd never stopped caring, even though I'd tried to put this place, and him, behind me.

Coming home again was hard. Memories I had no desire to dredge up lived here still. I'd been content to leave that part of me behind when I left Alabama in '93, but I owed Earl, and I couldn't tell him no. He was one of few people left in the world that had known me as a child.

I had hoped to never again see the lake where the badness went down, to never come within a hundred miles of it, but what could I do? It was a dying friend's last request.

"Come on now, Russ," Momma called from the door. "Get your shoes on before we're late for church. The new pastor's gonna be there today."

I frowned at my shoes, hand-me-downs from my cousin Clint, who had the feet of a sasquatch. I pulled them on and followed Momma out the door. The inner sole had come unglued, and my foot slid around collecting blisters.

The church was newly-built within walking distance of our house. It was a modest building, only large enough to accommodate the folks who lived on the mountain. All told there were less than thirty of us on any given Sunday, so when Reverend Wilkins agreed to shepherd the church there was a call to make him feel welcome. Easter was coming up soon, and the congregation speculated about how the new pastor would celebrate the holiday.

Since Momma always sat with the choir, and Daddy never came to church, Clint and I could pretty much do what we wanted. We kept vigil on the back pew to be the first ones out when service was dismissed.

When the last notes of *Are you Washed in the Blood* faded, Clint shoved the wrinkled paper we'd been passing under my nose. Scrawled in his chicken-scratch was: *Let's meet at the Junkman's house.*

After what felt like a lifetime prayer ended. We slid out of our seats and headed outside.

"C'mon, Rusty," Clint beckoned me to follow. "We can cut through the woods."

I shook my head. "I gotta go home and change. Momma will have my hide if I get my church clothes dirty."

"You sure you ain't chicken? 'Fraid of the Junkman?"

The Junkman had gotten his nickname because of the junkyard he ran behind his house. It was a creepy, tetanus-infested graveyard of machinery. Clint knew I didn't like it there, which is why most of his dares brought us near it.

"I'm not afraid."

"You look scared," he said.

"Yeah, well, you look stupid." It was a lame comeback, but I couldn't think of a better one. I was sure I'd think of one later, when it didn't matter anymore.

He smirked. "I'll meet you at the end of his driveway. Last one there does the first dare!"

I groaned. He lived closer and he knew it, and with these shoes I couldn't run.

Before I could knock, the front door swung open, and a man I hardly recognized stepped onto the porch. His face broke into a huge grin.

"Rusty! C'mere and let me look at you." He pulled his

glasses down from his forehead, settling them on his nose. "I ain't seen you since you was knee-high to a grasshopper."

I hadn't been called Rusty in years.

Earl was shorter than me, shriveled by age. As I stood there, hesitating to shake his arthritis-gnarled hands for fear of hurting them, he pulled me into a crushing hug. He'd always been stronger than he looked.

I pried myself from his Bengay-scented grasp and flashed a grin. "That's one Helluva grip for an old man."

He patted my shoulder. "That's from all them years as a grease monkey. You still work on cars?"

I shook my head. "Nah. I did for a long time, though. I was able to save up some money and go to college. I'm an engineer now."

"Engineer, huh? That's a good livin'. You got a girl? Ever get married?"

"I..." I looked down at the mildew stains on the porch. "I guess I just never met the right person." It's hard to trust someone to share your life. Through the good and the bad? It seemed more like a fairytale than reality.

He held the door and waved me in. "C'mon in an' let me get you somethin' to eat."

I'd been gone over twenty years, yet the inside of the house hadn't changed a day. I felt like a kid again as he motioned for me to sit at the table.

"How 'bout some coffee?"

"You don't need to go to any trouble on my account."

"Ain't no trouble at all." He placed a chipped mug down in front of me. His hands trembled as he filled it, and then his own. "I'm glad you came."

I cupped my hands around the mug and breathed in the acrid scent of scorched coffee. "Earl..." I started.

He lifted a hand to silence me. "Don't say you're sorry, Rusty. I've lived a long life, and I'm ready to be with Harriet again."

I looked at my coffee, afraid I'd tear up if I met his eyes. "I'm glad you called me. I didn't think I'd ever come back here. Not after..." I didn't know what to call it. How does one name the event that shatters their childhood?

"That's part of why I called you, Rusty. I don't know how much you remember about—"

"I don't want to talk about it." I'd spent years of my life and thousands of dollars in therapy talking about it. I'd made peace with it; an uneasy peace that helped me sleep at night.

"I'm sorry, but we're gonna have to talk about it, son. There's things you ought to know."

I ran as hard as I could from my house to the Junkman's driveway. I knew it wouldn't matter; there was no way I could beat Clint there unless his momma held him up, and that wasn't likely. She was usually too busy dipping into the cooking sherry to take an interest in him.

When I got there Clint was propped against a tree, waiting for me. He adjusted the backpack on his shoulder. "Took you long enough."

"Yeah, Momma was on my case."

"You didn't tell her where you was going, did you?" He searched my face with narrowed eyes.

"Naw, she's on me about church. Says I don't take it seriously enough, and I oughta get more involved now that we've got a preacher."

Satisfied he pushed off from the tree and stood, at least a foot taller than me. "You gotta do the first dare."

The junkyard was an overgrown field, large enough that we could sneak along the edges without risk of being seen from the Junkman's house. We weaved in and out of the yard, through the derelict remains of vehicles, and crouched low behind a sweetgum tree.

Clint leaned in close. "You're gonna look for his wife."

"What? We can't do that." He was getting bolder. Usually Clint's dares were simple, like throwing rocks at a windshield — something I could do from a distance.

"Scared?" He smirked.

I swallowed the lump rising in my throat. "No. It's stupid. That's just an old story."

Clint grinned. He could tell I was afraid, and he was enjoying it. "Uncle Lonnie said the Junkman hit her in the head with a wrench and killed her. Didn't even bury her... just stuck her body in the trunk of one of these old cars, and no one ever saw her again."

Clint's Uncle Lonnie was a drunk, and most of his stories were plots of movies he watched. He replaced the characters with people he knew and told the tales like they'd actually happened. Clint believed his every word, no matter how ridiculous.

"That's bull." My hands trembled.

"Well, then prove it." He unzipped his bag and handed me a crowbar. "Pick a trunk to search."

I surveyed the yard on my tiptoes. I'd pick the closest car I could find, but out here along the edge of the yard it was mostly pickup trucks.

I nodded toward a maroon Buick Skylark two rows over. Clint crouched down to follow.

We crept behind bumpers and tailgates, casting furtive glances toward the house before darting to the next row of vehicles. I yanked on the Buick's door, on the off chance it might be unlocked. It didn't budge.

I circled behind the car and knelt by the trunk, where I wedged the crowbar under the lip. Though I pried until the metal groaned, the lock held fast.

"Clint!" I hissed. "Help me."

He grabbed the crowbar and pushed, grunting with effort.

"It's easier to open if you have the key," came a voice from behind. The Junkman loomed over us like a giant oak.

I froze. The crowbar hit my foot as it fell, but the pain didn't register. Clint took off, abandoning his backpack. My brain screamed *run*, but I was locked in place.

"I... I'm sorry. We were just..."

I flinched as he bent down and picked up the crowbar. To my surprise, he offered me the handle.

"Name's Earl, and this here's my junkyard, but I expect you knew that already."

I swallowed hard and nodded. He wore no shirt beneath his grease-stained overalls, and judging by the corded muscles of his chest he was a strong man. Strong enough to hit someone over the head with a wrench and kill them, I'd wager.

"What's your name, son?" he asked.

"Russell Freeman." *Crap. Why didn't I lie*? "Uh, sir... please don't tell my parents I was here. They'll tan my hide."

"I ain't gonna say nothin'." He looked me over, and I suddenly felt self-conscious in my patched-up hand-me-downs and bare feet. "You need a part or something?" He nodded toward the old Buick.

"No. My cousin dared me to open it." I took a half step backward.

"What kinda dare is that?"

"We were looking for bodies." I blurted.

He threw his head back and laughed. "Bodies? Is that what folks 'round here are sayin' about me?" He doubled over and hooted. "Bodies!"

Of course it was ridiculous. I felt the tension melt from my body.

"Well, look here, Russell," he said, collecting himself. "Not too many years ago I was a mechanic, but I had to quit." He held up a swollen hand. "Arthritis, y'see?"

I nodded at his puffed and twisted fingers.

"I opened this junkyard when I sold my garage, but now it's so big I can't keep track of it anymore. I could use an extra set of hands around here to help out."

"Like, a paying job?" I thought of my parents' last

fight, when Daddy fussed at Momma for buying new curtains and a new dress. For wanting to buy me a pair of church shoes. If I closed my eyes, I could still hear him shouting. *Goddamn it, woman! You spend more money than I make.*

"Yes siree. I'll pay you for every part you take off, and if your friend wants work I'll pay him too."

"I'm leaving everything to you," Earl said. "Harriet didn't want kids, and I ain't got no other family." He glanced at the framed photograph on the wall. In it Earl stood tall and straight, looking sharp in a suit and bowtie. He wore a flower pinned on his lapel, and grinned at Harriet like the love-struck fool he'd been. Her dark skin contrasted beautifully with the white wedding gown. "Back then it was still taboo for couples like me and her."

I nodded, unsure how to answer. I'd grown up on the mountain. Earl and Harriet had always been looked down on. No doubt their child would have suffered the same treatment, but I didn't think I could admit it out loud.

Earl settled into the chair across the table. "You're the closest thing to a son I ever had."

I hesitated a moment to find my voice. There was a time when I had looked up to him like a father. Hell, there was a time when I wished he *had* been my father. "I appreciate everything you did for me. Giving me a job when we first met. Hell, you could've called the cops, but instead you took me in, taught me a skill. I want you to know I didn't forget that."

He chuckled into his coffee cup. "One look at you and I knew you needed somethin'. Truth be told, I think I needed somethin' too. I got lonely after Harriet died, so when you showed up half-starved and dirty, in your sewn-together rags, I thought maybe the Lord had sent you to me."

I felt my face flush. "I know I didn't do a good job of keeping in touch after I left."

Earl pushed back from his place at the table and stood. "I don't blame you. You were a kid, and you went through somethin' tragic. I thought the best thing might be for you to move on, but it's different now. You're a man, and you need to know the truth."

"I know the truth." I opened my wallet and removed a well-worn piece of newspaper that I'd carried since I'd left. It was yellowed with age, and soft like tissue from being folded and unfolded many times.

Earl slumped back down into his chair. He looked weary, his age written in the lines on his face.

The next Sunday Brother Wilkins caught us as we tried to slip out the back after church. "You know, you young folks are the future of this church. The future of the community."

Clint nodded awkwardly, while I pushed dirt around with my toe.

"Easter is coming up, and I'd like to have a special service. I want to get you boys involved."

Momma answered before I could. "That sounds wonderful!" I wondered if it had been her idea, if she'd put the preacher up to it. She had a way of getting what she wanted.

I cleared my throat. I needed to get out of this. "Actually, we're busy. We're goin' fishin'."

Momma glared. I was going to pay for that one later.

Wilkins chuckled. "That's just fine. Go on and get your fishing poles and meet me up by the rectory. I'll show you a secret fishing spot. You don't mind, do you, Mrs. Freeman?"

"I'd be mighty pleased, Reverend," she said, practically glowing.

Later that afternoon we met by the rectory. Wilkins led us down a path where a break in the scraggly pines formed a ring around a pristine lake, and on the shore water trickled over an old stone dam.

Before the church and rectory were built no one had known or cared much about the lake. It had been rediscovered when the land was cleared for construction. Now that the fence was removed, and most of the equipment gone, it looked like a good enough spot to test out my new fishing pole.

"Ya'll ain't ever been up here to Heaven's Lake, have you?" Wilkins asked.

I shook my head. Compared to our usual fishing holes this place was huge, and clean. No crushed beer cans or styrofoam cups in sight.

Wilkins had brought a pail of chicken livers for bait. "The catfish up here are the size of Volkswagens. They've been in the lake so many years and just kept eatin' and growin' until they turned into monsters."

Clint cleared his throat. "You said somethin' about a special church service for Easter?" He tried to sound casual, but he was concentrating a little too hard on threading the liver onto his hook.

"Ah, yes." Wilkins replied. He inspected his reel, and cast his line into the lake. "I'd like you boys to have a starring role in the Passion Play."

Clint turned to look out at the water. I could tell he was thinking it over.

I hadn't had the chance to tell him about Earl's job offer, so I butted in to answer. "We can't. We took an after-school job. We won't have time to rehearse or anything."

"Both of you?" Wilkins looked over my head, but before he got an answer his pole tugged. He jerked, then started to reel. "Get the net!" he yelled.

I jumped out of my seat and stood to watch him haul the fish from the water. Clint tore off his shirt and grabbed the net, soaking himself as he wrestled the largest catfish I'd ever seen onto the shore.

Wilkins roared with laughter. "I told you so!"

The late afternoon sun was high over the lake when we finally gathered our gear and set out for home. We took the path through the woods that led back to the rectory. Wilkins had caught three fish, Clint two, and I hadn't had so much as a nibble all afternoon.

Wilkins brought us around back where he had a make-shift table set up near his shed. "Do you know how to clean them up? Get them ready to cook?"

"Naw," I answered. "We never caught anything worth bringing home before."

"Well then, I'll show you how."

I'd never known myself to be squeamish, but the sight of the fish being sliced open and gutted was more than I could handle. I closed my eyes, but there was nothing to distract me from the smell, like rust, water and salt. I emptied the contents of my stomach at the edge of the woods.

Wilkins offered me a share of his fish, packing it into a cooler for me. He only needed a little, he said, since he lived alone. Part of me thought he just didn't want me going home empty-handed. "Why don't you give it to your momma? I'm sure she'll cook it up." I nodded, but had no intention of eating fish again for a long time. Possibly ever.

I grabbed the handle of the cooler and turned to Clint. "You coming?"

He shook his head. "I've got another fish to clean."

My stomach churned.

From the rectory I headed to the junkyard. Earl was rocking in his chair on the porch, listening to the radio. He stood when he saw me walking down the driveway.

"Hey there, Rusty! What brings you out here?"

I put my rod and cooler on the porch. "I brought you something." I opened the cooler to show him the fish.

He nodded, rubbing his chin. "You catch that yourself?"

My cheeks flushed. I didn't want to admit I hadn't caught anything. "Brother Wilkins, the new pastor up at the church, took me and Clint fishing at Heaven's Lake."

Earl's eyes widened. "The lake up behind the church?"

"Yes sir."

He waved a dismissive hand. "Nuh-uh. No thank you. That lake's *polluted*. I wouldn't go near it, if I was you."

I closed the cooler's lid and sat on the swing, letting my feet slide across the bare planks of the porch. "What do you mean, polluted? Wilkins said ain't nobody been up there in at least twenty years. How'd you even know about it?"

He leaned forward in the rocker. "Years ago, back before the church was built, I had a ugly old mutt named Simon. Nobody really went up to the lake back then. Legend says it was cursed, but I don't know if that's true or if it was jus' stories folks made up. Folks around here like makin' up stories."

I ran my hand along the rusty chain of the swing, waiting for him to continue. When he didn't I glanced over at him. He sat with his palms on his knees, but remained still.

"What does the dog have to do with the lake?"

He stared out at the sea of rusted cars in the yard. "I took him up there with me. It was a hot day, real hot. When we got to the lake Simon ran over and started splashing around and drinking. After that it was like he'd changed. He sat around like he was in a trance, didn't want to hunt or play. Wouldn't eat. Kept goin' missing, but always turned up at the lake."

"What happened?"

"He lost his joy. I reckon he forgot he was a dog."

I looked at my feet, wondering if I should hug him or pat him on the shoulder, but it felt insincere. "I'm sorry about Simon."

He pushed off his knees and stood again. "I reckon he's with Harriet. One of these days I'll go on to meet 'em. But, that's enough of that talk for now. Come on, and I'll put you to work."

I nodded and followed him to the backyard.

I unfolded the delicate paper and slid it across the table. "The official report in *the Herald* said it was toxic metals in the lake water that made everyone go crazy."

He looked down at the clipping, squinting against the faded newsprint. "Yeah, they *said*, but they were never able to prove it."

"By the time they came to investigate the lake had been drained. Someone blew the dam." I paused. How had I not seen it before? "It was you, wasn't it?"

His expression darkened. "I went to see the preacher man. He told me not to interfere, that he was doin' the Lord's work, then started talking about how easy it would be for an accident to happen at the lake. How the law don't like comin' up the mountain. I figured there wasn't gonna be any reasonin' with 'em. They had to be stopped, and the only way I could stop 'em was to do somethin' about the source."

"Why were you the only one that didn't end up..." I didn't have the words to finish. I don't know that I could have, even if I'd known what to say.

"Crazy?"

I cringed, but he wasn't wrong. "Yeah."

"I warned you 'bout that lake. Told you about Simon. I didn't know how bad it was, though, until things went too far."

"Clint." My mouth was bone dry. I took a sip of the bitter, black coffee.

He ran a hand over his balding head. "You remember I told you there were stories about the lake being cursed?"

"I thought you didn't believe any of that. You know how folks around here are, making shit up all the time." *Were*, I corrected myself. No one lived on the mountain anymore, no one but Earl.

"There's some truth behind most stories, even ones about Heaven's Lake. I did some digging. Looked up some old newspaper articles. I found out the lake was formed by a meteor that hit back around Civil War times. Most folks were so preoccupied with the war that it fell under the radar."

I swirled the coffee around my mug. "Meteor doesn't mean cursed. That's just nature."

"But that ain't all. That was jus' the start." He turned and pulled a leather-bound book from the cabinet. "Take a look for yourself."

The book contained a collection of photocopied news articles dating back to the early 1900s. Back then people were just starting to settle on the mountain, and there were only a few scattered farms. The first story, about a record growing season, was accompanied by a grainy photo of a man holding a cantaloupe-sized tomato. "So they had a bumper crop. What's weird about that?"

He nodded toward the book. "Keep reading."

In the article the farmer claimed his success was due to irrigating in water from the lake at the top of the mountain. He claimed the water had worked a miracle, single-handedly transforming the failing farm. It was like reading *the National Inquirer*.

I flipped another page. The same farmer had made the news again, but this time it was a darker story. "His entire family drowned... in the lake."

"Uh-huh. And it keeps on going, too."

I flipped another page, then another. I couldn't say how long I sat there, reading story after story. A history of tragic accidents, all tied to the lake.

I closed the book and looked up at Earl. "I don't understand. How did no one know this?"

"Know what? That weird stuff was happening? They must've; it's probably how the story about the curse started, with people noticing bad stuff happening up there. Folks kept away from it for a time, long enough for it to get overgrown. Forgotten, until..."

"...until they built the church." I finished for him.

He nodded.

Brother Wilkins stood behind the pulpit with his arms spread wide. "Glory, glory! The Lord has spoken."

Beside me, Clint muttered, "Amen," under his breath. His face was pale, like he wasn't feeling well. His glazed-over eyes stared forward the entire time, never leaving the preacher.

"The Lord has told me..." Wilkins continued, his words settling into a rhythm, "... that we shall have... a revival. And hallelujah, we shall spread His glory."

More mutters of amens and hallelujahs came from the surrounding pews. Wilkins was in rare form today, jumping and shouting, stomping and running. *In the spirit* is what folks would say after church. Usually Clint and I laughed to see grown men act that way, but one glance at Clint and I didn't think he'd be laughing.

After service was dismissed the revival was the only thing Clint would talk about. He practically dragged me over to Wilkins. "We want to help out."

A band of sweat ringed the preacher's collar. I shook his offered hand and noticed the damp stains under his arms. Despite the heat of the Alabama sun his skin felt cold and clammy.

"That's mighty good of you boys. We're gonna set the revival tent up by the lake. Have our Passion Play outside, right by the water. It'll be part of the service."

"Are you sure the water's safe?" I couldn't forget the expression on Earl's face when I'd mentioned the lake. Something had spooked him.

He and Clint turned and looked at me as if I were

speaking in tongues. "Safe?" Wilkins asked. The way they turned, almost in unison, caught me off guard.

"Yeah," I rubbed the back of my head. They were standing too close. I retreated a step. "You know Earl, down at the junkyard? He thinks something might be wrong with the lake."

Wilkins chuckled, but his expression was serious. "The junkyard man? Russell, that man doesn't come to church. He's a bad influence, and you ought to steer clear of him. Besides, you were just with us at the lake last week. You didn't notice anything dangerous, did you?"

I looked at Clint who was staring up at Wilkins, nodding in agreement. There was no use arguing. I stood silent while Clint volunteered to help set up the tent and chairs.

"Since when do you care so much about church?" I asked when I finally pulled Clint away from the preacher.

"Since now, and you should too. We have to spread the gospel."

"Spread the... do you hear yourself? You're talking like Wilkins!"

He shoved me hard, and I fell onto the ditch beside the road. "This isn't a joke, Russell. We've got to *save people's souls*." He'd never called me Russell before.

I sat there in the dirt, scraped, bruised, and too surprised to move.

Later that night I lay awake in bed. Something about the way Clint acted had me on edge. Not just the church stuff, either. He seemed changed, somehow. I thought it was a virus or something, but I couldn't explain the way he'd looked at Wilkins, practically hanging on the man's every word, or the way they'd both turned on me when I suggested the lake might be dangerous.

The sound of muffled voices drifted down the hall from my parents' room, but it didn't sound like their usual arguing. They never bothered to hide their fights, but this was hushed. Too quiet. I kicked off my sheet and crept down the hallway of our single-wide trailer, toward their bedroom.

The hiss of my father's voice carried. "For Christsake Jean, it's the middle of the night!"

"I know, but it's important. It's a short walk, just up to the lake. It won't take long."

From through the door I heard the shuffle of my father's footsteps. I fled on tiptoe back to my room and climbed back into bed. There was no way my parents would go to the lake in the middle of the night.

A minute later I heard the screen door creak open and shut — slowly, as if not to be heard. Drawn by wonder and worry I slipped on my shoes and followed my parents into the looming dark.

"You remember coming here an' telling me about the revival?"

"Yeah." I rubbed my eyes. "But if we were infected by something, I could have imagined it all." At least that's what a string of failed therapists had tried to persuade me.

"What if it was all a hallucination?"

"Rusty, I don't know what all you remember, but that preacher was sick. He didn't look right. His skin was gray, and he was sweatin' buckets. It was like he was bewitched, or somethin'. If you were infected you woulda looked like that too."

The memories rushed back in fragments, like pieces of a jigsaw puzzle locking into place. "I thought it was a virus. Everyone started acting weird. One night, before the revival, I followed my parents out. It wasn't like them to leave the house in the middle of the night, and Daddy had never taken an interest in anything to do with church." It was hard to speak, and the words nearly stuck in my throat. We were drawing too close to the memories I'd tried for years to block out, the ones I'd run from when I left Alabama.

Earl leaned against the counter. The mint-colored paint was peeling off in strips. "What did you see?"

I sobbed. "I don't know. It was dark, and I was scared. I saw my parents meet up with Wilkins and other people from the church. I wasn't close enough to hear much of what they said."

But I'd heard enough to know something wasn't right.

I peered out from behind a large pine. Lightning bugs danced through the night sky, leaving whispers of light in their wake. Moonlight glittered across the lake's surface and lit up the forest. From this distance I could see my parents approach the water, Wilkins standing just beyond them. My heart pounded so fast I thought they might hear it.

Beside Wilkins was a faint silhouette I recognized as Clint. But, why was *Clint* here? I felt a stab of envy. *Why let him in on the secret, and not me*?

I ducked back behind the tree as the forest came alive with the sound of footsteps. People emerged from all sides, approaching the lake. Even in the dark there seemed nowhere to hide, but they didn't see me. They passed right by, as if in some kind of trance.

Brother Wilkins lifted his arms, the same way he'd done in church. "I thank you all for coming out tonight. Now, we all know that God rewards his faithful. I want those of you with faith in the Lord to step forward."

The group, almost as one, stepped forward.

Wilkins placed his hand on Clint's shoulder. "This young man has volunteered to demonstrate his faith."

Clint stared up at Wilkins with that same glazed-over look in his eyes. Wilkins waded out into the lake until he was waist-deep, Clint at his side, both now brightly illuminated by the reflection of moonlight on the water. The other congregants stepped into the shallows, watching and waiting. Clint raised his hands into the air, and a collective gasp went out from the crowd.

"Behold! He bears the marks of Christ!"

I squinted, stepping closer to try and see what mark Wilkins meant, but I saw nothing. The congregants called out their *amens* and *hallelujahs*. I stole a glance at my parents and saw tears in my father's eyes. Those tears terrified me more than anything. I turned and broke into a full run, not stopping until I was back home.

I hid under my blanket for what seemed like hours until I finally heard the creak of the screen door.

In the morning, as soon as sunlight hit my window, I threw on my clothes and took off running to the Junkman's house.

"Stigmata."

Earl frowned. "Come again?"

"That night by the lake, Wilkins said, 'He bears the mark of Christ.' I didn't know what it meant then."

"Who had the mark?"

"Clint. Only, I didn't see it. He wasn't bleeding, there were no wounds."

"Hallucinations."

Now it was my turn to be confused. "But I thought you said it was real?"

"I don't mean *you* were hallucinatin'. I mean *them*." Earl flipped through the pages of the leather-bound book. "There were other accounts of it happening. People thought they saw things, always up by the lake. One family swore there was some kind of lake monster up there, like Nessy. Of course people thought it was a fraud, a publicity stunt, but the family was insistent."

I eyed the book warily. "Could toxic metals cause that?"

"Hell if I know, son." He shifted his weight and looked down at his feet. There was something more, something he wasn't telling me.

The following week the congregation gathered at Heaven's Lake for the revival. The tent was enormous, almost the size of a building. It backed right up against the lake, with a make-shift pulpit right on the shore. Easy access, I thought grimly. Beyond the tent the dark water frothed and rippled with unknown menace.

I entered with my parents, where we took seats behind Clint's family. Even his Uncle Lonnie had shown up, but, then again, so had my dad. It might have been shocking if not for what I'd witnessed that night at the lake.

Whatever afflicted Clint and Wilkins had spread throughout the community. The pale, clammy skin, the sweats... they all looked infected. I searched every face, trying to find someone who looked normal — someone who, like me, could tell something was wrong here. Was I really the only one?

The low murmur of the crowd quieted as Wilkins walked up the aisle and placed his Bible on the podium. "Brothers and sisters. We are God's chosen, here to undertake His divine mission."

A sound like low chanting drifted from the back of

the tent. I turned to look, which earned me a warning glare from Momma.

Brother Wilkins droned on about his divine task, without explaining what it might be. No one else seemed concerned, as if they all knew something I didn't. My palms were sweating, and I wondered if the sickness had finally spread to me. Between the blank stares and the strange meeting at the lake my nerves were on edge. The more I looked around the more I wanted to scream. *What's wrong with you all?* I nearly cried out. But I saw Clint, and the protest died in my throat.

He stood at the end of the aisle, by the tent's entrance, dressed in a white robe and sandals, hunched beneath the weight of a large, wooden cross. He began his walk, dragging the cross along the dirt, past the rows and toward the pulpit. I watched, frozen in horror. I'd always hated the big Easter productions of the Passion Play, but at least I finally understood why Clint had no time for me lately, why he'd been so excited for the revival. He had the starring role.

Of course, one thing still nagged at me. Why hadn't he told me about it?

The chanting from the back grew louder, and four men emerged from the sides of the tent just as Clint fell to the ground. The men lifted him, slipping the robe from his shoulders. I tried not to think back to productions I'd seen in the past. It had always seemed a little too real when they drove home the nails.

I tugged at Momma's sleeve. "I think I need to—"

"Shhh!" She hissed, and pinched the inside of my thigh.

Clint's eyes were closed, his brow slick with sweat. His head lolled as the men carried him and his cross out to the lake. I looked from my parents to Wilkins. They seemed calm and collected, reminding me that it was all a show, that none of it was real.

Clint lay sprawled over the cross. I cringed and squeezed my eyes shut at the hammer's first strike. The sound resonated: a metallic strike, then a squishing noise. I could never watch that part. Just the thought of it made my stomach do flips. They'd pulled out all the stops to make it authentic, right down to the sound.

When the hammering finally stopped I peeked through my fingers in time to see the men raise the cross in the waist-deep water of the lake. I tugged Momma's sleeve hard. "Why is he out there?"

I was silenced with another pinch, harder than the first.

Wilkins raised his arms to the sky and the chanting stopped. "Glory to God, who sent His only son so that we might be saved from our sins."

"Amen." The congregation stood. I scrambled off the pew to stand beside my parents. Wilkins reached under the podium and drew out a goblet. Holding it reverently he approached the cross, and without a word the congregation followed.

Momma gazed forward, not sparing me a glance as I lagged behind. I didn't want to be near the front for what came next.

Even from the back of the crowd it looked too real.

Clint hung, limp and pale, as if he really were dying on the cross. The red that seeped from his wrists was thicker and more crimson than the usual food coloring.

I felt the bile rise in my throat, but swallowed it down. I wanted to hide my eyes, but it was Clint's big day. I'd watch for his sake.

One of the men who'd erected the cross stepped forward, pointed stick in hand. I thought he would use it to help steady the cross, but instead plunged it like a spear between Clint's ribs. I groaned and doubled over, ignoring the glares of disapproval from the people around me. *It's not real,* I told myself, over and over. *Clint didn't move, didn't cry out in pain. If it was real he would have screamed. It isn't real.*

Wilkins waded into the water with his goblet held high. "Then Jesus said unto them, 'Verily, verily, I say unto you, Except ye eat the flesh of the Son of man, and drink his blood, ye have no life in you. Whoso eateth my flesh, and drinketh my blood, hath eternal life; and I will raise him up at the last day. For my flesh is meat indeed, and my blood is drink indeed. He that eateth my flesh, and drinketh my blood, dwelleth in me, and I in him. As the living Father hath sent me, and I live by the Father: so he that eateth me, even he shall live by me. This is that bread which came down from heaven: not as your fathers did eat manna, and are dead: he that eateth of this bread shall live forever.'"

He held the goblet up to the fake wound in Clint's side, filling it with fake, gushing blood. The chanting started back up among the congregation. Louder now, I could finally make out the words: "Dwelleth in me, and I in him. Dwelleth in me, and I in him. Dwelleth in me, and I in him." He turned to face the crowd. "Come, brothers and sisters."

At his command the waters of the lake surged to life around him, churning and bubbling as if it boiled. Around the foot of the cross strange forms breached the surface. *Things* with faces like catfish, but the teeth... the claws... God, they were half my size, at least.

By ones and twos they emerged from the water, scaling the cross with razor-tipped fins.

I grabbed the woman beside me and shook her shoulder. "What's happening? What's wrong with the lake?" Without peeling her eyes from the spectacle she shoved me hard, knocking me to the ground.

Kneeling on skinned knees I felt my eyes drawn against my will back to the lake, back to my cousin on his cross. The creatures swarmed him now, all gaping maws and needle teeth, staining his pale flesh red.

Before the cross, indifferent to the carnage, Brother Wilkins raised the chalice overhead. It glinted in the light of the setting sun. As he touched it to his lips the lake around him seethed, vomiting mutant creatures from its depths — all eager to answer the call of flesh and blood.

The congregation waded into the shallows, chanting loud enough to drown the hideous splashing. A damp patch spread down my leg. I turned and ran.

⟡

"Why did you blow it up?"

"You know why. I had to. You came runnin' to my door like a bat outta Hell, rantin' and ravin' about something crawlin' from the water. I knew something goin' on up there wasn't right. After you settled in and fell asleep, I went to see your folks. They didn't even know you was missin'. Treated me like I was crazy, and kept tellin' me to mind my own business, so I went up to the lake and saw for myself."

I grabbed the edge of the table to still my shaking hands. I didn't want to ask, but the words spilled out before I could stop them. "What did you see?"

"A wooden cross, still out there in the lake. Dark shapes writhing on the shore, slithering out there in the darkness. I saw what was left of that boy's body, all torn up and covered in blood." He dabbed at his eyes with a handkerchief.

As far as I'd known Clint's body was never found. I'd told myself he'd just run away, that none of what I saw had happened. I'd imagined it all, infected by the same thing that made everyone else on the mountain sick. "Why didn't you tell me before?" The question came out a hoarse whisper.

"How could I? You were just a boy, and near-broken from the loss of your parents. I didn't have it in me to heap more on you."

"So, you'd rather me live my life thinking I was crazy?

That I imagined it all?" I shook my head. "All these years I thought I was delusional, and I thought that taint had affected me too. But it never made sense." When the lake drained the whole congregation went catatonic. It was like someone flipped an off switch in their minds, and the official reports never mentioned the church, or Clint.

He let out a breath that sounded like I'd knocked the wind out of him. "Rusty, there was somethin' wrong with that lake, somethin' infecting their minds. Maybe it was toxic metals or some alien disease brought in on that rock, I don't know. But what if next time it was you they hung up on that cross? Fed to them things?"

"You... saw them, too?" It couldn't be true. Every person I'd ever told about my childhood all said the same thing, that it couldn't have happened. I must have imagined it.

He knit his brows. "It's what I've been trying to tell you, boy. After I blew the dam an' the water drained out, it left them creatures floppin' about like sittin' ducks. I took my gun up there and I picked 'em off one-by-one till they was all dead."

My eyes stung with tears. I couldn't imagine Earl lying to me, but I knew he wouldn't have brought me here just to tell me this. "Why did you ask me to come back here? Really?"

I could hear the creak and pop of his joints as he pushed himself off his chair. He crossed the room slowly, and lifted an ancient-looking set of keys from a hook on the wall. "Russ, I ain't gonna be around much longer. I need you to take over for me."

"Take over what? The junkyard? Why?"

"I've spent all these years standin' watch, keepin' people from moving up the mountain. Son, there's somethin' up there still, bidin' it's time. I can feel it sometimes, right down to the marrow of my bones. It's calling out to be set free."

"It isn't true." I felt a tear slide down my cheek. "It can't be true." Had Earl gone delusional in his old age? Maybe he'd been traumatized too, reliving that night over and over in his mind. Maybe, from too many years on the mountain, the lake had affected *him*?

With a flick of his wrist, he tossed me the keys. "The shed out back."

Keys in hand, I went behind the house to the dingy, old shed. The roof was green with moss, the walls choked with weeds. The only thing in good repair was the chain that barred the door.

I fumbled several keys until I found one that fit the padlock. I hesitated a moment to turn it. "There's nothing in there," I whispered aloud. "The water's made him crazy." I opened the lock, and held my breath as I opened the door.

It was hard to see in the evening gloom - I hadn't realized how late it had gotten. As my eyes adjusted I made out a plywood table against the back wall, a shadowy lump sprawled across it...

I gasped. My heart skipped a beat.

It was a fish, but not, with fins like wicked claws. The sawdust of clumsy taxidermy spilled from a shotgun wound in its side. But, even shrunken and desiccated, I recognized the needle-teeth that lined its snarling mouth.

I closed my eyes, and saw those teeth sinking into Clint's pale flesh.

I scrambled back and slammed my spine hard against the door. I turned aside and retched.

I closed my eyes, waiting for my heart rate to slow, willing myself to calm. *It's dead. It's real, but it's dead.* I stepped forward for a better look and reached out a hand, tentatively, as if the creature might come back to life and bite me. The surface was hard, reminding me of the fish Clint's uncle Lonnie had hung up in his trailer. He claimed he'd caught it himself, but everyone knew he'd bought it at a yard sale.

Tears filled my eyes, unbidden. It was all real. Something in Heaven's Lake had mutated these creatures, and infected the minds of my family and neighbors. Something that might be there still.

That meant what happened to Clint was real.

Part of me had hoped that the therapists were right — that, in my temporary insanity, I'd invented it all. It wasn't a stretch to believe, since, Lord knows, I wasn't right in the head for years after it happened. I'd even held out hope for Clint, telling myself that maybe he'd run away. I folded myself into a ball and wept.

I don't know how long I sat there rocking back and forth on the floor of the shed, but it was fully dark when I noticed Earl next to me holding a flashlight. He knelt down beside me and pulled me into a hug.

"You gonna be alright, son?"

I'd spent so many years convinced I was crazy, driven insane by toxic metal poisoning, but the truth… the truth was so much worse than that.

"Okay," I said in a hoarse whisper. "I'll do it."

Holley Cornetto

About the Author

Holley Cornetto writes dark fantasy, horror, and weird fiction. To date, her writing appears in over a dozen magazines and anthologies. To indulge her love of books and stories, she became a librarian. She is also a writer, because the only thing better than being surrounded by stories is to create them herself. She can be found online at https://hcornetto.wixsite.com/mysite or lurking on Twitter @HLCornetto.

Jelly

M. B. Vujačić

Lenny paced around his swimming pool.

It was July, the sky blue and cloudless, the wind nonexistent. He wore nothing but his swim trunks and his slippers. The sun shone in his eyes, but that wasn't why he frowned as he made himself stop and look at the newspaper again. The headline read:

JELLYFISH POPULATION BOOM
DUE TO OVERFISHING

He exhaled loudly. Those Goddamn money-grabbers and their disregard for the environment had finally done it. He'd been expecting something like this ever since the first reports of increased jellyfish sightings appeared on the-

"Good morning, Lennard. A fine day, is it not?"

Lenny halted in his tracks, wondering when he'd started pacing again. His neighbor, Mr. Clemens, watched him over the hedge that separated their backyards. He was an old guy, seventy-something, with gray hair perpetually slicked back and whose pencil mustache was perfectly trimmed at all times.

He glanced at the newspaper in Lenny's hand. "Still worrying about that marine business?"

"No, no. It's nothing. I just haven't slept well. How can I help you, Joe?"

"Oh, it is just that I have read an article concerning the increasing medusa populations. It reminded me of a conversation we had some months ago, so I dropped by to tell you about it. I see you have already perused it."

"Ah, yeah, I did."

"Their numbers really are growing, are they not?"

Lenny had to resist an urge to roll his eyes. *Well of course their numbers are growing,* he thought. With over-sized nets destroying swarms of fish, and pollution taking care of the sea turtles, not only was there no animal left to prey on jellyfishes, they now had all the plankton to themselves. Between that and global warming it was only a matter of time before tropical jellies, the ones whose sting could kill you in three minutes, would be everywhere.

"Yeah," Lenny said, "sure looks like it."

"I do hope those reports are exaggerated. Jasmine is awfully afraid of the slimy buggers, and I myself am not particularly fond of them, to say the least. It would be a shame if we had to worry about them every time we went for a swim."

"Well, that's why you should get a pool."

"Oh, but it is not the same."

Lenny shrugged. “Better safe than sorry.”

“Forgive my nosiness, but you seem a little white in the face. Are you still experiencing those stomach cramps?”

“I’m *fine*.”

They exchanged a few more words and then Clemens returned to his wife. Lenny waited until he went out of earshot, then crumpled the newspaper and flung it at the fence. He lowered himself into the pool, closing his eyes and diving to the bottom, letting bubbles pop from his mouth one by one. He loved being underwater. It was cold and quiet, and it made him feel like he still had a thick head of hair. Moreover, it was full of chlorine and not at all salty, and that made him feel safe becau-

Something grabbed his calf. He screamed, the sound coming out bubbly and garbled. He thrashed to the surface and, in a single frantic move, grabbed the edge of the pool and heaved himself out. He took a deep breath, gasped, then closed his eyes and sneezed hard enough to spray water and spittle halfway across the backyard. His leg felt like it had been dipped in napalm.

“Oh fuck! *Fuuuuuuck*!” Lines of raw red flesh criss-crossed his thigh. When he tried to stand up the pain went into overdrive. “Christ, shit, oh God,” he mumbled, wiping the tears from his eyes. He looked at the pool, then froze.

A spherical shape - sickly beige, about two feet wide - drifted under the surface, trailing string-like tentacles.

“How...How the Hell?” he said, staring at the jellyfish in his swimming pool.

No time to worry about that now. He rolled on his

belly and, doing his best to keep his injured leg in the air, crawled into the house. He got to the bathroom, opening the cabinet above the sink and taking out a bottle of vinegar and a tube of hydro-cortisone cream. He spent the next five minutes rinsing his calf with vinegar, then another thirty soaking it in hot water. By the time the pain abated Lenny's face burned and he was shivering, his hands shaking as he slathered the cream over his leg. He considered seeing a doctor, but he hadn't been paying for his health insurance and he could no longer afford a private clinic.

He limped to his bed and fell asleep with his swim trunks still on.

In the morning Lenny called the pool company and demanded they send someone over immediately. Reason? Infestation. When they asked for details, then mentioned a waiting period, he threatened to sue. Eventually they gave in and told him an employee would come by around noon.

Lenny spent this time battling the jellyfish. He tried throwing kitchen knives at it, but only succeeded in cutting his thumb. He took the skimmer net and attempted to capture it, but it was deceptively fast. It dodged every swing, so he reversed the net and tried using it as a spear. The jellyfish reacted by wrapping its tentacles around the pole and almost yanking it out of his hands. After that he didn't dare come within five feet of the pool.

His stomach throbbed steadily by the time the pool

boy arrived. He looked lean, tanned and full of life, a high school student working a summer job. Lenny led him to the backyard, pointed at the pool, and said, "See for yourself."

The kid looked at the water. "Those are knives in there, sir. How did they-"

"Forget the knives, the damn *jellyfish* is the problem."

"Jellyfish? Where?"

"In my pool, where else?"

The kid looked at the water, then at Lenny, then back at the water. "I don't see it, sir."

"Jesus Christ, you must be blind," Lenny said, and went to stand at his side. He opened his mouth to say, *There, do you see it now,* and realized he couldn't see it either. He scanned the pool, his mouth hanging open. He was already starting to go red in the face when his eyes went to the deepest part of the pool.

"There! It went into the drain!"

"The drain, sir? But that's impossible, it-"

"What do you mean it's impossible? *I just saw it*!"

"But there's a grate on it, sir. Nothing can-"

"Jesus, kid, it's a jellyfish. *Jelly*-fish. They're ninety-five percent water, they can go anywhere they damn well please."

"Yes... But... Umm... I think they only live in the sea, sir."

"Well, you think wrong. *Craspedacusta sowerbii*, for example, is a common freshwater jellyfish. It originated in China."

"Oh... Okay. But wouldn't chlorine still kill it?"

"It *should* have. However, something's obviously *wrong* with the pool."

The kid licked his lips. "So... You want us to kill a jellyfish."

"Damn right I do! And clean the drain plus the whole pool. Make sure it's dead. I don't want it spewing its larvae and polyps and shit in my backyard."

The kid licked his lips some more. "I'll have to talk to my boss."

"Whatever, just do it fast. No waiting periods, I want it done this week. I have a *warranty*."

After the kid left Lenny went into the house and surfed the net for hours, searching for articles about people finding jellies in their swimming pools. He didn't find any, but he discovered something much worse:

NUCLEAR PLANT IN SWEDEN SHUT DOWN BY JELLYFISHES

Sometime during the previous October a swarm of jellies had clogged the pipes that supplied cold water to the plant's turbines. The operators had to scramble the reactor. They eventually cleaned the pipes and restarted the reactor, of course, but it still made Lenny want to throw his computer through the window.

It was happening, and nobody even cared. Nobody except *him*.

The pool people arrived two days later.

Rugged, blue-collar types, they came equipped with toolboxes and bored expressions. They pumped out all the water, opened the drains, cleaned them, and changed the filters. They scrubbed the pool's walls until they glistened in the sunlight, then sat down and had a few beers while waiting for it to fill up again. Afterward they chlorinated and shocked the pool, and threw in some algaecide for good measure.

One of them approached Lenny while the others packed their tools. "It's done," he said. He was tall and wiry, with leathery skin and a million lines around his eyes, like an old sailor. "Leave it overnight, then shock it again tomorrow. It's one pound of shock per ten thousand gallons, so you go buy some today. Use gloves and-"

"This'll kill everything in the pool?"

"All the pests, yeah."

"Pests? What about jellyfishes?"

One of the workers chuckled. Two others barely suppressed their grins. Lenny kept a straight face, but his cheeks burned and he fantasized about making them suffer.

The sailor's expression didn't change. "Yeah, sure. They're toast."

"If it comes back I'll take it up with your supervisor."

The sailor shrugged. They left. Lenny watched them drive away, then returned to the backyard and paced around the pool, looking for the jellyfish. It was nowhere to be seen. Satisfied, he sat in one of the easy chairs. The sun had gone down already and he felt exhausted. He closed his eyes and massaged his forehead. His belly ached.

"Troubles with the swimming pool, Lennard?"

Lenny grimaced inwardly. Mr. Clemens stood behind the hedge fence, puffing at his electronic cigarette. "It's nothing," he said. "Just had some pests."

"That is unfortunate. They are dealt with, I hope?"

"Yep. Got their asses kicked."

Clemens smiled. "Jasmine and I had a similar problem in our first house. It was an old place at the riverside, so insects were always besieging us. One time we had a veritable swarm come out of our bathtub drain *and* our kitchen sink. Apparently, a pipe had broken somewhere and they had gotten into the water." He let out a soft *heh heh* sound. "To this day I still mistrust tap water."

"That's... That *sucks*."

"Thank God we do not live there anymore."

They exchanged a few more words, and then Clemens returned to his house. Lenny didn't. He sat in the backyard for a long time, his mouth pursed.

Thinking.

Lenny rubbed his eyes with the balls of his hands.

He sat on the toilet, his briefs hanging around his ankles, thinking what a bitch life was. Four months ago, after he got fired, he told his then-wife he was glad he no longer had to worry about alarm clocks and going to bed early. That was the one great perk of unemployment: you got all the rest you needed. And yet, these days he couldn't stay asleep for more than five or six hours a night; the pain in his belly wouldn't let him. So here he sat, awake at seven in the morning, yawning yet unable to sleep.

Lenny felt a familiar tightness in his intestines and strained a little. He heard a satisfying plop, followed by a big, dry fart. It made him smile. He was reaching for the wet wipes when he heard another splash from the toilet bowl, then something wet and stringy slapped his buttocks.

It felt like being whipped with razor wire.

He jumped, shrieking. His feet got tangled in his briefs and he stumbled. He brought his arms up over his head, trying to fall on his side, and ended up hitting the washing machine. Its corner rammed into his hip, turning his scream into a hiss, and then he hit the floor.

Lenny lay there, moaning, until he heard another splash from the toilet bowl. *That's impossible!* he thought. He grabbed the edge of the tub, pulled himself up, and looked into the bowl.

A jellyfish floated in the brown water, its tentacles slithering over the porcelain. Lenny just stood there, staring at it. Drops of sweat ran down his forehead and climbed to the tip of his nose. He pressed the flush button.

The turds and the brown water were washed away, but the jelly remained. Lenny flushed again, and again. No use. The jelly was either too big, or it held on somehow. He grimaced and lowered the lid. Then, just to be safe, he put the laundry basket on top of it.

When he finished putting the vinegar and the hydro-cortisone cream on his ass he went to the living room and took the fireplace poker. He held it on the stove until it was so hot he couldn't hold it without gloves, and returned to the bathroom. He raised the toilet lid and screamed, "Die in a fire, bitch!" before stabbing the jelly with the poker. There was a hiss, followed by a cloud of vapor and an eye-watering stench. The jelly shuddered and wrapped its tentacles around the poker, only to have them burned off. Lenny waited until it stopped thrashing, then spat on it and flushed the toilet. This time it went down. Hell yeah!

Lenny closed the lid again and let the poker clatter to the floor. He splashed his face with water and leaned against the washing machine, triumphant. He wouldn't be able to sit for a week, and he'd be squatting over a bucket for the rest of his life, but still, it could've been worse. *Much* worse. The jellyfish could've gone after his balls.

"I need a bath," Lenny said to the empty house. He turned the bathtub tap, but instead of rushing out the water came out in a trickle. A deep gurgle rumbled from within the wall. He raised an eyebrow, turning the tap all the way. The gurgle grew louder, but nothing else changed. He tried the shower head and the same thing happened. He muttered, "What now?" and started unscrewing the shower head. He wanted to take a look inside, maybe -

The shower head burst from his hand, followed by a jet of gray water. Lenny screamed and jumped back. For a moment he just stood there, watching the water spray out of the wall, soaking his towels and his stack of toilet paper. Then he grabbed the tap and turned it back. The water stopped after a couple more spurts. Cursing, he screwed the shower head back on.

As he backed away from the tub his bare foot landed on something damp and spongy. He stared at the slimy lump he'd stepped on for what seemed like a long time, his brain unable to process it. He looked around and saw other such lumps wriggling on the floor, the towels, the sink and the bathtub. His stomach turned to ice.

Jellyfish larvae. The walls and pipes were full of them.

He shrieked and ran out of the bathroom. His foot slipped on another larvae, causing him to lose his balance and bang his shoulder against the wall hard enough to leave a bruise. He slammed the door behind him and pressed his back against it. *They can't survive on dry land*, he told himself. All he had to do was wait.

Lenny didn't take a bath that day, nor did he drink tap water. If the jellyfish could breed in the pipes it was safe to assume every water source in the house was contaminated. For all he knew the entire city might be affected. People could be ingesting microscopic jellyfish larvae and nobody would know, so he drove to the nearest supermarket and bought as much bottled water as could fit in his car. It took him three trips to three different supermarkets, but by the time the sun went down his garage was stacked to the ceiling with two-gallon bottles.

He spent the evening researching at his computer.

He couldn't figure out what the jellies ate in those pipes. By all rights those larvae should've starved. Perhaps they'd developed some new mutation, a new way to breed?

Not that that left many options. They already did everything from courtship and copulation to fission and fusion, and even external and self-fertilization. Some were hermaphrodites, others cloned themselves, others still were cannibals. A *Mnemiopsis* started laying eggs at just two weeks old - ten thousand eggs per day - without needing a mate, all while growing rapidly. Zombie jellies literally reincarnated after they died, like goddamn phoenixes.

He found no reports of people discovering jellies in their toilets or bathtubs. It made him wonder: what if the jellies targeted him, specifically? What if they were out to get him?

Lenny scoffed, rolling his eyes. They weren't *that* smart.

Lenny sat in his backyard, holding a can of lukewarm beer.

It'd been two weeks since the bathroom incident, and the pool was once again infested with jellyfishes. Big red ones with long, spiny tentacles, they floated on the surface like water lilies from Hell. They must've developed photosynthesis or something, because they kept spawning larvae even though they had nothing to eat in there. He needed to get rid of them, but he didn't know how. He wished he had some dynamite.

He'd gone to bed at eight in the morning, exhausted, and only slept for three hours before waking up with a splitting headache. The sun threw needles in his eyes, making it worse. He'd taken aspirin and donned not one, not two, but *three* pairs of shades, to no avail.

The pain in his belly was there too, made worse by the changes to his diet. He didn't drink as much liquid as he used to, what with bottled water being so expensive. He also ate less, and then mostly junk food.

"Goddamn slimy bastards," Lenny said, and flung the beer into the pool. It stuck the jellies and sank. He hoped they'd drink it and get liver cirrhosis, then eat shit and die.

He was getting up to get another beer when something stabbed him in the gut. He gasped, pressed his hand against his abdomen, and fell back in the chair. It broke with a hollow snap, plunging him ass-first onto the grass.

He lay there groaning. He waited for the pain to stop, but it refused to lessen, let alone go away. His throat felt parched, like he hadn't had a drink in days. He dragged himself toward the house, pushed the patio doors aside and crawled into the living room. He couldn't remember if he'd left any bottles in the freezer, so he went straight to the garage. His face felt clammy.

The garage was dark, save for the light spilling in through a small window opposite the door. Lenny looked at the stacked bottles, and thought he glimpsed movement. He leaned against the walls and propped himself up with his legs until he reached the light switch. He flipped it...And screamed.

Jellyfishes swam in the water bottles. Larvae, polyps and ephyrae mostly, but some were fully grown, their bulk constricted inside the bottles.

"*No, no, no, no*," Lenny shrieked. "*This can't be happening*!"

He rushed out of the garage. He walked aimlessly through his house, then thought of all the jellies he must've unknowingly consumed. He felt bile rise, and quickly pressed his hand to his mouth. He ran to the bathroom, puking through his fingers. There he fell on his knees, in front of the same bucket he'd been using as a chamberpot during the past weeks, and let it all out.

Halfway through something got stuck in his throat. Lenny tried to inhale, but couldn't even wheeze. He attempted to stand up, struck the sink with his shoulder and fell on his ass. His hands went to his neck. It felt horribly swollen, like there were live wasps trapped inside it. Moaning, Lenny wrapped his fingers together to form a single fist, then brought it down as hard as he could on his own belly.

Air rushed up his throat, doubling him over and pushing whatever blocked his airways up, up, up into his mouth. It squirmed on his tongue, searing the insides of his cheeks. He spat it out. It flew from his mouth and rolled on the floor: a purple jellyfish as big as a tennis ball.

Lenny tried to scream, but his throat hurt too much. He staggered out of the bathroom, a string of saliva dangling from his lip. He felt another stab in his belly. The fire in his stomach spread to his kidneys, his intestines and even his dick. The need to relieve himself became unbearable.

Lenny turned back toward the bathroom, remembered the purple jellyfish, and stopped. He couldn't bear to look at it again, or he'd go mad. For a moment he wondered if he had another bucket tucked away somewhere, then realized it was too late. He dropped his trousers and squatted in the hallway.

He closed his eyes and let his body function, and for a second or two the pain eased up. Then something that wasn't excrement plopped out of him and stung his ankles. He shrieked again, kicked at it and tried to run. His crotch felt like it had been injected with acid. "Oh no, God no, no, no, no!" he screamed. Then a tentacle came out of the tip of his penis.

Lenny ran through the house howling, calling the names of his father, his mother, his ex-wife and even his ex-boss. He grabbed the telephone, started dialing, and flung it away. There was no time. The jellies were inside him, and he needed to get them out. *Right now.*

He stumbled to the kitchen and opened a drawer.

Joseph Clemens adjusted his glasses.

He sat on his couch, holding his electronic cigarette in one hand and his e-reader in the other. Behind him his wife hummed as she placed dirty platters in the dishwasher, one of her ambient compilations playing on the stereo.

"Splendid breakfast you made this morning, Jasmine darling," he said.

"You bet I did."

He smiled. "Now, if I could only savor one of your phenomenal cappuccinos then this day would truly be off to a good start."

"I bet you will."

His smile widened.

"Why don't you invite mister Lennard over sometime?"

He frowned. "I intended to, but he always seemed so distracted."

"Well, of course he is. His wife left him not half a year ago. He must be very lonely. Go invite him over, he's our neighbor."

Indeed, why not? Clemens thought. He left his glasses and his e-reader on the table, and went out into the backyard. The air was so hot he could feel its dryness against his skin, the sun so bright it made even squinting difficult.

He made his way through the garden, careful not to step on Jasmine's flowers, and heard a faint moan. For a moment he wasn't sure if he'd imagined it. Then it came again, weaker this time. He approached the hedge fence, looking into Lenny's backyard. The patio doors stood open, but Lenny himself was nowhere to be seen. Clemens saw only darkness inside.

"Lennard?" he said. "Is everything alright?"

Someone groaned in the gloom. Clemens was about to ask again when Lenny stumbled out of the house. He was naked, his skin covered in sunburns. A carving knife glistened in his fist. The blade was spattered in red, and so was Lenny's hand, wrist and forearm. A huge gash gaped in his abdomen. Blood and...and *other things* dripped from it, painting his crotch and his legs crimson.

"Joseph," Jasmine called from the kitchen window, "ask mister Lennard if he wants some iced tea."

"I..." Clemens said, "I... I..."

Lenny whimpered, his eyes huge and his mouth full of redness. He raised his arms toward Clemens, taking a step. The knife fell from his hand and clattered on the floor. At the last instant he seemed to realize he was walking straight toward the swimming pool. His eyes grew so big that they looked ready to tumble from his head. He tried to turn back, but his knees gave out. He fell face-first into the pool.

Clemens watched the water splashing and turning pink, unaware that he was muttering "I... I... I..." over and over. Jasmine's voice echoed from another reality. She told him to tell mister Lennard they had strawberry jelly in the fridge.

Clemens swallowed.

"I... I don't think he wants any jelly..."

Mijat Budimir Vujačić

About the Author

Mijat Budimir Vujačić is an economist by trade, storyteller at heart. He is a published author of three horror novels written in Serbian: Krvavi Akvarel, NekRomansa, and Vampir. His stories appeared in SQ, Serial, Devolution Z, All Worlds Wayfarer, DBND, Turn to Ash, Crimson Streets, Encounters, Acidic Fiction, Double Barrel Horror, Creepy Campfire Quarterly, Under the Bed, 9Tales, and Infernal Ink magazines, as well as in professional anthologies Infinite Darkness, Toxic Tales, Silent Scream, The Nightmare Collective, Down With The Fallen, and The Worlds of Science Fiction, Fantasy and Horror Vol1. He believes a strong work ethic is the root of all success, and that it is best to err on the side of action. A fan of all things horror, he is also an avid gamer, occasional blogger, hookah enthusiast, and a staunch dog person. He lives in Belgrade, Serbia. You can reach him via e-mail: mbvujacic@gmail.com or check out his blog at: https://mbvujacic.blogspot.com/

Cry of the Hunger Fish

Lin Darrow

The Comprehensive Deep Sea Oceanarium was seven levels deep.

The first housed the arctic specimens: the electric narwhals, iceflow salmon and the like. As the floors descended the climate cooled. There were spackled shallow-crabs from Eastern Canada, then angel and devil fish native to the Germanic lakes on the second and third. By the fourth there were tropical whales with rainbow spots from off the shores of Sri Lanka, with golden octopi from the far-flung Pacific on the fifth. There were the crystal caves on level six for children to go running through, containing a thousand diverse species of candy-colored coral and spiked anemones, with flying fish on the balconies that overlooked the daily mermaid shows at the Siren Shallows.

The seventh level housed in the basement, was off-limits to visitors. It was accessible only by a slow, creaking elevator ride and a long, narrow hallway that led down to a metal door, which was red with rust and wet to the touch. Past the red-iron door was a stinking, pitch-black gut of a room that rumbled with the slow, digestive grind of some distant suffering sound.

It was this level that Elena Cortez had been hired to keep dry during the night shift.

Standing on the catwalk, illuminated only by the triangle of light from the rusted-red door, Elena stared into the inky darkness of the room. She breathed in sharply, the air scraping fingers down her throat. With an accordion-like wheeze she turned back to Dr. Hill.

"What's that sound?" she asked as a groan shuddered down the metal railing under her hand. "Sounds like—" There she paused, for the sound was half the whimpering cries of some animal in distress, and half the crushing of bones through cruel, chugging machinery.

"The pressure machines," Dr. Hill explained, keeping one hand on the door. "They keep the specimens comfortable."

The tour had been brief. The seventh floor was, Dr. Hill explained, where the rarest creatures from the deepest, most desperate wells of the sea were housed. There was the Black Angler, the sharp-toothed fish with red lanterns glowing at the end of nine long, slithering cords. Next came the Leaping Lampreys, which were mere winged cords of pearly flesh with gaping, sucking mouths. Another tank held the Phosphorescent Eels, their lumpy faces rolling back and forth against the water with an oatmeal-like consistency. Still yet were the Fringeheads, scaly fish that could burst open their mouths to twice the size of their bodies, and the Dracula hagfish, which could extend its fangs out several feet to spear prey with cruel precision.

But the crown jewel of the seventh level was the Clear-Skull Barreleye: just the one, about the size of a large man's torso, its body nothing more than a translucent mound of meat through which two glowing eyes could look in 180 degrees.

Elena kept her eyes averted as Dr. Hill led her through the darkened displays with a lantern, focusing instead on her guide. She was all polished spectacles and crisp, clipping heels, her hair slicked back severely to prevent even a single strand from flying loose. Her lab coat swished about her knees as she led Elena through the winding walkways, and even that small flicker of motion felt directed, purposeful.

"The pressure machine simulates the conditions found on the seafloor," Dr. Hill explained, light flashing through thick glass and spooking one of the infernal creatures back into the darkness. "For safety purposes we've programmed it to shut down for five minutes at the end of every hour so that it doesn't overheat. Sometimes the damp can get into the old thing's bones, and it takes a little longer to restart. If the machines fail to turn back on after five minutes it's your job to get them running again by pulling the reset switch."

In the meantime she was to keep the walkways mopped up, and report back if the creatures expressed any sign of distress.

"Do they typically?" Elena grunted as she stepped

back out into the light of the hall, breathing in deep. "Show distress, I mean?"

"Only if the conditions aren't kept to their liking," Dr. Hill replied, shutting the door firmly against the growl of the pressure machines. "You'll have to wear a headlamp; the creatures will be blinded by anything brighter."

Elena nodded. Dr. Hill reached to clasp her arm, and she started at the foreignness of the touch.

"By the way," she said, her gaze soft despite the severe professionalism of her appearance. "I just wanted to say that I'm sorry for your loss."

Elena must have stiffened, because Dr. Hill withdrew her hand with a sad smile.

"It came up on your background check," she said apologetically. "I know how difficult—well, I'm just sorry, that's all."

"Thanks," Elena said, throat thick with an old quiet.

Her first day was a Monday in June.

Elena's wife had been an artist, with pink streaks in her greying hair and a particular talent for analogies. She used to sit on Elena's lap and tease her for having the look of a wrinkled, old shirt, folded a thousand times in the exact same way and pressed down flat into the same drawer for decades. In her gentle drawl it hadn't sounded like an insult. Elena had always been rough-handed and well-worn, approaching most things in life with a threadbare simplicity.

A less practical woman might have noted the scratch marks latticed along the sides of the headlamp as she slipped it on.

"Last fella, he found it a bit spooky down there," the janitor for the upper levels rambled on, popping her chewing gum. She couldn't have been more than nineteen, though she carried herself with an almost comical air of authority, as though she considered herself a regular expert on the art of soap meeting water.

"Y'don't say," Elena commented blithely, watching as the janitor rooted a pair of rubber boots, overalls and a waterlogged safety manual out of somebody's locker.

"I'd let him out in the mornings all pale and quiet," the janitor drawled over her shoulder. "It was the dark that got to him. Thick as the inside of a coffin, he'd say! Always remembered the way he put that. Well, here you go." She stood, and tossed Elena's new uniform at her, grey and shapeless. "Jittery Frank's old gear—cleaned, of course, since he ditched the job halfway through and disappeared in the middle of the night."

Together Elena and the janitor heaved open the heavy metal door. It was such a trial to keep it open between them that the janitor had to clip the unyielding mass to a ring on the wall in order to keep it from slamming shut. A gush of hot, wet air rolled past their shoulders.

"Good luck down there, Ms. Cortez," the janitor said, finally swallowing her gum. "Now, the door's so heavy you'll need a second hand to open it, so I'll be here at seven a.m. sharp to let you out."

"Why not just leave it open?" Elena asked, glancing at the hook and chain. "Or is Hill afraid I'll run off too?"

The janitor shrugged.

"Must be for the specimens' benefit," she said. "Keep the sound disturbance to a minimum."

At Elena's grim look—typical for her face, though the janitor couldn't have known it—she added, "Well, maybe she thought it'd help with the jitters if you felt like someone'd be there at the end of the night. Empty rooms can get in a person's head."

"I'm used to that particular ache," Elena said, after a pause.

"Sorry to hear it," the janitor said, before saying goodnight and gliding the door shut with an echoing *thunk*.

Elena's feet slid against the slimy steps as she descended to the main floor of the aquarium. The headlamp illuminated a plate-sized portion of the floor as she went, one hand clutching the railing hard. The light flashed along the glass of one of the tanks, glinting down the circular rows of a lamprey's teeth as it clung to the glass. Disturbed, she flicked the light to the walkway and began to drag her mop through the thick layer of damp that had built up over the day.

The hum of the pressure machine pounded like a dull heartbeat in her head as she worked, stalking between the labyrinth of tanks with her mop and bucket. It whirred against her ears, like the scrape of glass across porcelain and the heaving breaths of some angry, skewered beast.

When the machine shut off at the top of the hour the

churning sounds were replaced by a strange, bubbling quiet. Without the labor of all those gears and parts all Elena could hear was the lap of the water against the tanks, the slosh of it down the glass walls and onto the floor. Hearing the specimens as they disturbed the water reminded her of their presence—the sucking lampreys, the toothy anglerfish, the disintegrating hagfish. Occasionally she would hear a dull *thud* in these moments of silence, as though the creatures were hurling themselves against the glass, just once or twice before the machine was turned back on and the churning, grinding music muffled everything else.

The path to the machines always took her past the barreleye's tank, which was situated just beneath the machine at the very back of the room. Its eyes, when she approached, would glow steadily through the dark. They moved in seemingly random circles back and forth, illuminating the veins and nerves that tangled beneath its translucent skin. It almost seemed to follow her as she climbed the sweaty steps and heaved on the switch.

"That eyeball thing—can it actually... y'know, *see*?" Elena asked one morning, almost a week into her shift.

Dr. Hill had dropped by to see how she was doing, and Elena was struck by the difference in her appearance: her bun was just slightly askew, and her eyeliner was smudged at the edges as though some private stress was weighing on her.

"We don't know. There's a lot we don't know about the seventh-floor specimens, hence the aquarium. How are you handling the conditions?" she asked professionally, scribbling down a few quick, efficient notes on a pad of paper.

"Well enough," Elena replied simply.

"Any strange dreams? The last janitor—Franklin—reported having a few nightmares."

"None about—work," Elena said. Then she opened her mouth, only to close it again.

"What? There's something," Dr. Hill prompted.

"It's nothing," Elena said, reluctant to admit a weakness even as she was touched by the doctor's insistence. "Just that the sound of those machines gets into my ears a little. It follows me home from my shift some nights—fades long before I tip into bed, though."

"Oh," Dr. Hill said quietly. She reached to tighten her bun and smooth down a few flyaway hairs. "Yes, I know the feeling. Does that bother you?"

"No," Elena replied. "Takes more than a few rattled eardrums to scare me off."

For the first time since Elena had interviewed for the job Dr. Hill's smile felt fully present on her face. She placed her hand on Elena's much larger arm and gave it a squeeze, which Elena felt all the way down to her ventricles.

"I'm glad to hear it," she said, and Elena wondered if she had been imagining that her smudged eyeliner was due to anything more than a slightly tilted mirror. "We're pleased to have you here, Ms. Cortez."

⟡

The weeks passed, and Elena's eardrums began to feel wet. The sound of the pressure machine had become second nature, beating through her like the pulpy matter of a second heart was squeezing in through her ears and trickling rust all down the insides of her veins. The ringing had, in her first week, lasted only an hour or two past her shift; now she could scarcely remember what it was like to hear the world without the ghost of grinding gears as a distant thrum.

At three weeks Elena began to anticipate the slowing grind of the machine, the hiss and release of steam as it prepared to settle and die. At four weeks she began to hear the nuances and subtleties to the churn, the shriek, squeak and hiss of its parts like a song played on loop a thousand times in laborious sequence.

At six weeks she began to hear the voice.

"Help!" the creak of grinding gears seemed to call out as it settled, its voice sharp and childlike. "Help! Help!"

Elena's heart gave a spark at the sound. For a long, dragging moment she stood paralyzed, her boots soaked through and her insides caught in the sensation of a sudden fall. The gears creaked and squealed constantly—they had a human sound to them at times, but she had never been so attuned as to imagine them actually speaking before.

For a moment—an elegant, glacial, irrational moment that seemed to warp the flow of time around her into hazy knots—she could only think of pink streaks in graying hair.

Then a *thud* slammed against the glass. Startled from the clutch of her reverie, she turned her headlamp just in time to see one of the Leaping Lampreys writhing against the glass, its milky eyes foaming. The press of its cord-like body against the tank wall was almost violent, as though it was being flattened by some invisible object, or as though it would rather be crushed than remain where it was a moment longer.

Shaking herself, she clomped through the water and restarted the machine, ignoring the gliding eyes of the barreleye as she passed. The machine roared back to life, and the squeaky voice was muffled. For the rest of the night Elena viciously shut down any lingering thoughts of color.

It came again not days later. This time the machine was still running, only a half-hour out from the last shut-off. The shrieking of its parts seemed to strain above the general roar, crying out, "Help! Help!" in a weeping tone, as though some specter was caught haunting the machine's very innards.

Elena was determined to ignore it, along with the dull twinge it put in her gut, but it persisted throughout the rest of the hour, scored by the occasional *thud* of specimens against glass until it was killed by the silence of the machine shutting off. When Elena restarted it again the voice was quiet.

Hill came almost every day to check how she was doing, looking more haggard and pale every time.

"How are you handling the conditions?" she would

ask, her voice crisp and professional despite whatever mysterious strain she was under.

"Fine," Elena would reply, quietly admiring Dr. Hill's evident fortitude and feeling somewhat ashamed at her own sensitivity. She couldn't pretend to know what kind of pressure the head of such an extensive research project was under, but Dr. Hill was never anything but kind, concerned and competent in her dealings with Elena. It made Elena determined not to add to her stress, and to hold her own even closer to the chest, lest some of it leak out and smudge Dr. Hill's eyeliner even worse.

Moira had always frowned at her for doing that.

One day, after answering Dr. Hill's questions, Elena decided to ask, "There's nobody else down there with me, is there?"

"Who would be down there with you?" Hill asked, quirking an eyebrow. "Aside from the specimens, of course."

"You've never heard anything strange down there?" Elena pressed.

Hill paused. Her pen pressed so hard against her clipboard that the ink made a stain on the paper.

"It's the sound of the pressure," she said. "There's something about the sound that—pulls at you. It's the same on the ocean floor."

"You've been to the ocean floor?" Elena marveled.

Hill nodded. "Two years ago. It was an intensive, experimental expedition. A week at the bottom of the sea to gather specimens, all the while surrounded by that sound."

She drew a breath, shutting her eyes for a moment before gathering up a bracing smile.

"Though, personally," she said, "I prefer it to silence."

At eight weeks Elena was hearing the voice every night. At nine she was hearing it even after she left the aquarium, spearing through her ear canals like the scraping of teeth. Every night it grew in pitch and tone, shrieking in echoes that rattled the specimens' glass cages. It followed her into sleep, piercing through her dreams of drowning, of swimming deep, deep, deep into inky pools of water after the white flash of a hand that was sinking just fast enough to keep her from catching it.

Sometimes she would tilt the headlamp into the tanks and imagine that she saw the white hands of her nightmares straining forward, before being pulled back into the inky depths. Other times she heard the banging of the creatures against the tanks, or the slosh of water over the edge of the glass, and felt a sudden panic that the specimens had launched themselves over the top and were now crawling, clawing and slithering their way across the floor.

Every morning she told Hill she was fine.

"I'm glad you're adjusting so well," Hill said at ten weeks, sounding relieved.

On that particular day Elena noted that Dr. Hill looked more polished than usual. Her stress seemed to come in bouts, and Elena silently measured her good days and bad days by the lines of her makeup and the wrinkles in her lab coat.

"It's been so hard to keep your position filled."

"It might help if the door wasn't shut every night," Elena suggested, feeling instinctively that Dr. Hill was used to being solitary in her work, and might appreciate someone who came to her with solutions instead of problems. "It *can* get a bit claustrophobic down there."

"It's best not to open the main door more than is strictly necessary," Hill said, tensing. "It disturbs the conditions—the air pressure, the sound waves. It's just a precaution."

"I take it the specimens don't like it?" Elena ventured.

"They're... very sensitive," Dr. Hill said, after a pause. "They're much more attuned to things like sound waves, or changes in atmospheric pressure. What we sense they sense a thousand times over."

Elena recalled the frantic press of the lamprey against the glass.

"And the machine, you're sure it doesn't bother them?" she asked.

"It shouldn't," Hill replied. "The noise of the ocean floor is much louder. That deep-pressure hum, it's... Well, they're just better equipped to handle it than we are. That's all."

She made a dismissive note on her pad, and Elena felt strangely as though she had failed to lift whatever was weighing so heavily on Dr. Hill's shoulders. Not for the first time she wondered if this was how Moira had felt whenever she had let her own private tensions show on her face without admitting to their existence.

"What if there's an emergency?" Elena asked, after a pause.

"There's an alarm that sounds if the machine isn't restarted within seven minutes," Dr. Hill explained. "And there's a back door just behind the pressure machine that leads up to the observation bay we use during the day. If there's ever an emergency that door is bulletproof, fire-proof, flood-proof—just about every 'proof' you can get. And it's unlocked if the alarm goes off longer than ten minutes. Exiting that way will be less disturbing to the specimens."

"Suppose that's something," Elena muttered to herself.

It was a Wednesday when Moira left, bundled in a faux-fur stole and a summer dress complete with long, white evening gloves. They'd been an impulse-buy some twenty years ago at an antique fair, promptly bundled into a drawer and forgotten until the opera had come to town. Moira, being Moira, had bought a single ticket in the back row, knowing that Elena couldn't care less for the theatre.

The memory wasn't much, but Elena had turned it over in her mind a thousand times, trying to stretch the edges and build something out of the wisps she was left with. Moira bustling around in the kitchen humming an aria; Moira phoning for a cab because she didn't want to drive at night; Moira waving goodbye with those long, white gloves as she swept out the door.

It was the gloves she remembered most: in her dreams

the fingers were long and spindly, almost boneless as they wriggled out a goodbye. The silk was impeccably smooth and white as steam-fresh china, scaldingly sanitary. In her mind's eye the wintery hue was always eerie against her dark, dark skin.

It was a Wednesday when she left; a Thursday when she didn't come back. Then it was every day afterwards that the absence settled in, made itself a home in their old rooms, as the police slowly stopped calling, the neighbors stopped asking and Elena stopped recognizing the world around her as a familiar, answerable place.

On her next shift Elena found the back stairwell leading up behind the machine to a small platform that overlooked the barreleye's tank. Her headlamp flashed down the dark glass of a window, and she felt her way to the doorknob. The door swung open easily enough, revealing a small pod with a desk and a few neatly-stacked folders.

The bright gaze of a young boy in a framed photograph watched her as she explored the contents of the desk. Tucked beneath the frame was a battered, old card proclaiming YOU'RE SIX, HAPPY BIRTHDAY! Briefly, Elena touched the corner of the frame, then moved on.

She flicked open a few of the folders, thumbing her way through crude sketches of half-formed sea-creatures, notes on height, width and weight. Illustrations of organs, intestines and optical nerves littered the pages, swathed in numbers that meant nothing to Elena. More personalized notations covered the sheets in a neat scrawl, a collection of scattered phrases like 'teeth, 14 centimeters' and 'glow varies depending on light density' and 'capable of digesting meat'.

At last she came to a folder that seemed dedicated to the barreleye. Underneath the heading, someone had written only one thing, underlined five times: '90 percent stomach, 10 percent eyes.'

Beneath that was another line: 'The other specimens don't like it.'

The usual sounds of the machine growling and crunching in the main floor was muffled by the walls as Elena read through the papers. It had nearly leaked entirely from her ears when the mechanical hum gave a sudden *twist.* A tea-kettle shriek, longer and more rusted than any noise that had come before, launched itself suddenly at the door. With a *WHAM* the glass began to shake unforgivingly, pounding and rioting in the frame as though phantom hands were banging desperately against it.

Elena staggered back against the wall as the shriek of a voice clawed its way through the seams of the soundproof door, crying out, "HELP! HELP! HELP! HELP! HELP!" in increasingly high-pitched tones, until at last it hit a crescendo in one final, steaming hiss that signaled the machine shutting down.

It took Elena nearly ten trembling minutes before she was able to peel herself off the wall and go restart the machine. The voice was silent for the rest of the night.

Elena went straight to Dr. Hill's office the next morning, only to find the room locked and dark.

"Where's Dr. Hill?" she asked the janitor, after wandering the halls for some time, searching for a familiar face. It took several waves before she could be convinced to yank off her headphones, which were trembling with disco music, and give Elena any attention at all.

"Taking the day unannounced, I imagine," the janitor said, scarcely looking up from the dials on her portable radio. "She does that sometimes."

"What, she just—doesn't show up for work?" Elena asked.

"It's worse this time of year," the janitor replied, blowing her gum into an obnoxiously large bubble. As it popped she finally looked up at Elena's furrowed brow and gave a sigh. "Listen, maybe you oughta know so you go easier on her. This month's the anniversary of her kid shufflin' off this mortal coil."

Elena's guts twisted, sour and cold.

"Oh," she said quietly.

"Three years," the janitor said. "I dunno what it was, exactly, only know it was sudden."

Elena recalled her first day, when Hill had haltingly offered her condolences, and her insides bowed miserably.

"I know," the janitor said, flicking off the radio and killing the muffled shrieking of her music at last. "Anyway, it never affects her work. Just means her vacation time is sporadic. She'll work nonstop for months, then disappear for weeks."

"I see," Elena said, mulling over the information.

The janitor shot her an anxious look.

"Don't tell her I told you, eh?" she said, fumbling with her headphones. "She wouldn't like it, and she won't take it well if you try to help her either."

"She's a pillar," Elena muttered, hearing the word in Moira's disapproving voice.

"Whatever that means," the janitor said with an airy shrug.

"She deals with—things, bad things, on her own," Elena said. "I know—I mean, I've been told I do the same thing."

The janitor popped her gum again. "Yeah?"

"I'll let her alone, then," Elena said with some gruffness, feeling the words hang unnaturally in the air between them. Stiffly, she turned away. "Thanks."

The janitor clapped her on the shoulder before shrugging her headphones back on and thumbing the volume dial up to 10.

When the machine went down Elena typically had five minutes to stand in the dark and listen. After the grinding pall of settling metal joints had faded into a muffled silence, the hidden noise of the aquarium floor began to pulsate through the black, curling up against her ears and digging deep. In her first weeks on the job the noise had been muffled and distant. Now, after weeks of being submerged into regulated five-minute blocks of silence, her ears had adapted, and she began to imagine a greater nuance of sound lurking in the quiet haze.

It was hard to imagine that she had ever been unaware of the hidden soundscape of the seventh floor, which was almost orchestral in its lush chaos. The lap of water against thick glass panels, the occasional thud of coiled bodies against the lids of the tanks, the burping gasps of specimens parting the water's surface before guzzling back down into the depths once more—it all struck her ears like a great mass of slimy, bubbling instruments all clamoring at once, tuning themselves as though preparing to launch into some louder overture.

The first time that the machine failed to start up on its own Elena felt the silence expand through her body, tensing her limbs and ringing through her ears. Propping her mop against one of the tanks she began the wet trek through the aquarium tanks towards the metal stairway that led up to the machine's landing.

As she approached her headlamp flashed along the glass of the barreleye's tank, pinging off a giant, dilated blotch that somewhat resembled a pupil. Her knees locked, and she stopped dead in her tracks. The blotch of a pupil wavered lazily back and forth as the fish floated close to the glass, its full body fading into the murky haze of water so that only the one glowing eye was fully visible. Elena's stomach churned under the creature's absent gaze—was the hideous thing actually *looking* at her, or were its great eyes merely roaming aimlessly through the surrounding black?

The machine had been shut down for 9 minutes. Then she heard it: a sudden, lurching, violin-screech of a sound vaulting up from the muffled noise of the room.

"Help!" it cried, prompting Elena to gasp and cover her ears. "It's me! *I'm here!*"

The sound seemed to be descending from above, echoing off the wet glass of two-dozen aquarium tanks to echo painfully in Elena's ears. The barreleye forgotten, Elena pushed through the paralysis in her legs and staggered up the stairs, slipping on the damp metal and clawing at the railing.

When she hit the landing the sound had all but disappeared.

"Where are you?!" she cried hoarsely into the dark, only for the sound to fade like mist into the black, swallowed up by the lap of water in the barreleye's tank. Helplessly, Elena moved to the railing and peered down into the water. The beam of her headlamp cast a glow like a silver dollar over the churning, black water, illuminating nothing except a few stray bubbles.

Her lungs expanded slickly in her chest. Each breath felt moldy and mildewed, as though her throat was filling up with tangled weeds, the water rising from her stomach and filling her mouth. She opened her mouth to cry out again, her gut heaving from the effort—only for nothing to emerge except a strangled wheeze.

She heard the first *thud* from a distance. One of the specimens had thrown itself so violently against its tank that she heard water splashing over the side of the lid. Another *thud* followed, then another and another, until the whole room was ringing with the sound of bodies against glass, water sloshing and splattering in a panic, and—Elena's stomach lurched most violently at this—the unmistakable sound of something fleshy landing with a *slap* against the aquarium floor.

Elena pushed herself back from the edge of the barrel-eye's tank and threw herself at the machine. In an instant the monstrous grind of the machine roared back on, blanketing the room in a deafening cacophony of noise.

By the time Elena had gathered herself enough to go inspect the tanks the Leaping Lamprey that had vaulted over the aquarium wall had already stopped moving. It lay in a ropey coil, soft and slimy to the touch, its eyes open and black as inkwells. Whether it had died from the fall or from suffocation she couldn't tell.

It was another two weeks before Hill returned to work.

"There's something wrong with the machine," Elena said to Hill then, after standing a long moment outside her office door. "Something—or some*one*, I don't know—it's like it's *trapped* down there."

"Are you suggesting the aquarium is haunted?" Hill

asked. Her hair was immaculately combed and pinned to the top of her head. Her dress was without a crease, and her lab coat was pristinely white. Whatever had passed in the two weeks she'd been absent she was here now, as though she'd never left, a paragon of untouchable professionalism.

"I don't know what it is," Elena admitted. "I don't know if it's making me mad, or if it's pulling some old madness *out* of me—"

"It could be one of the specimens making noise," Hill interrupted. "I'll join you for the night shift tomorrow to observe, how's that?"

Elena hesitated. "It—it takes some getting used to, down there."

"Oh, don't be silly," Hill said, making a sharp note on her pad. "I know the specimens aren't exactly pretty to look at, but I oversaw their acquisition myself. I've *been* to the ocean floor, Ms. Cortez, in a submarine scarcely larger than a coffin. I've heard the sounds of the darkest, deepest, most pressurized places on the planet. I would be a poor scientist if I was afraid of the very thing I captured for study."

"I'm not afraid of the things down there," Elena said. "It's not the dark, or the door, or even really the noise."

"No?" Hill asked, glancing up from her pad for the first time. "What is it, then?"

Elena was silent, feeling her lungs constrict and heave back open, seeped in the thick damp of the seventh level as though she would never breathe clean again.

"It's the not-knowing," she said at length. "That's all."

Hill considered her a moment. Elena felt as thin as water beneath that stare, and for a moment she considered saying something about the photograph she'd found in the pod, the old birthday card that had grown wavy from time but not neglect. But, as the quiet stretched on, she felt as though the invisible threads that were twining between them were best left untouched and unremarked upon.

"I'll see you tomorrow, Ms. Cortez," Hill said at length, before lowering her clipboard and turning away. "Perhaps we'll find some solutions to the ambiguity together."

The next shift marked the eleventh week of Elena's employment at the Oceanarium. She took a deep breath as she descended the stairs, the distant echo of the voice still yearning through her ears. The door shut behind her as usual, and the machine churned itself into its usual frenzy.

"I don't hear anything out of the ordinary," Hill commented as they walked along Elena's usual route, rounding the tank that crackled with occasional light from the phosphorescent eels, illuminating their lumpy, writhing bodies. "Are you sure you're not just hearing the machine?"

Elena shook her head. "It's more than just a bit of rust in the gears."

"I know! There are waterproof microphones in the tanks. How about I head up to the observation pod and see what I can hear?" Hill suggested.

Elena hesitated.

"I'll be *fine.* Back in a flash!" Hill assured her, her tone strangely light and girlish in a way Elena had never heard before. Almost as though the wet, dank cavern of an aquarium really was a sort of home to her—or that she wanted Elena to think as much.

Elena nodded, and Hill swept comfortably off into the darkness, the sound of her heels echoing off the tanks until it was swallowed up by the whisky-hum of the machine.

Elena mopped the floor. She followed the labyrinthine path through the tanks, heaving her mop against the glass, trying not to look at the milky eyes of the hagfish, the sucking mouth of the lampreys writhing against the tank wall. It wasn't until the machine shut off at the top of the hour that she began to wonder how long it took to check the microphones.

"Help!" came the voice, slithering soft and pitifully through the quiet.

Startled by the sound after such extended silence, Elena's head flew towards the sound. In doing so her headlamp flew off her head and smashed against the glass, shattering into pieces and flickering out. Her heart gave a sickly lurch as the darkness swept in all around her, swallowing every last vestige and pinprick of light, pressing in with the pressurized pumping *throb* of the machine rioting through her ears.

She staggered forward, one hand reaching for the glass wall of the tank, only to touch something spongy and thick with slime. Reeling back, her hands flew to her ears as the voice began to racket up in intensity, its high-pitched tone like a steam whistle in its shrieking desperation. Almost instantly she fell to her knees, one hand peeling free to scrabble for the broken headlamp and loop the straps around her wrist.

"Help!" it cried. "Help! Help! Help!" The voice hollered and wept, rusted and raw and friendless, until the mechanized tones of its cries began to bleed into something more familiar. "**ELENA**! *Help*!"

Elena lurched to her feet in a blind panic. She ran, feet sliding far too easily against the slime that coated the floors, staggering against the walls of the tanks at every turn. The glass shook as the specimens threw themselves against the glass, sending giant globs of water over the edge, thick with wriggling, fleshy *things* that grazed teeth down her back as they fell and flopped to the ground like the pulp of torn muscle.

All around her she could hear water splashing, glass booming and flesh slapping against the floor. Still she kept running, finding her way instinctively to the platform just outside the observational pod.

The platform that overlooked the barreleye's tank.

"HELP!" came the voice again, unobscured by the machine's rumblings from just below. Breathless, Elena grabbed the rail and peered over the side.

There it was: illuminated just barely by the glow of the barreleye's pupils, the faintest outline of a white, white hand was straining the water towards the surface.

Elena moved without thinking, vaulting herself over the railing and plunging into the tank, one hand seeking forward for the fluttering, empty hand. All around her the water swirled with a piano-key blackness, thick and beating with a panicked heartbeat, the trailing fingers of the hand dancing just barely out of reach. She was drawn deeper and deeper by the pale, phosphorescent glow of the receding fingers, struggling through the water as her lungs began to flood. Her ears began to ring, and all sense of direction was swallowed up by the encompassing dark. She could hear the cries for help pulsing through the water, the sound muffled and indistinct but loud, so loud it turned her bones to pulp and all her muscle into paste.

Gradually it became harder and harder to move; her body melted, disintegrated as it dove, her limbs trailing weakly at her sides to leave her as adrift as a cut puppet. Still the voice cried out, and Elena struggled to push past the lethargic mush of her body, ground her teeth against the frustration of the endless, dark search and the ever-fading light of the hand as it flickered out into the darkness. One last cry came, shattering through her every vein and tendon, twisting the last remaining strings of her into a helpless tangle. She was alone, without breath, lost in the water and utterly without direction—except, in some small torturous way, for the acute knowledge that the owner of the white hand was just beyond her grasp, adrift in the same darkness.

Then, all at once, scars of scarlet light burst through the black, illuminating the insides of the tank like a feral x-ray. Elena's eyes shot open as the scene flashed before her: eight rows of teeth growing taller with every straining breath, the thin membrane of skin stretching wider and wider to open the barreleye's mouth to ten times its original size, a furious pinwheel of fangs and a white, white tongue with fingerish tendrils snapping quickly back into its gaping esophagus.

Its teeth gaped open larger, one more row piercing through its fleshy membrane, body twitching as another cry emerged from deep within its throat. Again it struck Elena like a tranquilizer, but the effects were less: it no longer sounded half so innocent, so lost and desperate, nor even—as she strained to listen—*human*.

The barreleye's glowing eyeball twitched, and she saw it move to peer through the translucent stretch of its skin, trying to locate her through the net of its own teeth. The scarlet light burst on and off like a wounded lightning storm. Elena felt a shot of adrenaline panic burst through her, just enough to bend a leg against the glass wall of the tank—nearer than she'd thought—and push herself up, up, up towards the surface.

When she broke through the water she could hear the buzzing of the alarm coming from the office, the scarlet light coming from a light blinking on and off over the door. Her hands slipped against the rungs of the railing as she tried, weakly, to make her fingers grip the bars, to heave her muscles into action enough to pull her up onto the platform.

Then she saw a dark silhouette standing against the

window of the research pod, just beneath the frenzied alarm.

"Dr. Hill!" she called, fingers moving sluggishly against the bars as though she was still submerged. The water around her legs was clinging and heavy, and she could feel it swirling beneath her. "Help me up!"

"Ms. Cortez, you've got to get back into the water," Hill said, moving forward with an eerie calm. "You were right, someone *is* down there."

"There's nothing down there but the barreleye!" Elena coughed, feeling as though her throat was thick with slime and seaweed. "You were right—there's nothing there to find, just a trick to pull at a weak mind—"

"Of *course* someone is down there," Hill said, leaning over the railing. "The barreleye's teeth can expand to twenty times the size of its stomach. The pulse of its hunger strikes the human ear like—like the dilution of loss and longing into sound. That echoing, aching sound—what did it sound like to you?"

Elena was silent.

"When I first heard it down on the ocean floor..." Hill said, after a wounded pause. "I thought I recognized it too."

"Hill," Elena began, managing to get a decent grip by bending her elbow around the rung and dangling it there like an empty glove-finger.

"It needs to eat, Ms. Cortez," Hill said. "It needs to eat, or the sound of its hunger will drive me mad. It sounds too much—too much like *him*. And I don't know where he's gone, Hill; I don't believe in Heaven, so I don't know where my boy's gone, and there are some nights I think he's really there, in the belly of the barreleye, and when I start thinking that way, that's when I know it can't be put off any longer—"

"You should never have taken this thing from the bottom of the sea!" Elena growled, making another failed, slippery attempt to drag herself up.

"I know you're right. It upsets the other specimens, too," Hill said, her voice like a broken ripple. "But I couldn't leave it, not when it sounded like—but it's mad at me, I know, for taking it from its home. It pulled Franklin down first, but I swear I didn't know—I didn't know he'd lost his mother when I sent him down there!"

"But you knew about *me*!" Elena roared.

Hill peered over the rail, down into the water, avoiding Elena's seeking gaze.

"I thought you might be able to withstand it," Hill continued. "You seemed so strong, and it was so long ago. I thought, if it could only hunt you for a while, it might quiet the cries in my own head."

"You could have warned me!" Elena cried, voice raw and scraping. "We could have faced it down together!"

Hill's expression clouded with a clamor of grief and tears. "It doesn't matter. It never would have mattered. I understand what it needs, now. Grief alone gets swallowed down, but it never fully satiates its appetite. It has to eat—to have you, have *someone,* or else its hunger will only get louder and louder until all I'll be able to hear day and night are the cries of my son in its throat!"

The tank water began to suck at her legs, and Elena turned to see rows and rows of teeth emerging from the water, a long, white tendril of a tongue snaking out of the central mouth like an outstretched hand. The hulking thing shivered, and a funeral moan burst from its stomach, an elusive sound that still struck Elena's ears like a cry for help.

On the platform, Hill gave a shuddering breath at the sound. Then, with trembling fingers, she pressed herself to the railing and began to climb.

"It's him, I know it!" she wept, shoes slipping against the wet bars.

"Hill, get down!" Elena called.

"He's in there, he's trapped in its stomach," she cried, stretching out a hand towards the barreleye's fingered tongue. "What am I supposed to do, Elena? How am I supposed to—I can't *listen* to him crying out and do *nothing—*"

"You can't *do* anything!" Elena cried. "You can't—that's why it's so hard! *Hill*!"

Hill's outstretched fingers brushed against the fingered tendrils of the barreleye's tongue.

"Let go!" Elena cried, using one last burst of strength to haul herself up.

Hill sobbed, her eyes hazy in the flash of the alarm.

"I can't," she said, before curling her fingers around the barreleye's tongue and letting it drag her over the rail.

Then the teeth descended, the water swirled, and the glow of the barreleye's gaze fizzled into nothing.

It was 4 a.m., and the sky was streaked with pink and grey when Elena stood on the front steps of the Oceanarium.

Her hands were white. She clenched them tight until the blood began to flow again.

Lin Darrow
About the Author

Lin Darrow holds a PhD in Victorian literature She wrote Slipshine Studio's award-winning sci-fi comic Captain Imani and the Cosmic Chase, as well as Mysteries of the Spectral Hour. She is the author of the webcomic Shaderunners (published by Hiveworks Comics), and has written prose stories and comics for anthologies such as Valor: Cups and Valor: Wands, QueerSciFi, Malaise, Come Together!, Heartwood: Sylvan Tales of Non-Binary Fantasy, Tabula Idem, and Moonlight. Her first novella, Pyre at the Eyreholme Trust, combined noir and fantasy, and was published by Less Than Three Press in 2018. Lin is based in Canada.

Euphoria

Chris Bannor

Nothing ever happened in their quiet town. The adults thought of it as safe, and the tourists thought it was quaint. Andrew Sampson knew better than anyone that it was just boring.

On the weekends he and his friends went to the movies and hung out in the mall parking lot. Sometimes one of them got an older sibling to buy them beer, but usually it was a waste of time.

Tonight was no different than any other. The beer was gone, and the others were just sitting in the back of Jack's truck talking shit about moving out of the country, going away to college or moving to the city.

None of them had any plans to leave home; it was just shit talk and grandstanding. He was tired of it.

"This is lame," he said as he hopped off the back of the truck. "I'm leaving."

"Like you got better places to be, Sampson?" Jack asked.

"Better than here." He walked across the parking lot, towards the fields on Grant Road.

The strip mall disappeared behind him, and the sounds of his friends died away. There wasn't much out past the main street, but it was quiet, and sometimes he liked to think under the stars.

It was here he'd quietly filled out college applications and written scholarship essays. No one thought he was smart enough, but he wanted more from the world than Wolverton would ever offer. Neither of his parents had gone to college, and they were both happy to stay where they were. His older brother worked at the same auto shop his dad did, and his mother did nails over at Barb's Salon. *Special discounts every Saturday if you brought a friend.*

Their whole family was there, and no one ever thought of leaving. He was alone in his desire to see the world, to know more than the small town could offer.

He jumped a fence that separated the street and a local farmer's land. He didn't know the man, but there was a river that ran through his property that Andrew liked to walk alongside. In the summer he'd go out and let his feet rest in the cool water, and maybe swim if he wasn't feeling too sleepy.

He didn't usually take the shortcut across the farmer's property, but tonight he wasn't in the mood to walk around and pick the river up on the other side. The moon was bright tonight, and the path was well lit as he picked his way across the field until it ran into a copse of trees. He followed it further until he was deep in the woods.

The night breeze was cool, the summer warm and lightning bugs dancing over the grass and through the trees. It was a beautiful night, and he was happy enough to be under the moon tonight.

He found the water's edge, noticing the river was bloated tonight. Heavy rains over the last few weeks had raised it high above its usual banks, and if it rained again it might spill out and flood the area. That's what the adults were all talking about.

Small town gossip and weather.

He continued walking, but stopped to pick up a couple of rocks along the path. He rolled them in his hand, leisurely tossing them into the river one-by-one as he let his thoughts drift.

A noise broke the usual sounds of the night and he stopped, listening to see if he heard it again.

Softly, ahead and towards the river, he heard the neigh of a horse. He stilled, the sound repeating again.

Andrew carefully walked ahead, making sure to step lightly so he wouldn't make any noise. He didn't know if it was just a stray horse, but he didn't want to scare whatever it was.

He came to a small clearing by the river to a place where a large rock split the waters. He'd spent hours on that rock, alone or with friends, swimming in the deep pool when the rains had been good.

In the center of the river, resting on the rock, was a dark horse. His hair and coat were so dark they blended in with the night, but they had a sheen that caught the moonlight.

It was ethereal, like the stories of fairies his little sister liked him to read to her at bedtime.

The light of the moon reflected off the water and washed it in an eerie green. Its mane was so long that it brushed the water, the hair dancing around almost like it was alive. Its tail disappeared into the pool, swirling with the gentle current.

He took a step closer, but the leaves under his feet made a crackling sound. The horse snorted and turned its head towards him, though it didn't try to run away. It stared at him, intelligence in its eyes. He'd never seen or heard of a black horse around town. Maybe it was wild and had managed to stay hidden, or maybe it had escaped from some Hell and was enjoying freedom for the first time. It was stuck on the rock though, and he didn't want to leave it there.

It wasn't a good idea to approach a wild animal, but he came back to the horse's eyes. Thoughts were going on behind there, and he believed he could help it.

"Shhhh," he said softly as he neared the river. He kept his hands in front of him and made his way to the water's edge.

The horse whinnied as he stepped into the water, but it didn't move away. It stayed remarkably calm.

"You aren't hurt, are you?" he asked in a gentle tone. "If you are, I'll take care of you, don't worry. We'll get you back across the water so you won't be trapped here."

The horse shook its mane as he stepped knee-deep into the river; another stride and the cold water was up past his waist. The riverbed dropped off then, leaving him to swim across to the rock.

He tried to keep up the soothing sounds as he moved through the water, but there was only so much he could do as the water splashed up into his face. The horse still made no move to get away.

He pulled himself up onto the rock and sat for a moment, catching his breath and letting the horse get used to him. The horse seemed more curious than scared, and it continued to whinny and shake its mane as if encouraging him.

He reached out a hand and carefully patted its nose. He felt a sense of comfort ~~and~~ as he crept forward, gently resting his hand down on the horse's mane. The horse didn't respond to his touch, and he ran his hand down over the wet mane.

"What did you get into?" he asked the horse. The hair that looks so beautiful in the moonlight was slimy to the touch.

He started to pull his hand away, and was surprised when it seemed to be stuck. His fingers were trapped in the fine hairs of the horse's mane.

"Hold still," Andrew said as he tried to pull his hand away. It was still wrapped tight, though it seemed a little tighter.

He pulled again and felt the slime slide further down his wrist. "What the Hell is that?" He stood on the rock, but his hand was stuck fast. It wasn't hair though; hair didn't move like that. It slithered up his forearm to his wrist, gripping him firmly there.

Even as he tried to back away the horse began to stand. He used his other hand to try to pull away, but when he put it on the horse's body to try to brace himself it was quickly covered with the same substance.

"Stupid horse! Let me go!" he yelled this time.

As the horse stood he was lifted off his feet. He looked down to try to find the ground, but was horrified when he saw that the horse's hooves were backward. "What the Hell are you?"

The horse stood up on its back legs and pulled him up behind it. He was tossed into the air, and as the horse's front feet fell back to the rock Andrew landed squarely on its back.

"Let me down!" He yelled as he struggled against the creature's movements. He felt something wrap around his waist, looking down to find that the tail moved the same way the mane did. It slithered around him, holding him tighter.

Old legends flashed in his mind, stories his mother had taught them as children, stories he still read his sister. Stories of fairies and monsters, stories of creatures that roamed the banks of rivers, lakes and oceans.

"Kelpie," he gasped, just as the beast jumped high into the air before plunging into the water.

He felt the push of the current against his body as the kelpie began to swim towards the deeper section of the river. He was held tight to its body even as he continued to fight against it.

The kelpie leaped through the water as if it had firm ground beneath its hooves. Andrew screamed for help, but he was in the middle of nowhere. As they came to the deepest part of the river the kelpie splashed into the water, then rolled.

Andrew was still firmly held, the hair wrapped up past his elbows now. As the water crashed around him he couldn't do anything. He was trapped on its back. He held his breath, but his lungs burned and his body ached for oxygen.

He was caught by the strands, but he pulled hard enough to jerk the kelpie. It reared back and they rolled again, breaking the water's surface. He gulped in deep breaths of air, but the kelpie was already rolling him under again.

He pulled harder with his arms, using legs to try to get leverage against the beast. He used the hair-like reins to try to control the kelpie, but it didn't work. He'd surprised it before, but now it took him back under the water and dove deep.

Andrew kicked at its flank with his heels, but it was no good. The creature took him deeper into the river until he could barely see. Water filled his nostrils, the air escaping his lungs as fluid rushed in.

He couldn't stop himself. His body gasped, trying to get much-needed oxygen, but water was what he breathed in.

He felt a calmness take over his body, a sort of euphoria that he hadn't known before. He'd never been truly happy here, never able to settle. He'd wanted so many things, but this was good too. The quiet of the world was good.

He saw something shimmer in the dark waters, and he saw where they were headed. In the deepest part of the river was a nest. He could see the two small kelpie foals that waited, sharp-toothed and eager for a meal.

Hair-like appendages reached out, more clumsy than their mother's, but they draped over his face and across the rest of his body. They pulled him close as he closed his eyes, filled with the euphoria of water in his lungs.

He felt teeth rend his flesh, but there was no pain. There was no fear or panic anymore. Fate called him to the river tonight and he had met it. The kelpie would feed, and it's young would survive.

He felt his arms released, then the hair around his waist was gone. Andrew was left to the young who pulled him into the nest with them.

The kelpie came up and nudged his head higher, almost as if it knew he was admiring the swirling current of his own death. Needle-like teeth sunk into his neck, and soon he felt the final call of sleep. The water turned red like a fine, dark wine, and he watched as it swirled beautifully with the moonlight streaming into it from above.

The euphoria of death was his fate, and she had never been more spectacular.

Chris Bannor

About the Author

Chris Bannor is a speculative fiction writer who lives in Southern California. Chris learned her love of genre stories from her mother at an early age and has never veered far from that path. Her stories have been published in over two dozen anthologies and range from horror and science fiction, to fantasy, romance, and steampunk.

The Shadow Over Innsmouth High

S.O. Green

Cat found her locker halfway between biology and culture. She seemed to find herself there a lot in life.

It was the problem with starting a new school in the middle of a semester. Everyone else was focused, settled, but there she was, standing in the middle of the corridor with a slip of paper, a combination lock and a bewildered look on her face. Probably giving off all kinds of prey vibes.

She checked the number on the locker against the slip of paper, then pulled it open.

A half-dozen dead fish fell out.

She didn't scream. Her scream reflex was pretty underdeveloped, so she could hold it back like a champ. It didn't stop bile from rising at the sight of those dead, marble eyes and all those slimy, grey scales.

Other students flitted by, trying not to notice the seafood spillage around Cat's black high-tops. Conspicuous by their non-movement, a trio of girls led by a bottle blonde in a too-small Innsmouth High School tee and blue jeans loitered at the corner, trout-pout lips curled into savage sneers.

Predators testing the waters.

Cat grabbed the only fish still in her locker. Her stomach quailed at what she was about to do, but she was the master of her own biology. She stuck the thing in her mouth, felt the scales breaking on her teeth, then bit its fucking head off, making the most gratuitous eye contact she could.

Their self-satisfaction crumpled under the weight of their disgust. Victory. Cat watched them walk away, trying not to vomit.

The moment their backs were turned, she spat, spat, drank soda, spat again and vowed to find a strong acid in chemistry class to use as mouthwash.

"Damn, girl," someone said. "You know how to make a statement."

'Someone' turned out to be a girl Cat hadn't noticed. Black hair tied up in bunches, dark eyes shadowed like bruises, a crop-top printed with what might have been a still from a tentacle hentai and denim cut-offs. Lots of fishnet. Innsmouth High didn't have a uniform, but she might have been pushing it just a little.

"Welcome to Innsmouth, bitch," she grinned.

"Can't let them see that I don't like it," Cat said. "Blood in the water."

"That's the spirit." She clapped Cat on the back. It almost made her puke. "What's your name, Fish?"

"Cat."

The other girl sniggered. "Catfish?"

"It's short for Catriona."

"Ooo, Polish? I like a Pole every now and then." She stretched out against the lockers next to Cat's, easy and boneless, and Cat wondered if there was a single drop of shame in her. "Name's Shell. Y'know, I wish half the inmates were as interesting as you."

"I'm not that interesting."

New girl politics dictated that she keep a lid on 'interesting' for at least the first few months. She didn't want to turn any heads, not in a place where the welcoming committee put dead fish in your locker.

"You say *inmates* like this is a prison."

"It is. Place is a piranha tank, nothing but fences and walls. Screws everywhere. Try to leave and they'll send the cops to bring you back."

"If I decided I was going to escape they couldn't catch me."

Shell's eyes glittered; the tough talk seemed to be impressing her.

"If this *is* a prison shouldn't I pick a fight with the biggest, meanest bitch in here?" Cat asked, slamming her locker shut

She'd clean out the sea water later. "Establish dominance?"

"You don't want to go and do a thing like that," Shell said, putting an arm around her shoulders. "*I'm* the biggest, meanest bitch in here."

The school stank of low tide. Actually, Cat had noticed the whole town stank of low tide. It was an old place, and the buildings were pitted and barnacled like ancient piers. Here and there newer buildings, prefabs and redbricks, popped out of the neighbourhood like garish tourists. Outsiders.

Innsmouth High was no exception. New math building, new science labs and an ancient, cobbled quadrangle that looked like it had once hosted a fish market.

Smelled like it too.

"So, what brings you to Innsmouth?" Shell asked. "No offense, but moving school senior year? Not a smart move."

"I moved here with my mom. She goes where the work is."

"And the work's in *Innsmouth*?"

"Right? Actually, she works in renewable energy. You know those turbines in the harbour?"

"No shit? Pretty cool."

"Wind turbines are cool?"

"Hell yes! She's saving the world like some kind of bad ass Captainess Planet."

"A female captain is still a captain."

"I know that. My mom was a captain."

"Oh yeah? Fishing?"

"Pirate."

They laughed together as Shell led her into the gym.

It had new equipment, but the building itself was old. Cat tried not to imagine grainy, black-and-white footage of men in vests and moustaches vaulting off pommel horses and preparing for war.

It was nice to have a friend on her first day. Frankly, she hadn't dared to hope.

"What's the sport here anyway?" They'd moved for her mom's work, so details about the school had been sketchy. "Football? Lacrosse?"

"Those are landlubber sports, Fish. Swim team's the good shit in Innsmouth. Remember that guy who won gold in, like, *every* water-based event in the Olympics last year? Innsmouth, born and bred. We live for the water. Check it out."

She marched through the gym to a door so new they hadn't even peeled the labels off it. She flung it open, and chlorine grappled with the salt stink in Cat's nostrils.

The pool was an Olympic-sized, state-of-the-art facility, a ten-lane, touch-panelled megalitre of shimmering, blue water. It looked like it had been air-lifted into Innsmouth and dropped into the middle of the school, and it probably cost more money than Cat would ever have in her life.

And it wasn't just the school board that seemed to take swimming seriously. The stands were packed with spectators. Half the school seemed to take their lunch and free periods there.

At poolside a gaggle of girls in swimsuits were reclining on loungers in the humid air and rippling light. Cat saw her blonde friend eyeing her over a pair of sunglasses, and she felt the fish head repeating on her.

"Hey, Shell. Picked yourself up a chum?"

"You know I like a girl who's got a taste for fish, Sally."

If Cat and Sally agreed on nothing else it was their reaction to Shell. Still no sign of that shame.

"One of these days it's going to be just you and me in the water, Shell," Sally said.

Shell looked delighted. "It'll be a bloodbath."

A horn blared. The boys lined up on the diving podiums sprang into the water and surged the length of the pool. Everyone started cheering, their attention immediately captured. Cat admired their form. She'd been a Hell of a swimmer at her old school, but it hadn't really been a big deal.

Here, it seemed like the biggest deal.

The winner was pretty clear. He'd climbed out of the pool before the others had even finished their length. Cat's eyes followed him up and up and up as he rose to his full height. She tried not to stare as he walked over, like an animated statue made of muscle, dark hair and scowling. The swim trunks were little more than a decorative bow.

"What did you think?" he asked. It took Cat a moment to realise he wasn't talking to her.

"I wasn't really watching," Shell said, with a shrug. "Maybe you should try it again."

His scowl deepened. His eyes passed over Cat, and she felt a knot of fear tying itself in her stomach. He marched back to the diving podiums without another word.

"Who the Hell is that?"

"That's Finn," Shell said. "He's mine. Don't worry, we're not exclusive or anything."

She flashed a sharp smile. Cat would spend the rest of the school day trying to figure out what that meant.

"So, how about it?" Shell asked. "Wanna try out?"

Her hands encompassed all that water, and Cat felt the rebellious stirrings of nights spent swimming lengths, trying to find her centre, arms and feet churning the water until exhaustion took over and she clambered out, limbs turned to jelly and head on straight.

"Well," she said, hesitating, "I *did* bring my swimsuit."

She was the last girl out of the locker room. That was her design. She'd been too sedentary during the move, and her costume didn't fit so great anymore. She wished she'd kept up the training; this wasn't how she'd wanted to find out she'd put on weight.

She slunk back to the poolside with her arms crossed. Shell had been limbering up by the pool, but the moment she spotted Cat she stopped and waved.

"Hey, what took you so long?"

"Probably took her a few minutes to shoehorn her ass into that suit," Sally jeered. "You look like a manatee."

Cat scowled. "You ever been slapped by a manatee?"

Shell cackled. It made the words and disparaging looks a little easier to shrug off, knowing the other girl had her back.

They lined up at the podiums. Cat was between Sally and Shell, but it didn't matter. Not when you were swimming. None of it mattered: not the new school, not the smell of seaweed, not the crowd cheering and whooping and screaming above you...just the frothing blue below.

She stretched out, ignoring the way the suit hugged and pinched at her limbs.

The moment the air horn sounded she sprang into the water, then everything was white noise and movement. She didn't have time to think about Sally or Shell, or Finn and his dark, brooding eyes. She was ploughing through the water, and part of her thought that maybe she was going to win.

Then something grabbed her by the ankle and dragged her under. She flailed, trying to kick it off, but it didn't let go. Not until it had sunk its teeth into her calf. She exhaled bubbles and her scream popped on the water's surface.

Then her attacker was gone. She was kicking herself up, lungs burning, brain darkening, leg *aching*.

She burst up into the air and paddled like a dog across the other lanes to the edge. She hadn't even finished her length.

The other girls were rising out of the water, each like Venus clad in black spandex. Shell looked like the overall winner. As she watched Finn wrapped an arm around her and kissed her in a way that wouldn't get PG-13 certification. Sally seemed more interested in Cat than the medal table.

She grinned right at her, and her teeth looked sharp.

Cat's hand quested down to her calf, where a circle of bleeding holes marked the muscle. She winced, her fingers coming away sticky-red.

"Hard luck, Fish!" Sally called. "You need thicker skin if you want to swim in this pool!"

She patched her leg with a sanitary pad and duct tape - always useful - and changed out of her swimsuit before anyone else came into the locker room. It was time to call it a night.

As far as first days went it hadn't been spectacular. She'd bitten a fish in half, made an enemy for life (or at least until graduation) and then gotten mauled when all she'd wanted to do was swim. She slipped out of the building and beat feet home in full retreat.

Maybe she'd just stop going to school. She could pretend like she was leaving in the morning, then spend all day hiding out in the woods because it was the furthest place from that stinking, slate-grey slice of ocean.

One year. That was all it would take to get away. Finals. Graduation. Freedom. So long, Innsmouth.

She swung her bag against the wall under Mom's new coat rack, nailed it to the wall herself, and collapsed against the door. Outside the sound of pounding surf rolled against her back and forth, back and forth. ***Little fish, little fish, let me in.***

She kicked her sneakers off and swore; she'd bled on her insoles.

Mom glided through from the lounge, patrolling like a shark. "Cat, we talked about swears."

"Sorry." Cat looked up at her and blinked. "What are you *wearing*?"

Mom resisted the urge to check over her black minidress. She'd decided, months ago, that she was going to stop apologising for every decision she made. "What's wrong with it?"

"It's kind of...short."

"Yeah, but it goes with the pumps and purse. I'm going out with someone from work. I want to look nice."

'Nice' wasn't the word Cat was thinking of. Actually, she couldn't say that word in front of her mother.

"Glad you made a friend," she said.

Sympathy creased Mom's otherwise immaculate expression. Cat wondered if she'd still look that young when she reached that age. Today alone felt like it had added ten years to her.

"Rough day, huh? Don't worry about it, kiddo. You'll make friends. I know you will."

"I don't know, Mom. The kids in this town are... weird."

She needed a stronger word than that, but she'd already been chided for cussing once. She didn't know how else to describe Shell and her perverse mania, Sally and her needle teeth or Finn and his *eyes*.

It wasn't just them. The school, the town, the ocean slamming against it over and over again...none of it felt right.

"There's something wrong with this place."

Mom sighed. The anguish in her eyes was like a harpoon in Cat's gut. "Don't do this, Cat. Please?"

"Do what?"

"Do that whole 'dramatic teen' thing. I know this wasn't what you wanted, moving out here, but I go where the work is. Do you know how hard it is to get people in this country to give a damn about the planet they're standing on? The people here really seem to get it."

They got *something*. Cat wasn't sure exactly what it was, but the people in Innsmouth weren't anything like the ones she was used to. There was something fishy going on.

"I need you to try. This was supposed to be a fresh start for us, remember? We were going to put it all behind us."

"I know that, but..."

"Is this about your father?"

"God, Mom, no! I literally haven't thought about him once the whole time."

She'd had her hands full with survival.

"Good. We can make it on our own, you know? We don't need him. You'll make friends if you just give it some time. If your mom can do it, so can you." She hesitated, scooping out her phone. "Listen, can you fix dinner? I need to go. I have a...date tonight."

"No shit, really?"

"Yeah, really."

It was probably the free pass on her bad language that did it. That, and the little smile tugging at the corner of

Mom's lips, which, she suddenly noticed, were a darker red and glossier than usual. She was excited. Cat couldn't remember the last time she'd seen her mother legitimately excited. There had been the move; in the car the few possessions they'd deigned to bring with them were packed in two boxes in the trunk, and she'd been laughing and joking and singing along to the radio. Now she was practically glowing.

Cat needed to try. She owed her that, which was why she wasn't going to show her the weeping bandage on the back of her leg. If she did that forget date night, forget everything.

It was a bad idea anyway. Mom couldn't deal with Sally for her; she was going to need to find her own way.

"Have a nice time," she said, and she really hoped the smile looked genuine.

"Thanks. Wish me luck."

Cat didn't dare ask her what she needed luck for. Instead, the moment the door shut out the sound of sea again she stormed up to her room and thumped her face in her pillow.

"I don't wish I was dead. I am not a cliché."

Cat wasn't a cliché, but her life was turning into one. Someone tapped on her window.

It was Shell, sitting in the boughs of the tree outside. Cat regretted picking this room, even if it *was* the one that didn't overlook the water.

"What the Hell are you doing?" she asked, once she'd slapped back the bolts and Shell had unfolded into her room. She waited, hands on hips, as the other girl assessed her living space. The little nod seemed to denote satisfaction.

"Visiting."

"How the Hell did you know where I lived? Did you follow me home?"

"I was worried about you."

"What you meant to say was 'yes.'"

It occurred to Cat that no one had ever been so concerned about her well-being that they'd stalked her before.

"You okay, Fish?"

"No, I'm not fucking okay. Didn't you see the *bite mark* on my leg?"

"What do you want me to say? Swimming gets competitive around here."

Cat glared at her. Was that it? Limping, wincing, struggling home, and she was getting a pep talk about the dangers of competitive sports?

"Besides, some girls like to get bitten."

"Probably not by a girl they hate."

"What about by a girl they like?"

It was worrying how much time Cat spent in mute disbelief around this girl.

"For what it's worth, I was pretty sure you were gonna smoke her." Shell nudged her. "Smoked Salmon. Get it?"

"Her name's *Salmon*?"

Cat hesitated. No wonder that girl was so pissed. Maybe she had no right to judge.

"Look, Fish. Don't worry about her, okay? She's trying to make out like she's a whale in a koi pond, but she's a minnow like the rest of them. Seriously, you can handle her." Her grin faltered a little, and what might have been a blush, but could just as easily have been a bruise, passed across her cheeks. "Besides, I like you. Finn likes you too. He told me so."

"He told you he liked me?" Cat asked dubiously.

"He said you looked strong; that's basically the same thing. Oh, and he said you looked good in a swimsuit. Trust me, that's practically Byron for him."

It was Cat's turn to blush. She thought about those fearsome eyes again, and all that solid muscle, and about how he and Shell weren't exclusive, apparently.

"You want to come and hang out with us?" Shell asked, loitering by the window. "There's this place we like to go sometimes, down by the water. A lot of the kids around here go there to hang out. Want to see it?"

She wanted to say no. She wanted to shower, eat and sleep, not necessarily in that order, and she never wanted to be 'down by the water' again. It had been a rough day, and the bloated sun hadn't even given up spilling its grey light yet.

I need you to try.

"Yeah," she sighed. "Sounds great. But can we use the front door?"

They walked down towards the coast, following the cobbled road through Old Innsmouth. Cat stared up at the sun-bleached seaweed on the rooftops and wondered how it got there. She looked out over the ocean. The sun was perched somewhere behind her, bouncing off the rippling waves like a ping-pong ball into a beer cup. The wind turbines they'd already erected spun ceaselessly in the wind whipping across the bay. They were the most modern thing for miles; as far as Cat could see there wasn't even a lighthouse around here.

Those bleak, colourless surroundings were ancient and held untold secrets, but even they were being dragged into the future to play a part in the modern world.

Thick mist was rising by the time they reached the end of the cobbled road. They descended a worn, coastal path to the base of a cliff that overlooked the sea. This felt like the stretch of rocky beach where bodies washed up after falling, where shipwrecks were usually found with skeletons lashed to the wheel.

Where they'd find poor, stupid Catriona, the girl who hadn't just chased dinner with an early night.

There was a cave at the bottom of the cliff. Shell turned, waggling her eyebrows, and Cat couldn't tell what she was supposed to be excited about.

She wasn't excited, she was terrified.

"You want to go in *there*?"

"It's fine. We hang out here, like, all the time. You'll love it. Wait until you see what's inside."

She skipped into the darkness, oblivious to the fact that she'd just hit Cat's problem right on the nose. She *couldn't* see inside.

She breathed deep and took baby steps into the shadows. She expected to be blind, but her eyes adjusted almost immediately. The black lifted, and eerie, green light started to pulse from the walls with the slow, steady rhythm of a heartbeat.

Finn was looming next to her like a tall, angry-looking statue. Cat jumped away from him, clutching her chest. He didn't smile, but she thought she saw a twinkle of amusement in his eyes.

"I told you she'd come," Shell said. "She wants this just as much as we do."

"Wants what?" Cat demanded. She kept her distance from them and tried to remind herself that a wounded animal was more dangerous, even if she didn't *feel* more dangerous.

"We got you a present."

Shell waved to a mural painted on the wall in what looked like squid ink. It depicted something massive rising out of the water over a town that might have been Innsmouth. It held out a hand, and the people fell to their knees in rapturous worship. Half of them turned to fish and swam away; the others only turned into half-fish.

There was, predictably, a stone altar under the mural. Someone was tied to it with mooring rope.

Actually, it wasn't someone. It was Salmon.

"What the shitting Hell is going on here?"

"We're tired of Sally," Shell said with a shrug. She'd produced a curled and curiously-patterned blade from somewhere, and was tossing it back and forth between her hands. "They gave her a gift, but she's petty and mean. There are better uses for the gift, and we've decided that you'll do a better job. Plus, this way you can get even with her for being such a bitch to you all day. Won't that be nice?"

Cat looked at Sally. They'd stuffed seaweed in her mouth as a gag. Her eyes were wide, terrified. Not laughing now.

"Give me the knife."

"That a girl!"

Shell grinned as she handed Cat what she could only describe as 'the ritual knife'.

The only thing worse than being kicked by a swimmer was being kicked by a swimmer who'd trained in karate for five years, which was why Shell went down like a concussed brick when Cat roundhouse kicked her in the jaw.

Finn lunged for her. She aimed the knife at his throat, and he stopped short of impaling himself on the blade. If looks could kill...

"Get the fuck away from me." He didn't back down, but neither did she. "Come any closer and I'm going to give you a brand-new set of gills, fish-boy."

He finally smiled.

She whipped the blade behind her, slicing the ropes off Sally's wrists. It was so easy, and the thought of how the knife would have pared her flesh down to bone left her nauseated. She waited while Sally pulled her feet free and retched out the seaweed, then Cat grabbed her wrist and ran.

Only the way she'd come was no longer the way out. The cave twisted, and pretty soon they were lost in the darkness. Somewhere she could hear Shell laughing.

Cat stopped to fumble out her phone. When she finally got the flashlight switched on she realized they weren't at the entrance. They were standing on a narrow, stone walkway around a huge, underground lake.

Thoughts of the Innsmouth High pool came unbidden into her mind. What lurked beneath those still waters?

"What the Hell did you do?" Sally croaked.

Cat scoffed. "You're welcome."

"Bitch, we have to go to school with those lunatics!"

"Guess I'm bringing a knife to show-and-tell tomorrow."

"You're dead in the water, Fish. Don't you realize that? This is Innsmouth! You don't fuck with this cave or that knife."

"Would you rather I killed you? Because that was the other option on the table."

She didn't get the chance to find out if death was the preferable option. A hand wrapped around Sally's mouth and nose, wrenching her back into the darkness. Cat could just make out the silhouette of someone massive and grim in the shadows. Shell reappeared. She'd bled all over her hentai shirt.

"You shouldn't be here," she said. Her eyes weren't on Cat, they were on the water. "It's dangerous."

"More dangerous than a pair of knife-wielding maniacs?"

"*Much* more dangerous. We just want a taste, but *it* will swallow you whole."

"What the fuck are you talking about?"

"Come back with us. We forgive you. It's a lot to take in, we know, and everyone gets nerves their first time. But you belong here, with us. Finish what you started! Then you can be part of the family, you and your mom."

"Don't talk about my mom!"

Shell was coming closer, hands raised to pacify. Cat didn't want to be pacified. She wanted to get out of that cave, run all the way home, grab her mom and drive, drive, drive out of Innsmouth. She wouldn't even look in the rear-view until they were in a land-locked state.

She took a step back.

Too close to the edge.

Something wound tight around her ankle. She let out a strangled scream that turned to a gurgle, and then she was nothing but a cluster of bubbles popping gently on the surface. Pop, pop, pop.

Her phone slipped from her fingers, tumbling, screen still bright. Tentacles bristling with suckers swayed at the edges of the light, then the water found the battery and it fizzled out, plunging her into the black.

She sank down, down, down, and Cat was reminded of burning lungs and a darkening brain and an aching leg as she kicked, kicked, kicked because she'd been here before, hadn't she?

Only the waters hadn't been so deep.

She hacked into the meat of the thing wrapped

around her leg. It was slimy under her hand. It bled, but it didn't seem to care. It wouldn't let go. Its sucker pads had chewed through denim and into her leg, seeking the wound Sally had left back when they'd been enemies eight hours ago.

She hacked again, arms burning, tiring. The thing let go and a screech reverberated through the water and through her. Everything was blood, and all Cat could do was kick to the surface, trying not to die.

She saw the light shining on the surface, and the thought of that first, glorious breath sustained her long enough to burst up and breathe and retch and spit and then breathe some more.

Oxygen. Sweet, sweet oxygen.

She wasn't in the cave anymore. She'd been dragged out into the open ocean, which meant that, somewhere under her high tops, was the creature with the tentacles that had tried to drag her to a watery grave. There were eyes down there, watching. A mouth, hungering.

She swam for the craggy shoreline, still clutching the knife in her hand.

Cat dragged herself out of the water and realized she didn't know where she was. She followed the coastal road back towards town because she needed to know how to get home. Her phone was gone; she'd have to wait until Mom came back before she could leave.

She clutched the blade tight. Let them try something.

She was shivering. Why? Cold? Blood loss? The knowledge that, at some point tonight, she was probably going to have to stab someone?

The water trail she was leaving diminished to squelching footprints, stained with the blood from her ripped leg. Every other step was like being shocked in the hip. She felt heavy, and not just because she was full of liquid.

Car headlights threw her shadow on the asphalt ahead. It looked like seaweed had become sentient. She turned, shielding her eyes, and saw Mom gaping at her through the windshield. Cat hadn't cried in years, but she thought maybe today would be the day.

She stood like an idiot until the car pulled alongside her. Mom jumped out. Mom's friend looked on, concerned. Quite a catch by anyone's standards. Dark hair, dark eyes. Lean, athletic physique. Related to someone? Or were these just the specimens Innsmouth produced?

"Cat, what happened? What are you doing out here this late? Where the Hell did you get that knife?"

"I had a bad day at school," she said. The laugh that followed sounded maybe just a little hysterical.

"Come on. Get in the car."

Mom steered her into the backseat by the shoulders. Cat mutely accepted, glaring at their driver, daring him to try something. She had a knife.

Mom sat beside her and said, "Take us to the cave."

"Wha-?"

"Cat, I told you this was a fresh start for us. You need

to go back to the cave and finish what you started. Do you understand?"

She grabbed the knife by the blade. Cat felt it cut flesh and let go with a scream. Mom didn't seem to care. She tucked the knife away and wiped the cut on her soiled dress. The blood looked and smelled like red seawater.

She put a hand on Cat's shoulder and bled on her already-sopping tee. Her eyes implored.

"This place will be good for us," she said, bubbles popping at the corner of her mouth. "I need you to try, like I'm trying."

S.O. Green

About the Author

Simone Oldman Green is a genre-fluid writer and editor living in the Kingdom of Fife with husband, John. Author of over 70 published works with imprints including Dragon Soul Press, Black Hare Press and Eerie River Publishing. They also won 3rd Place in the British Fantasy Society's Short Story Contest 2018. Writer, vegan, martial artist, gamer, occasionally a terrible person (but only to fictional people). They thrive on the unusual, which might explain why there are so many cats.

Reef Encounter

Chris Hewitt

Ali stretched over the side of the boat and ran her hand through the water. Bioluminescent plankton slipped through her fingers, leaving long, green streamers trailing in their wake. She loved the reef, especially on moonless nights, and now that they'd cleared the light pollution of Innisfail the constellations were clear to see. She sighed as her fingers entwined with the plastic rings of a discarded beer pack. How far would they have to go to escape all the town's pollution? Unwinding the trash from her fingers she wished she could wave a wand and rake all the toxic waste from the struggling reef.

"Ali, we're here. Suit up, Sis," said Steve, climbing down from the bridge as the drone of the boat's engine cut out. He ruffled her hair on his way to check the oxygen tanks. A strapping six-feet of bronzed muscle, Steve, or Stevo to his mates, fancied himself a professional surfer. He was never happier than when he was hanging ten, although his chances of going pro had slipped away several seasons ago along with the discs in his back.

Kate appeared from below deck, sleep-styled blonde hair snaking across her face in the whisper of wind. Stretching and yawning, she blew the loose locks aside. "We here?"

Ali held up the tangle of plastic.

"I'll take that as a yes. Bloody tourists," said Kate, tying back her errant hair. "I'd like to shove that up..."

With a swoosh, Doug slid down the ladder, landing with a thud. "Right, ladies. Are you ready for the biggest orgasm of your life?"

Kate and Ali rolled their eyes. Doug owned the boat; he was Steve's best mate, and he scratched a living chartering the cruiser for summer fishing trips far off the reef in the deep water. Years in the sun had aged him well beyond his forty years. Leathery, tanned skin and greasy, greying hair made him look sixty. Kate pushed past him to retrieve her diving kit. "Like last weekend? Promises, promises."

"Hey, it happens to us all. You wouldn't hold that against a fella, would you?"

"I wouldn't hold anything against you," mumbled Ali, spitting in her goggles.

"Or any fella if the..."

Doug gasped as an oxygen tank to the thorax knocked the wind out of his sails. Any idea of protesting vanished, along with Steve's easy-going surfer dude persona. No one messed with Ali with her big brother around.

"Thanks, mate!" Doug gasped, sliding on the tank and shooting daggers at Ali. Ali smirked back at him and adjusted her wetsuit.

"If we don't get the monster of all money shots this time I ain't coming back," said Kate, pulling on her flippers. She had a knack of defusing a situation, having plenty of practice teaching at Innisfail East State school.

Doug dropped the boat's anchor. "Trust me, I got a good feeling. Tonight's the night!"

The friends readied their diving gear, hoping Doug had timed it right for once. Predicting the yearly reef spawning was an inexact science, but once a year in mid-November, when the temperature and the tides aligned, the largest organism on the planet indulged in an oceanic orgy. For twenty frenetic minutes every coral polyp, starfish and clam across the reef orgasmed in one of nature's most spectacular events. In all the years Ali had lived and dived around Innisfail she'd never seen it; few townsfolk had. Doug had, and he never stopped talking about it.

The way he described it, it was a winter wonderland of jizz.

With a third splash Ali stood alone on the boat, checking over her diving kit one last time. She could see the bubbles of her friends as they descended to the reef twenty meters below. During the day the location was a popular tourist destination, thanks to its proximity to the continental slope that always ensured a wide variety of sea life. The ideal spot, in theory, to see this epic wonder of the natural world.

Ali adjusted the straps on her oxygen tank and waddled to the boat's stern, almost forgetting her flashlight. Latching the large flashlight's strap on her belt she leaped into the darkness. She hated that first step into the void. Thanks to the movie Jaws some part of her brain always screamed *'shark'*, but as the flurry of bubbles subsided, and she could see the others' lights below, she relaxed and swam down to join them.

Reaching the rocky reef she returned a thumbs-up from Steve as she came to rest beside Kate. The Great Barrier Reef never slept, and night saw a rainbow of critters flitting in and out of their artificial lights; vivid, primary colors were made all the more brilliant by the surrounding darkness.

Kate grabbed Ali's arm and pointed to a crevice, and Ali's heart skipped a beat at the sight of the most feared monster on the reef. The blue ring octopus was no larger than her thumb, but that didn't stop it claiming at least one foolish tourist every season. They were lured to their death by its mesmerizing, iridescent rings and devastating cuteness. *At least with a shark you stood a chance*, thought Ali, watching the tiny, tentacled terror slink away in search of another hapless day-tripper.

For half an hour the friends explored the familiar reef. There was always something new to see, no matter how often they dived. But, after forty minutes, their oxygen and patience ran low. Kate signaled to Doug, using a hand gesture that would have earned one of her students detention. She tapped at her chunky dive watch, and Doug shrugged. Ali sighed, creating a long column of bubbles. It looked like they'd miss the spawning for another year.

Ali had completed her preparations to swim to the surface when she saw Steve waving his flashlight at a stunning, red, tree-like coral covered in spidery threads. As they watched the currents teased the fine filaments into long strands that stretched out several meters. All around them the crystal-clear waters had turned opaque, almost milky. Ali shined her torch at Kate, and her friend appeared to do something akin to a jig. A muted scream of excitement reached Ali's ears.

It was happening.

Doug's description of the spawning proved to be spot-on. Within a minute it seemed like a blizzard descended over the reef, and Ali lost sight of her friends. Only their dingy flashlights backlighting the flurry of eggs and ejaculate assured her she was not alone. If it wasn't for those lights, she could have believed she'd been transported to another world, a realm of silence, save for the sound of her breathing punctuated by the gurgling regulator.

Ali felt something slide past her cheek and panicked, clutching a hand to her face. Other things slipped past in the darkness, brushing her arm, stomach and thigh; her flashlight only catching the fleeting shadows of her attackers as they weaved in and out of the oceanic orgy. She'd lost track of her friends' reassuring lights, and was about to kick for the surface when a silvery-yellow wall loomed out of the gloom, glaring at her with a thousand eyes. The cyclone of yellowfin goatfish threatened to tear the goggles from her face in their feeding frenzy. Enveloped by the circling fish, Ali's fear melted into wonder as she floated in the eye of the maelstrom.

Ali giggled with glee as hunting tuna darted in and out of view, causing the school to twist and turn in spectacular, undulating patterns. She could almost forgive Doug for all his bullshit as she ran her fingers along the shimmering edge of the shoal. He'd delivered a once-in-a-lifetime experience.

Training her light on a knot of thrashing goatfish, she watched four large tuna launch themselves towards her, narrowly missing her head, and what pursued the fleeing fish turned her blood to ice. Ali screamed as the reef shark bore down on her, its razor-sharp teeth flashing. The shark had a similar reaction, and it was all it could do to miss her. In its dogged pursuit of the tuna the shark's pectoral fin slapped against Ali's leg as it vanished back into the night. That was enough for Ali.

The fear of larger predators had her kicking for the surface. Except, to her horror, she went nowhere. Instead, something coiled itself around her ankle and pulled her down into the depths. In the inky gloom long arms slid around her torso and she saw two glinting eyes staring at her. Bringing her flashlight to bare, she found herself face-to-face with Kate; sheer joy in her friend's eyes as she hugged Ali and squealed in her ear. Reaching down Kate clicked off the light, and the friends stared up into a spinning, pulsating, bioluminescent galaxy. The friends bathed in the afterglow of the spent reef until, out of air, they swam for the surface.

Doug and Steve were already aboard when Kate and Ali surfaced. Steve helped them out of the water, and before they could unbuckle their tanks Doug appeared, beaming. "Well, ladies?"

Kate wiped her glazed face. "Now that's what I call a money shot!"

"Didn't I tell you?" said Doug, high-fiving Kate. He turned to Ali, but she left him hanging, shaking her head wryly.

"Turns out you're not totally full of shit," she grinned.

"As long as you're satisfied," Doug winked.

"Yuck!" said Steve, a long strand of gloopy goo dangling from his fingers. "How do we get this spunk off?"

"It's good for your skin. Nature's conditioner, right?" said Kate, grinning at Ali.

"Oh yea, better than that expensive retinol serum the stars use."

"Really?" Doug asked, rubbing the gunk between his fingers.

Kate sniggered. "Oh yea, it'll take ten years off you.

All those long protein molecules and stuff."

Doug dabbed at his face. "Cool."

Steve moved to intervene, but the glares from Kate and Ali warned him off. "You know he's got a thing about his looks," he hissed at the girls.

"Hey, it might work," said Kate, washing the worst from her hair. "Isn't that what you lads always say?"

Steve shook his head and smirked. "You two are terrible."

While Doug piloted the cruiser back to Innisfail the others cleaned themselves off. Over a fair few beers, they compared notes about their incredible reef encounter.

Kate looked at her watch, sighing, and pounded the car's horn. A moment later Ali appeared, falling out of the front door and stumbling down the path towards the car.

"Christ, you look like shit," said Kate, as Ali slumped into the passenger seat.

"Don't," Ali moaned, turning down the radio and curling up. Her sunglasses did little to block the early Monday morning sun.

Kate reached over and unlatched the glove compartment to reveal a bottle of vodka. "Hair of the Dog?"

Ali groaned and kicked the glovebox closed.

"So, a good family get-together then?" Kate asked, a little too loudly.

"Ugh, I don't remember."

Ali remembered the BBQ starting early, even if she couldn't remember having quite so much family. The few fragments of Sunday she could recall came tainted with guilt or shame; things may have gotten out of hand. Ali remembered Steve throwing a blanket over her before throwing up behind the sofa, and she shuddered at the realization he was unlikely to have cleaned up his mess.

"What time did it finish?"

Ali shook her head, regretting the move instantly. "Too late."

As the car pulled away Ali wound down the window, hoping the fresh air might help the situation, and removing any barriers if her stomach followed through on its threats.

"I'm still buzzing after Saturday. It was incredible," said Kate, turning out of the road and heading for school. Ali nodded; at least those amazing memories remained intact. Why couldn't her life be like that all the time? Most of the time she loved being a librarian, but not today. Today she'd find a dark corner to sort books, some lowly shelf where the kids wouldn't find her before midday.

"Oi!" said Kate, waking Ali in the parking lot. "Let's get you some coffee."

"Coffee," intoned Ali. The cure-all for all her woes. She fell out of the car, and Kate helped her stagger towards the school.

"Okay, settle down," said Kate, closing the classroom door. She'd left Ali, coffee untouched, face-down at her desk in the library; she'd have until the end of first period before the kids would find her.

"I hope you've all had a great weekend, and that you've completed your homework."

The mention of homework elicited a collective groan from the class. Kate noted the usual worried faces as she sat down and opened the register. Reaching for a pen she knocked over her cup of coffee, much to the amusement of her students.

"Okay, okay, settle down," barked Kate, wiping the coffee from the sodden books. As she dried off her hand a quick headcount confirmed everyone to be present; she'd do the paperwork later. "Right, let's pick up where we left off. What can you tell me about photosynthesis?"

Kate pushed on through the lesson, engaging the kids in the intricacies of the biochemical process. Twenty minutes in and she was feeling a little odd: shaky, with a raging thirst. She regretted skipping breakfast as she wrote on the old blackboard. "So, we have the sun," Kate croaked, sketching a large circle. "And a plant, with its leaves and roots." Hand trembling, she drew a sketchy looking shrub. "And of course..."

As she went to write the word 'water' a sound like fingernails dragged across a board screeched through the classroom.

"Ewww!" cried the kids.

"S... sorry," said Kate, glaring at the chalk before

turning her attention to the white dust along the edge of her hand. She tried to wipe away the chalky mark, but it wouldn't come off. Kate scrutinized the discoloration, running her finger along its rough edge, feeling tiny bumps.

"Are you okay, Miss?"

Kate continued examining the hard skin on her hand until, stifling a scream, she buried her fist into her armpit.

"Miss?"

"Yes, I'm err..." Kate, looked up at the clock. "Break time. Let's take an early break."

The class didn't need a second invitation, and within a minute Kate was alone, clutching her arm. As she pulled her hand from her armpit she prayed it had been a figment of her imagination. It wasn't. There, along her hand, several delicate, fleshy tendrils wiggled and waved from pits in her skin.

Kate rushed to the toilet, clutching her hand. The sight of her pallid reflection in the rest room mirror sent a cold chill down her spine as she held her hand under the faucet. The cold water flowed over her callused skin, exploding every pitted pore into a wiggling, rosy tentacle. Her skin became mottled, hard, before erupting into new pulsating polyps. Kate snatched her hand from the sink and, seizing a handful of paper towels, she patted the throbbing extremity. As the towels mopped up the moisture the polyps retreated into their fleshy hidey-holes. She could still feel them wiggling under her skin as she applied more towels. An overpowering smell of ammonia made her eyes water; a smell that had little to do with the toilets. Kate didn't need her degree in biology to spot the similarities with the coral polyps they'd...

"Shit, Ali!" she cried, sprinting from the toilet.

An almighty crash announced Kate's arrival into the library, and Ali's head shot up. "What? Shhh, this is a library."

"You're okay!"

"Hardly," said Ali, reaching for the lukewarm coffee.

"No!" cried Kate, knocking the paper cup from her friend's hand; sending the coffee spilling across the floor.

"What the fuck, Kate!?"

Kate laid her hand on the table. "Look!"

Ali tried to focus, rubbing sleep from her eyes. "What!? What am I looking at?"

Kate pulled back the paper towels to reveal her blotchy hand.

"Ooh, nasty," said Ali, examining Kate's hand before rummaging in the table draw. "I've got some moisturizer for that."

"Watch!" said Kate, spitting on her hand.

Eager polyps unleashed their moisture hungry tendrils and Ali sprung from her chair, back-peddling from the table. "What the Hell is that!?"

"I don't know. It appeared when I was teaching."

Ali retrieved a pencil from the drawer and poked at the pink tendrils. "The skin looks like some kind of infection. But these…" she said, as the tendrils wrapped around the writing implement. "These are something else." It took a firm tug before the polyps gave up their prize. "They look like the corals from the other night."

Kate nodded, re-bandaging her hand. "I know. You ever heard of anyone getting infected by coral?"

Ali shook her head and laughed. "No, I've never heard of anyone getting an STD from a reef."

Kate pouted before nodding at Ali's hand. "Try yours."

Ali looked down at her hand, her mouth as parched as any desert.

"Here," said Kate, grabbing her friend's wrist and helpfully spitting in her palm. Ali closed her eyes and looked away. When nothing happened, she opened an eye and glanced at her hand before snatching it back. She breathed a sigh of relief, until she saw Kate's face. Tears welled in her friend's eyes and a teardrop trickled down her cheek, its progress marked by a reddening of her skin. Ali pulled up her sleeve and wiped the tear away, but not before a pair of polyps erupted on Kate's cheek.

Kate leaned into Ali and buried her face in her friend's shoulder to stop the tears.

"It'll be okay," said Ali, hugging Kate and wondering what to do with her sodden hand. As Kate sobbed Ali patted her friend on the back. When next Kate looked up Ali struggled to hide her disgust at the polyps popping up around her puffy eyes. "Let's get you some help."

In the school office Ali spun a story about Kate's

sudden food poisoning; one look at Kate's face and the principal had little doubt. Ali offered to drive Kate to the hospital - much quicker than calling an ambulance.

The wind had picked up as they rushed across the carpark to Kate's car. The blue skies belied the chaos the first storm of the season would bring. Five minutes later Ali drove Kate's car down McGowan Drive towards the hospital. Kate sat in the passenger seat rubbing her hand, chewing her lip.

Ali glanced over at Kate. She'd not said a word since they'd gotten in the car. Several new sores ringed her friends' nostrils, and a small polyp lashed its tendrils at the corner of Kate's mouth. Ali struggled to pull her gaze from the probing, thirsty strands. Couldn't Kate feel them? Ali shivered at the thought and jammed her foot to the floor, the car lurching forward.

"Shit, Steve!" cried Ali, glancing at her watch. "He'll be heading to the beach. If he's...oh, God..."

Steve never missed an opportunity to catch the big waves, and the approaching stormfront guaranteed monster breakers.

Kate pulled out her phone and tapped Steve's speed dial; the call went to voicemail. "Hi, you're through to Steveo. I'm on surfabout at the moment. Sah, leave a message, and I'll catch you on the flip side."

"Steve, it's Kate and Ali. I know this is going to sound

crazy, but stay out of the water. Until you see us stay away from water."

Ali leaned over. "It's not a joke, bro. I need to speak to you. Don't go in the water!"

Kate hung up, and Ali banged the steering wheel. "Bloody idiot! He never turns his phone on."

"What about Doug?" said Kate, dialing his number. The two-tone beep signaled an invalid number. "Have you got another number for Doug?"

Ali threw her phone over, and Kate scanned down her phonebook. "It's the same number."

Ali's hands curled tighter around the steering wheel. "I'll get you to hospital, and then..."

"No, Doug's on the way. Five minutes won't make any difference."

Ali would have argued, but Kate grabbed the wheel.

"Right, here!" Kate cried, steering them down the slip road towards the dock.

The car skidded to a stop at the harbour, and Ali could see Doug's boat moored up in its usual spot. There was no sign of Doug himself.

"At least he's not at sea," Ali consoled herself as she exited the vehicle. "Stay here. I'll check if he's onboard."

Kate nodded, her smile failing to hide her pain as she cradled her twitching arm.

"Doug!" shouted Ali, walking down the boardwalk.

As Ali climbed aboard, she could see the small hatch that led to the cabin was open. Doug had to be around. “Oi, Doug?!”

Ali made her way down into the compact living area; her eyes taking a second to adjust to the dim cabin. It was as she remembered, even down to the empty beer cans they’d knocked back on Saturday. Doug lived on the boat. His boudoir, as he liked to call it, was at the bow. A wooden, slatted door blocked any view into his den. “Duggy! Are you back there?”

Silence. Ali turned to leave, but a guttural groan stopped her in her tracks, and she stared at the door. “Doug, is that you? Stop messing about.”

The strange noise repeated, louder and with urgency. “Doug!?” cried Ali, racing across the cabin. The handle turned in her hand, but the door refused to open. The rasping, gasping sound became a pitiful cry as Ali shoved her shoulder against the door. “It’s stuck!”

Taking a step back she launched herself at the door, and it yielded a little. The overpowering stench of ammonia escaped through the gap, choking her. Ali took a few steps back and gasped down a deep breath before throwing her full weight forward. The door flew open. Ali fell into the darkened cabin, slipping on the slick surface. Staggering to her feet, she fell against the wall; her probing fingers dancing over a peculiar, slimy surface until they found the light switch.

The lights flickered on, illuminating a rocky grotto, every surface covered with a calcium veneer. The slimy things wrapped around her fingers, now visible, were tentacles that snaked from a myriad of polyps studding the wall. Fine, yellow capillaries laced every pitted surface, and she traced the filigree of veins towards the bunk, stifling a scream at the sight of Doug encased in the calcium cancer. A network of throbbing, yellow veins emanated from his nose and mouth as his face squirmed. Against every instinct Ali reached out a trembling hand. "Doug?"

Whatever remained of Doug didn't react as Ali inched across the cabin. As she reached the bunk the gurgling stopped, and she froze. "Doug?"

Ali leaned in closer, and this time she heard him.

"Water," Doug hissed.

Ali gasped. "Water? I can't. This stuff, it..."

Doug's hand shot out with a crack and grasped Ali's arm. Tight, razor-sharp, pockmarked skin grated against her flesh. "Please, you're hurting me."

"Water!" he repeated in a long, rattling breath.

Ali squirmed, trying to free herself, but Doug's vice-like grip only tightened. Fearing he'd break her arm Ali scanned the cabin, searching for what he demanded, but the spreading corruption had left nothing. She felt warm blood trickle down her arm, and she tried again to lever his rock-like fingers from her arm.

"Ali? Doug?" Kate called out.

"Kate!" cried Ali, both relieved and horrified to see her friend appear at the hatch. "Stay there, don't come any closer."

"Why? What's... "

"I need water."

Kate stared at her friend in disbelief and held up her hand. "You gotta be joking, right? I can't..."

Ali cried out as a wave of agony shot up her arm. "Please, Kate!"

The pain in her friend's voice spurred Kate on, and rummaging through the cupboards she found an unopened two-liter bottle of lemonade. "Will this do?"

Ali nodded, and Kate launched the bottle down the cabin, the lemonade bottle bouncing across the floor before coming to rest just out of Ali's reach.

"I'll get it," said Kate.

"No," barked Ali, waving her back and stretching out a foot to drag the container close. Holding the bottle between her thighs she twisted the top off in a fountain of foam, jamming the bottle into Doug's gaping mouth. The effervescing liquid fizzed down Doug's gullet and he convulsed, threatening to tear Ali's arm off. She cried out, Kate moving to help her.

"Stay there!" Ali screamed, and with one last, desperate yank pulled herself clear, staggering towards the exit.

"Ali, what's going on? What is that?"

Ali looked back at the bunk and saw a huge, pulsating mass explode from Doug's mouth; his head arching back as the large, twisting tentacle lashed out. Ali had seen enough. "Go! We've got to go!"

Heart hammering, Ali dragged Kate back into the sunlight and along the boardwalk to the car.

"You're bleeding," said Kate as they buckled up.

Ali wasn't listening. She sat shaking at the wheel, staring back at the boat.

"Where's Doug?" asked Kate, touching her friend on the arm. "Ali!"

Ali winced at her friend's touch. With adrenaline pumping she started the car. She had to run, to flee from the sickening terror. The stench of ammonia still hung thick in her nostrils.

"Ali! Did you see Doug?"

"I... he... he's gone," Ali stuttered, reversing the car and heading for the highway. Glancing in the rear-view mirror she half expected to see Doug, or the creature he'd become, chasing them.

"What do you mean 'gone'?"

"He's dead, and Steve could be next. I have to get to him," she said, not taking her eyes from the road as a pick-up truck blared its horn and swerved to avoid them.

"Dead? How? How did he die!?" shouted Kate, holding out her hand. "It was this, wasn't it? He died because of this!"

Ali nodded as she took the road along the coast to Etty Bay.

"Ali, slow down," cried Kate, as the car scraped the barrier that separated the road from the cliff edge.

Up ahead Ali could see the long, golden curve of the beach. A handful of surfers rode the waves whipped up by the approaching storm, and Ali tried to spot Steve among the distant, dancing dots.

"Try him again," said Ali.

Kate pulled out her phone and dialed. The call directed through to voicemail again.

"Fuck it! Try texting him."

Ali honked the horn and slowed the car behind a dawdling RV intent on taking photos of the sweeping bay. When she glanced back across at Kate her friend was sobbing, her fingers scratching at her smartphone. "I... I can't...."

Kate bit at the hard skin on her fingertips, and Ali reached across and held her trembling hand, feeling the spreading cold, hardening skin. "It's okay. We'll be there in a minute. Keep an eye out for his van." She squeezed Kate's hand. "It's going to be okay."

Kate nodded and wiped the tears from her face.

Dark clouds gathered in the distance as they pulled into the parking lot.

"There! Behind the hut," said Kate, pointing to the back of Steve's campervan. Ali stopped the car and jumped out, running over and pounding on the VW's windows. "Steve! Steve!"

She tried the locked doors and peered in through the window at the empty interior. Steve's surfboard was missing from the roof rack, and Ali ran to where the beach started as she looked along the length of golden sand.

"I can't see him," cried Ali, scanning up and down the expanse of sand.

"There," said Kate, catching her up and pointing to a figure carrying a surfboard.

"Steve!" screamed Ali, sprinting after her brother.

She'd never run so fast in her life, despite the soft sand's efforts to slow her progress. Her world became a long, dark tunnel, and at its end her brother ignored her breathless pleas to stop. She couldn't stop him walking into the lapping waves. As she neared, she could see the wetness of the sand, and she roared.

"Stop!"

A wave of relief crashed over her as Steve turned. Seeing her he smiled. "Hey, Sis! What's up?"

Ali's wave of relief turned into a wave of dread at the sight and sound of the large breaker hissing its way up the shore. "Run!" she screamed, but it was already too late. The wave broke over Steve's ankles as it bubbled up the beach.

"What?" asked Steve.

Ali tiptoed backward as the wave slid towards her, and as it ebbed, she looked at her brother's bemused expression. "Thank God, you're okay?"

"Err, yea?" said Steve, looking around perplexed. "Are you tripping, Sis?"

Ali laughed and fell to her knees, exhausted. "I hope so," she panted, looking back over her shoulder towards Kate. Halfway down the beach her friend struggled to catch up, floundering in the unforgiving sand. Ali's thoughts flashed back to Doug's face being torn apart, and she turned to Steve. "You need to get out of the water."

"Why? Is there a shark?" he asked, looking over his

shoulder at the rolling waves.

"Please, Steve," Ali implored, holding out her hand as another wave broke on the shore and slid past Steve. As the ocean retreated Steve stared into his sister's eyes. "Alright, alright, what's going on?" he said, taking a step towards her. His body moved, but his feet did not as he almost tripped. He looked down at his feet, and Ali followed his gaze. At first, she thought his feet had sunk into the sand, but on closer inspection she saw they were stone.

"Ali? What's happening!?" cried Steve, trying to move. He fell onto his hands and knees as the next wave broke. When the waters receded, Ali screamed. Steve's hands and legs had turned to limestone, long tentacles snaking from bubbling sores on his hands to coil up his wrist.

Ali moved to save her brother, but seeing the unfolding nightmare Kate threw her arms around her friend and pulled her away from the encroaching water. Ali fought to escape her friend's grasp. "Let me go!" she wailed as Kate dragged her up the beach.

The next wave rolled in. Ali watched it lap against Steve's chest and chin, turning his torso and neck to alabaster. She stared into her brother's terrified eyes and, seeing the next wave about to crash, buried her face in Kate's chest and held her tight. There was no scream, only the gentle hiss of the spent wave. When next Ali looked up only a crumbling, white mound remained of her brother, a vanishing island in the golden sand.

Kate stroked Ali's face, scratching her cheek with callused fingers. Ali didn't notice, didn't care. She couldn't believe the chalky mass being reclaimed by the sea could ever have been her brother; so full of life, so full of dreams. Kate spoke to her, but it was as if her friend was on some distant shore, drowned out by the rushing blood in her ears. Or was it the hiss of that last wave? Ali couldn't tell as she stared out at a spectacular rainbow arching across the bay, bright against the darkening clouds.

"Please, Ali. We have to go."

Ali winced as something hit her eyelid, and lifting her hand she felt the first raindrops on her palm. Kate's hand slid and entwined with Ali's. The next raindrop hit the back of Kate's hand, and her skin turned white before collapsing into a small crater through which another eager tendril snaked up to meet the rain.

Realizing the danger Ali spun about, and she found herself face-to-face with Kate. Her friend tried to smile as raindrops scarred her face, her eyes melting into pits of twitching, writhing eyelashes. Ali pulled Kate to her feet and dragged her blind friend down the beach, trying to outrun the storm. They reached the car, soaked, and Ali bundled a shivering Kate into the back seat before climbing into the driver's seat.

"Let's get you to the hospital," said Ali, turning on the headlights. The rain beat down on the roof as the darkening clouds turned day into night. Ali continued to babble, her mind trying to find sanctuary in small talk with her best friend. "They'll know what to do, won't they? Some antibiotics will sort you right out."

Ali pulled out of the parking lot, and an all-too-familiar, guttural, gurgling noise came from the rear seats. She'd not gotten the stench of ammonia out of her nostrils, not since Doug's boat. The suffocating odor stung her eyes and stole her breath.

"You never know that Doctor you like. Paul, wasn't it? He might be on today, and you... "

Ali adjusted the rear-view mirror, so she didn't have to watch her friend writhing and spreading across the back seats. "Hang on, Kate. It's going to be fine."

Something struck Ali's arm, and out of the corner of her eye she saw Kate's hand resting on her shoulder; long tendrils licked at her neck as she tried to keep the car on the road. "Not long now, Kate. We're almost there."

A deafening crack resounded, and Ali's seat jerked forward as she fought to control the speeding car. Kate's hand slipped away, but Ali kept driving; tears welled in her eyes, turning the oncoming traffic's headlights into dazzling stars. She sobbed, almost veering into the beckoning traffic. At the last moment Ali skidded the car to a halt, before slumping against the steering wheel. Eyes closed tight she listened to the pitter-patter of rain on the roof before reaching into the glove compartment and retrieving the bottle of vodka. Unscrewing the cap, she raised the bottle to her lips and took a good slug of the fiery liquid. Why her? Her brother, her friends, all dead. Why had she survived?

"Why!?" she screamed, punching the steering wheel, the car's horn a howling cry against the tempest outside.

She took another swig of vodka and stared at the bottle clenched in her hand. Her palm appeared magnified by the curve of the glass, and what it revealed made her laugh. In anguish she thrashed and screamed, staring at the wiggling things pressed hard against the bottle. She hadn't escaped, and she would share the fate of her friends.

Ali adjusted the rear-view mirror until she saw her blotchy face and bloodshot eyes. Two polyps on her lip licked at her saliva, and she poked a tongue at the grateful horrors. She didn't feel a thing. It wouldn't be the same at the end. Upending the bottle, she drained its contents, and resolved to step out into the traffic. It would be quicker that way. She wouldn't die in agony like her friends, like her brother. She took one last look at her reflection in the mirror and stepped out onto the rain-lashed road.

"Your place, or mine?" asked Alan.

"Hang on, mate. I'm bursting," said Gus, one hand against the wall, the other taking care of business. The sounds of revelers leaving the pub echoed down the darkened alley.

"Tell me about it," said Alan, unzipping his fly while juggling his beer. He groaned as he relieved himself.

"Fuck off," slurred a figure rising from the gutter.

Hot piss snaked down Alan's leg as he stumbled backwards, almost catching his manhood in his zipper. "Jesus!"

"What the fuck yer doing? I was laying there," shrieked the woman. Gus could see her now. She looked ancient. Grey, matted, piss-stained hair framed a blotchy, wrinkled face, and a red nose that told its own tale of excess and self-destruction.

"Oh, fuck off Ali, you pisshead," spluttered Gus, turning and buttoning up his fly. "Why you out here, frightening folk?"

"Is that you, Gus?" hiccupped Ali as she squinted across the alley. "Yer friend don't have any manners."

"Well, if you pass out in the gutter, what do you expect, you crazy old bitch? One of these days..."

"Yea, yea, one of these days...if I'm lucky," cackled Ali, snatching Alan's half-full beer.

"Yer better get home, Gus. Rain's coming," said Ali, lurching off down the alleyway.

"Oi! That's my beer, you bitch," Alan shouted after her.

"Leave her," said Gus, dragging his friend away. "She's harmless, just down on her luck."

"More like down on her knees," Alan shouted, gesticulating at his piss-stained crotch. He could just make out Ali flipping a long, wiggling middle finger as she threw the emptied bottle against the wall before vanishing into the gloom.

"Fucking Ali Cat, that's what you are!"

"Leave her, mate. She ain't worth it. You know, she used to be a school librarian. Lost her brother, her friends and her marbles."

"Fuck, that was her? I heard it was some nasty toxic smack."

Gus nodded. "Yea, it sent her proper scatty. She reckons, if she ever sobers up, she'll die like her mates. I mean, what a basket case."

Alan threw an arm around his mate. "Nah mate, she ain't crazy. She's got the right idea. Come on, let's get a nightcap."

The first drops of rain hit the cobbles as the friends staggered back into the pub.

Chris Hewitt

About the Author

Chris resides in the beautiful garden of England, Kent UK and in the odd moments that he isn't dog walking he pursues his passion for all things horror, fantasy and science-fiction.

Blog: https://mused.blog/
Twitter: @i_mused_blog

Shoney's Revenge

Julie Sevens

Ben ran his tongue along the edge of his ice cream cone as it melted down his fingers. Alicia couldn't remember the last time she'd eaten a big, soft-serve ice cream like this, but something about the hot sun beating down on her shoulders and the seagulls cawing non-stop had made it seem necessary, and the *Dairy Queen* logo had made her feel nostalgic. She laughed as she tried to race the sun in consuming her own ice cream.

They were sitting on a bench staring out at the ocean, an enormous statue of King Neptune emerging from the boardwalk. A particularly persistent seagull was eyeing them, edging closer, and Ben stomped his foot in its direction to scare it off. Ben leaned back, soaking in Virginia Beach. His forehead was sunburned like her shoulders, but they were happier on this vacation than they'd been in a long time. Or was it a vacation?

Ben had finally defended his dissertation in May, just in time for their first anniversary. He had spent three years studying and writing about how increased public transit options improve the lives of people around the world, but when he was done all he wanted to do was get in their car and drive. Alicia had been laid off from her job in June, but she had known she would quit soon anyway. Ben had been on a few interviews, but, academia being what it was, none of the jobs he had gone to grueling interviews for ended up being filled by anyone. Their lease near campus expired on July 3rd, so they had decided to take the opportunity to float around a bit until they ran out of savings and had to figure out their next move.

Loading up their car they'd waved goodbye to the last six years of their lives and driven towards the ocean. The color had started coming back to Ben's face after their first night in their vacation rental. That morning in bed Ben had focused his wide, brown eyes on her, and she ran her fingers through his hair as they finally took a minute to exhale. They had lived for months being terrified of the cliff they were running straight towards, unsure where they would live, what they would do or how they would become functioning adults. But now they'd jumped right off that cliff, and it didn't turn out to be that bad to land on a two - or three - month vacation. The blissful moment as the fog of sleep dissipated hadn't lasted that long, as vacation sex was pretty irresistible, but the new sense of freedom that had replaced the dread had stayed with them as they pulled on their swimsuits and shorts and ventured out to find coffee somewhere.

"Let's just get in the water and swim until we find a

deserted island. We can live there. We'll just eat coconuts and not pay any bills." Ben said, gesturing widely towards the horizon.

"Well, we wouldn't get scurvy. We should bring some rum though." Alicia sighed at the thought of rum, a dull ache at the base of her skull reminding her that she had had too much of it the night before. "After the beach I want to show you the Smokey Mountains! We can get a cabin with a hot tub and lots of privacy," she said, running her hand under the sleeve of his t-shirt.

"Alright, alright," Ben said. He hoped Alicia wouldn't make him go hiking, but everything else about the plan sounded good. His wife was pretty awesome, and he wasn't sure how he would have gotten through the last year without her. He studied her newly freckled face, enjoying the way she looked with no makeup and frizzy beach hair. Her swim cover-up was open suggestively at the top. "Hey let's go back to the apartment, huh?" he said, waggling his eyebrows at her cartoonishly.

Alicia laughed and punched his arm. "Let's see what else is here. Maybe there'll be a corny arcade where we can play Skee-Ball." They sauntered aimlessly down the boardwalk, eventually settling on their towels at the edge of the dry sand, letting the waves bury their toes. Ben's toes sank into the wet sand as a wave washed over the beach in front of them, and he remembered the long summers of his childhood divided between a similar beach and his family's houseboat.

Alicia was scraping her finger through the sand, carving around a seashell, when a wet, jet-black creature rolled up the beach toward Alicia, riding the front of a wave. It stopped in front of her. It was cone-shaped, one end coming to a dull point, the other a blobby mess that could have been a mouth. "Gross," she muttered, holding her legs up in the air as the blob paused below them.

"That's very dead. What was it?" Ben wondered as he watched the sea swallow it back up. Alicia pulled her arms tighter to her chest. The next wave crashed up, splashing their towels and pulling the creature back to sea. She tentatively rested her feet back down, uncomfortable now.

"I don't know. David Attenborough never talked about one of those," she mused, eyeing the surf for any other dead critters. "You getting hungry?" Alicia asked, squinting at the colored circles on the tourist maps she had insisted on stacking in her purse at the visitor center.

As the sun started to lower over the deck of the tourist-trap restaurant they had picked Alicia pointed a mozzarella stick at a marina. "What do people do with their boats in the winter?" she asked Ben.

"We always kept ours in a big barn. You can pay people to take care of them, even haul them for you." His parents had sold their boat when his younger brother had started college, but he and his brother often wished they hadn't.

She nodded, gulping down an inch of her beer. "We should go look at the boats when we're done." Alicia had only been on a friend's pontoon boat a couple of times, but she had always loved to sit out on the dock and watch the water lap up against the posts. Looking for boats with dumb names was one of her favorite beach vacation activities.

After another round of beers to wash their dry burgers down they made their way to the cluster of marinas. The first two docks they found had a locked gate at the entrance, but the third was held open by a stick. Just tipsy enough to feel emboldened, they snuck through the gate.

Ben called out, "This boat is called *Hook, Line and Sink Her*." Alicia snorted as she caught up to him. It was a classically trashy boat name, very befitting for a boat whose seats were all built-in coolers.

"Benj, look. This one's called *Shoney's Revenge*. I wonder who Shoney is." They paused to look at it. It was a beautiful boat, bigger than most of the others in the dock. A deep-blue awning covered a seating area towards the back, and they could just see a living room inside under a second-story captain's deck.

A woman popped up from a bench seat on the deck as they were admiring it. "Hey! You folks here about the boat?" A visor separated her permed hair from her face, which was beaming at them. "It's Kathleen, we talked on the phone?" she called as she clambered down the narrow steps. "Come on, come on, I'll show you everything!"

Alicia and Ben froze, not sure what to do. Then Alicia stepped forward, smiling broadly. "Hi Kathleen! Nice to meet you!" she yelled back. Ben's mouth fell open, but he quickly shut it, waving at the woman on the boat.

"All aboard!" Kathleen said, holding her arms wide to welcome them. Ben nervously glanced at his wife, who was shaking hands enthusiastically with the boat owner, baffled that Alicia had gone along with the woman's assumption they were interested in buying her boat. His pulse rang in his ears as Alicia nodded at everything she heard as they toured the boat. She examined the waxed, wood panels carefully, oohing and aahing over the chrome fixtures. Alicia opened and closed the mini fridge, pumped the sink faucets, ran her hands along fixtures; familiar things he had seen her do every time they went apartment hunting.

Soon they had seen the whole boat, and Kathleen and Alicia were chatting near the door back to the dock. "Alicia and Ben? I thought you were—" But Kathleen waved her hand around her head like she was shooing away flies and dismissed the thought. "I've talked to a lot of people on the phone lately, never mind." Alicia seemed thrilled with herself.

Ben wandered up the stairs to pretend to check out the top deck, futzing around with a chair. He sat there, one hand on the steering wheel, watching the sun cast long shadows toward the sea as the sky turned scarlet and orange. He breathed in deep, convincing himself that the fishy, salt air was a nice smell. For a moment he pretended to have a different life entirely, one in which he was the kind of man who wore leather loafers and aviator glasses, a beer in his hand as he hosed off a boat that he owned. Reality crashed back down on him and he jumped down, impatiently waiting for Alicia to give up the ruse.

"Thanks for the flyer, Kathleen. Yep, yep we'll call you, okay?" Alicia smiled as she climbed off the boat.

"Nice to meet you, Kathleen, thanks for the tour," Ben said, unable to meet Kathleen's gaze, still wondering why they had toured a for-sale power yacht.

Kathleen looked like she wanted to say one more thing, but instead she decided to tell them to have a good night and waved as they headed off.

As they walked back down the dock, out of earshot, he whispered, "What the fuck was that!?"

"I always wanted to see what a big boat like that was like. Don't be mad! It was serendipity. She was expecting people to come see her boat, and we did!" Alicia was grinning mischievously at him. "Besides, what if we really did buy a boat?"

Ben stared at her. "I mean, sure, but not a fifty-foot Bayliner. That boat is a mid-life crisis for an investment banker, not a first boat for a laid-off gym teacher and a failed academic." He couldn't help but look back at the boat, gleaming in the last rays of sun as it towered over its neighbors.

"Maybe. You said you'd love to go diving again, and I saw you up there in the pilot seat," she teased him. "Is it really any crazier than ditching our lives to go on vacation for a whole summer with no idea what to do afterwards? Maybe we could just become boat people. We could find somewhere to open a beach bar, and you could buy a bunch of shirts and never button them."

Ben laughed and tousled her hair, sure now that it had been a harmless prank. "Okay, okay, good joke. It was a nice boat. Let's go find a beach bar someone else already opened and hang out."

"Kathleen says she wants to sell *Shoney's Revenge* fast, because it reminds her too much of her late husband. She said it's paid off, and just wants to make sure it goes to someone who will take care of it; she's selling it for half the appraisal value," Alicia laughed, "But yeah, we don't even have that much, I guess."

The next morning Alicia woke up early, her heart pounding in her chest. Ben had seemed to forget about the boat entirely by the time they left the marina, but Alicia hadn't been able to. She sat at the kitchen table, eating a stale croissant dipped in Nutella. The flyer Kathleen had given her was on the table next to her plate, and her thumb worried the corner. She hadn't told Ben, but they really did have enough money to buy the boat, in cash. Just barely. She had invested all the cash they were given for their wedding, and her grandpa had given them more than Ben knew about. Probably he had intended for her to buy a house with it, but he wasn't around anymore to ask, and, besides, she thought he would approve.

Maybe.

She punched out a text to Kathleen's phone number asking if the boat were still for sale. Her phone buzzed with the reply as Ben stumbled into the kitchen, scratching his chest. Alicia gazed out the front porch of their vacation rental at the ocean. It seemed so limitless, so full of possibilities. She caught her husband off guard when she looked back at him intensely. He paused with his scruffy chin buried in a coffee mug and waited, eyebrows up.

"We should buy the boat. She says it hasn't sold yet, and we would never find another deal like that."

Ben snorted in disbelief, the breath forming waves on the top of his coffee. "With what money?"

The next morning Ben and Alicia eased into a parking spot at the marina. Alicia gripped the neon-orange, foam floaty attached to their new boat's keys so hard her knuckles were turning white. She felt afraid that if she dropped them their new life would crash down with them. They were in a dream, maybe, where things were finally going okay.

It took several trips back and forth from the car to bring in the groceries and all the things they'd bought for their boat. Ben had practically flown to the store to buy wetsuits for them when Kathleen casually mentioned there was plenty of old dive gear in the closet that they could have. Alicia smiled as she wiped down all the counters and seats, thinking that she had been right to take this risk now that her husband was pinging around the boat like a kid with a new toy.

Digging through a stack of maps, Ben pointed at handwritten notes. "The old owner must have loved to dive at shipwrecks," he mused. "We should check one out. Maybe the *Morgan*? Sunken Navy boat." He tapped his finger on a circled spot on the map. "No, that one is probably too deep for you. The *Brass Spike* is better, let's check that out."

"Yeah, okay. Let's take it pretty slow the first day. You know I haven't been scuba diving, except for the lessons we took in Nassau on our honeymoon." Alicia settled back into the seat, the upholstery squeaking like a diner booth. "Which is starboard and which is port? Left and right?" she asked, figuring she should know now as a boat owner.

Ben patted her knee, "Starboard," his finger waggled to the right side of the boat. "You ready?" he asked, flipping little red switches. Two screens on either side of the helm flickered on, maps appearing. Alicia wasn't sure if she was ready. Getting out of the slip at the marina seemed impossible; surely they would bang into the dock, or another boat? He whooped as the engines roared to life, slapping the polished, white console. Soon Virginia Beach was slipping away behind them, and Alicia started to relax.

She let the wind whip her hair, closing her eyes as she imagined their lives on a boat. It would be nearly impossible to live aboard the boat all the time, but they could spend the amount of the future she felt like thinking about right now on the boat. She stretched her legs out, letting a flip-flop dangle. Ben's shirt flapped in the breeze, and she admired the way he looked captaining a boat. She pulled a corny old captain's hat out of a box in the corner and snugged it on his head. "O captain, my captain!" she yelled, pretending to salute him. He was grinning ear-to-ear.

⟡

"The Garmin says we're about there, Al!" Ben called from above. He cut the motors down and let the boat rock gently. She was laying out the dive equipment Kathleen had given them, wiping it all down carefully. "They had a ton of stuff. I'm surprised she didn't want to keep any of it. They must have even had extra stuff for guests," she called back.

He kissed her forehead and said, "You mean *we* have extra dive stuff for guests! Did you find any more tanks, or just the ones we had refilled?" Picking up his wetsuit he started to get changed.

"Just the ones we already found. It's so sad that Kathleen and her husband loved being out in this boat so much, and now she doesn't even like to look at it. She must miss him a lot." Alicia mused, imagining Kathleen looking wistfully out a window toward the ocean.

"What do you think happened here?" He held up an old pair of goggles with a shattered lens. Running his hand across the cracks in the plastic, he wondered, "Maybe somebody dropped them, though these things are usually pretty tough." The dive goggles looked like they'd been hit hard, as the plastic had cracks radiating all over. Hopefully whatever happened hadn't been while someone was wearing them.

⟡

In the water Alicia and Ben waved at each other. Alicia gave a thumbs up, and Ben turned to head down. He seemed to be moving in slow motion, the long, yellow fins on his feet gliding through the water. A trail of bubbles leapt for the surface from his mask. She followed him down, remembering the scuba tips she'd learned. Deep, slow breaths. Alicia could still pop her ears without opening her mouth, a trick that helped a lot on airplanes.

She looked off into the steady, blue around them. The ocean floor was still a pale shadow below them, but they were getting closer. Ben reached his arms out wide, coasting for a moment. He felt so free; he'd always loved how being underwater made him feel weightless, how he could move any direction unbounded by gravity. He pointed at the silhouette of the wreck they had come to see, making sure Alicia saw it too. They adjusted course slightly, slowing down so they wouldn't scare off all the fish that were surely populating it.

Ben turned on his dive light and shined it on the decomposing, wooden hull. The algae waved in the current, fish darting away from the light. It was so weird to see something so human on the floor of the ocean, surrounded by bare, shell-studded sand and not much else. He pointed out a lobster picking its way across the sand near the bottom of the hull, and she gave an excited thumbs up when she saw it too.

Bobbing up and down in the water near their boat, Ben and Alicia pulled their regulators from their mouths. "Oh my God Benj, that was really cool!" Alicia bubbled over. Ben was thrilled that she had liked it; it had been hard to tell with all the equipment in the way. They pulled themselves up their swim ladder and sat on the back of the boat's platform.

"Hello? Heeeello?" a woman's voice called from behind them. Startled, they turned sharply to the left. A Coast Guard boat had pulled up beside them. "You okay here?" one of the coasties called. Ben's brow furrowed, but he called back "Yeah, thanks!"

"Great, great. We had an abandoned fishing boat in the area last week, so we're just doing extra patrols," she yelled, waving. She squinted at the name of their boat across the stern, trying to place it. "*Shoney's Revenge*?" she mouthed to herself.

"We're the new owners!" Alicia explained, wondering if Kathleen and her late husband had gained some sort of reputation. Ben was troubled that the coastie seemed to recognize the name of the boat. Maybe it had just been a frequent presence on the water?

"Well, congratulations on the new boat then," she offered, mustering a smile, "Dive safe, okay?" Satisfied, the patrol boat pulled away. Out of habit from the dive, Alicia gave them a thumbs up.

"What do you think that's about, Al?" Ben watched the Coast Guard boat as he pulled down their diver flag. Alicia didn't know what to say. She wanted to say it must be nothing, but who would abandon a boat a couple miles off the coast of Virginia Beach? Where had they gone? Maybe they'd been picked up by someone else, and there was more to the story of why they didn't come back for it?

"Dinner's here!" Ben yelled. Alicia was drying off from her shower. She had felt thoroughly salted, the fresh water from the showerhead like moisturizer on her skin. Pulling her fingers through her hair she studied herself in the mirror. She felt different with a new life opened up in front of her. She could be a boat person living her life on the water, on the beach or next to the beach. They didn't have to settle down, anchoring themselves in some suburb after finding new jobs.

Not yet, at least.

Ben pulled out some plates and shoved aside the maps from *Shoney's Revenge* to make room for dinner. While they ate his finger absentmindedly tapped one of the circled spots on a map. The one they had picked today had been carefully circled and labeled in permanent marker, along with several others in the area. The one his finger kept finding, though, had been circled much more dramatically, ovals looping over each other, with no hints to what could be found there.

"Let's try that one tomorrow," Alicia gestured with one of her chopsticks.

They set off early the next morning, the tourists still sleeping. They greeted all the regulars at the marina, some already returning from break-of-dawn fishing trips. It still felt surreal as they glided out of the marina on their very own boat.

"X marks the spot!" Ben told her. Alicia perched on the bench seats next to him as he piloted the boat, dipping pretzels into a jar of peanut butter. She looked out across the water, the straight line of the horizon splitting the view into blue sky above and blue sea below. The wind was calm this morning, the sky mostly cloudless. She wanted the summer to soak into her bones. Ben had his shirt off already, another step in his transformation from grad student to boat guy. Alicia didn't mind this new confidence.

They soon closed in on the spot they were seeking and cut their engines. With their gear triple-checked and their red diver down flag hoisted they sat on the swimming platform. Ben stuck his finned feet in the water, watching as the surface distorted his feet into bizarre appendages springing from his calves. He flipped them a couple of times, the water stirring around.

"You ready? I hope I don't have to pee again while we're down there." Alicia seemed ready to dive, delighting Ben. He had been worried she wouldn't like it, and couldn't remember her being that impressed on their honeymoon. Ben wished they could give up the boat and just live in the water like Poseidon and Amphitrite. He shoved off from the boat, and they fought their way down from the surface.

At first they didn't see anything that would justify the

emphatic circle on the map. They swam along the ocean floor, startling camouflaged flounder out of the sand and racing to see them skate along to a new hiding spot. There were no promising shadows indicating any shipwrecks, but Alicia pointed at a vague spot of darkness that had been just beyond visibility when they came down. It didn't have much of a shape, but it could be a wreck, so they pulled their anchor line along in a new direction.

Ben pointed his dive light at a dark hole in the sea floor. The gaping hole was at least the size of the shipwreck from yesterday. The endless sand dropped out like a falling elevator at the edges, disappearing. Whatever was at the bottom of the hole was far enough away to be invisible. Alicia gave a thumbs down, but Ben motioned for her to come anyway. He headed towards the hole, and it only seemed to get bigger as they approached. She hung back, feeling uneasy about being over the top of the hole instead of above the sea floor. Yet she also didn't want to be alone, suspended on the edge of the hole like an olive speared on the rim of a martini glass, so when Ben didn't hesitate she followed. The water chilled as they approached, and they felt goosebumps rising on their skin.

A few feet into the hole the water was punctuated by angular blobs whipping themselves around. A dozen of them gathered around Ben and Alicia, attracted to their movement. They seemed slimy, coated in some sort of protective goo. Shining her dive light at one Alicia recognized it as the same creature that had rolled up the beach at her, dead. Except now she could see that the flat end of the cone had a gaping, toothed mouth about the size of a quarter.

She retreated back above the sand. The jet-black things hovered, and she felt like they were looking at her, although she had noticed they were eyeless. She couldn't stop looking behind her, and under her. They were not that big—they could fit in the palm of her hand—but together, in a pack, they threatened. Ben's seam of air bubbles still floated from inside the hole but Alicia drifted in place, the hugeness of the ocean closing in on her. Studying the sand near the hole she realized there were no other fish in sight. There was nothing in sight, in fact, and she had never felt so alone in her life.

Shuddering on the swim deck, Alicia scolded Ben, "That was creepy! Why did you make me stay down there?"

"Oh, don't be such a thalassophobe!" Ben teased her, "That was so cool. I wonder what made the big hole?"

"Well, you knew I didn't like it, but you made me wait for you for so long. We're supposed to come up if either of us is uncomfortable." Alicia's words had a streak of anger.

"Okay, I'm sorry. You're right, we have to stick together," Ben moved her wet hair out of her face as she refused to look at him. "I get it. I shouldn't try to get you to do dives you don't like."

"Yesterday was really fun. Today..." Alicia said, "Just don't do that again. I felt trapped down there."

They peeled off their gear and their wetsuits. Ben took it as an invitation that Alicia didn't go to the cabin to take hers off and moved closer, kissing her shoulders. "Let me make it up to you," he whispered, running his fingers softly down her back.

Alicia turned and kissed him back. She ran her hands over his shoulders, down his back, then jumped back and yelled, "Turn around!" She stared in horror, her hand instinctively reaching out, but pausing midair. "One of those things, it's on you. How did it get in your wetsuit? Like. It's burrowing..."

Panicked, Ben slapped his hands behind him. The worm creature was just out of his reach. "Al! Get it off!"

"Okay, okay...oh, my God, I can't..." she said, but she knew she had to. It was wriggling and twisting, and with each movement more of it disappeared into Ben's back. She grabbed its pointed end, trying to get a grip. It pulled out, slightly, but wouldn't let go. She ran to the galley and grabbed a grilling fork.

Ben was nearly sobbing when she returned with it. He saw the sharp, two-pronged instrument in her hand and nodded. She stabbed the creature with both tines, yanking it outward. Ben screamed in pain as its teeth released, leaving a bloody, jagged circle in his back. An even narrower hole in the center bled freely, obscuring the translucent tail of a smaller worm as it disappeared inside Ben's body.

The jet-black blob on their deck was dead, laying in a puddle of seawater mixing with the blood dripping from Ben's back. Alicia opened the bench seat and pulled out a first-aid kit, toweling him off. She decided not to mention the hole the creature had bitten in his wetsuit; he was still so shaken, squirming in his own skin.

"It's okay, Benj," she comforted him, "it's dead. We'll get you patched up." Dabbing the wound with gauze she reassured him, "It's not so deep. You won't need stitches." He gritted his teeth. As she disinfected and bandaged his back, neither of them noticed the wriggling disturbance on his skin from something inside moving up his neck. "There." She pressed the last bit of bandage tape against his skin, "Let's just rest now. You want a beer?"

Ben sighed as he looked at Alicia, who was sleeping on the couch next to the galley. He paused for a second, wondering why he was doing this, and then let himself fall into the water.

Awoken by a splash, Alicia looked around the boat. The sun was still bright; she hadn't been asleep very long. She didn't see Ben. "Ben?" she yelled, bile rising in her throat. He was nowhere to be found, not even when she looked off the sides of *Shoney's Revenge*. There was no way he would dive alone, was there? Without telling her?

Ben was diving alone. He was swimming straight downwards, much too fast, straight towards the hole. Its hypnotic pull dragged him towards it, sucking him in like quicksand. He wasn't entirely sure what he was doing, and his ears hurt. He knew he should slow down, or, better yet, stop and slowly make his way back to the boat. Yet down he went. Hesitating above the hole, his pulse quickened. He didn't want to go back into it, but he couldn't stop himself. His fins beat the water, churning him downwards. The muscles in his legs protested, but there was nothing he could do.

A long, gelatinous tentacle floated like a silk scarf caught in the beam from his dive light. Ten-foot-long filaments floated from it, suspended in the dark. This single tentacle was nearly as thick as his leg but translucent, the blackness from beyond it seeping through. Soon another joined it, twisting and curling. One of the black worms that had dug into him floated by, then another. Moving the beam of his light upwards, he saw that the water teemed with them. They swam like a school of herring, seeming to have one mind.

Drawn towards the center of this flurry, Ben found himself at an enormous mouth. Rows and rows of needle-sharp teeth formed a spiral bigger than Ben himself. Each tooth was as long as his hand and spindly, almost clear at the edges they were so thin and sharp. They jutted inward, an adaptation he knew would mean that any prey that struggled would only find the teeth digging in deeper. A pulsating throat beckoned him from the center of the spiral.

The edges of the mouth were pitch-black and glossy with slime. A ring of dark, hazy eyes watched him carefully from around the mouth. Feathery fins beckoned him, the enormous tentacles enveloping him from behind and pulling him closer. The filaments stung his skin, although he barely felt it. The enormous creature's body tapered off into the dark.

The thousands of tiny versions of itself it had sent out to find prey all faced him, floating, the audience for his arrival. The flurry had stopped, and though they still surrounded him they barely moved now.

Ben knew now why he was here, and he was not surprised when he felt the teeth pierce his wetsuit. He calmly unbuckled his dive pack and let it sink away, the regulator pulling from his mouth as he surrendered himself.

Staring upwards, expressionless, Ben saw the outline of his boat. He gave a helpless wave as the teeth closed around his waist, the kind of wave you give someone you recognize but can't quite place.

Alicia paced the boat, wondering what to do. Ben hadn't fallen in, his dive gear was gone, but he had told her again and again that it was never safe to dive alone. He hadn't put up the diver down flag or run an anchor line so he could ascend safely back to the boat. She looked back and forth from the radio and the emergency kit to the rest of the gear. If she called for help the time she spent waiting might be too long if Ben was in trouble.

Hands shaking, she slapped her dive gear on over her swim coverup and splashed into the water.

Her heart sank when she didn't see Ben or his yellow flippers anywhere nearby. Treading water she looked toward the hole they had visited earlier with trepidation; her pulse raced as she launched herself down. The ocean felt enormous around her, as if she'd been swallowed up by the sea. She could hear the echo of Ben's reassuring voice reminding her to breathe, to slow down. Doing her best to breathe, instead of cry, she pushed on.

A cloud of sediment had been kicked up from the hole, muddying the water. She drew closer, wishing she could call out, then she remembered the trick her dive instructor had used: banging a large bead he kept on a bracelet against the tank to make noise. She didn't have a bead, but she had a compass watch, so she flailed her arm behind her until she heard a clanging sound.

Making as much racket as she could, hoping Ben would hear her and appear out of the depths, she slowly drew closer to the hole. A few of the bizarre worms swam past her, one skating along her thigh to dart in and out around her leg. She kicked at it, making contact.

Suddenly she was swarmed by them, flying at her out of the hole like bats out of a cave. They pelted her, bouncing from her skin and yanking at her hair. Then they were gone. She hung there, gazing into the now-quiet hole in the cold water.

Something else was moving down there, floating gently upwards out of the dark, a ribbon of bubbles pouring from a hole pierced in the side. Ben's dive tank moved in slow motion through the stillness, his mouthpiece trailing behind it. Alicia screamed, almost losing her regulator.

She shone her light frantically around the abyss. Her fin caught something at the edge, in the sand, and sweeping at it with her hand uncovered part of a leg. Sand-blasted and rotting, it couldn't be Ben's — it had clearly been there several days, maybe more. Alicia dropped it and froze in horror as she turned back towards the hole. In one glacial second she realized the danger she was in, and the hopelessness of going further and meeting this predator.

Grabbing the anchor line she ascended. She could barely see as her mask fogged up with tears, but she felt herself break the surface of the water, felt the sun on her face again, and yanked her mask off. Sobbing, she pulled herself to the deck of the boat and lay there gasping.

Alicia crawled toward the emergency kit, tipping it over. An orange boat-in-distress smoke bomb rolled out. Weakly she ripped it open, lobbing it into the water. The orange smoke drifted with the wind, high into the air. She leaned back and stared at the sky. The closest boats turned toward her, coming to her aid. Why had Ben gone down there again? Why had he gone alone? She howled into the drifting, orange haze, the loss like shards of glass piercing her heart. Unfortunately, she didn't notice the creature attached to her stomach flagellating against the gauzy white fabric of her shirt. It was digging itself deeper and deeper, deep enough to release its freight.

Soon enough Alicia would find out why Ben had returned to the hole.

Julie Sevens

About the Author

Julie Sevens is an Ohioan who transplanted to Philadelphia and Berlin before finally settling in the Chicago area with her family. She loves falling down rabbit holes researching the times and places her stories are set in. When she isn't writing out her nightmares, she copy-edits nightmares written by other people.

Find her at www.juliesevens.com

The Sea Reaches Up

Mason Gallaway

The patio was a plane of industrial steel, the yard a rippling square of water infused with a blue-violet glow. The view--what view there was--was a deep vista of cerulean filled with the dull radiance of dissolving sunbeams. All around, the structure hummed, holding its own against 100 feet of ocean water.

It was like no back porch Chase had ever lounged upon. Small, a bit claustrophobic for his tastes, but unique and exciting. It was designed mainly for quick passages and transitions, allowing divers to get from cabin to sea, but there was plenty of room for a curious daughter and a proud dad who was well on his way to being the 'cooler' parent.

Chase reclined in the lounge chair at the edge of the moon pool while his nine-year-old daughter, Leila, knelt on the rubber mat by the water, looking for fish. Her gaze would hop from the pool to the glass window above it, hoping to see something 'big' like a shark or octopus.

Chase hoped she would see something too, only nothing too big. He knew his daughter's wonder often gave way to doubts and what-ifs, and eventually full-fledged terror.

"See anything yet?" he asked

Leila shrugged without looking at him. "A few little fish, no big ones though." The lilt of Leila's voice told him that her disappointment was not too heavy, not enough to ruin the wonder and excitement of the trip; if anything it was driving it.

Chase and Leila had arrived at the underwater cabin an hour before, had taken a quick tour of the residence to check out the bedrooms, bathrooms, kitchen, living area, and the two large viewing portals in the living room-–one showing the shallower, sun-dazzled and coral-strewn side, the other a dark blue expanse just over a slope into the midnight depths.

Chase's buddy, Jon, had found great success in real estate in recent years, which had outgrown its size on land and found its way to the sea. Jon, along with a few investors, endeavored to build a series of underwater cabins near the sun-plashed Florida Keys. Not a resort, per se, more like a hi-tech, well-supported, 'glamp'-ground. There would be security staff patrolling the water, easy access to the offices and restaurants near the surface and clear communication between cabins, resort staff and the surface world.

It was a self-contained, fully functional aquatic hideaway; a way to be immersed in the ocean without actually being *in* the ocean. But now it was just Chase and Leila-–and of course Jon and his new model girlfriend in the neighboring cabin.

"How about we hop in the pool for a swim?" Chase asked, slipping out of his chair. As novel as the wet porch was, he felt canned in. He thought a dip in the pool might refresh them both. Chase had brought his dive suit and planned on doing a deep dive with Jon at some point, stopping at each window of his cabin so his daughter could wave and marvel. But he felt like a good bonding session should come first.

"What do you say?" he said, nudging her. She looked up at him, her gray eyes glinting and rippling. She glanced back down at the water, then up at the large window showing nothing but sun-washed blue. When she looked back at Chase her smile was gone, her sparkle shadowing.

"What?" Chase asked.

Leila shrugged. "What if a shark actually *does* come up?"

Chase laughed and sighed. "Sweetie, I told you they won't. They have better things to do. Plus, a big one couldn't get his fat head under here."

Leila snickered as she envisioned a cartoonish version of what Chase described.

Without another word Chase pulled off his shirt and cast himself into the glowing water. He didn't dive, fearing he might slip out from under the protection of the cabin and be overwhelmed by sea. The pool was nine feet by five and just five feet deep, its bottom a grated platform several inches above the sea floor. It was caged in on three sides, leaving the side below the window open to the sea for easy access.

Though far down, the cabin was still in the euphotic zone where the sun's rays still held sway and wildlife abounded. Jon had assured Chase and Leila that no dangerous creatures would come within the tiny space of the moon pool.

Chase did a few backstrokes, tossing glances at Leila who was smiling from the edge. After a while she hopped in too, and for several minutes they swam back and forth. They splashed each other, talking about how lucky they were, about all the fish they'd seen and about how scared her mother would have been down here.

Chase promised Leila they would see amazing things, probably in the morning when the sun was high and bright. And then, after breakfast, Jon would be by with the small submersible and they'd tour the entire campus. She'd see more wildlife than she could ever hope to.

That seemed to light Leila up, but instead of sparking more talk or more questions it sent her into a quiet reverie.

Chase too grew quiet as his thoughts drifted to his ex-wife and the guy she had been seeing. How much money did he make? What was he like in bed? Was he really as kind as Leila assured Chase he was, and did Leila thinking the guy was nice make Chase feel any better?

"Dad!" Leila cried suddenly. Her voice boomed within the hollow chamber, shaking Chase from his thoughts.

"What?!" His eyes shot down to the pool's surface, expecting to see a dark shape rising toward Leila, but the rippling purple-blue water was clear.

Chase looked at Leila, confused. She smiled at his

reaction and giggled.

"Don't do that!" he chided. She quickly composed herself after catching his glare.

"Now what?"

"Sorry! I was just thinking about that hand thing in the cabin."

Leila tilted her head, her brow turning to ridges and valleys.

"Hand thing?"

"Behind the glass. There are coins and a *weird hand-looking thing*."

"Oh! Jon's diving collection. Cool, huh?"

Leila nodded and slowly spun around to the large glass window. The water seemed to carry her toward it. Chase followed her gaze to the pane of varying blues. A few yellow-tailed snapper darted by. One stopped and hovered a moment near the glass, observing them.

Leila smiled with appreciation. "Isn't Jon afraid that people will steal them?"

"Well, the people who will be staying here probably won't care about making a buck. Plus, those things aren't worth as much as you think."

Leila looked down at her hands as she swept them over the surface of the moon pool. Looking at the yielding water as if to clarify her muddled child thoughts.

"I bet the coins are worth a lot more than that hand. That thing is *creepy*."

"Creepy, but cool."

"Whose hand was it?"

Chase laughed. “The creature from the Blue Deluxe Suite?”

“Dad, I mean really!”

“ I don’t think it’s a real hand. It’s just a piece of coral that looks like a hand.”

“But it really does look like a hand.”

“It does.”

“Like a claw or something.”

“A *monkey’s paw.*” Chase raised a brow and lifted a gnarled hand from the water, giving her his best creepy-cute pose.

She glared at him, her face quivering as she stifled both a whimper and a smile. “Hey, I don’t like that story!”

“Fine. If anything, it looks like some kind of fetish or talisman. Maybe someone long ago found some coral and made it look like a hand.”

“Talis-*what*?”

“Items that people carry for power, protection or to make things happen. Different cultures, like Native American ones, believe that talismans have real power.”

“Like good luck charms?” Leila asked.

“Yeah, sort of.”

Leila nodded as the fear and consternation left her eyes.

“I like that. Maybe it’s here to help us have a great time.”

“Good idea, but I don’t think we’ll need any––“

A sound stifled Chase’s thought. A tapping, scraping noise came from above. Like a branch rapping against a window, or tickling the side of a car. Chase looked up at the glimmering steel ceiling. There was only open water out there; no branches, no finger-like limbs. He looked back at Leila, expecting to see her peering at him with fear and confusion, but she was gazing out the window and smiling.

"There!" she said, pointing to the window. She hadn't heard the strange sound. Chase regarded the fish, more snappers and a lone, hefty grouper, and smiled.

"Very nice," he said. He turned his attention back to the ceiling, then to the window, seeing the group of fish dart away. The moon pool seemed safe and contained, but there was no denying that it left part of their lower halves vulnerable to the ocean. Broad snouts and gaping jaws couldn't get to them easily, but a jellyfish could bobble its way in. Tentacles could snake their way in, or a cold, squamous hand could reach up, desperate for connection and warmth.

A chill ran through Chase, as if the pool's temperature had dropped a couple degrees. He blinked away the thought and replaced it with the mandate to be more forgiving of his daughter's fears and whims in the future.

"Okay, sweetie," he said, slapping his wet hands together. "Time to get out. Too much of this pressure." He turned and pulled himself onto the side of the pool.

Leila smiled and emerged from the radiant moon pool with no objections.

The cabin was compact, but cozy, efficient and stylish. It had a sleek, post-modern design with lots of smooth surfaces. Stainless steel, fiberglass, water-resistant leather and thick glass. All the walls and furniture were slick and streamlined, facilitating movement and short-term comfort as though it were designed to swim through.

The wet porch fed into an entry lock that fed into a small, but fully-functional, galley. Next to the galley was a dining area and a sunken lounge space. A hall from there flowed to the two bedrooms and bathrooms, and between the short hallway and the lounge room was a front access door that led to a glass elevator to the surface. Next to this door stood the glowing display case holding the coins--and the hand-like coral.

After stepping out of the entry lock Chase stopped to again marvel at the cabin. He was in a pit of luxury, comfort and style, in a place of the world where those things should have been watery dreams. Leila brushed past him and went straight to the couch, throwing herself on it.

"Hey, you're not dry enough," Chase said.

"It's all waterproof!"

"Yeah, but I'm not. Go wash and dry up for dinner."

Leila sighed and pushed herself up from the couch. She headed toward the hallway, but stopped at the entrance to the cabin before the illuminated display case. Within the case sat six coins, doubloons, Chase had explained, of varying sizes. Silver, bronze and gold. At least they looked gold, though Chase told Leila they probably weren't.

Leila fixed her eyes on the peculiar, hand-shaped piece

that sat between the coins. It lay there, palm upward, ready to hold. Ready to grasp. It didn't take much imagination to see something hand-like or claw-like about it. When you focused closely on its porous surface it was just a unique piece of coral, but when viewed in its entirety it became something alien. Something human eyes shouldn't see. Leila didn't really conceptualize these thoughts vividly. She just focused on the fingerlike extensions, the awaiting palm.

Ready to hold.

Ready to grasp.

Chase noticed her fixation from the kitchen.

"I didn't raise no thieves," he called out.

"I'm not! Just pretending that it really is a charm," she said.

"What do you mean?" Chase set down the pan and stepped into the living room.

"I'm going to ask it to help us have the most incredible trip ever, so we can tell all our friends and make them super jealous." She turned back and flashed a smile full of impishness and brand new teeth. Chase gave her the OK symbol.

"Just don't tell your mom. She thinks most fun is evil. Prayers to hand-things would seem even evil-er."

"Dad!" Leila rebuked, laughing. "It's just for fun." She turned back to the glass case and leaned into it.

Chase walked closer, wanting to see her expression as she concentrated on the hand. He was poised to crack a silly remark that would make her laugh or roll her eyes, but when he saw Leila's face his playfulness chilled. She was no longer glowing or smiling. Her brows were furrowed again, more so than a little girl's should. It made her look severe and troll-like. Chase was hit with an uncanny feeling that Leila deserved more of his respect. He cleared his throat and prepared himself for the show.

"Oh great hand of the sea, you have grabbed and held lots of things. Bring us lots of excitement and crazy moments. Help us have an amazing trip we will never forget."

She stopped, meditating. Her eyes went to the floor as she searched for words. Chase watched her, feeling almost like an intruder, a voyeur to the sacred. Leila looked as though she were hearing not her thoughts, but some oracular voice. Her eyes widened as an idea came to her. She nodded in assent and turned back to the hand.

"A trip with really amazing animals. Creatures no one else has ever seen. Creatures that could teach us things, wow us, blow our minds."

Her eyes narrowed, sharpening their gaze on the talisman. Then she squeezed her eyes shut, as though to seal her supplication. And, in that moment, Chase found himself adding something to the request. *Yes, make this trip incredible, and make me the cool parent, the better parent. Better than Craig will ever be.*

He felt guilty for thinking it, but where was the harm?

When Leila opened her eyes, she turned to Chase, showing her usual playful diffidence. Chase laughed as he pulled her in for a hug.

"I'm so stupid," she said through laughter.

"I loved it!" Chase said. "I bet it comes true."

She looked back up at him, reflecting his optimism and cheer, but then her eyes grayed over.

"Mom would be so freaked." She turned back to it, regarding it now with suspicion.

Chase squeezed her. "*You* are brave, and you have the best imagination of anyone I know."

The sun in her eyes returned as her cheeks reddened. "Maybe so."

"But, if I wake up tonight to a big ol' squid eye staring at me, I'm blaming you," Chase said. The image glared in his mind, and he immediately regretted the joke. It had always been Chase's aim to skirt and soothe the darker sides of Leila's imagination, while also nurturing it. He'd love to say that her wild imagination came from her mother alone, but he knew that was not true.

He braced himself for her reaction to the joke, maintaining his smile.

Leila's eyes broadened, filling with light. And to his relief, she laughed.

"You're so crazy, Daddy."

Chase lay awake in his plush bed, draped in the cotton sheets while staring out the broad window. If not for the blue-violet LEDs over the outer side of the window the view would have been a fortress of black, impenetrable to the eye. But now it had a whimsical, easy glow, making it seem more like a night light than a glimpse into a black wilderness.

With his stomach full of burgers and his head full of dad things, ex-husband things and single-guy things, Chase stared at the luminous portal. Seeing it as a soothing mantra, a window into peaceful emptiness, nothingness.

And just as his mind began to slow and his stomach began to settle, the portal to the deep became the display case in the cabin's foyer. And the coral hand, no longer lying on its back, was plastered to the window, its fingers gently raking in and out over the glass like the bell of a jellyfish––or a slowly beating heart.

Chase awoke gasping, his heart pumping hard. Darkness surrounded him.

The window light was out. The room was near black.

Chase slid out of bed, disconcerted by the blackout, yet comforted by the cloaking darkness. The room held only whispers of light from the windows in the living room and his daughter's bedroom. Otherwise he might have had trouble even finding the window. But his feet took him right to it, and his hands touched the thick glass. Chase looked, but there was only black looking back.

He wondered, as his fingers pressed the glass and his eyes pressed the inkiness, how thick the glass really was. Thick enough to keep the water out, but was it thick enough to keep out...what? What else might he want the glass to keep out? *Whatever is on the other side of this glass looking back at you.* Chase took a step back and inhaled deeply, feeling shaken and chilled, and when he exhaled a laugh escaped him. He was supposed to be the brave parent, the cool parent, right? *Faith and fun. No fear, my dear.*

But he found himself wondering how black the black before him really was. How dark the dark. It was near absolute to him, but most of his life was spent in the light. His sight depended on it. Whatever could be out there, whatever *was out there*, could probably see Chase just fine.

Chase looked away from the window and massaged his brow, rubbing his third eye as though to close it. Nightmares. Overthinking. Anxiety. Ever since splitting with his wife he'd had more anxiety and paranoia, and sleeping alone had gotten to him.

It wasn't that being alone scared him, like it might a child. It was that he often felt, physically felt, someone in bed with him in the wee hours. Like a phantom.

He'd feel the weight and heat and energy of a body lying next to him, just as he was waking up. The more awake he became the clearer the sensation became, until he was wide awake and still sensing a presence that shouldn't have been there. He'd hold his breath and reach over to seize whoever it was, but the sensation would suddenly disappear, and he'd be alone again––the space beside him cold and empty.

Chase moved away from the window and eased himself back to bed. As he pulled the covers to his chin he heard a scream like the shrill, ear-rending screech of office fire alarms and abruptly-halted tires. But those sounds never sent his stomach and heart slamming into one another like this one did. He knew this scream, had heard it only once before. *A beloved family cat, smeared on the road a couple years ago.*

Leila.

Chase threw himself out of bed and ran to Leila's bedroom. When he reached it he found that the room still held the blue-purple glow from the window, though less of it. Leila had pulled down the shade. But the bed was empty, and Leila was nowhere in sight.

"Leila? Leila!" He called out, his mind racing, not making sense. There were thoughts of sleep-walking. Or maybe she decided to take a night swim, and she got her wish. Something big and amazing had swum right up to her. Chase bounded through the living room, through the kitchen and found her small form standing before the door to the entry lock and the wet porch. Her hand was reaching for the lever.

Her back was to him, her head was down, her shoulders fallen. Chase went to her and spun her around. She looked up at him, then gasped and blinked. Something fell from her hands onto the floor. Chase didn't notice it right away; instead he dropped to her level and cupped her face in his hands. Her eyes seemed to clear of haze, to see him.

"Daddy? What are you doing? What happened?"

"Sweetie, I heard you scream. Are you okay?"

Leila frowned and fluttered her eyelids. A look of confusion and shame came over her.

"I don't know. I was asleep, but--" She paused, her eyes going wide. She was looking down to the floor at the object she'd been holding. The hand from the case. It lay at their feet, fingers to the ground, ready to skitter away.

Chase bent down and picked it up. "Why did you have this?"

"I just had a dream. I felt like the hand shouldn't be here." She looked up at him, her eyes twitching. Suddenly, her eyes broadened with clarity. "Yeah, I was giving it back. I had to give it back. I was told to do that. Something that was sleeping, for a long time. We woke it up, and..." Her voice was breathy, full of relief, as though her remembering cleared her of wrongdoing.

"Giving it back? To who?"

She looked up at him, her eyes going distant, gaining depth.

"I––I don't know. But it felt real." Suddenly, her gaze narrowed onto the hand her father held, and she took a step back. "But I don't think I like that thing anymore. I don't think I like this place at all."

"Honey, you just––"

From behind his daughter rose a faint soupy, sloshy sound from the wet porch. For a moment Chase's sleep-clouded brain supplied him with an easy, benign image. A bathroom. His wife was in the bathtub after a hard day, and had now decided to break from her warm loll and start washing herself. The water was breaking and falling from her naked body in drips and streams.

But there was no wife beyond those doors, or anywhere in his life for that matter. There was no humid hideaway of a bathroom, no place of comfort and solace. There was only a dark, damp, wet porch, and beyond that an unforgiving ocean whose mysteries, wonder and monstrosities were equalled only by darkness and immense pressure.

There was no bathtub, but there was a moon pool, and something was splashing around in its waters. That something didn't sound playful or relaxed.

Chase and Leila looked at the steel door to the entry lock, then at one another. Leila's eyes registered fear, but not heavy fear. They were edging with fear, inquisitive and pleading, ready for her father to give a sane, comforting explanation. But Chase's eyes remained wide, confused and frightened. All he could do was shake his head and motion for her to get away from the door.

She threw another glance at the door, then she pranced over to him and leaned in close.

"Daddy! What is it?"

He absently rubbed her shoulders as he tried to sort out a reasonable, not-so-terrifying explanation.

"Probably just an animal, sweetie."

"I'm sorry. I didn't mean to--"

"You didn't do anything. It's nothing to worry about. I want you to go into the living room while I look. If I yell, run into your room and lock the door. Buzz Jon--no, the cops. Can you do that?"

She gulped and nodded, then walked into the living room. When she reached the edge of the lounge pit she turned and watched with anticipation. Chase gave his best reassuring wink, then he opened the door to the entry lock and stepped in.

He pressed his ear against the door to the wet porch and heard a whir of emptiness and hollowness, as if he'd put his ear to a sea shell - only the shell was huge, and he was inside of it. He turned the lever, flicking on the porch light as he did so. Not wanting to create unnecessary suspense he cracked the door without hesitation and peered in. The wet porch was clear, but there were puddles and smears all around, the moon pool's water dancing with recent activity.

Chase crept in for a better look.

The water that had fallen from his and Leila's bodies hours before was dry by now. This was freshly dropped water, and there were patches of it leading up to the door. A late-night visitor. A lonely traveller who had seen a faint glow in the wet emptiness.

He whirled around to face the moon pool, as though its water could lurch upward to seize him and drag him into the depths. Something had been here, had climbed up from the pool and walked here. *Walked.* The small puddles of water appeared to be prints of some kind.

Chase looked at the coral hand in his. Pieces of his daughter's mock incantation, and his own, flashed through his mind. *Stupid. Better not let her think that you think it's real.* Chase set the hand down, backed out of the room, and shut the door quietly.

Leila's eyes were full of excitement and relief.

"What was it?" she asked.

"Nothing there."

Chase went to the living room and grabbed his laptop. He had to check in with Jon. Maybe it was Jon playing a stupid, drunken joke. Either way, Chase would tell him about all the weirdness; though he wouldn't mention the hand they had tampered with, or the strange prayer they'd said to it.

"Nothing? Nothing at all?" She stepped closer to him, ready for the truth. Chase sighed and looked up at her. He wanted to reaffirm, but he couldn't. Her eyes flashed to the large window. It was still glowing, still showing the dark ocean night. Leila went rigid. Chase turned, expecting to see a hand pressed against the glass, an alien face projecting cold, intelligent eyes at them.

But there was nothing there. He meant to get up and close the curtains, but Leila hurried around the sofa and hit the button herself. The ocean slowly disappeared from view as the curtain fell. Chase took a breath.

Then he turned back to his laptop and made the FaceTime call. He didn't want to sound any alarms or cause panic. Chase wasn't sure if he and his daughter were even in real danger, he just knew something was very wrong.

Finally the call was answered. Chase's computer became a window into Jon's cabin, but neither Jon nor his girlfriend appeared.

"Hello?" Chase leaned closer. "Jon, you there?"

There was no answer. No movement. Chase considered the scene before him: at the bottom of the screen was the surface of a coffee table, and a piece of what may have been an overturned bottle. Part of the kitchen bar was on the left side, but most of the upper portion of the screen was glowing blue-purple. The living room window of Jon's cabin had its curtain wide open. Jon's laptop was positioned to give Chase a view of the dark sea he had just tried to veil moments ago.

"Jon? Jon, what the fuck is going on?"

Suddenly a shadow passed over the table. The screen flickered and shook, as though the table had been rocked by something, but nothing appeared on screen. Then Chase noticed details he hadn't initially. On the window were small dots or specks, dark in color. Brown or black or red.

Spatters.

Then the blue-violet of the ocean view began to shift and shutter. There was movement just beyond the reach of the lights. A strange waving, fluttering undulation. Something swimming there, hovering in the penumbra. Fins, no, *arms*, rising and falling as legs kicked and pumped hypnotically. Swimming in place, but not quite in place. The figure was slowly moving closer to the window, becoming more defined. A head with a face, a face with elongated shadow eyes and a wide-open shadow mouth.

Chase slammed the laptop shut to prevent Leila from seeing whatever the hell was taking shape outside of Jon's cabin window. He looked at the curtained window above him, wondering what waited outside.

"Let's get our things and--" Chase turned to find Leila gone.

He heard the entry lock door snap shut. There was a shriek, then a splash.

“Leila!” Chase shot up from the couch and ran to the wet porch.

Leila was gone. Water was everywhere. The moon pool rocked and splashed, tossing spittles of water onto the porch. Chase ran to the water, wanting to dive in, but not finding the courage. His knees hit the wet steel and he slid to the edge.

Leila broke the surface. Her eyes were clenched shut, her mouth wide open to either breathe or scream, but she did neither. Chase reached for her, grabbed her, but she slipped from his grasp back into the water. His hand clasped hers before she could slip from the moon pool and into the sea completely.

“I’ve got you!” Chase screamed. He could see his daughter’s distorted form underwater, but nothing more. He knew something held her, was pulling her, and Chase thought he could see something wrapped around her leg––a hand, an arm, or a tentacle, but he couldn’t be sure.

“What do you want!?” he screamed as he tried to pull his daughter up. Her face broke the surface; Leila sucked in a breath of air, and she also spat a word out. Maybe it was *help*, *hurt* or *hand*, but she went back under before he could grab her with his other arm.

Chase, desperate, knowing nothing to do but hold on, frantically looked around the porch. The coral hand lay within reach, upturned and calling for his grasp. Chase suddenly realized what he had to do, or at least the only thing he could do. He snatched up the hand, fired off a quick, jumbled mental incantation, and then raised the hand above him.

"Here! Here, take it back. Take it back, Goddammit!"

The hand sailed from his own, splashing into the moon pool and slipping out from under the covering into the open sea and out of sight, like a released fish swimming away. Chase closed his eyes and kept his grip firm on his daughter's, but he felt his daughter's soft skin slide through his palm. And, in a flash, she was gone.

A bellow rose from within Chase, a deep, mournful cry. But it never escaped him, only reverberating within his chest, shaking his bones. His hand closed, feeling nothing but cold ocean. Then he opened his hand, hoping it would once again fill with his daughter's grip.

Something did fill his hand.

A palm pressed against his, something like fingers draped themselves over his wrist and knuckles. There was an immense, crunching pressure, and something needle-sharp dug into his flesh.

The hand gripping his didn't feel like flesh, more like water somehow concentrated; solid, but not frozen. Intensely alive and knowing, it squeezed and squeezed. Chase screamed, feeling as if his hand had somehow been dipped into the crushing realm of the Mariana.

Then the grip loosened and slipped away, and Chase felt strips of his flesh go with it. He ripped his striped, bleeding hand from the water, holding it before him as water and drops of blood rained into the moon pool.

Then Leila exploded from the water, choking and coughing. Chase seized her and pulled her onto the deck.

He drew her to him, hugging her tighter than he ever had before, wiping the water away from her and hoping the nightmare would go with it.

Dazed and rattled, Chase and Leila gathered their things and went to the elevator door. They looked into the cab for a moment, then they looked at one another.

"Safe?" she asked him.

"I think so...I don't know," he said, knowing he couldn't lie. His eyes went to the open display case, now holding only the doubloons. He went to the case and gathered the coins.

"What are you doing?" she asked. Her eyes were curious, impatient.

"Just in case. Maybe they want a tip. Hell, maybe pirate ghosts are out there too," he said shrugging. He wasn't sure if he meant to be funny or not. Leila smiled anyway, but the smile faded before it could reach full form.

Chase opened the door to the elevator and stepped in. Leila stood at the threshold, looking down at her feet. Chase held out his bleeding hand, but she didn't move to take hold of it. His hand just floated there, waiting for hers. When she finally reached out and took it she squeezed, hard. Leila didn't mind the blood, and Chase didn't mind the pain. But still, she didn't move, too afraid to make the slow ascent to the surface while the sea looked in from all sides.

"You can close your eyes. We both can," Chase said.

She looked up at him and smiled, drifts of shame rippling her eyes. He smiled back. Those few seconds at the moon pool--when Leila was gone and Chase's hand held nothing but cold, crushing ocean--had felt like an eternity.

He could wait a little while longer.

After all, isn't that what the cool parent would do?

Mason Gallaway
About the Author

Mason Gallaway is a writer of dark, weird, and scary stories. His work has appeared in various publications, such as Dark Moon Digest, Flint Hills Review, Calliope, and The Chattanooga Pulse. He began writing seriously after reading Stephen King's Night Shift and thinking, like a fool, how hard could it be? He and his lovely, ever-supportive wife (who once shunned the horror genre) live with their cat and poodle in Tennessee.

You can catch him on:
https://www.instagram.com/masongway/
https://masongallaway.com

Long Pork

R. L. Meza

The knife hovered at the end of his arm, its steel tip pressed into the *Lear*'s oaken hull. It took a tremendous amount of his waning strength to draw the blade down, to carve a notch beside the others, but Edmund made the sacrifice. To keep the count. His fingertips grazed his handiwork, trembling slightly. Thirty-nine.

Thirty-nine days since the wind had abandoned them, left their sails hanging slack.

There was a knock on the door, and Edmund straightened. He combed his fingers through the coarse, copper-blonde hairs of his beard and rubbed his cheeks, trying to bring a flush of life to his sallow, haggard visage. Edmund's mouth was parched, his tongue swollen and furry. Clearing his throat, he said, "Come in."

"Captain Ryder." Simon Acker shuffled into the cabin, bald head ducked low between his broad shoulders, and said, "I tallied the supplies again."

"And?" Edmund massaged his temple, where a headache was forming. During the second week of their voyage a violent storm had assaulted the *Lear*, invading the hull and destroying a substantial portion of their food stores. Edmund had charged his trustworthy first mate with managing the crew's rations, but in the following weeks, discrepancies had crept into Simon's tallies. Even with the hold's door locked and the two keys closely guarded, the food supply continued to dwindle without explanation.

Simon's eyes darted to the lantern, the chest in the corner, the journal on Edmund's desk. "I've found the source of the discrepancy," said Simon. "I think you'd better come and see for yourself."

The simple act of standing made Edmund feel light-headed, but he followed Simon to the hold, ignoring the erratic flutter of his heartbeat and the drunken weave that had replaced his once sure-footed stride. Simon's key rattled in the lock, and the heavy door swung inward. Raising the lantern high, Edmund's lip curled at the irony of the crowded hold. It was packed tight, not with the food and water that they so desperately needed, but with barrels of rum destined for trade in West Africa.

"Come on out, boy!" Simon Acker's tone was stern, but not unkind. A boy stepped out of the shadows, a scarecrow of a lad with more dirt than muscle covering his bones. Edmund gasped and fumbled for something to slow his crumbling descent, as his knees buckled beneath him. Shouldering his bulk under Edmund's arm to steady him, Simon said, "Easy, now. I knew it'd be a shock. I should have warned you, and for that I'm sorry."

Edmund squeezed his eyes shut. The boy had been an illusion—a scrap of memory conjured by a starved mind that suspected it would never see home again. Groaning, Edmund said, "Is he...gone?"

Simon's breath was warm in his ear. "No, Captain."

"I'm sorry, Poppa." The boy's voice was so soft that it could scarcely be heard over the sound of waves lapping against the hull.

Edmund kept his eyes closed and willed the waif to disappear. Small hands clasped his calloused fingers, imploring him to look upon the face of his son who had just turned nine last spring. Edmund finally relented, and tears trailed down his weathered cheeks. "Thomas," he said, stroking the boy's cheek. His words were choked with emotion, a croaked whisper. "How is this possible?"

Thomas lifted his chin, and stringy, blonde hair fell back from his forehead. His eyes flashed crystalline blue. *His mother's eyes.* A fresh wave of grief swept through Edmund at the thought of Elizabeth Ryder, waking on the morning of his departure to find Thomas's bed empty, searching their tiny home in New England and becoming more frantic as each lifted blanket and torn open cupboard failed to produce her son.

"He's made himself a hiding spot, there in the back—between that last row of barrels and the hull," said Simon. "I was shifting things around, searching for any stray supplies that might have been mixed in with the rum barrels by mistake..."

"Foolish boy," Edmund said, wondering how many

days' worth of rations had been nibbled away in the late hours of the night, after the men were asleep and the ship had gone quiet. "Why are you here, Thomas?"

Thomas hung his head. "I wanted to see Africa," he said. "It was supposed to be a surprise. If I'd come out too soon, you might have turned back. And then there was the storm…I overheard you shouting about the ruined food, and I was afraid you'd be angry. I just wanted to have adventures—be a real sailor, like you."

"So you've been down here, alone, all this time," Edmund said. He scratched his beard, reluctant to ask the question that loomed unspoken in the darkened hold. "Simon, how long before the remaining supplies run out?"

"One—" Simon's voice broke, and he coughed into his hand.

One week. It would be tight, the crew might get unruly, but Edmund could dip into their rum stores to soothe the tension—a reward for their discipline.

"One meal remaining, Captain Ryder. Maybe less now that…" Simon tipped his head towards Thomas. There was a sinking in Edmund's chest, as if his heart had been lashed to an anchor and dropped into the icy depths of the sea, and all he could manage in response was a slow, stunned shake of his head.

From above Edmund heard a shout. Other voices joined in, feet drumming across the deck, and Edmund shoved Thomas into the shadows, saying, "Hide. Do not come out for anyone, unless it's my voice calling you. Do you understand?"

Thomas nodded and slipped between the barrels, vanishing like a specter. Simon closed and locked the door behind them as a man came running down the corridor. Edmund turned to greet him, and the lantern's light illuminated the red flush of Geoffrey Keane's cheeks. His brown eyes were feverish with excitement.

"Captain," Keane said, gasping for breath. "There's…a man. On…a raft. Come."

Edmund followed Keane, certain that the man was mistaken. When combined with the prolonged sun exposure, hunger and lack of clean drinking water blurred the lines between reality and hallucination. On the previous day Charles Staple had rallied everyone with ecstatic shouts, insisting that a flock of seagulls was circling on the horizon. When his fellow crew members were unable to locate the birds, Staple became confused and distressed, then infuriated, convinced that they were playing a mean-spirited trick on him. He had tried to start a fight, then fainted from exertion. The men had carried Staple to his bunk without a word, each fearing that he would be next.

Emerging onto the deck beneath the baleful eye of the afternoon sun Edmund winced. After the darkness of the hold the sunlight stabbed at his eyes, like little glass slivers pushed through his pupils to poke at the tender, dehydrated grey matter shriveling in his skull. The crew had gathered on the port side of the *Lear*, several of the men leaning out over the water while others dangled from the rigging. They turned as one to mark their captain's approach, parted, then fell silent.

There was, indeed, a man on a raft. He was facing away from the *Lear*, sun-scorched skin stretched tight over the ridge of his spine, as though the man had also weighed the likelihood of encountering a ship adrift on the open ocean and turned his back to the illusion. The raft was a rudimentary construct, a collection of split planks and various other pieces that might have been salvaged from a wreck, bound together with fraying rope and cracked lengths of sinew. Water chuckled between the boards and pooled around the man's naked parts.

"You there!" Edmund leaned over the side of the *Lear,* hands cupped to his mouth, and said, "What is your name? How did you come to be out here, floating alone?"

The man did not turn his head at the sound of Edmund's voice, but the raft turned—a smooth rotation, like a leaf spinning on the surface of a pond—until the man was facing the *Lear*. His eyes were like chips of emerald, glittering in dark sockets, and they fixed on Edmund. He might have been younger than Edmund's forty-three years, or ten years older; the chapped, peeling lips and the deep creases in his leathery skin made it impossible to estimate the stranger's age. The man tipped his head from left to right in a child-like movement that was both inquisitive and incongruous with the man's grime-streaked nudity. His right hand tugged absently at his exposed genitals, while his left flew up to scratch at the matted dreadlocks behind his ear. With a grin that revealed the blackened stumps of his teeth, the man said, "You there! What is your name? How did you come to be out here, floating alone?"

Edmund scowled. He did not have the patience or the clarity of thought for such foolish games—not from a mouth he could not afford to feed. Simon said, "Do we bring him aboard, Captain or..."

Let him drift. The thought was tempting, but Edmund dismissed it. "Yes," he said, "Mullens! Hall! Bring him up."

While his crew fished the bedraggled stranger from the raft, Simon sidled up to Edmund. Under his breath the first mate said, "Captain, do you plan to inform the men of the depleted rations?"

Edmund rubbed his eyes. Thomas's visage hovered against the glowing orange of his closed eyelids so Edmund opened them, preferring to squint against the harsh sunlight. As he watched the crew haul the naked man aboard, Edmund said, "What would you do, Acker, if it were you and not me?"

Simon removed a stained kerchief from his back pocket and mopped the sweat from his brow. "If it were me, I'd say nothing of it until morning. Double the rum ration and pray they don't notice."

"They'll be eating crumbs," said Edmund. "They'll notice."

"Men make poor decisions under the cover of darkness, Captain."

Hall and Mullens lowered the stranger to the deck and approached their captain, grimacing and wiping their hands on their clothes. Behind them the man folded his long legs and patted the deck with his hands, uttering a high, gibbering laugh. The crew kept their distance, as though they feared his madness might be contagious. To Hall and Mullens, Edmund said, "Did he have anything with him? Weapons? Any means of identifying him?"

Mullens shook his head, but Edmund noticed the way that Hall had first opened his mouth to speak, then—after a sidelong glance at his companion—pressed his lips into a thin line. "Mullens, go fetch a drink of water from the barrel—*a small one*," said Edmund. "Simon, accompany him."

When they were alone, Edmund drew Hall close and said, "Out with it."

"Sorry, Captain. It's just that Mullens can't read, and I didn't want to—"

Edmund raised a hand, cutting Hall short. "What did you find?"

"His name, I think, scratched into the wood of the raft. Over and over. There was no weapon, but with his fingernails missing, I think he might have—"

"Please, Hall. Calm yourself and tell me his name."

"Yates, Captain."

Edmund trained his fierce brown eyes on the stranger. Crossing the deck, he said, "Stranger, is Yates your name?"

When Edmund's shadow fell over him, the stranger looked up. He rocked back and forth, releasing more unsettling laughter, and Edmund tried to hide his disgust at the awful odor wafting up from the man's gaping mouth. The odor far exceeded the foul scent of tooth decay—it was the reek of bloated whale carcasses beached beneath the hot sun, dribbling pink fluids that mingled with the brine and seaweed; the smell of tangled kelp and rotting fish. Swallowing his bile, Edmund said, "Yates. Is that your name?"

"Yates." The stranger bobbed his head. At first, Edmund interpreted this as an affirmation, but then the man said, "Is that your name?"

Hall said, "What do we do with him, Captain?"

Mullens had returned, bearing a sip of water with slow, careful steps as though the cup was brimming with molten gold. Kneeling, Mullens brought the cup to the man's mouth. The water had hardly trickled over the stranger's cracked lips before the man spat it out again, spraying Mullens in the face. Cackling, the stranger said, "What do we do with him, Captain? What do we do with him?"

Mullens wiped at the wasted water, eyes wide with disbelief. Angry mutters rippled through the crew. Hall said, "We could lock him in the hold."

"No!" The simultaneous declaration earned Simon and Edmund the full attention of the men. Before their surprise could turn to suspicion, Edmund said, "We can't risk him getting into the rations."

"But...we are going to tie him up—confine him somehow?"

Hall edged away from the man called Yates, who twirled a dreadlock around his finger and mimicked Hall's nervous tone, saying, "Confine him somehow. Confine him somehow?"

"Hall's right," Simon said. "Until we know whether he's a threat to us or himself—"

"Fine," said Edmund. "Bind his wrists and take him below deck. Stow him in Cooke's bunk."

Cooke had been lost to the storm, taken by the waves. There was a murmur of dissent from the crew, but Edmund held up a hand. Silent and sullen, the crew milled about the deck, leaving Hall and Mullens to bind Yates's wrists and lead him below.

Supper was a bleak affair. Each man received a small chunk of hardtack and a scrap of salted beef. Cups were issued with a thin layer of beer sloshing at their bottoms—enough moisture to soften the hardtack so that it could be chewed and swallowed. The food portion fit in Edmund's palm; the men's rations were half as much. For the past week, Edmund had declined the Captain's portion as a show of solidarity, but that had been before the discovery in the hold: the thieving, stowaway son. Edmund felt the eyes of the crew upon him as Simon distributed the full ration to his captain. They continued to watch Edmund, brooding and chewing their food a hundred times over, as though delaying the act of swallowing might convince their grumbling stomachs that an entire feast was being consumed, and not a single mouthful.

Edmund pretended to chew, but slipped the entire portion into his pocket to give to Thomas, forgoing the fleeting comfort of a final meal. The doubling of the rum rations did not lift the crew's spirits as Edmund had hoped, as it was offset by his decision to feed the stranger. He sensed their quiet outrage, heard the faint rumbles of discontent at his back when he retreated to his quarters, like the ominous thunder of an approaching storm.

It was a sleepless night. The men turned in to their bunks, the ship creaking softly on the placid waves, and then Yates began to sing. Edmund heard it from the hold. He had waited until the men were quiet to call his son out from the shadows and deliver the portion of food that he'd concealed in his pocket. Yates's song echoed through the ship, a strange mix of jovial shouting and disconsolate wailing, as if Yates had been unable to decide between a sea shanty and a dirge. His voice rose and fell; the inconsistent pitch and varying intensity obscured the song's structure, blurring lines and lyrics into a series of unintelligible vowels and consonants. Locking the hold's door behind him, Edmund crept towards the crew's quarters as Yates reached what could loosely be considered the song's chorus: a repeated segment punctuated by two short barks and a howl. Edmund drew closer and realized that it was not distance obscuring the meaning of Yates's words, but a different language altogether—one he did not recognize.

Yates fell abruptly silent, his song replaced by a muffled percussion that quickened Edmund's steps. Lantern raised, Edmund entered to find the men piled on and around Cooke's bunk. At the sound of their Captain's shout, the men fell back. Edmund searched their faces, saw eyes shadowed with guilt, chins jutting out in defiance, bloodied knuckles and clenched fists. Yates was sprawled on the bunk, his head canted at an ugly angle. Broken bones distorted his features, jutting outward to form taut tents of bruised skin. Edmund clenched his teeth against the rage building in his chest and said, "Who did this?"

The men exchanged glances, but no one came forward. Edmund sighed, the rage fleeing as quickly as it had come. There was nothing he could do—no threat he could impose upon the men that would be worse than the impending starvation they already faced. Yates had been a stranger and a madman. Edmund supposed the killer had done them all a service, but the knowledge provided no relief.

"Get him up to the deck," Edmund said. "Toss him over the side."

"Captain." Mullens stepped forward, hands knotted over his sagging belly, and he said, "Maybe we ought to consider..."

Mullens trailed off, eyes flicking towards his companions, but the others would not look at him. Watching them stare at their feet, smeared with the blood spattered across the floor, Edmund knew that they had already been discussing something in his absence, plotting a course of action so terrible that the words had died on Mullens's lips.

"No," said Edmund. "Under no circumstances."

"I think you should hear us out, Captain." Walter Bray rose from his bunk and crossed his arms. Beneath his tanned skin muscle bunched like coils of rope. Edmund had been reluctant to hire the man, had heard at least a dozen different accounts regarding the origins of the blue tattoos that decorated Bray's neck and arms, but they had been a man short on the morning of their departure, and Bray had been there at the docks, ready to climb aboard for half pay. Bray's lips pulled back from chipped teeth—a snarl masquerading as a smile—and he said, "Considering what you two've got tucked away in the hold, hearing's the least you could do."

Shoved from behind, Simon Acker emerged from the shadows. The lantern illuminated the fresh bruises on Simon's neck and chest, and his blackened left eye was swollen shut. "Your first mate's told us all about the tally," Bray said. "Took a little convincing, but hungry men have their ways. Now, I don't know about the others, but I would have liked to know it was my last meal I was eating—might've chewed it longer, right boys?"

With Bray's black eyes boring into him, Edmund felt like he was staring down a feral dog. It would be a fatal mistake to take his eyes off of Bray and allow his attention to wander to the growling, bristling pack behind him, already closing the circle to prevent his escape. Showing fear would be the same as opening his own throat with the knife on his belt, and so Edmund mimicked Bray's pose, squaring his shoulders and crossing his arms. Edmund's voice did not quaver; it was commanding—all steel and edge and force.

"Speak," Edmund said, as if Bray was nothing more than mangy cur begging for scraps from the table. "Speak, God damn you."

"We eat him," Bray said, sneering. "Plenty of good meat on those bones."

"And the rest of you—do you agree? You would consume this man? Look at him before you answer, because that is what he is: a *man*. And you would eat him?" Edmund scanned their faces and saw vacant eyes staring back at him, heard only the nervous shuffling of feet, a throat being cleared and the rasp of hands scratching beards.

"He *was* a man," said Bray. "Now he's only meat. Unless you've got something more tender to offer us..."

Disgusted, Edmund shook his head. They were not asking for permission; the decision had already been made. Bray's implication was clear: Edmund could let them eat Yates, or Bray would reveal Thomas's presence to the men. Better to maintain the charade, pretend that he still held control, and protect his son for as long as possible.

"Very well," Edmund said, turning to leave.

"You'll be the one to do it, Captain," Bray said. "It's fitting, don't you think? Since you kept us in the dark about the food running out."

"I won't," said Edmund, but a metallic clinking gave him pause. Edmund felt the weight of the hold's key in his pocket, but the second key belonged to Simon. Turning, Edmund saw the key dangling from Bray's fist.

Bray jiggled the key on its ring, his snarl spreading wider. "You'll be the one to do it."

Yates was dead, his head twisted so far around that, even after Bray flipped the man onto his stomach and shoved a knife into Edmund's hand, Edmund could still see the man's blank stare. Like vultures eyeing a carcass the crew gathered around, as Edmund sank the knife into Yates's left buttock and sawed the blade back and forth, using his other hand to pry back the chunk of flesh, inch by inch. Progress was slow, and Edmund understood why when he looked up from the dull, chipped blade to the grinning man who had provided it.

Bray urged him onward with a nod. When Edmund peeled back the glistening cut once more, separating the meat with a soft, sucking sound, the ragged sigh of the knife's blade was drowned out by a new sound that flooded Edmund's veins with ice water: Yates was laughing. It was impossible, and yet the rotted mouth hung open, the good-natured chuckle escalating into a wild howl.

Keane fled, tripped on a coil of rope, and vomited onto the deck. Others simply turned away, seeking escape from Yates's pungent breath and the tears welling in his unblinking eyes, streaming down the cheeks of a head turned backwards on its shoulders. Edmund's hands shook as he turned Yates onto his back and pressed a hand to the man's hitching chest in search of a heartbeat. There was movement in the cage formed by Yates's ribs—not a beat, but a hectic, irregular thumping, as if some part of Yates was trapped inside and seeking a way out.

Edmund detected motion in his peripherals and fell back just as Bray drove a heavy barrel down on Yates's head to silence the laughter. Stunned, Edmund brushed at the moisture clinging to his cheeks and saw clots of gray and flecks of bone stippling the red smear across the back of his hand. Bray rolled the barrel away from the flattened pulp above Yates's shoulders and smiled. "I'll take care of the rest, Captain," he said. "Go get cleaned up for supper."

Reeling from shock, Edmund stumbled across the deck and disappeared below, no longer concerned with the image he presented to the men. Yates had been dead. *Dead.* His mind whirled with conflicting thoughts. Instinct urged Edmund to save his son, get the boy far from the hungry, desperate crew, but there was nothing but open ocean for hundreds of miles in every direction.

As Edmund struggled to unlock the door to the hold, dropping the key twice in the process, an idea occurred to him: he could build a raft for the boy. The chances that Thomas would run across another ship and be rescued were slim—more likely he would die, desiccated by the sun or drowned by the sea, but it was a better fate than what awaited the boy's tender flesh after the crew had finished digesting Yates. Their insatiable guts would begin to growl once more, urging them to seek new prey.

The crew was busy pulling Yates apart, sectioning and portioning. They did not see Edmund steal about the ship, collecting rope and wood fragments. When the fire was built, and pieces of Yates were roasting beneath the eerie light of the moon, the men began to sing. Their boisterous chorus was strained; it possessed a manic, forced energy, but the noise disguised the sounds from below the deck. Edmund broke apart empty barrels, battering the sparse furniture from his quarters and lashing everything together with rope. When he had finished a small raft lay in the corner of the hold, covered by a scrap of canvas. Edmund pressed his forehead to Thomas's and said, "My son, whatever happens to me you must escape."

From his pocket Edmund withdrew a silver bell. "Your mother's. Do you know the sound it makes?"

"Yes," Thomas said. It was his mother's most prized possession, given to Edmund at the start of every voyage to bring him good fortune and keep him safe.

"Good," said Edmund. "When the raft is ready, I will come and fetch you. If you should hear this bell, it means that something has gone wrong, and you must put the raft into the water yourself. Climb aboard, and get as far away from the ship as you can. I've fashioned paddles from the—"

"Poppa. The raft is too heavy. How will I—"

Edmund clapped a hand over his son's mouth. The singing above them had stopped. He removed the hold's key from his pocket and folded Thomas's hand around it. "I will drag the raft up after the men have eaten, when they are all asleep."

Edmund heard a low grumble, and Thomas hugged his belly. "Could I have something to eat?"

"No!" Thomas recoiled from the shout, and Edmund reached out to catch the boy before he could flee back to the shadows. He drew his son into a tight embrace and said, "There is no food left on this ship. Do you understand me? Only men."

"No food." Thomas released a shuddering sigh.

When Edmund emerged onto the deck the smell of roasted meat flooded his mouth with saliva. Bray approached him, brandishing a club of flesh that might have passed for an elongated turkey leg, if not for the blackened fingers curled at its base. "Your portion, Captain," said Bray, shoving Yates's forearm against Edmund's chest. "Be sure to eat it all. We need to know that you're with us—that there won't be any...misunderstandings about what transpired, once the wind has returned us to dry land."

Eyes shone in the firelight, watching Edmund, waiting. Edmund brought the meat to his lips and sank his teeth into Yates's skin, swearing to himself that it was a necessary decision made to keep his son safe, and not to satisfy the ache in his empty stomach. Juices spilled down his chin. He chewed, then swallowed. The next bite was easier. The one after that required no thought at all.

The men lay in their bunks, snoring loudly, when Edmund crawled from beneath the shroud of sleep to carry the raft to the deck. After affixing a simple pulley system with ropes to lower the raft into the water, Edmund tossed the scrap of canvas over his handiwork and went to retrieve his son. When he passed the place where they had butchered Yates a stain on the deck seized Edmund's attention. The men had scrubbed the deck clean. Edmund had watched them, his eyelids drooping from the fire's heat and the satisfaction of a full stomach.

Frowning, Edmund lit a lantern and knelt to examine the stain, like black ink spilled across the wood planks in the rough shape of a man. It was growing. As he watched the stain expanded, nearing his boots, and Edmund reached out to touch it. Dark tendrils sprouted from the rough planks, stretching towards his fingertips, and he jerked his hand back in fear. Something rolled over in his stomach with a sickening, slippery heat as Edmund lurched to his feet. He had intended to fetch his son, to help the boy make his escape, but now—with his hand pressed to his distended stomach, feeling a distinct squirming sensation against his palm like snakes nesting beneath his skin—Edmund felt compelled to check on the men.

The retching sounds reached his ears first, followed by the horrendous smell. The reek of Yates's breath had been magnified, liquefied and spewed across every surface of the crew's quarters. Ichor dangled from the men's mouths in thick ropes, coating their hands and bulging bellies with fluid that shone like tar in the lantern's light. Hall collapsed and began to seize. The pale skin of his chest split, white knobs protruding from the weeping flesh to shred Hall's right nipple and spread down his arm, up his neck and across the bubbling surface of his stomach.

Edmund wanted to run, but he remained frozen in place, eyes fixed on the bony growths that covered Hall's entire body. They were like hideous, malformed barnacles, their beak-like centers clicking and chattering. Keane tumbled from his bed, tearing at his scalp and issuing high, breathless shrieks as his eyeball bulged from his socket and ruptured, the deflated cornea pushed aside by a pulsing, muscular tentacle that explored his hair before burrowing into his ear.

Bray stood facing the wall, cloaked in shadow. The blue tattoos across his naked back rippled, guttural laughter rising above the retching and the raw, unfettered screams from Edmund's crew. Turning, Bray moved towards Edmund, his steps halting and uneven. "Captain." Bray belched and pressed the back of his hand to his lips. He chuckled—a wet sound, like stones being dropped into thick mud—and said, "Oh, Captain. I think our friend Yates was tainted."

With a groan Bray fell to his knees, diaphragm hitching beneath the arch of his spine. Another belch tore from his chest, vibrating the planks under Edmund's feet as something long, slick and sickly-yellow was birthed from Bray's throat. It wiggled between his lips until Bray's jaw reached the limits of expansion. When the girth of its eel-like body became lodged between Bray's teeth the creature retracted, surging forward with renewed vigor, and Edmund heard a meaty pop from Bray's dislocated jaw. He saw the corners of Bray's mouth rip and streak the creature's jaundiced skin with blood.

The thing flailed between Edmund's boots and whipped around to batten onto Bray's right cheek. Releasing terrified, agonized moans, Bray pawed at the monstrosity blocking his airway. Unable to grip the slippery form he tried to work his fingers beneath the creature's flat, pulsing mouth, but its teeth kept it hooked in place. Bray toppled forward, eyes rolled back to whites, and Edmund's paralysis finally broke.

He ran.

Up.

To the deck.

Under the starry night sky Edmund fell to the deck and clutched his stomach. There was something inside of him—he was sure of it now—a writhing tickle deep in his sinuses, creeping up from the root of his tongue and crawling under his skin like a tide of ants. A bass rumble traveled through the ship, and Edmund craned his neck to look up at the sails. The air was still; there was no wind, and yet the canvas billowed outwards, filled by an invisible breath. A blue-green light beckoned to Edmund. He crawled on hands and knees to the place where Yates had been butchered; no longer a stain, but an opening: a gateway. Dark forms were pressing through, dripping shadows with alien features illuminated by the bioluminescent glow that poured through the opening. They spilled over Edmund's hands, licking up his arms and into his eyes like poisonous, dancing tongues of flame.

Mesmerized, Edmund felt his consciousness drift outwards. The tether of a nagging memory—some unfulfilled, crucial task—tugged him back, away from that alluring glow. Something shifted in his gut, transferring its weight to his bladder. The skin beside his navel stretched tight over a protruding force, and when he moved to loosen his belt Edmund's arm brushed against something in his pocket. He removed the bell and stared at the metal, glowing blue-green in the night air. Thomas, his son, was still waiting in the hold. Cramps seized his entrails in a merciless fist, and Edmund fell to the deck gasping. He rang the bell again and again until the pain became too great, then the darkness welcomed him with unrelenting hunger.

It was morning when Thomas finally dared to venture out of the hold and onto the deck. The bell had fallen silent hours before, but the shouts, screams, thumps, howls and chittering laughter had haunted the ship for the remainder of the night, fading only when dawn spread its warm fingers through the starless sky. The silver bell lay on the deck beside a contorted mass of twisted flesh wrapped in his father's tattered clothes. Thomas retrieved the bell and wandered towards the raft. There was no other living soul aboard the *Lear*, yet he could not stay. The ship was listing, taking on water. Whatever had visited their vessel the night before had been ruthless in its retreat—rending, splintering, and splitting. Thomas yanked back the canvas to reveal the simple pulley system that his father had rigged. Two paddles—flat boards with cloth-wrapped handles—were lashed to the raft's center. Thin arms flexing, Thomas heaved the raft over the side of the ship and took a last look around before climbing on to lower himself down.

A faint breeze blew across the deck, carrying with it a tantalizing scent that made his mouth water. Evidence remained from the feast the night before, and Thomas abandoned the raft to investigate the semi-circle of barrels on which the men had gathered. The pile of ashes, and the blacked scraps of meat, still clung to the makeshift spit. Glancing around, as though he was afraid he might be caught, Thomas reached out, peeling a scrap of flesh from the spit and popping it into his mouth. Charred gristle crunched between his teeth. He had never tasted anything so delicious. Thomas picked the spit clean, running his teeth under his fingernails to glean every last morsel, then climbed aboard the raft.

Drifting on the open ocean Thomas folded his legs beneath him and waited for rescue. While he waited he fidgeted, his restless fingers seeking some action with which to distract his young mind. Thomas's stomach gurgled. His fingers twitched. On the wooden plank beside him Thomas's thumbnail scratched three furrows that met in the center to form a "Y".

Three days passed, and the boy looked up from a raft covered in letters—one name, repeated, smeared with blood from his frayed fingertips—to see sails on the horizon. Pulled aboard by strangers, the boy laughed. He spit the water they offered back in their faces. Reading the scratches on the raft, they said, "Yates? Is that your name?"

The boy bobbed his head.

"Yates," he said.

And then, "Is that your name?"

R.L. Meza

About the Author

R.L. Meza lives in a century-old Victorian house on the coast of northern California with her husband and the host of strange animals she calls family. When she isn't writing horror stories, roaming through the forest, or painting, she can be found with a cat in her lap and a book in her hand.

Into the Depths

David Green

"If you tell me we're lost," Danene growled, "I'm throwing you off this fucking sub, and I couldn't give a shit if your sorry arse drowns."

She ground her teeth as Jacob, head of navigation on the Sabre, shrank into his seat. *Spineless bastard,* Danene thought, staring instead at the submarine's radar, its beep echoing around the command room. *Fucking Hell, relax. He's doing his best, like everyone. It's not your fault, or theirs.*

A scientific expedition into the Mariana Trench, funded by an eccentric Singaporean billionaire, Danene's team aimed to explore the ocean's deepest point further than anyone before. Time dictated their need and haste; scientists had discovered mining potential in the Trench, and the world's wealthiest entrepreneurs and corporations scrambled to map the Mariana first.

Their benefactor spared no expense, providing innovative equipment and a bespoke submarine for the task—a sleek vessel built for a small scientific research team and able to withstand the crippling pressures of the Trench. He even let Danene, Britain's foremost Oceanographer, handpick her crew from around the world. They'd cut corners on the testing periods, their claim at being pioneers overriding common sense. Anytime an issue cropped up she pictured the money sunk into this project, and the trust placed in her.

They'd passed the previous marked depths of the Mariana Trench three days ago. Their charts, data and systems disagreed on their position, and even on what direction their nose pointed in.

"Danene," Jacob stammered, tracing the radar screen with his index finger, "the telemetry makes no sense. The readouts are bogus. The more I look at it, the less I understand. I need a break, please."

"Malfunction? All the systems wouldn't fry. Too much of a coincidence. What about the backups?" Danene grated.

"Sabotaged," Jacob whispered.

Danene bit her lip as her fists curled into balls. Jacob kept his eyes averted as he hunched over the radar, his hair slick with sweat. She felt a hand squeeze on her shoulder. Turning, she discovered Mateo, a marine biologist, and someone she'd grown a little too close with during their training. The rest of the team knew and accepted it. Not that she cared; they were single, and there weren't rules against crew relationships, this being a civilian mission. Plus Chen and Zoey had hit it off too; living in close quarters did that. Mateo's amiable nature calmed her, and with tensions running high since they entered the Trench she appreciated him, though the man appeared tense himself.

"He's on the verge of bugging out," Mateo whispered. "Some R&R wouldn't go amiss. Shit, we could all do with it. I'll look at the data, see if he's missed something. Maybe the water pressure is messing with the sub's systems and we can fix them."

Danene sighed. "Alright. Get to your bunk, Jacob. Rest up, and we'll figure this out." The navigator stayed in his seat, rocking back and forth. "Jacob? You hear me?"

"French!" Mateo barked, kicking his chair. Jacob spun, a frenzied look in his eye. "You okay, man?"

"Yeah," Jacob muttered, glancing around him like he'd forgotten his location. "Yeah, just tired."

He got to his feet and shuffled away, hunched over himself.

"No way is it sabotage. Who'd do that?" Mateo said, shaking his head as he watched Jacob disappear into the bowels of the sub. "Cabin fever, I'd guess."

"Tell me about it," Danene replied, leaning her forehead on Mateo's shoulder. "All I can think about since we entered the Trench is escaping. I walked by the airlock today, and part of me wanted to tear it open."

Mateo narrowed his eyes. Danene felt her cheeks burn as he studied her face. Sometimes the intensity in his stare made her self-conscious. "Reckon you need some downtime, too. I'll call if I make any sense of the readouts."

"Wanna take charge, huh?" She said with a smirk.

"Maybe later," Mateo replied, subdued.

Danene couldn't argue, she needed the rest. She'd lost track of time as they plunged deeper. *Feels like I'm drifting through a dream,* she thought.

"Yeah, I know what you mean," Mateo said. She blinked, not realizing she'd spoken aloud. He stared into the middle-distance.

"See you later, big guy," she whispered, slapping him on the backside, a normal act meant to put herself at ease. It didn't work, and Mateo didn't react. Turning to the comms station she forced the dread welling in her chest back down to the pit of her stomach. "All crew, listen up, this is Danene. Sub's coming to a halt till we figure out this radar malfunction. Hang tight."

Danene's footsteps echoed down the corridor as she walked to her cabin. The sub had come to a full stop, and her head spun. They'd spent the last four weeks at sea, and her senses had gotten used to the constant motion. The lack of it seemed alien to her. Danene hugged herself tight as she hurried to her destination. She'd spent her entire life dreaming about the oceans, even dedicating her studies since childhood for the chance to chart them.

The opportunity to explore the Mariana sent tingles of excitement through her body, the expedition being what she'd worked toward all her life. The Trench fascinated her even as a child, and she'd lay awake at night imagining the awesome scale of it. *Seven miles deep,* she thought, glancing around the grey, soulless corridors of the Sabre, *and forty-four miles wide. One-thousand-five-hundred-and-fifty-four miles long.*

Danene often gave her imagination free rein when she thought of the secrets the Mariana Trench might hold, but now, as a tiny speck in the abyss' maw, she could only think of the cold, dark, crushing water surrounding her in that vast well of emptiness.

Her heart thudded in her chest, and Danene's breath pumped in a short, fast, uneven rhythm. Her neck muscles tightened as she imagined all the weight outside the sub's hull squeezing her.

"A fucking panic attack?" She breathed, leaning her forehead against the metallic wall. She closed her eyes and racked her brain for anything safe, but visions of black water crashed into her mind. Danene beat her fist against the smooth surface, its clang giving her something to latch on to. "No," she growled, "I'm not afraid."

"You and I are the only people in this tub that ain't, Cap," a voice drawled to her right.

Danene half-jumped as she spun to face Brett, the ship's medical officer, and a man she regretted bringing onboard. He'd charmed her when she'd interviewed him, and his knowledge of medicine and experience in the US Navy impressed her, but his abrasive, arrogant nature soon revealed itself as they disembarked for the Trench. A loner, the rest of the crew gave him a wide-berth unless they required his help. He appeared to like that just fine.

She punched him hard on the shoulder. Brett rolled

with it and threw her a lopsided grin as he leaned against the wall.

"Fuck, Anderson," Danene snapped, using his surname, "almost gave me a goddamn heart-attack. Sneaking up on people? For fuck sake."

Brett raised his eyebrows in mock surprise. "Well, I passed Jacob shambling towards his cabin, muttering about sabotage. Thought I'd come find you, to say that, in medical terms, your boy's in danger of going full-on wacko." He smiled again. "You ain't looking much better."

"Go fuck yourself," Danene growled. She had to thank the doctor for the seething anger now obliterating the panic that threatened to overwhelm her. "If he needs meds, or an evaluation, go do it. You don't need my permission."

"Too right," Brett replied, peering at his fingernails as if he tried to decide which one he liked best. "Can do the same for you. There's eight crew onboard. I'm the one who can relieve you, on medical grounds, if I feel necessary. Don't forget it."

"That a threat?"

Brett shrugged, then met her brown eyes with his piercing blue ones. "What did Jacob mean by 'sabotage'?"

Danene pulled breath into her lungs and counted to five; better that than unleashing her anger on the sub's only medic.

"Nav's having trouble telling us where we are," she replied, smoothing her voice as best she could. "Mateo reckons the water pressure has messed with the systems.

Jacob's spooked."

"Oh? Your boyfriend would know better than a navigator, I suppose," Brett smiled with a wink.

"He's not—"

"I don't care, we're all adults here." Brett replied. He lifted an index finger and pointed it towards the ceiling. "Go up. Break water. Get a readout. Send an SOS. Problem solved, then the crew can stop their descent into fucking madness. It ain't just Jacob."

"Thanks, Brains," Danene laughed. "Dilemma's this: without the nav, we don't know where that is. We're swimming blind; we could surface, but our position might have us too close to the Mariana's sides, or something might lie above us. If we're floating the correct direction, that is. If you don't mind, I've got some downtime."

She pushed past him and tried to ignore his eyes burning holes into the back of her head as she descended deeper into the sub's belly.

Danene set her alarm for four hours and slipped into an uneasy slumber. The lack of motion unsettled her, and she kept jerking herself out of her dreams. Not that she complained as she drifted in the space midway between waking and sleep; images of an inky darkness smothering her haunted her, as did Brett, holding his finger up to the ceiling and mouthing *"Up."*

"You ever wonder what's going on beyond the

Trench?" Someone croaked from the end of her bed.

Danene scrambled backwards, her back slamming against the wall as she pulled her covers up to her neck. Jacob sat in a chair facing her, the whites of his eyes glinting in the low-lit gloom. To Danene they appeared fevered.

"What the fuck are you doing in my room, French?" She half-yelled, remembering to use his surname like Mateo did back on the bridge. It got through to him then.

"I wanted...no, *needed*, to talk," Jacob replied. He sounded somewhat short of lucid. "Have we always existed here? On this sub, in the Trench? I try to remember my life before, but it's like I'm trying to catch smoke in the wind."

"Jacob," Danene whispered, her instincts screaming at her to run. The way he peered at her through the dark made her hackles rise. "You're tired and spooked. I am too. Get some rest."

"Can't sleep," he muttered, looking away as he nibbled on the skin surrounding his fingernails. "My blood feels twisted, like it's running the wrong way. You know?"

He leaned forwards.

Unblinking.

"Yeah," Danene said, attempting a smile. "Sure, I understand. The lack of motion doesn't help, huh?"

"We're still moving," Jacob laughed, a sound filled with despair. The noise curdled Danene's stomach. "Down. The Trench is pulling us in. It has us now, and it'll never let go."

What the fuck? Danene thought. "Jacob, as soon as the nav's back online, we're golden. We'll figure it out."

"What do you know?" He yelled and aimed a trembling finger in her direction. "You brought me here, didn't you?"

Danene glanced around without moving her head. She felt defenseless. Alone. Trapped.

"Jacob—"

The cabin's comm unit chimed, and breath exploded from her lungs in a rush.

"Danene," Mateo said, "sorry, but we need you on the bridge. Gonna call the entire crew in."

"Okay," she replied, her quivering voice weak in her ears. She locked eyes with Jacob. "Don't bother calling French, he's with me."

"Jacob's in your cabin?" Mateo asked in a flat tone.

"Yeah. Talking shop. We'll see you in five. Danene out."

They stared at each other, Danene aware for the first time in weeks of the metal beams and supports creaking around her.

"You mind leaving so I can get dressed?" She said.

Jacob blinked, his lips curved in what she couldn't call a smile.

"Sure," he replied, getting to his feet. "I'll wait outside."

The doors slid open, then shut as he left. Danene buried her face in her hands, her shoulders heaving as she wept.

She gave herself sixty seconds, then brought her tears to a shuddering halt. She had work to do.

Jacob trailed behind as Danene entered the bridge. Silence, broken only by the steady beep of the radar, welcomed her. The rest of the crew sat in chairs around the meeting table, all lost in thought. Mateo looked up, wearing a pensive frown instead of his usual good-natured smile. He narrowed his eyes at Jacob.

Chen and Zoey sat next to each other, her head on his shoulder. They made no effort to hide their affection. As marine biologists they had plenty in common before their relationship bloomed. Macy sat with them. Danene nodded at her.

"Cap," Macy said with a sad smile. "Not holding together too well."

Danene felt a pang of sympathy for the oceanographer. They got on well. The young woman kept to herself, but they both shared a love of the sea and spent hours discussing its minutiae.

"Hang tight," Danene said, taking her seat at the table's head. "We'll pull through this."

Macy spread her hands. "I just don't know what I'm contributing. I feel useless, and...no, it doesn't matter."

"What?" Danene said, looking around. The rest of the team appeared to ignore their conversation, except Brett. He watched, looking all too interested. His regard almost distracted her; she noticed an empty chair.

"Dreams," Macy whispered. "Nightmares, really."

Danene reached out, and patted her on the shoulder.

"They're going around, don't dwell on them."

"Sure, Cap."

Danene glanced at Mateo, pointing at the empty seat. "Where's Danvers?"

"Pinged his comm a few times, but no answer. Spoke to him this morning. Said he'd perform some system tests before his break. He's on downtime, so maybe he switched it off?" He replied, not meeting her eyes.

She ignored his sullen behaviour. "He's the bloody sub's engineer, and he ain't here yet? Let's give him a few minutes before we start. I presume you've bad news, so I want him here to offer solutions."

Danene glanced around at her team. Brett nodded back, a sly smile on his lips as he lounged in his seat like he hadn't a care in the world. Jacob twitched as he peered towards the radar screen. Chen and Zoey huddled close, and Macy stared in silence at her fingers splayed out on the table. Danene felt she could taste the tension. *That just leaves Paul Danvers,* she thought. *Where the fuck is he? Lazy bastard. An engineer should be all over this.*

"This can't wait," Zoey snarled, "we've come to a fucking full stop somewhere in the deepest trench in all the planet's oceans, and I don't know about you, but I'm on the verge of freaking out."

"It's not as bad as that, is it?" Chen asked, a pleading note to his voice, like he needed to hear soothing words. "We've options. This sub's state-of-the-art."

"Fine," Danene said. "Mateo, what's the word?" She nudged him, and he tore his eyes away from Jacob.

"We're fucked," he whispered.

"Jesus Christ," Brett laughed. "You sulking because our glorious leader and Twitchy McGee had a private one-to-one? Grow a pair, man, and do your job."

Mateo lunged from his seat. Danene grabbed him and pulled him back down.

"Hey," she shouted, looking around at her fractured team. Brett threw her a lopsided grin, his eyes twinkling. "I get it, we're scared. God knows all that water out there is getting to me, but we're a crew. We have to stick together. Like Chen said, the Sabre's cutting-edge. Let's figure it out. Together. Mateo, we'll talk later, right? For now what's the word?"

The marine biologist sniffed, then nodded to himself as if he'd arrived at some decision. *Now's not the time for fucking pouting,* Danene thought.

"Okay, there's no way to sugarcoat this: we've no idea where we are. We could try to surface, but we could end up deeper in the Trench, or hit something. Then we're one-hundred percent fucked. We're out of comms range. That's it."

"What happened to the nav system?" Zoey asked, slapping the table with her palm.

Mateo shrugged. "Full malfunction. No one's gone as far into the Mariana as we have. The water pressure would have crippled any other sub. Listen: you can hear it, can't you?"

"Fuck off, man," Chen muttered, glancing around him as if he expected to see the ocean pouring in through the bulwark at any moment. "No need for drama."

"It wants us dead!" Jacob screamed. "It did this to us. We don't belong here."

The crew shifted in their seats, refusing to make eye contact. *Mateo's right,* Danene thought. *Cabin fever, the lot of us. Well, I refuse to get frightened. This is the life I wanted.*

"Backup systems?" she said, putting steel into her voice.

"Down," Mateo said, shaking his head. "Two reasons spring to mind: the pressure's one."

"The other?" Danene asked.

"Sabotage," Brett said, staring at Jacob.

"Enough," Danene snapped. She wanted to slap the man. "Who in their fucking right minds would do that?"

The doctor pointed at the rocking navigator. "Does he look 'right' to you?"

Danene ignored his barb. "We do a full system re-start. That gives us our best chance." Mateo shrugged and looked away. "Macy, you're quiet. What do you reckon?"

"I'd like to know what Danvers thinks."

"Where the fuck is he, anyway?" Brett asked. Getting to his feet, he pushed the sub's intercom button. "Paul. Meeting on the bridge started ten minutes ago."

They waited in silence as the seconds trickled by. Brett pushed the button again. "Paul? Come in, you lazy sonofabitch."

"Go check on him," Danene said. For once Brett didn't smile or respond with a quip before leaving. "How long will a restart take?"

"I want to hear what Danvers says," Macy repeated.

"And I want some fucking options," Danene snarled.

"Four hours," Chen muttered. "Give or take."

Danene looked around at the frowns and bleak stares. "We can do this. Let's pull—"

"Cap," Brett's panicked voice blared through the intercom, "I need you at Danvers' cabin now!"

The crew surged to their feet as one and raced into the corridor. Danene pushed her way past them as she ran, the metallic floor ringing with their heavy footsteps. She saw Brett up ahead, sat on the floor with his back to the wall outside the cabin. Zoey got there first.

"Fuck!" she screamed, scrambling back from the doorway. Danene came to a stop. Brett looked at her, shaking his head. She took a breath and entered.

Danvers lay on his bed. Years ago Danene saw photographs of Jack the Ripper's victims. Walking into the cabin felt like stepping into history. Spread-eagled, the corpse's stomach and chest gaped open, intestines and other organs spilling from the wound. Blood pooled from the now-red sheets onto the floor. Danvers' lifeless eyes stared at the ceiling, his face stuck in shock.

Danene took it all in with a clinical detachment. A part of her mind gibbered and wailed at what she witnessed, but a cold reasoning took over. She scanned the former engineer and discovered another wound; a clean one across his Adam's apple. She turned and left the cabin.

The crew waited outside. Brett still sat on the floor, head bowed. Chen hugged the sobbing Zoey.

"He's dead," Danene said, making eye contact with

Mateo. She wanted to go to him, desiring his comfort, but she needed to show her strength as a leader. He flinched away from her stare. No doubt Zoey had told them what she'd seen in the cabin. "I have to ask where you all were. I saw Mateo on the bridge four hours ago, and the doc around the same time."

"You accusing one of us?" Macey snapped, glaring at Danene.

"Danvers didn't do that to himself," Mateo said. "I know who my money's on."

"Zoey, Macy and I have spent all day in the labs running some tests. You can check the logs if you like?" Chen cut in.

Zoey noticed someone missing. "Where's Jacob?"

Mateo glanced around. "Bingo. I'll find the little fucker," he said, stalking away. Danene suppressed a shiver. *Could Jacob do this?* She remembered the way he watched her when he appeared in her room.

"There's nothing the rest of you can do. Brett, examine the body. Chen, Zoey and Macy: do a system restart, then rest up. The sooner we surface the better."

The crew drifted away. Danene heard Brett get to his feet and enter the cabin. Alone, she sank to the ground, the images of Danvers' massacred body hitting her. Silent sobs wracked her, and fear bloomed in her chest.

Lost in the ocean's deepest trench, seven crew members remained alive on the Sabre, one of them a killer.

Danene stood in the sub's mess hall, hands curled around a steaming cup of coffee. She stared into the liquid as Brett poured hot water in his mug. He'd insisted on staying with her, though she didn't know if he did it for his own safety or not.

"From the way the blood congealed he died no less than two hours ago, and no more than four," the doctor said with none of his usual abrasiveness.

"When Jacob went for downtime," Danene muttered.

"And you."

"I didn't do this," Danene yelled, squaring up to him.

"No," Brett said, shaking his head. "I don't think you did. Not Jacob either. He's cracked, but I couldn't imagine him doing this. We're marooned with a system failure, and the expert in that field's dead; that isn't a coincidence."

"What would make someone flip like that?" Danene said, almost to herself.

Brett shrugged, and took a sip of his coffee. "We're in uncharted territories. I don't mean to act glib, but we're deeper than any humans ever reached. There's only so many simulations you can run. We've no way of telling what effect reaching these depths has on us, both physical and mental. We're dealing with changes in oxygen levels, massive water and mental pressure, isolation and experimental tech. To be honest, I'm surprised someone didn't flip already. You've noticed it, haven't you? The muttering, the sour looks, the dreams. We're all getting them."

Her mind wandered back to Danvers' cabin, returning to the horror. After leaving she returned to her cabin with

Brett waiting outside, and vomited her stomach empty before changing, afraid that the stench of death clung to her clothes. She checked in with Zoey, Macy, and Chen; they'd busied themselves getting the sub ready for the restart. Of Mateo and Jacob she'd heard nothing. Danene attempted to reach them both on comms, but neither answered.

It's all falling apart, and I can't trust any of them, she thought before letting out a shaky laugh, *except Brett. Unless he's a damn good actor...* She'd seen his reaction to Danvers' body up close. Staring into his eyes she saw the walls he raised to protect himself, and she witnessed the same fear she felt. *I'm glad I'm not alone, but he's out on his feet.* She smiled, took his hand in hers and gave it a squeeze.

"Go get some rest," Danene said.

"Can't," Brett replied with a sigh, "incidents mean reports, and deaths require lots of paperwork. Sure you don't want me to stay?"

"No, I'm fine. Stay safe."

"Don't get all soppy on me now, Cap."

She watched him go, fighting the urge to flee back to her cabin and lock herself in.

"Danene," Chen's voice crackled over the intercom. "Are you there?"

She shuffled over to the mess' intercom and thumbed the button. "Yeah. All good?"

"Just about ready to reset. Macy volunteered to restart the backup."

"Alone?" Danene replied with alarm.

"What else can we do? We need two on the bridge,

and fuck knows where Jacob and Mateo are." *Or if they're still alive,* Danene thought. "The lights will shut down, then Macy will spin up the backup and the emergency systems should kick in while the system resets."

"*Should*?"

"Listen, Cap, I'm doing the best I can. Our expert's dead."

Danene kicked a chair leg in frustration. "Right, I know. I'll make my way over to Macy's location. Danene out."

Glancing around, Danene pulled open a draw and took a kitchen knife. *Better to be fucking safe than Goddamn sorry,* she thought. Her footsteps echoed as she headed to Macy and the engine room. Even though she knew it would happen panic bloomed in her chest when the lights snuffed out. She'd grown used to it, but the sudden lack of vibration and hum from the Sabre's engines disturbed her. Danene came to a full stop and held the knife out in front of her, peering into the darkness. More than ever she felt the oppressive presence of the Mariana Trench surrounding them, with only inches of metal between her and the vast unknown.

"Come on," she whispered as the seconds dragged. The sub vibrated, and Danene sighed in relief as the emergency lighting system kicked in, though her comfort faded as the red illumination gave the corridors an ominous slant. She picked up her pace.

Turning a corner to the engine room Danene slipped and crashed to the ground, striking her head against the wall, and collided with something on the walkway. Her knife fell from her grasp. Dazed, she shook her head and glanced around.

Beside her, Macy's body lay on the deck, her skull caved in on one side. Grey matter and gore splattered the wall where someone had slammed her cranium against the bulkhead multiple times. One eyeball stared into Danene's, the other hanging loose against her cheek. Adrenaline surged through Danene's body, and her brain made a connection that sent her scrambling to her feet.

"She just turned the generator on," she said, grabbing the knife from the floor and holding it in two hands. "Macy died in the last few minutes."

The intercom crackled into life, and Danene's heart tried to escape through her throat. A strangled cry rang out across the sub's speakers, only to cut off as soon as it sounded.

"Chen," Danene said. She raced towards the bridge, the red emergency lights guiding her way. She glanced down as she ran as her empty stomach protested, though she had nothing left to vomit. Macy's blood caked her blue jumpsuit.

We're civilians, she thought as she tore through the corridors, *we're trained in our jobs and the expedition, not on dealing with a fucking serial killer.*

Danene drew near the bridge and slowed her pace. She knew others who heard the scream over the intercom would follow. Creeping, she slid up alongside the entryway and peered through. In the crimson gloom she saw

Chen and Zoey slumped across their stations, their blood splashed over the equipment. Someone stood over them. She turned the corner; the knife held out in front of her.

"Jacob," she called, "why?"

The navigator spun. The whites of his wild eyes stared at her through a mask of blood.

"No," he cried, taking a juddering step forward. "I found them!"

"Don't come any closer," Danene yelled, the knife trembling in her hand. "I suppose you just found Macy too, huh?"

"What?" Jacob shouted. He staggered, a hand raised to his head. His fingers came away bloody, and Danene gasped as she saw the gash cut into the side of his scalp. "I heard the scream, someone—"

Danene fell to the ground as someone barged past her. Mateo cannoned into Jacob, knocking him to the floor.

"You sick sonofabitch," he cried, raining blows down on the stricken navigator. Danene scrambled to her feet as Brett ran in behind her.

"Stop," she screamed, grabbing Mateo. "We need answers. I won't have you beat him to death."

Mateo struggled, and Brett lent his strength to bring him under control. They pulled him off the prone Jacob; Mateo spat at him and sank his boot into the man's ribs.

"He's had enough," Brett cried.

"Check on the others," Danene said, grabbing Mateo's face and staring into his eyes. Hard hatred glared back. She pulled away from him.

"Why?" Mateo growled. "They're fucking *dead,* just like Danvers and Macy. This piece of shit murdered them. Couldn't handle the fucking pressure."

"How do you know about—"

"He's unconscious, but alive," Brett called, peering at the wound on Jacob's head. "He's taken a nasty blow before the beating. If you want answers help me get him to my station. He's losing a lot of blood."

Danene bent to lift Jacob's legs, and Brett cradled his neck. She looked up to see Mateo standing between Chen and Zoey's corpses, staring into space as if two dead bodies didn't surround him.

Danene and Mateo watched through the medical room's glass doors as Brett worked on the sedated Jacob. She kept the knife in her belt, away from Mateo. He hadn't spoken in the hours since they'd discovered the triple murders. Danene wanted nothing more than to run, to curl into a ball, or to throw open the airlock and let the ocean claim them. Fear etched itself into her bones. The man next to her, the one she'd welcomed into her bed and spent hours whispering about her hopes and dreams, felt like a dangerous stranger. *I'm not giving in,* she thought. She'd insisted he stay with them at the medical office. They were the last four crew members, and Danene didn't want any of them out of her sight. Mateo had grunted in response. *If timid Jacob's a killer,* she thought, *any of them are capable. No doubt they think the same about me.*

"What were you and Jacob doing in your cabin?" Mateo croaked. Danene glanced at him. He stared through the doors, his eyes burned with a fever.

"I woke up to find him there, watching me. Said he needed to talk. Went on about the Trench holding us."

"That's all?"

"Yeah, what the fuck do you think? I'm screwing the whole crew?"

Mateo shrugged in response.

"You and the doc seem to be getting awful close. You made a mistake hiring Jacob," he whispered. "Something always bothered me about him."

"We don't know he killed them," Danene said, though the evidence pointed that way. His erratic behaviour, the times spent missing, him being on the scene of the last murders...*It doesn't explain it all, though.* "What about his head?"

"Macy fought back," Mateo replied, still staring through the doors. "Jacob's not the strongest. Look, he's covered in blood. On his hands, his face. You think that's all his? No."

"I don't know what to think," Danene said, turning to face him. Something Mateo said back on the bridge had bothered her, and he'd pressed her buttons again. "How did you know about Macy?"

"You told me," Mateo answered, his face smooth.

"No, I didn't. You already knew, back on the bridge."

He frowned at her, then smiled. "You gaslighting me?"

"This isn't fucking funny," Danene snarled, "you knew. How?"

The smile wiped from Mateo's face, as if it never existed. "I followed you. Saw her body. I couldn't find Jacob, so watched you instead. You and he were the only people alone when Danvers died."

"And you."

Mateo's expression slid off his face, like it'd never expressed an emotion before.

"We don't belong here, don't you see? The Trench doesn't want us exploring, and this sub is too damn stubborn to let it crush us."

Mateo let out an abrupt chuckle. Alarm bells rang in Danene's head. Madness filled his laughter.

"You sound like Jacob," Danene said, taking a step backward and letting her hand fall to her belt.

"Didn't you say it yourself? '*All I can think about since we entered the Trench is escaping. I walked by the airlock today and part of me wanted to tear it open.*' It whispered to you, too, but you didn't listen."

"Do you know who sabotaged us? Jacob?" she bit her lip. "You?"

Mateo laughed again. "Oh no, the Trench did that. The way out is easy. We just go up, but it didn't want you to know that."

Danene jumped as Brett rapped on the glass. "He's waking."

"Be right there," she answered, staring at Mateo. Sweat beaded on his forehead.

"What are you going to do with that knife you're fingering?" he said, taking a step forward.

Danene raised it, and Mateo grabbed her wrists and squeezed. It fell from her grasp and he thrust his forehead into her nose, lights exploding behind her eyes. Dazed, she fell to the floor. He took the knife and opened the doors.

"No!" Danene screamed, flopping onto her front. She watched him plunge the knife between Brett's shoulder blades, his blood spurting like a fountain as Mateo withdrew the blade. He kicked the falling doctor over and approached Jacob. Dropping the knife he took the navigators head, pulling him from the operating table.

"Not going to escape this time, my friend," Mateo said. "I'm here to finish the job."

Mateo beat Jacob's cranium into the ground. The sub groaned and creaked as Mateo slammed Jacob's head in a steady rhythm. Danene could do nothing but watch, her limbs like water as the pain in her head made her weak.

Mateo let Jacob's body drop to the floor, the collapsed mess above its neck unrecognisable. He turned to Danene, his white teeth flashing in his crimson face. Mateo got to his feet.

"One left," he said, "then the Trench will claim us."

Mateo jerked forward. *Brett,* Danene thought.

Somehow the medic had staggered to his feet and retrieved the knife, plunging it into Mateo's ribcage. He sagged to the floor, a confused look on his face. Mateo pulled the blade from his side, then collapsed in a heap.

"Brett!" Danene cried, scrambling past Mateo's prone

body. Brett lay on his back nearby, blood pooling beneath him.

"Oh, hey Cap," the medic croaked between shallow breaths. The colour had retreated from his skin, leaving it chalky. "Think I might take some downtime, if it's alright with you?"

"No, we're going to the bridge and getting out of here," she said, putting a cheery note into her voice, though she knew Brett's time drew short.

"You do it for me. You owe me one."

"I know. You saved me," Danene whispered, clasping his hand. "Sorry for thinking you were a prick."

"Well, thanks for letting me know," Brett replied, the corners of his mouth lifting into a small smile. "I never knew you did."

Danene laughed, but it turned into a sob as tears leaked from her eyes. She glanced at Mateo, then forced herself to look at what remained of Jacob. "They're dead. My entire team. Mateo...he killed them all. He must have. You, too."

Brett wheezed and looked her in the eye, but it seemed he saw through her. "Mateo's right. We don't belong down here in the depths. I hear its call, too. Escape while you can."

His grip around her hand slackened, and his pupils turned to glass.

Danene screamed as the lights flickered from red to white; she felt the floor beneath her purr as the systems reengaged. The Sabre returned to life as Danene's last crew member died.

She climbed to her feet and made her way to the bridge, ignoring the groans of the surrounding structures and the clang of metal that echoed in her wake. Her only company. Chen and Zoey's bodies lay where Mateo had slain them. Danene picked her way around them and approached the nav screen.

A broken chuckle bubbled from her lips, morphing into a howl as tears streamed down her face.

The Sabre lay in clear waters, facing the correct direction. If she'd gambled on blowing the ballast they'd have escaped the Trench.

Her trembling fingers punched in the command and the sub obeyed, the familiar motion kicking in as the Sabre rose. Danene fingered the S.O.S prompt, useless at this depth but it would emit once the sub reached a suitable level. She slumped over the console.

"I never wanted to hurt you." She spun. Mateo waited inbetween the dead, a hand clutched against his bloody ribs. "The Trench. I hear it whispering to me, forcing me to stop you. It told me to kill the others. I couldn't say no. I tried, believe me, I did."

"You're mad," Danene said, her fingers fumbling around her for a weapon of any kind. They came up short. "It's cabin fever, a lack of oxygen. You said it yourself, and so did Brett. We just needed to figure it out."

"No," Mateo replied, taking an uneven step forward. "That's what you *want* to believe. You understand better. The Mariana claims all life. We don't belong here."

"Mateo, please—"

"Then I think about you and Jacob. What you did today in your bed. I'm not stupid," Mateo said. His eyes burned as he bared his teeth. "Were you fucking Brett, too?"

Run, Danene thought, *hide. The sub will surface soon, and they'll hear the distress call. I can make it.* She pointed at the corpses.

"Look at what you did," she bit out, adrenaline building in her veins. "Take a long, hard look. Can you do it?"

Mateo shook his head and glanced at the dead crew members. Danene surged past him, slamming her shoulder against his side to knock him off balance. She placed one foot in front of the other.

Then slipped on the blood-slick floor.

She crashed to the ground as Mateo threw himself on top of her, fury etched into his face. Danene tried to wriggle free, but his extra weight pinned her down. He gripped her throat and raised another above his head.

She acted on instinct and drove her knee into his groin. Breath escaped Mateo in a whoosh as he cried in pain. Danene used the momentum and swung above him, straddling him and squeezing her knees against his ribs. He gasped as she dug into the knife wound in his side, forcing the blood out of it, struggling to push her away as the strength ebbed from his limbs.

Danene smashed her forearm into his face, then again, then a third time. Blood pumped from his nose, dripping onto his stained, broken teeth as she clasped her fists and brought them down against his head. Dazed, she clutched his throat, throttling him.

She felt his kicking legs slow down beneath her as his body stilled. Mateo's arms flopped by his side as he stared into Danene's eyes, pleading with her to stop. She looked away as the life choked out of him.

The minutes passed as Danene held on. Her fingers ached, but still she squeezed, staring into the distance, tears flooding down her face. Her hands cramped and she let go, falling forward onto Mateo's corpse. She lay there until her crying stopped.

Pushing herself up, Danene turned and left the bridge. She walked through the empty corridors, wandering by Brett, Jacob's and Macy's lifeless shells before finding herself at her cabin. She entered, locked the door and climbed into her bed.

Danene pulled the covers over her head, waiting for her rescue and her escape from the Mariana Trench.

"We never belonged here," she said, rocking herself as she curled into a ball, "I hear the whispers too."

David Green

About the Author

David Green is a writer of dark fiction. Born in Manchester, UK and living in Galway, Ireland, David grew up with gloomy clouds above his head, and rain water at his feet, which has no doubt influenced his dark scribblings. David is the author of the Pushcart Prize nominated novelette Dead Man Walking, and is excited for his fantasy series, Empire of Ruin, debuting in June 2021 from Eerie River Publishing.

Newsletter: https://tinyurl.com/y6ah8brp
www.twitter.com/davidgreenwrite
www.davidgreenwriter.com
https://www.facebook.com/davidgreenwriter

When you are finished reading this collection of stories please take a moment and review it on Amazon, Goodreads, and/or BookBub.

More from "It Calls From" series
It Calls From the Sky

SENTINEL
By Drew Starling

www.ingramcontent.com/pod-product-compliance
Lightning Source LLC
Chambersburg PA
CBHW020327030826
48979CB00021B/467

* 9 7 8 1 9 9 0 2 4 5 2 0 6 *